THE WRITINGS OF CHRISTINE DE PIZAN

OTHER BOOKS BY CHRISTINE DE PIZAN
PUBLISHED IN TRANSLATION BY PERSEA

The Book of the City of Ladies
Translated by Earl Jeffrey Richards

A Medieval Woman's Mirror of Honor:
The Treasury of the City of Ladies
Edited by Madeleine P. Cosman
Translated by Charity Cannon Willard

The Book of the Duke of True Lovers
Translated by Thelma S. Fenster
With lyric poetry translated by Nadia Margolis

ALSO OF INTEREST

Christine de Pizan: Her Life and Works
A biography by Charity Cannon Willard

THE
WRITINGS
OF
CHRISTINE
DE PIZAN

❦

SELECTED AND EDITED BY

CHARITY CANNON WILLARD

PERSEA BOOKS

NEW YORK

For permission to quote excerpts from copyrighted material, acknowledgment is made to the following publishers:

E. J. Brill, for "The Tale of the Rose" and "Letter of the God of Love," translated by Thelma S. Fenster, from *Poems of Cupid, God of Love* (Leiden: 1990) copyright © 1990 by E. J. Brill Publishers.

Persea Books, for *The Book of the City of Ladies* by Christine de Pizan, translated by Earl Jeffrey Richards (New York: 1982), copyright © 1982 by Persea Books, Inc.; *A Medieval Woman's Mirror of Honor: The Treasury of the City of Ladies* by Christine de Pizan, translated by Charity Cannon Willard (New York: 1989), copyright © 1989 by Bard Hall Press and Persea Books, Inc.; and for *The Book of the Duke of True Lovers* by Christine de Pizan, translated by Thelma S. Fenster (New York: 1991), copyright © 1991 by Persea Books, Inc.

All other translations are published by arrangement with the translators. Write to Persea Books, Inc. for information.

Persea Books, Inc.
60 Madison Avenue
New York, New York 10010

LIBRARY OF CONGRESS CATALOGING-IN-PUBLICATION DATA

Christine, de Pisan, ca. 1364–ca. 1431.
    [Selections. English. 1993]
    The writings of Christine de Pizan / selected and edited by
Charity Cannon Willard.
    p. cm.
    Includes bibliographical references.
    ISBN 0-89255-180-1 (cloth) — ISBN 0-89255-188-7 (pbk.)
    1. Christine, de Pisan, ca. 1364–ca. 1431 — Translations into English. 2.
    French literature — To 1500 — Translations into English. I. Willard,
    Charity Cannon. II. Title.
PQ1575.A27   1993
841'.2 — dc20   92-41941

Designed by Hh Design
Typeset in Monotype Janson by ComCom, Allentown, Pennsylvania
Printed on acid-free paper and bound by Haddon Craftsmen,
        Scranton, Pennsylvania
Jacket and cover printed by Lynn Art, New York, New York

FIRST EDITION

CONTENTS

❧

INTRODUCTION

❦

TRANSLATING the writings of Christine de Pizan is in no
way a new venture. Christine had scarcely established herself as
a court poet during the final years of the fourteenth century when
Thomas Hoccleve, one of Chaucer's disciples, produced an English
version of her first long poem, "L'Epître au Dieu D'Amour" *(The Letter
of the God of Love).* Somewhat later, William Caxton translated and
printed two of her works, *The Book of the Fayttes of Arms and Chyvalerye*
(1489 – 1490) and *The Morale Proverbes of Christyene* (1478). There was
also an English translation of the *Livre de la Cité des Dames (The Book
of the City of Ladies)* (1521) as well as a Portuguese translation of her
Livre des Trois Vertus (1518). We are therefore following a long and
honorable tradition in presenting to English-speaking readers the
works of Christine de Pizan, but in this volume we are making available an unusually wide selection of her writings, much of which has
never been collected.

Christine de Pizan was no ordinary woman. [1] At the time when she
wrote she was altogether phenomenal, but in view of the scope and
variety of her works she would have been impressive in any era. [2] In
recent years it has been her valuable writings on the place of women
in society and history that have attracted particular attention. Yet
Christine is equally important as a vivid witness of the times in which
she lived, as an educator of the young with ideas well in advance of
her times, and even as a political commentator comparable to some of
the men who were her contemporaries.

She has sometimes been criticized for not taking a more revolution-
ary view of the shortcomings of the society in which she lived, but this
is to misunderstand the nature of that society. In common with most
of her contemporaries Christine believed that the form of society as
it existed was initially ordained by God. This concept is illustrated by
John of Salisbury in the *Policraticus,* a book well-known to Christine.
Society is there represented as a human body with the prince as the

head to guide it, the military as the arms to protect it, and the common people as the feet to support it. Little was to be gained by decapitating the body; it would be more useful to encourage the various parts of the body to work together better. This idea is particularly evident in Christine's *Book of the Body of Policy*.

Christine's intellectual heritage was exceptional. She was the daughter and granddaughter of university educated men, and her youth was spent in the shadow of the French court of Charles V, one of the most intellectual and forward-looking monarchs of his day. In one of the towers of his official residence, the Louvre, Charles V had established an important library to which he constantly added works he himself had commissioned, including a significant number of translations of the classics of the past.[3] He also liked to gather about him learned men, scholars from the University of Paris and elsewhere, to advise him on various affairs. Christine's father was one of these men. Few courts of the day gave evidence of such respect for learning.

Little is known of the details of Christine's early life and education beyond what she herself includes in her autobiographical *Vision*. She apparently demonstrated a precocious love of study, which was encouraged by her father but regarded by her mother as unsuitable for a girl. Nevertheless, her father's influence was to prevail. Perhaps she studied with her two younger brothers, learning enough Latin to be able to make use of it in later years, as she herself suggests. Certainly her education was limited by her marriage at fifteen, a normal enough age for the times. The husband chosen by her father was a young notary, a man about ten years Christine's senior with a university degree, Master Etienne du Castel. He came from a good Picard family, which still flourishes in France today. He also enjoyed useful connections at the court, and in 1380, the year of the marriage, he was appointed a royal secretary, a position that frequently opened the way to a promising future. His position in the royal chancellery bears witness to his association with a group of young intellectuals who were to become France's first humanists, young men who cultivated Latin prose, read Petrarch and Boccaccio, and corresponded with such Italian counterparts as Coluccio Salutati. By her marriage, Christine was assured of a continuing association with educated men.

The early years of the marriage, as might be expected, were devoted to normal domestic life, the birth and rearing of three children, a daughter and two sons. As Christine often wrote in later years, this was the happiest period of her life. The prospects for the future seemed very bright. To be sure, the death of Charles V the year of the marriage and the minority of the new king, Charles VI, accompanied by a struggle among his uncles for control of the government, brought an end to the fortunes of many of the men favored by the former king. Thomas de Pizan's health was failing, too, and his death, probably in 1387, made Etienne du Castel head of the whole family. Fortunes continued to prosper for another ten years.

Then Etienne suddenly and unexpectedly died, apparently the victim of one of the epidemics that repeatedly swept over Europe following the Black Death of 1348. The family's fortunes plummeted, producing the series of misfortunes that Christine describes in the *Vision*.

At the age of twenty-five, Christine found herself responsible not only for her three children but also for her widowed mother and a niece who had been left in Paris when her two brothers returned to Italy to claim family property in Bologna. Like most widows of her day, Christine was completely unprepared for the tasks that lay before her. Her only advantage was that she was endowed with intelligence, character, and the perseverance required to rescue herself from the sort of situation that had proved ruinous for many other women. In solving her own problems, she became the champion of all such women. Widowhood and its frustrations became a persistent theme throughout her writings.

Ten years were to pass between Etienne's death and Christine's emergence as a recognized court poet. It is not certain how she survived this trying period of her life, but the most plausible explanation is that she worked as a copyist, or perhaps a corrector in a workshop where manuscripts were being prepared for the expanding book trade. This occupation, having been secularized since the days when it was carried on primarily in religious communities, was flourishing in Paris at the end of the fourteenth century. There, as in Italy, it provided one of the few professional opportunities open to women. It is known, for instance, that the daughter of the fourteenth-century book illustrator, Jean Le Noir, was his assistant, and Christine herself speaks of a woman named Anastaise who was a skilled illuminator. It is quite possible that Christine had learned the book-hand to be seen in some of her manuscripts that are thought to be autographs from her husband. Royal secretaries, along with their assistants, are known to have worked at home sometimes, preparing letters and other documents for the royal seal. Sometimes they even had a special room set aside in their homes for this purpose, which might account for the little study to which Christine refers and in which she is portrayed by miniaturists. The best manuscripts of her writings certainly testify to a close association with her illustrators and suggest her personal involvement with the flourishing Paris book trade.

Christine's first literary success grew out of her contacts with the court of Louis of Orleans, the king's younger brother. His wife was an Italian, Valentina Visconti, daughter of the Duke of Milan, who was a notable bibliophile, and the head of Valentina's household was Giles Malet, a friend of Etienne du Castel's family, who was also in charge of the royal library in the Louvre. It was to the Duke of Orleans that Christine dedicated several early works, notably her successful *Epître d'Othéa (The Letter of Othea to Hector)*, composed around 1400. At around the same time, she asked the duke to act as judge of the lovers' debate, which is the subject of her *Débat de Deux Amants (Debate of Two Lovers)*. Shortly after this she described in her *Dit de la Rose (The Tale of the Rose)* a festive evening in one of the duke's residences in Paris. It was probably at the Orleans court that she met John Montagu, Earl of Salisbury, a close friend of King Richard II of England and a poet himself who admired Christine's poetry. Salisbury offered a place in his household to Christine's son Jean, now thirteen years old. Although the venture turned out badly as a result of Richard's downfall, the ultimate outcome was that some of Christine's writings came to be known in England, notably *The Letter of Othea to Hector* and *The Letter of the God of Love* (translated by Thomas Hoccleve as early as 1402).[4]

It is possible that her son's return to France precipitated Christine's departure from the Orleans court. She undoubtedly hoped that the duke would help her provide a suitable place in life for Jean; she had asked him for this favor in a ballade. Unfortunately, nothing came of this request, and several comments scattered through Christine's writings suggest that she found that frivolous entertainers were more generously rewarded by the duke than serious writers.[5] In any case, by 1404, Jean had been given a place in the household of the Duke of Burgundy, and Christine was writing a ballade praising the excellent qualities of the duke and his court.

It could also have been possible that Christine had become entirely disenchanted with the frivolity of the Orleans court. The last work she dedicated to the duke, the *Livre de la Prod'hommie de l'homme (The Book of Man's Integrity)*, later included in her collected writings as *Le Livre de Prudence*, shows an interesting talent for social satire. This work, basically a translation of a treatise on virtue erroneously attributed to Seneca, provided Christine with a point of departure for calling attention to some shortcomings of the society around her. The work marks a significant transition from Christine the courtly poet to Christine the social commentator so evident in her later works.[6]

It was only shortly before this that Christine had become involved with some former colleagues of her husband's at the royal chancellery in a literary debate over the merits of Jean de Meun's ever popular continuation of *The Romance of the Rose*. What is remarkable about this affair is that a woman of the day should have had the courage to talk back to men who thought they knew all there was to know about women.

The debate inspired Christine to write two of her most interesting works, *The Book of the City of Ladies* and *The Book of the Three Virtues*, known in later printed versions as *The Treasury of the City of Ladies*. These contributed to Christine's reputation as a writer who was not afraid to speak her mind.

As has already been mentioned, Christine is undoubtedly best known to modern readers for these writings on behalf of women, and there is no doubt that they are landmarks in women's history. They are also important for their influence on the first generation of women to play a visible role in public life: Louise of Savoy, Marguerite of Navarre, Diane of Poitiers, Anne of Beaujeu and, especially, Marguerite of Austria all owned and read these books.[7]

By the time Christine had written these two important books on women, she had firmly established herself as a writer. She then went on to comment further on the problems of France. It is important to see her evolution as a writer in order to understand the various phases of its development. She has sometimes been accused of repetitiousness, but it should be pointed out that when she repeated herself it was because she was considering some problem from a new angle. It is illuminating to follow the way in which certain favorite themes develop over the years.

This collection of translations is intended to give some idea of the variety of Christine's writings and her developing ideas along with her evolution as an appealing human being. Unfortunately, it is possible to include only a limited selection in a single volume. The basis of choice has been to invite scholars who have made a close study of certain texts to provide translations of passages that seem important to them. The editor has undertaken to fill in gaps once the selections were made. All notes on the texts have been made by the editor, except in the case of "Christine's Vision," where the notes were made by the translator. The source of the translations is indicated at the end of the selection.

It must be understood that in common with other writers of her day, Christine de Pizan is difficult to translate into language that is easily understandable or appealing to modern readers. At the beginning of the fifteenth century, it was the style in prose to imitate complex Latin sentence structure, the result in part of excessive admiration for the Latinized style of early Italian humanists. The effect in French is often ponderous, although Christine's prose is sometimes quite lively, especially when she is speaking to other women or when she is describing something she has experienced personally. Her poetry, of course, is based on the fixed forms popular in her day, following the traditions practiced by Guillaume Machaut and described by Eustache Deschamps in his treatise on writing poetry.[8] These poetic models are based on early song forms, and it was only after the days of Machaut that poets ceased to be songwriters at the same time. The poetic patterns they favored were complex, and Christine, in common with other poets, obviously enjoyed the challenge of playing with these elaborate forms. Rhymes often turn on plays on words that do not make sense when translated into English literally, but the point of the game is diminished if the poetic patterns are not observed in translation. This aspect of Christine's poetry is less important in the long poems where the pattern is simpler, perhaps merely a case of rhyming couplets. Sometimes it is better to avoid the more elaborate verse forms in favor of blank verse, and in the case of *The Book of the Duke of True Lovers,* prose has been substituted for verse in order to dramatize the psychological implications of the love affair that forms its basis. This long poem is best appreciated as a forerunner of the psychological novel.

It has been the objective of each translator to provide the modern reader with examples in English of Christine's writings in the hope of demonstrating the spirit as well as the varied subject matter of this increasingly popular writer.

The editor is most appreciative of the contributions of other scholars to this volume, and would like to express particular gratitude to Professor Angus J. Kennedy for reading the text and offering some excellent suggestions.

NOTES

1. Biographies of Christine de Pizan include: M.-J. Pinet, *Christine de Pisan: étude biographique et littéraire* (Paris, 1927); reprint Geneva, 1974; E. McLeod, *The Order of the Rose: the Life and Ideas of Christine de Pisan* (London, 1976); S. Solente, "Christine de Pisan" in *Histoire littéraire de la France* XL (Paris, 1974); C. C. Willard, *Christine de Pizan: Her Life and Works* (New York, 1984).

2. See, for instance, Joan Kelly, *Women, History and Theory* (Chicago, 1984), p. 66.

3. Some idea of this library can be gained from the catalogue of the exhibition *La Librairie de Charles V* (Paris, Bibliothèque Nationale, 1968). See also L. Delisle, *Recherches sur la librairie de Charles V* (Paris, 1907).

4. The *"Epistle of Othea"* translated from the French text of Christine de Pisan by Stephen Scrope, ed. C. F. Bühler (London, 1970); *Poems of Cupid, God of Love*, eds. T. S. Fenster and M. C. Erler (Leiden and New York, 1990).

5. This is suggested, for instance, by a passage in *A Medieval Woman's Mirror of Honor: The Treasury of the City of Ladies:* "A person reputed to be wise was summoned there for all to hear and appraise his talents.... Simultaneously, the court was frequented by one reputed to be a fool, who entertained the lords and ladies with jokes, flattering remarks, gossip, and idle chatter to make them laugh. When the time came to reward them, the fool was given a gift valued at forty crowns and the other a gift of only twelve crowns" (p. 117).

6. C. C. Willard, "Christine de Pizan: From Poet to Political Commentator," *Politics, Gender, and Genre*, ed. Margaret Brabant (Boulder-San Francisco-Oxford, 1992), 17–32.

7. C. C. Willard, "The Manuscript Tradition of the *Livre des Trois Vertus* and Christine de Pizan's Audience," *Journal of the History of Ideas* 28 (1966), 433–44, and essays on these women in *Women Writers of the Renaissance and Reformation*, ed. K. M. Wilson (Athens, Ga., 1987).

8. Eustache Deschamps, *Oeuvres complètes*, ed. G. Reynaud (Paris, 1891), VII, pp. 266–92; N. Wilkins, "The Structure of Ballades, Rondeaux and Virelais in Froissart and Christine de Pizan," *French Studies* 23 (1969), 337–48.

THE WRITINGS OF CHRISTINE DE PIZAN

I

CHRISTINE'S AUTOBIOGRAPHICAL VISION

❧

ONE OF THE most significant and most interesting aspects of Christine's literary production is her willingness to talk about herself. A modern reader would like to know a great deal more about her than she told, but she is the first woman to give any significant account of her formative years, her marriage, and how she came to be a writer. Although a certain amount of personal revelation is scattered throughout other works, the most significant account of her life is to be found in the third part of her tripartite *L'Avision-Christine*, written in 1405 when she was around forty years old and already well launched on a successful writing career.

The influence of Petrarch, a contemporary and possibly an acquaintance of her father's in Venice, is apparent in the form of this work, as well as in Christine's concern for her ultimate reputation and her evaluation of herself as an individual. It is evident that at this point in her career she had ceased to think of herself as an amateur. In describing her struggle to overcome the problems of her early widowhood when she sought in vain the help of others, she bears witness above all to her remarkable stamina in dealing with both Fortune and Opinion, two of the allegorical personages she discusses here.

Like Petrarch in his autobiographical *Secretum*, her revelations about herself and her ideas about her place in the world take the form of three dialogues. Although all three of Petrarch's dialogues are with Saint Augustine, Christine speaks with three allegorical women. The first of these is a Crowned Lady, a representation of France. She rehearses with Christine various significant epochs of the country's history, dwelling at length on the contemporary problems resulting from Charles VI's ever more frequent spells of insanity. In 1405 these troubles had finally led to open conflict between the rival dukes of Orleans and Burgundy. The Crowned Lady concludes her complaints about France's misfortunes by begging Christine to continue writing on the country's behalf.

The second part introduces the reader to the environment of the University of Paris. There, Christine recognized the lady who speaks to her about the world of learning as Dame Opinion. She eventually reminds Christine that it was she who stirred up the debate over the merits of *The Romance of the Rose*. She adds the interesting detail that it was she who allowed certain critics to say that Christine herself was not the author of her writings because no woman would have been capable of such work; she insists that only ignorant men would have uttered such nonsense. Nevertheless, the result is that some praise Christine while others blame her for what she writes. Dame Opinion urges her to continue her work, although Christine's reply is to accuse Dame Opinion of being the daughter of Ignorance, thus explaining her power over ignorant men in this world.

At the beginning of the third part Christine describes her difficult ascent into a high tower, where she finally reaches a handsome hall painted with murals representing the sciences and their derivative knowledge. There she also finds seats where scholars may sit to listen to readings by their masters. Soon she hears another feminine voice, that of Dame Philosophy, with whom she holds her final dialogue and to whom she recounts the story of her life up to that point. Dame Philosophy is undoubtedly inspired by Boethius' *Consolation*, which she has earlier spoken of reading. In her long complaint to this lady, Christine undertakes to examine her evolution from a well-brought-up, sheltered young woman and devoted wife and mother to a widow beset by tribulations due in large measure to an unsympathetic social order, and then to the writer who was not afraid to become the defender of women and, indeed, of France.

Her conversation with Dame Philosophy and this lady's admonition lead Christine eventually to the realization that it has been her studious life that has above all given her pleasure, and that if her husband had lived, she would never have discovered this truth. Dame Philosophy points out to her not only the uncertainty of worldly wealth but also the folly of expecting too much happiness in life. She insists that deprivation makes a person more sensitive to the needs of others than does abundance, and that humankind is misguided to expect true felicity except in Eternity.

Christine's vision of the Holy Trinity at the end of the *Vision* inevitably recalls Dante's *Divine Comedy,* as does the beginning in which the writer finds herself at the midpoint in life's journey. After all, Christine was one of the first writers in France to have read Dante and to have been influenced by him.

Clearly, Christine's basic intellectual formation was Italian and strongly influenced by her father's tastes. What she says about her father here and in other writings makes this unquestionable. We will probably never know whether it was her father's influence or ten years of happy marriage to an educated husband that provided her with the intellectual stamina to overcome the obstacles that lay in her path when she was obliged to make a new life for herself. However, the revelations Christine makes about herself here, taken together with the miniatures depicting her in her study among her books, allow her to become for the reader a living person.

CHRISTINE'S VISION

❦

Christine's Complaint to Philosophy

Most reverend Lady to whom I have proclaimed obeisance, I pray that the narration of my fortunes will not tax you in its prolixity, and that you will deign to lift my lowly thoughts with your counsel. Oh, dearest mistress, note how capricious Fortune has been the cruelest of stepmothers to me ever since the days of my childhood:

I was born of noble parents in the city of Venice in Italy, where my father, a native of Bologna the Fat,[1] where I afterwards spent my tender years, went to marry my mother, a Venetian, whom he had met through his long acquaintance with my grandfather. Now my grandfather, a native of Forlì, was a clerk and doctor of the University of Bologna and served as counselor in the city of my birth.[2] Through him, my father got to know the Venetians, who were so impressed by his knowledge that he was also engaged as counselor to the rulers of that city, where he remained for a while and acquired both honor and riches.[3]

Was it not because of Fortune, I ask you, that quite soon after my birth my father returned to the said city of Bologna the Fat to conduct business and visit his lands, where invitations reached him simultaneously from two excellent kings who, because of the great renown and prestige of his knowledge, both wanted him to come to their realms and promised a generous salary and other gifts? One of these was the sovereign Christian king, Charles V the Wise, and the other the king of Hungary, justly known by posterity as the "Good King of Hungary."[4]

Because his respect for the said princes would not allow him to put these offers aside, my father resolved to serve the king deemed surpassing in excellence. As he also wished to see the Parisian schools and the splendor of the French court, he decided in favor of the French monarch. His plan was to enter that king's service and visit the said schools over the course of a year, then return home to his wife and family, whom he enjoined to remain on his estates in Bologna the Fat. When these arrangements were made and authorization from the Venetian rulers obtained, my father left for France, where the said wise King Charles welcomed him grandly with every honor. Soon afterwards, Charles, in recognition of his wisdom and knowledge, retained him as special privy counselor and came to appreciate him so greatly that when the year drew to a close, he was unwilling to grant him leave to return home. Offering to pay all expenses, the king urged my father to send for his wife, children, and family so that they could spend the rest of their lives near him in France; and he promised properties, annuities, and pensions so that they might live in honorable estate. Hoping to depart, my father delayed for about three years; however, he finally consented, and we left Italy and took up residence in France.

The good and wise king was eager to welcome in joyous ceremony the wife and children of your beloved philosopher, Master Thomas. And thus it was brought about in the month of December, soon after our arrival. Dressed in richly decorated Lombard costume befitting women and children of high estate, our family, accompanied by honorable relatives, was presented to the king in the palace of the Louvre in Paris, where we were greeted warmly and given many generous gifts.

Christine Speaks of Her Good Fortune

Fortune was most kind to us while the good and wise King Charles lived, bringing us honor and various bounties, which made for a full and happy life. Now it is natural for every loyal servant to rejoice in the success of his good master, and thus Thomas, from the time he entered the king's service, thanks be to God, counseled him in various matters, including those of warfare, according to the science of astrology,[5] and Charles's fortune prospered as he won several victories and conquests over his enemies; I call on princes still living and others from those days to witness the truth that the good of the prince constituted the supreme joy of his faithful servant. And despite the fact that, as is customary with philosophers, my father's savings amounted to nothing—which practice, with all due respect, I consider not at all praiseworthy for married men whose duty it is to provide for their families, who could fall into poverty after their death as a result of their prodigality—nonetheless, despite my father's liberal ways, the good king's generosity took care of every need in the household of his beloved servant.

Coming to the peak of my good fortune, the time arrived when I was approaching the age at which girls were customarily given in marriage. Although I was still quite young, I was nonetheless sought after by several knights, other nobles and wealthy clerks; and this should not be construed as boasting, for my own worth was not the cause, but rather the respect enjoyed by my father, for whom the king showed great love and esteem. Now as my father valued above all knowledge and a worthy life, he singled out a young Picard nobleman who had completed his studies and who had more virtue than wealth.[6] It was to this man, whom my father regarded as his own son, that I was given; and I do not complain at all about Fortune on this account, for as I have stated, judging by all suitable qualities, I could not have found a more desirable partner. Soon afterwards, our prince, who held him in much favor, recognized his merits by granting him the position of notary and court secretary that had fallen vacant, along with wages and other rewards.

Christine Begins to Speak of Her Misfortunes

This prosperity lasted for several years. However, Fortune, envious of our honors, wished to cut them off at the source. Was it not through her, dearest mistress, that there came about the terrible loss to the kingdom that struck such a severe blow to the household of Master Thomas? The excellent and wise prince, not yet old in nature's course, but at forty-four still relatively young, fell ill and died soon after.

Alas! Truly it often happens that good things last but briefly. For even today, had it pleased God to prolong that life so necessary to the realm, which is faring badly in comparison with those days, the king would not be all that old. Thus was the door opened onto our misfortunes, and I, still a very young woman, entered in. Now frequently after the death of powerful men, major changes are brought about at court and in their lands because of numerous wills that come into conflict. And it can scarcely be otherwise unless great wisdom intervenes, as is clear from the example of Alexander, after whose death disputes broke out among his barons despite the measures he had taken to divide up his lands.

Thus, upon Charles's death, my father lost his generous pensions. Income from his properties added to gifts came to less than a hundred francs a month, which was much less than the amount to which he had grown accustomed. The promise the king had made to grant him and his heirs lands yielding five hundred pounds a year, plus additional benefits, went unfulfilled, first through oversight and then because of the king's untimely death, and my father was retained by the governing princes on a greatly reduced and falteringly paid stipend. As old age had already come upon him, he grew ill and feeble and had to endure many hardships that the money spent earlier could have alleviated. For this reason, I deem prudent saving a wise practice in youth, as it provides comfort in old age.

His full faculties remaining intact until the end, and acknowledging his Creator like a good Catholic, my father died at the very hour he had predicted.[7] For this, he was renowned among clerks as the man most skilled in the mathematical sciences and astrological predictions not only in his own time, but for the preceding hundred years as well. He was truly missed by princes, colleagues, and friends for his integrity, good deeds, loyalty, truthfulness, and other virtues, among which there was nothing blameworthy, save perhaps his excessive generosity towards the poor to the detriment of his wife and family. And I do not say this out of partiality, as there are still many people alive today, royal and otherwise, who knew him and who can bear personal witness. He was a man rightfully mourned.

On this Same Subject

Thus it came about that my young husband, a man both prudent and wise and beloved of princes and all those who worked with him, became head of the household, and by his prudence and wisdom he was able to maintain our financial situation. But as Fortune had already placed me on the downward side of her wheel and was bent on casting me to the very bottom, she did not suffer this good man to remain with me much longer. Because of her, Death struck him down in his prime when he was on the verge of attaining his intellectual peak and acceding to the highest ranks of his office. He died in the bloom of youth at thirty-four years of age, and I, at twenty-five, was left with the responsibility of three small children and a large household. I had good reason to be filled with bitterness, and longed after his sweet company and my vanished happiness, which had lasted but ten years. Seeing a vast wave of tribulation about to rush upon me, I desired death rather than face living. And remembering my troth and the love I had pledged him, I wisely resolved never to have another. I had fallen now into the valley of tribulation. For Fortune, once she has decided to bring down kingdom, city, empire, or individual, gathers from far and wide her adversities to visit calamity upon the object of her fury — and thus it happened to me. For I was not with my husband when he was carried off by a sudden plague in the city of Beauvais where he had gone with the king (nevertheless I thank God he died a good Catholic). As he was accompanied only by his servants and an unfamiliar retinue, I was not able to get full and precise information on the state of his affairs. For it is customary for married men not to discuss financial matters in detail with their wives, a practice that often leads to great problems, as I have learned from experience, and does not make any sense at all when a woman is not stupid but prudent and wise in her dealings. [8]

Thus it behooved me to set to work, I who had been indulged and pampered as a child and had no experience in such matters, and take the helm of the captainless ship in midstorm, by which I mean the bereft household far from its homeland. [9] Troubles surged upon me from all sides, and as is the common lot of widows, I became entangled in legal disputes of every sort. Those who owed me money leaped to the attack to prevent me from asking payment. And God is my witness that one man with whom my husband had placed money claimed to have returned it, producing a paper my husband had supposedly signed to that effect; but his fraud was discovered, and he was too embarrassed to persist in his lie. Shortly afterwards, I was prevented from claiming property my husband had purchased. Since it was turned over to the king, I was responsible for the payments and could not derive any revenue from it. I engaged in a lengthy dispute in the *Chambre des comptes* with a pitiless noble from whom — among others — I have yet to receive satisfaction. As many know well, he did me great injustice and even today, having grown old in his sins, remains indifferent to the wrong he caused me.

These problems were not the only ones besetting me. For I had agreed that my young orphans' guardians place what little savings they had in the hands of a reputedly honest merchant so as to increase their value, and at the end of a year's time the savings had grown by approximately half. When the merchant was tempted by the evil one, he spread the rumor that he had been robbed and took flight. I lost even more money trying to pursue him.

In addition, I was faced with problems stemming from properties on which were asked considerable arrears, none of which were mentioned in the purchase deed. The best lawyers advised me to resist staunchly in this matter, assuring me that since I was in the right, the judgment would turn out in my favor. They recommended I have a summons issued to the parties responsible for the sale. But since those individuals had already died penniless in a foreign land, there was no recourse to be had.

Fortune, eager to bring me to the height of adversity, visited upon me, as she had Job, a long illness. As this and insufficient funds prevented me from pursuing my cases, I ended up paying court fees and reached the bottom of my meager purse. It was astonishing how Fortune could hound me with such vengeance! For in every manner that it was possible for a person conducting her affairs in prudent and orderly fashion to incur losses, I did so; and as God knows, I was trying my very best. What happened to me was against all reason.

Patience! I never possessed you in large measure, and so you were often overtaken in me by great bitterness. There came the day when I found myself a defendant in four different courts in Paris. I swear to you upon my soul that in this I was the victim of injustice! When I realized that the ridicule to which I was being subjected was an attempt to force me to relinquish, as I am of a peaceful temperament and found all of this so hateful, I finally yielded and incurred considerable expenses as a result. Do not think these troubles went on for a year or two but rather more than fourteen in all: when one misfortune went away another came in its place, and still others so numerous that the recounting of them by half would be long and tedious.[10] Thus that leech Fortune continued sucking my paltry savings until she had consumed them all, and I had nothing more to lose. At that point my legal disputes came to an end, but not my woes.

Sweet mistress, how many tears, sighs, complaints, and lamentations do you think I poured forth in those days when I was alone in my retreat, how many pains I endured? What anguish when I looked at my young children and poor relatives, and compared past days to my present misfortunes that cast me down and seemed beyond my power to redress. In those trials I pitied my family more than myself. One day, someone remarked that I had no cause for complaint, since I was like a single person with no burdens or responsibilities; I replied that he had not looked carefully enough, as I was three times my double. As he didn't understand what I meant, I explained to him that the one person he saw was really six.

In addition to this, can you believe that my heart was heavy with the fear that my plight might be discovered by outsiders or neighbors, a plight brought upon me by my predecessors and for which I was not responsible? Ignorance made me so bitter that I would have preferred death to financial ruin. Oh, what a heavy grief for a heart set on maintaining a former way of life when Fortune is against it—no suffering can equal it! No one can understand unless he has experienced it himself. God knows what sorrows people have endured for this reason in the past and continue to do so today. I assure you that my trials were little evident in my demeanor and dress. Under my fur-lined cloak and fine surcoat that was carefully mended but seldom replaced, I was often shivering, and spent many a restless night in my handsome, well-draped bed. But my meals were modest, as befits widows; in any case one must go on living. God knows what torments assailed me when the bailiffs would come to carry off some of my dear possessions. However great the loss, what I feared most was the shame. When I had to borrow money to avoid greater problems, dear God, how I made my request with embarrassment and blushing, even if it was to a friend. And still today I am not cured of this indisposition, and would rather fall ill with fever than have to borrow again.

Alas! How vividly I remember many a chilly winter morning spent in that palace, shivering from the cold while waiting for those representing me so I could remind them of my case or urge them to action, only to hear at the end of the session decisions that made me burst with outrage, or else puzzled me; but what hurt even more was the expense I could ill afford.

Our Lord Jesus Christ suffered to be tormented in every part of His body in order to teach us patience, and so Fortune sought to torment my heart with every manner of heavy burden. What greater evil can befall someone who is innocent, what can vex one more deeply than to hear oneself unjustly accused, as Boethius relates in the *Consolation?*[11] Was it not rumored throughout the city that I was romantically involved? Suffice it to say that this was but another of Fortune's many blows. For such rumors arise easily and often unjustifiably, either because people frequent the same circles or because the situation appears possible; but I swear to you that the party in question did not know me personally, nor did he even know who I was! No man or creature born had ever seen me with him in public or in private, for my path never went his way, nor did it have any reason to do so. May God be my witness that I speak the truth! Moreover, given his situation and mine, such an interest could never have arisen, nor was it likely, nor did it have any basis in fact. Thus I often marveled at how such tales could arise, spreading from mouth to mouth that would repeat: "I heard it was so." And I, knowing my innocence, was sometimes distressed when the story reached me, and other times would smile and say: "God and he and I know that these rumors are without foundation!"[12]

My trials were not over yet. As I always tried my best to parry Fortune's blows, when I realized the dire situation I was in, I decided to make use of notes that had been certified by the *Chambre des comptes* concerning wages still owed my husband, and obtained an order from the king that they be paid. Thus was I forced by need to undertake an irksome quest in which I was batted back and forth by diverse favorable and unfavorable replies over a period of several days. That the process is tedious and bothersome I call to witness those who have gone through it. And as the ancients say, it seems more onerous now than ever before. You can well imagine how it was for me, with my woman's strength and timorous nature, to make of necessity a virtue and run after them—a difficult and costly matter, since my situation would not allow me to go about unaccompanied. Most days I had to sit idly in their chambers or waiting rooms with my casket and royal order, only to receive after a long while some ambiguous reply. The wait was long indeed! Dear Lord, what annoying remarks, what sly glances, what jokes I endured so often from men bloated with wine and the flesh of ease, only to pretend I had not and turn away, or else cast off lightly and make believe I had not understood, lest I should compromise my case! May God reform all evil consciences, as I came across so many!

In my need, I could not find a charitable soul anywhere, in high quarters or low, even after I had asked several nobles to intervene in the hope I could convince them of their obligation towards widows and orphans; but it was to no avail. One day, discouraged and disconsolate, I composed this ballad through my tears.[13]

Ballad

Alas! where shall they find solace,
Poor widows who have lost all?
For in France, which used to be their harbor
Of safety, and where women without shelter
And without protection would find refuge,

Now they find no offer of friendship,
No sign of pity from nobles
Or from clerics great or small,
And princes are deaf to their pleas.

From knights, no offer of help,
From prelates, no good counsel.
Judges give no protection,
And officials no encouragement.
The powerful are often their exploiters;
Before the great scarcely
Can they get anywhere.
They must try elsewhere—
And princes are deaf to their pleas.

Where can they flee? In France
They find only
Empty hopes,
Deadly counsel,
Treacherous words
Prodding them to damnation.
No one espouses their concerns,
Seeming help turns to harm
And princes are deaf to their pleas.

Worthy, valiant men! Let your good instincts
Be awakened, else widows are destined
To suffer many wrongs; with a glad heart
Come to their aid and believe what I say,
For no one cares about them,
And princes are deaf to their pleas.

   I was forced to pursue my cause in person, despite my aversion to such matters, since when I sent a messenger in my stead, he could not gain audience. When I did go to them myself, calling attention to my widowhood and bowing before them to beg for help, I encountered not the least semblance of compassion. This unpleasant matter, like others, was not quickly resolved, but stretched out over six years during which I presented my plight to various nobles and finally received, at different times, part of the modest sum I was seeking, the rest of which still remains due.

Christine Continues Her Complaint

When, sweet mistress, you learn about those merry early days of my widowhood, you can well imagine how eager I was for romantic dalliance! Despite all that I had suffered at Fortune's hands, that faithless one, about whom I have already written one well-justified complaint,[14] was not finished with me yet. For the pain in the tooth soon draws the tongue.[15] I will continue, therefore, along the same lines, relating how Fortune continues to assail me even now.

During those trying days, as I have said, I was resolved to conceal my problems from others, for the reason that charity is rare, and a little of it can easily lead to servitude. But as it is indeed burdensome to contain one's sorrow entirely, Fortune could not assail me to the point of depriving me of the company of the poets' muses. Your banishment of poetry from Boethius notwithstanding (you had worthier fare in mind for him),[16] I was moved to compose plaintive rhymes that lamented my dead husband and the days that had passed, as is clear in the early poems of my first collection of *One Hundred Ballades*.[17] Then, in order to pass the time and also to cheer myself somewhat, I began writing gay love poems expressing others' feelings, as I state in one of my virelays.[18]

Christine Relates How She Changed Her Way of Life

As my youth was already largely behind me, as were most of my outside obligations, I returned to the way of life that suited me best: seclusion and quiet. In my solitude, there came back to me some remnants of Latin and the beauteous sciences, along with sayings from the authors and rhetorical pieces I had heard my beloved father and husband recite but, in my frivolity, had remembered quite poorly. Despite the fact that my nature inclined me to learning from my earliest years, my duties as a married woman kept me otherwise occupied, as did the burden of frequent childbearing. In addition, youth, that tender enemy of good sense, will prevent even children with good minds from applying themselves to study, unless fear of punishment is brought to bear. And as this was not done in my case, the desire to play won out over intelligence and inclination, so that I could not be constant in the labor of learning.

Christine Complains of Youth

Oh flighty youth, so blind and capricious! You do not realize what is good for you; you take pleasure only in vain and worthless things, and pursue nothing else. Truly he who follows your way treads the path of perdition and stumbles in his own blindness. I should bear you great resentment, for when I was right beside those two founts of philosophy, so clear and pure, I was too young and foolish to drink my fill, even though those limpid streams pleased me greatly. Like the fool who sees the sun shining and does not give a thought to the rain, thinking he will always have sunlight, I paid no heed, believing I could recover what was slipping away. Ah, Fortune, what a treasure you took from me! My possibilities were greatly diminished when you did not let me keep those two until I had advanced in learning. You harmed the very character of my soul! For if I had the benefit of the clarity of their knowledge now, with my present desire not for vain activities and delights but for study only, I would fill myself so, that I would surpass all other women of this day and many generations preceding. Alas, when I had those learned masters beside me, I did not give much thought to study! And now I hunger in mind and spirit for that which I am no longer able to possess: the knowledge of you, sweet Philosophy! Ah, savory, honeyed treasure, sovereign above all others. Happy are those who delight in you fully! I nonetheless find small tastes of you in the subordinate branches of science. As I can reach no higher, I can only imagine the supreme delight of those who love and take relish in you completely. Oh, children and youths! If only you knew what good is to be found in the delight of knowledge, and the evil and ugliness in ignorance — if only you knew better, you would not complain about the labor of studying! Does not Aristotle say that the wise man naturally leads the ignorant, as the soul governs the body? What can be more beautiful than learning? And what uglier than ignorance, so ill-befitting human nature? One day, a man criticized my desire for knowledge, saying that it was inappropriate for a woman to be learned, as it was so rare, to which I replied that it was even less fitting for a man to be ignorant, as it was so common.

Christine Relates How She Turned to Study

Thus I arrived at the age when one naturally attains a certain level of knowledge, and looking back over my past life and ahead to the inevitable end, like a traveler who has just passed over a dangerous route and who, turning back in amazement, resolves never to go that way again but to find a better path, I came to the realization that the world is full of dangers and that there is only one good: the way of truth. So I turned to the path of study, towards which I was inclined by nature and constellation.[19] I closed those gates that are the senses, which no longer wandered amongst external things, and took up those beautiful books with the intent of recovering part of what I had lost. I was not presumptuous enough to delve into the obscure sciences, whose language I could not understand, for as Cato says, "to read and fail to understand is not truly to read."[20] But like a child who first learns the alphabet, I began with the ancient histories from the beginnings of the world, then the history of the Hebrews, the Assyrians, and the early kingdoms, proceeding from one to the other and coming to the Romans, the French, the Britons,[21] and several other historians, and then to what scientific learning I was able to grasp in the time available for study.

Next, I took up the works of the poets, my knowledge increasing all the while. I was glad to find in them a style that seemed natural to me, and took pleasure in their subtle allegories and lovely material hidden beneath delightful moral fictions, as well as the beautiful forms of their verse and prose adorned with polished rhetoric, subtle language, and piquant proverbs.[22] For this science of poetry, Nature rejoiced within me and directed: "Daughter, be glad when you have fulfilled the desire that I give you, studying all the while and understanding certain thoughts better and better." I felt then a certain dissatisfaction growing within me. Nature willed that from my studies and experience there be born new works, and commanded: "Take up your tools and hammer out on the anvil the material I shall give you, as lasting as iron and impervious to fire and everything else, and forge objects of delight. When your children were in your womb, you experienced great pain bringing them into the world. It is now my wish that new works be born from your memory in joy and delight, which will carry your name forever all over the world, and to future generations of princes. Just as the woman who has given birth forgets her suffering as soon as she hears her child cry, so too you will forget the toil of your labor once you have heard the voice of your writings."[23]

Thus I began to write short pieces in a lighter vein, and like the workman who perfects his technique by practicing, I learned more and more new things through the study of diverse disciplines, and refined my style with greater subtleness and the use of nobler material. Between the year 1399, when I began writing, and the present, 1405,[24] I have composed fifteen principal works, not counting some shorter ones, all of which fill seventy thick quires, as can easily be shown. I do not say this, Lord knows, to boast or seek praise, as my works are not remarkable for their subtlety, but recount it in the context of my good and bad fortunes.

The Pleasure That Christine Took in Study

Thus I had adopted a different way of life, but my fortunes did not improve. Misfortune, as though jealous of the comfort and peace of my solitary contemplation, persisted in her malevolence not only towards me but towards my friends as well, which I see as proof of her animosity towards me.

It is true that news of my studious way of life had already spread, contrary to my wishes, even among princes; but since this was so, I sent those nobles a number of my meager writings as gifts, thinking they might appeal by way of their novelty; and the gifts were accepted joyfully and with a graciousness befitting the nobles' rank. I attribute this reception not to the value of my works but rather to the fact that they had been written by a woman, a phenomenon not seen in quite some time. Thus, quite quickly, my writings became known and were read in many different lands.

At about that time, the daughter of the French king was given in marriage to King Richard of England, and a certain noble Count of Salisbury came to France for that reason.[25] As this gentle knight loved poetry and indeed wrote beautiful poems himself, after seeing some of my works he had several nobles persuade me, despite my reluctance, to send back with him to England my elder son, a rather clever child of twelve with a gift for singing,[26] so that he could serve as companion to a son of his of about the same age. Because the count was very generous with my child and promised even more for the future, I placed my confidence in him, and am certain that he would have kept his word, as he could well afford to do so.

Note, dearest mistress, the truth of my earlier statement that Fortune, by robbing me of my good friends, showed that she was enemy to my prosperity. Misfortune, who had visited so many ills upon me before, could not allow me to enjoy these friendships for long, and soon afterwards brought calamity down upon the said King Richard of England, as is well known. The good count remained loyal to his rightful lord and as a result was beheaded, which was an act of grave injustice.[27] Thus my son's initial worldly good fortune was brought to an end, and since he was young and in a foreign land beset with such turmoil, he had good reason to be alarmed. What followed? King Henry, who seized power and still holds the throne, saw some of the many books and works I had sent for the count's pleasure, became aware of the situation, and took my son into his household, providing for him generously.[28] Then he charged two of his kings of arms, Lancaster and Falcon,[29] to invite me to come to England, promising a generous recompense. Under the circumstances, and as the prospect did not tempt me in the least, I feigned acquiescence in order to obtain my son's return. To get straight to the point, after laborious maneuvers on my part and the expedition of some of my works, my son received permission to come home so he could accompany me on a journey I have yet to make. Thus I rejected an opportunity for both of us, because I cannot believe that the faithless person can come to any good.

How happy I was to be reunited after those three years with my beloved child, whom Death had left my only son. My joy notwithstanding, his return added to my already burdensome expenses. I doubted, moreover, that he would be happy to come home after the grand way of life to which he had grown accustomed, for children, who have little discernment, are readily attracted to what appeals most to their eyes and their comfort. So I sought a situation for him in the household of a great and powerful lord; but as the talents of this young boy did not stand out among those of the many great men at this court, I remained responsible for his support myself, and reaped nothing from his service.[30]

Thus had Fortune deprived me of one of my good friends and one of my best hopes. But since that time she has visited even worse upon me.

Christine Complains of Fortune, Who Took Her Good Friends from Her

As I related earlier, I had by this time achieved some fame, since many of my works had been given as gifts — not by myself but by others — to princes in foreign lands, and these were regarded as new works written from a woman's perspective. As the proverb says, novelty pleases;[31] and I do not say it out of boasting, as that does not enter in. Thus, the first Duke of Milan in Lombardy heard of me, perhaps in a way more flattering than I deserve, and offered me a generous lifetime income if I would come live in his land.[32] This can be verified by several nobles from that country who served as ambassadors in this regard. But Fortune, true to her ways, would not suffer any improvement in my ruinous financial situation. So she took this benefactor away from me by death—not that I would have left France easily, even if to return to my native land. Nonetheless, she did me harm when she deprived me of this good friend, inflicting upon me no small loss, for as certain worthy individuals have told me, my books would have won his support even if I had decided to remain in France.

More on the Same Subject

There remains for me to relate the death of the prince who, after wise King Charles, represented the greatest loss for me. Now the most venerable and powerful Prince Philip, Duke of Burgundy, brother of Charles the Wise, had in his benevolence extended his affection to me after he became familiar with some of my works, which I had only recently sent him because I had considered them unworthy to be opened in his presence. In recognition of the constancy of my application rather than of any great subtlety found in what I wrote, he praised and remunerated me generously, and graciously took my son into his service. Moreover, he deigned to pay me the great honor of asking me in person to record as an example for all posterity the noble life and deeds of the said wise king. Was it not a sure sign of the heinous envy of my perverse enemy that soon afterwards she took him from me in death, just as his benevolence towards me was increasing? His death marked a renewal of my adversities, as well as a grave loss to the kingdom, as I sadly recount in the book he had commissioned, which was not yet finished at the time.[33]

Christine Concludes Her Complaint

Thus, reverend mistress, have I related the causes of my past tribulations, but not all. For God knows that many other evils and trials assailed me at the same time; but the account of these would be too long and too tedious. And even today I do not see an end to my ills.

As for the present, I have had to make numerous entreaties to French princes still living because of the many losses suffered at Fortune's hands; and I have implored them to aid my little family and me far from my native land, not because of any merit of mine, but in memory of my father, who left his homeland to serve them, and did so with such devotion. I am not being either untruthful or ungrateful when I say that the value of the modest help I received from some of these noblemen has been somewhat diminished by the difficulties I encountered in obtaining it from their treasurers. What is your opinion in the matter, dearest Lady? What a trial it is for a woman like me, who is rather retiring by nature and little concerned with material possessions or money, to be forced by my financial responsibilities to seek out various officials, only to be tormented day after day by their smooth words! Such, honored Lady from whom nothing is hidden, is the plight of widows today. You know well how little interested I am in amassing riches or bettering my estate, for I wish only to maintain the one I inherited; although I am foolish to be concerned even with that, since I recognize that worldly goods are like the wind. As you know also that I have no desire for superfluous adornments or delicacies, I call upon you to witness that my sole concern is for my elderly mother, now totally dependent upon her only daughter, who has not forgotten all she has been given and desires to pay her debt, as is only just. I grow saddened and bewildered when Fortune thwarts my will and does not allow this noble and honorable lady to live in the manner that she deserves and to which she is accustomed. And add to this the burden of poor relatives for whom I must find suitable husbands, and other friends I must aid: nowhere do I see Fortune inclined in my favor.

Continuing in this vein, do you not think I consider myself unfortunate when I see other women living happily and comfortably with their brothers and families, and reflect that I am away from my friends in a foreign land? My two brothers, fine and worthy men both, had to return home to the estates inherited from my father because they were fortuneless here.[34] And I who am tender by nature and open with my friends ask God why a mother has to live far from the sons she misses, and I far from my brothers. Thus you can see, dear mistress, that Fortune has served me contrary to my wishes and still perseveres in her evil doings.

And that I speak the truth, God, Who is You, and You who in fact are He, know full well. Thus I return to my earlier statement that

Fortune has been my adversary in the past, and continues to assail me with burdens difficult for the heart of a woman to bear. What troubles me even more is the fact that my studies are interrupted by these many ills and worries, which so distract me that I cannot devote myself as I want to the delights of the mind.

∞

More on the Same Subject (Lady Philosophy's Consolation)

For the love of God, let us go further and determine what you could be asking of Him, or blaming on Fortune. I seem to perceive in you great ingratitude, as well as a lack of recognition of the multiplicity of gifts and graces He has bestowed upon you and continues to do so each day; for not only do you not thank Him, you actually consider yourself wronged, as though you deserved to have not only a better lot but indeed everything according to your desire.[35]

To demonstrate the truth of my statement, call to mind the considerable gifts and blessings you have received from God in your unworthiness and still receive each day. If you would reflect well and wisely, you would realize that those events that you now regard as personal misfortunes have served a useful purpose even in this worldly life, and indeed have worked for your betterment. I will demonstrate this to you forthwith, although your corporeal nature prevents you from seeing the real truth.

I observe that there are three worldly goods that humankind regards as chief among its joys and glories. Without some or all of these three, I maintain, there are no riches that could content the heart of man, nor could any treasure of Fortune be found that one would not give to possess them. Two of these are external, and the third is within oneself.

The first of these goods is to be born of noble parents, and here I mean the nobility of virtue; the second, to have a body free from deformity and reasonably attractive in appearance, plus good health, a good constitution, common sense, and reasonable intelligence. The third benefit, which is far from negligible, is to have charming, attractive children who have good sense and are upright in their behavior and God-fearing.

Are you not ungrateful, woman? Do your consider yourself as lacking these gracious blessings, or many others that God has given you? It would appear that when you see yourself as so unfortunate, you forget the gifts with which you have been blessed. Is there a woman among all those you know who can boast of more glorious parentage than your own? Have you forgotten the dignity of your noble philosopher father who spent so much time in our schools that we sat beside him on the chair of philosophy, discussing our secrets with him? In his day, his knowledge earned him the reputation of master of our speculative science; moreover, he remained throughout his life a true Catholic until the end, and was so virtuous that I call upon you to judge whether you value and profit more from the fruits of his wisdom that have remained with you than from any other good, despite your complaints about the lack of what you might have learned from him. Think whether or not you should be content with what you have!

And what shall I say of your noble mother? Do you know of a more virtuous woman? Since the time of her youth, has she ever neglected the life of contemplation in the service of God, notwithstanding whatever duties she might have had to attend to? I believe not. This worthy woman has never succumbed to tribulation nor lost heart through impatience. What an example she has set for you to follow, if you would only pay heed! Reflect on what a special grace God continues to bestow upon you, along with all the rest, by allowing such a noble and virtuous mother to remain with you in her old age. How often she has comforted you and brought you from your impatient thoughts to acknowledge your God! And if you complain that it pains your heart not to be able to provide for her as you think she deserves, I answer that such a desire, patiently endured, is meritorious for both of you. Truly, her worthy behavior and lofty way of life single her out among women. And that is a well known and blessed fact.

As for the second of your blessings, is it not true that God has given you a body that is strong and well-suited to your station in life? Could you ask for anything more at present? Be careful that you use the understanding He has given you well, lest it be better for you to have less knowledge.

On the subject of your third blessing, do you not have children who are good-looking and endowed with good sense? Your first-born is a daughter who entered the noble order in Poissy to dedicate her life to the service of God, contrary to your own wishes but in response to God's call to her. In the flower of her youthful beauty, she lives the life of contemplation and devotion so well that you often derive great comfort from speaking about her and from those sweet and devout letters she writes in her young innocence, full of good sense and wisdom, consoling you and exhorting you to despise this world and worldly success.

Do you not also have a son who is fair and well-mannered? Despite his years numbering no more than twenty, from the time he began his studies, scarcely could anyone be found surpassing him in natural aptitude for grammar, rhetoric, and poetic language, nor anyone of subtler understanding. And the truth of what I say is obvious and can easily be verified.

I am not telling you these things to engender in you a sense of false pride, but so that you will give thanks to God, the source of all good, Who has given you these blessings and many others. It is not Fortune who bestows these gifts, but God, solely out of His grace, and to whom He pleases.

I shall not reply to the other complaints you express with regard to members of your family whom you cannot see because they are far away. For since this world is but transitory, you must hope that, through your good mother's prayers and their own righteous lives, they will be led into the city of joy through God's mercy, where you will all be together for all time.

CHRISTINE M. RENO

(Translated from ex-Phillipps Ms. 128)

NOTES

1. The Bolognese nickname "la Grassa" (in French "la Grasse") was proverbial during the Middle Ages because of the region's fertile soil, which yielded in abundance grapes, oil, corn, and hemp.
2. Tomasso Mondino da Forlì was, like Christine's father, a doctor of medicine.
3. Thomas of Pizan worked as a doctor for the Venetian Republic between 1357 or 1358 and 1364; see Elena Nicolini, "Cristina da Pizzano, l'origine e il nome," *Cultura Neolatina* 1 (1941), p. 145; Charity Cannon Willard, *Christine de Pizan: Her Life and Works* (New York, 1984), pp. 19–20; and Guido Ruggiero, "The Status of Physicians and Surgeons in Renaissance Venice," *Journal of the History of Medicine and Allied Sciences* XXXVI, 2 (April 1981), p. 173.
4. Louis I the Great, King of Hungary (1342–82) and of Poland (1370–82), was the son of Charles I, founder of the Angevin dynasty of Hungary. His reign marked a period of prosperity, with concomitant support of the arts and sciences.
5. An example of Thomas of Bologna's magical military strategies is described by Lynn Thorndike, *A History of Magic and Experimental Science*, 8 vols. (New York, 1923–58), II, p. 802. On various aspects of Thomas's career, see Christine de Pisan, *Le Livre des fais et bonnes meurs du sage roy Charles V*, ed. Suzanne Solente, 2 vols., (Paris, 1936–40), I, pp. vii–xiv; Charity Cannon Willard, "Christine de Pizan: the Astrologer's Daughter," in *Mélanges à la mémoire de Franco Simone*, (Genève, 1980), I, pp. 95–97; and Willard, *Christine de Pizan: Her Life and Works*, p. 22.
6. Christine's husband, Etienne du Castel, is the subject of a tender portrait in her

twenty-sixth "Autre Balade." See *Oeuvres poétiques de Christine de Pisan,* ed. Maurice Roy, 3 vols. (Paris, 1886–96), I, p. 237.

7. One may well wonder whether Christine's insistence on her father's orthodoxy, which she will again make a point of further on, is born of religious conviction or is rather a reaction to criticism or suspicion.

8. This passage can be seen as an example of a characteristic of Christine's work already pointed out by Sheila Delany: that the author takes every opportunity "to influence men in favor of educating women." See "Rewriting Woman Good: Gender and Anxiety of Influence in Two Late-Medieval Texts," in *Chaucer in the Eighties,* eds. Julian N. Wasserman and Robert J. Blanch (Syracuse, 1986), pp. 83–86.

9. The image of the captainless ship receives a much more dramatic development in the *Livre de la Mutacion de Fortune,* ed. Suzanne Solente, 4 vols., (Paris, 1959–66), I, vv. 1160–1416.

10. Some details of Christine's legal difficulties, including archival references, are given by Suzanne Solente in her edition of the *Livre des fais et bonnes meurs du sage roy Charles V,* I, pp. xvi–xvii.

11. Glynnis M. Cropp demonstrates in meticulous detail that Christine worked with an anonymous fourteenth-century verse and prose translation of the *Consolation,* the most popular Boethian translation circulating in her day. See "Boèce et Christine de Pizan," *Medium Aevum* 37 (1981), pp. 387–417. In the *Chemin de long estude,* Christine pictures herself in her study, reaching for her familiar copy of Boethius in an attempt to find some solace in her troubles (ed. Püschel [Berlin, 1887], vv. 171–303).

12. The legend of Christine's amorous attachments is recounted by Gianni Mombello in "J.-M.-L. Coupé e H. Walpole: Gli amori di Christine de Pizan," *Studi Francesi* 16 (1972), pp. 5–25. See also Raimond Thomassy, *Jean Gerson, chancelier de Notre-Dame et de l'Université de Paris* (Paris, 1843), pp. 142–44.

13. This ballad was also included by Christine in the collection of "Autres Balades," of which it is the sixth in the Roy edition. See *Oeuvres poétiques de Christine de Pisan,* I, pp. 213–14.

14. Reference to the *Mutacion de Fortune,* completed in November 1403.

15. One of the many proverbs that Christine, like many of her contemporaries, used as a stylistic embellishment (cf. her description of the style of the "poets" in the section "Christine Relates How She Turned to Study"). A variation of the proverb is found in James W. Hassell, *Middle French Proverbs, Sentences and Proverbial Phrases* (Toronto, 1982), p. 145.

16. Reference to the *Consolation of Philosophy* I, Pr. 1.

17. The qualification "first" is found only in the final version of the *Avision* that has come down to us in ex-Phillipps 128 (f. 61r); it is not found in either of the slightly earlier manuscripts: Paris B.N. fr. 1176 and Brussels B.R. 10309.

18. Christine is referring here to the fifteenth of her "Virelays" found in the *Oeuvres poétiques,* I, pp. 116–17.

19. The French is "constellacion," which has unmistakable astrological connotations.

20. The quotation is from the end of the prologue to Cato's *Distichs,* a book that was widely used in the Middle Ages as a primer.

21. As Suzanne Solente has demonstrated, this description refers to one of Christine's principal sources for historical information, the *Histoire ancienne jusqu'a Cesar.* See *Le Livre de la mutacion de Fortune,* I, p. lxvi.

22. Christine's theory of poetry appears to derive mainly from Boccaccio's *De Genealogia Deorum.*

23. For a discussion of the feminine model of creation proposed here, see Sylvia Huot,

"Seduction and Sublimation: Christine de Pizan, Jean de Meun and Dante," *Romance Notes* 75 (1985), pp. 361–73.

24. It should be remembered that Christine is calculating by the medieval system, in which the new year began on Easter; in 1405 it began on April 19.

25. Isabelle of France, daughter of Charles VI, was married to Richard II of England in November 1396; after Richard's death, she would return to France and marry Charles d'Orléans. On the missions surrounding the marriage with Richard, see James C. Laidlaw, "Christine de Pizan, the Earl of Salisbury and Henry IV," *French Studies* 36 (1982), pp. 129–43.

26. There is a curious discrepancy in the three manuscripts of this work—all the product of Christine's workshop—regarding the age of Christine's elder son Jean du Castel. Ex-Phillipps 128 gives the figure twelve, and the other two manuscripts, Paris, B.N. fr. 1176 and Brussels, B.R. 10309, give his age as thirteen. See Christine de Pisan, *Lavision-Christine*, ed. Sr. Mary Louis Towner (Washington, D.C., 1932), p. 165.

27. Lord Salisbury fell to a crowd at Cirencester in early January 1400.

28. Henry had the reputation for being a patron of the arts. One of his first official acts was to grant pensions to the elderly Geoffrey Chaucer and the young Thomas Hoccleve, who in 1402 would translate Christine's *Epistre au dieu d'Amours*. See *Poems of Cupid, God of Love: Christine de Pizan's Epistre au dieu d'Amours and Dit de la Rose, Thomas Hoccleve's The Letter of Cupid, with George Sewell's The Proclamation of Cupid*, eds. Thelma S. Fenster and Mary Carpenter Erler (Leiden, New York, Kobenhavn, Köln, 1990) and James Hamilton Wylie, *History of England under Henry the Fourth*, 4 vols. (London, 1884–98), I, p. 200.

29. Richard Bruges or Del Brugge, herald in the service of John of Gaunt, Duke of Lancaster, was promoted king of arms by Henry IV in 1399; John, named Falcon King of Arms in 1394, was, like most heralds of the time, known only by his first name. See Hugh Stanford London, *The Life of William Bruges, the first Garter King of Arms* (London, 1970), pp. 1–4, 78.

30. The lord in question is Louis d'Orléans, to whom Christine wrote a ballad recommending her son Jean to his service. It appears as the twenty-second of the "Autres Balades" in the *Oeuvres poétiques*, I, pp. 232–33.

31. On this proverb, see Hassell, *Middle French Proverbs, Sentences and Proverbial Phrases*, p. 177.

32. Christine refers here to Gian Galeazzo Visconti, a ruler of enormous and unscrupulous political ambition, as well as an enthusiastic patron of the arts, who died of the plague in 1402.

33. The *Livre des fais et bonnes meurs du sage roy Charles V* was completed on 30 November 1404; the duke died on 27 April of that year. The second part, begun at the time of his death, opens with a moving lament (I, pp. 108–11).

34. This property is identified as being in the parish of S. Mammolo by Giovanni Fantuzzi, *Notizie degli Scrittori Bolognesi*, 9 vols. (Bologna, 1965) (orig. ed. 1781–94) VII, p. 57 and n. 15; reference given by Suzanne Solente in her edition of the *Livre des fais et bonnes meurs* (I, p. xv).

35. The following description of the worldly gifts Christine enjoys is based on Lady Philosophy's similar reminder to Boethius in the *Consolation* II, Pr. 3 and 4.

CMR

II

THE COURTLY POET

❦

A S C H R I S T I N E herself explained in her *Vision*, her first poems were composed to console herself for the loss of her husband and to distract her mind from the tribulations of her widowhood. These early poems of widowhood are, in themselves, original. Their distant model might have been women's complaints about their lot as expressed in earlier Provençal *chansons de toile*, which women are thought to have sung as they wove, complaining of troubles brought on either by an absent lover or a brutal husband. Christine's more immediate inspiration for writing poetry, however, was Eustache Deschamps' *Art de Dictier (The Art of Writing Poetry)*, which was circulating in Paris, at least in manuscript, at about the time she was writing her first poems. Some years later, in February 1403, she would address a poem to Deschamps in which she refers to herself as his "disciple and well-wisher." He would reply by calling her an "eloquent muse among the nine."[1] It is evident that in her poetry she made use of the same fixed forms he recommends — the rondeau, the virelay, but most especially the ballade. These popular poetic forms had originated as dance patterns and then developed into songs to accompany the dances. The ballade, in particular, had been perfected earlier in the fourteenth century by Guillaume Machaut, who had composed both words and music. By the time Christine started to write, poets were limiting their efforts to words alone.[2]

Christine sets the date of 1399 as the beginning of her literary career, but in fact she had composed some poems several years earlier. In one of them she speaks of the fifth anniversary of her husband's death, which would place the poem around 1395.

> For five long years now do I mourn —
> So often with a tear-stained face —
> Since the day he left me so forlorn
> And turned my joy into disgrace.

My good, wise man by death displaced,
Whose loss has brought to me such pain
That I've wished as rage my joys replaced
That I need not in this world remain.[3]

It was on the seventh anniversary of her husband's death that she
wrote the first of her rondeaux: "Like a mourning dove I'm now all
forlorn." The best known of these poems of widowhood, however, is
the ballade that begins "Alone am I, alone would I be," in which she
mourns her unending, though chosen, solitude.[4]

In spite of her unhappiness, Christine must soon have discovered
that she had a certain facility with words and relished the challenge
of fitting them into intricate patterns. During her lifetime she composed nearly three hundred ballades. Eventually her poetry not only
treats a greater variety of subjects, but it also reveals an experimental approach to these traditional fixed forms, which enjoyed a great
popularity in court circles and in poetic contests organized there.
Such contests might well have been a particular incentive to her, as
her May Day poems suggest. May Day was the time traditionally
favored for poetic competitions. But as her poetry began to show a
greater diversity of inspirations, she was at pains to make it clear
that much of this poetry, especially when it spoke of love, was in no
way autobiographical:

Some people beg me to compose
These verses on them to bestow.
They claim my verses talent show,
But save their grace, I would not know
To write good verse, but even so,
As out of kindness they have asked me
In response, though ignorance I show,
I'll try to please them graciously.[5]

Indeed, this is the ballade that introduces her first poetic cycle, the
Cent Ballades (One Hundred Ballades), which she put together before
1402, the date that can be assigned to the first manuscript of her
collected works.[6] In addition to the poems inspired by her widowhood, one finds here several reflecting the program of reading she had
undertaken to improve her education. There are also sequences that
tell the story of love affairs, usually from the point of view of a young
woman although in at least one case presenting the emotions of the

lover. Another sequence consists of a dialogue between a lover and his lady. These are seldom happy love stories. Christine was obsessed by the instability of Fortune in human affairs. She has been aptly called the poet of love's ending, rather than its happier beginning.[7]

Her attitude toward love stems from her disapproval of so-called courtly love, the usual inspiration for poetry of this sort in her day. Because courtly love was usually illicit, between a man and an older married woman, she could see little happiness in it for a woman, and perhaps not even for an honorable man. She developed this idea at some length in her *Livre du Duc des Vrais Amants (The Book of the Duke of True Lovers)*.

A particularly interesting aspect of these early poems is that they introduce themes that will be developed at greater length later. One learns, for instance, of Christine's reading of Ovid's *Metamorphoses* and the history of the Trojan War, ever popular throughout the Middle Ages. One of the poems inspired by the undependability of Fortune refers to her reading of Boethius, whose *Consolation* was a principal source for her autobiographical *Vision:*

> In general all of us hold more dear
> Fortune's promises than Nature's good,
> But this is false, for these can disappear,
> So one should not put faith in such falsehood.
> Boethius makes this affirmation
> In his book of Consolation,
> Warning against Fortune's glory
> If we believe some wise men's story.[8]

Although certain poems inspired by events of the day or dedicated to important personnages are less interesting, these sometimes provide a useful context for their composition and help to date them. Several of these are related to the early years of Christine's career when she frequented the court of the king's brother, Louis of Orleans. Several poems are addressed to this duke, and there are three ballades celebrating a jousting match between knights from his court and English knights that took place on May 19, 1402. Of greater interest are references to her participation in the debate inspired by *The Romance of the Rose*, or the ballade in which she appeals to the Duke of Orleans to find a place in his household for her son, Jean, recently returned from England. As it is evident that the duke turned a deaf ear to her plea, we soon find her praising the Court of Burgundy where Jean had been given an appointment, in a poem dated 1403. There is also a lament inspired by the death of the Burgundian duke, Philip the Bold, in April 1404. It was he who had commissioned Christine to write the biography of his brother, the *Faits et Bonnes Meurs du Sage Roi Charles V (The Deeds and Good Character of King Charles V the Wise)*.

In all of this, there is abundant evidence of Christine's pleasure in experimenting with verse forms. In her ballades these experiments involved verse and stanza length, and rhyme sceme. She rarely wrote two poems using exactly the same pattern. In a few cases the experiment seems more important than the content, as is the case in four poems called *Ballades d'Estrange Façon (Ballades in a Curious Form)*, which includes one in which the verses can be read from the beginning or the end.[9]

Her rondeaux, though fewer in number, show a similar variety of pattern. Some have twelve verses, some have ten, and a few have only seven verses. Christine truly excels in these shorter poems. Her virelais, in general, show fewer innovations, and are similar to those written by other poets of her day.

Some attention should be given to two other sorts of poems that are to be found in her collections: these are the playful *Jeux à vendre,* which might be called *Songs for Sale,* and the *Enseignements* and *Proverbes Moraux (Moral Teachings and Proverbs)*.

The *Songs for Sale,* taken from a sequence of nearly one hundred poems, seem to involve a sort of poetic game, one that continued to be popular for some time after Christine's day. They are playful and amusing, although of slight poetic significance. One can imagine that they might have provided an engaging way to entertain children. The *Moral Teachings* and *Proverbs* are more important because they mark the true beginning of Christine's enduring interest in the instruction of the young. The *Moral Teachings* and *Proverbs* were quite evidently composed for her son, for they begin by admonishing him:[10]

> Son, I have no great treasure
> To make you rich, but a measure
> Of good advice which you may need;
> I give it hoping you'll take heed.

The last collection of Christine's poetry, the British Library Harley Ms. 4431, shows at the beginning of these quatrains a delightful miniature of Christine instructing her son. Some of her advice, however, is sufficiently general to apply to other categories of young people. She especially recommends the value of cultivating the mind, saying:

> Read willingly fine books of tales
> As much as you can, for it never fails
> That the examples such books comprise
> Can help you to become more wise.

On the other hand, she warns against reading such texts as *The Romance of the Rose* and Ovid's *Art of Love:*

> If to live chastely you propose
> Don't read *The Romance of the Rose,*
> Nor Ovid's *Art of Loving Well*
> For that can only trouble spell.

She particularly disapproved of the widespread use of Ovid as a school text.

Christine quite evidently understood the value of verse as an aid to memory in the learning process, a technique that has been used many times in books for the young, including the *New England Primer,* which taught so many of our forebears to read.

A similar inspiration undoubtedly accounts for the *Moral Teachings* and *Proverbs,* very possibly suggested by the *Distichs of Cato,* also a widely used school text throughout the Middle Ages. Christine's proverbs were sufficiently popular to be translated into English by Anthony Woodville, King Edward IV's brother-in-law. They were printed by Caxton in 1478.[11]

The best-known theme of her poetry, however, aside from the poems on widowhood, is the history of love, including poetic debates about love of the sort that was a popular form of entertainment in courtly circles, at least from the days when Andreas Capellanus wrote his *Art of Love.*[12] Christine's love poetry is unusual not only because it presents a woman's point of view, but because the love she describes is not entirely idealized and so is often an interesting revelation of more realistic relations between men and women at the end of the Middle Ages.

Christine first made use of this theme in two groups of poems in her *One Hundred Ballades,* composed before 1402, and she continued to develop it in a variety of ways until she wrote her *Cent Ballades d'Amant et de Dame* (*One Hundred Ballades of a Lover and His Lady*), perhaps as late as 1410.

For a modern reader, it is interesting to consider these dialogues in the light of Nathalie Sarraute's theory expressed in an essay entitled "Conversation et Sous-Conversation" and setting forth the idea that conversation is the only valid representation of reality in literature.[13] Although far removed in time from the invention of such a novelistic technique, Christine understood the merit of attempting to externalize an inner drama, especially as it reveals conventional relationships between men and women.

The first example of the love theme is introduced by the twenty-first of the *One Hundred Ballades,* which begins a series of twenty-eight telling the story of an unhappy love affair from the point of view of a disillusioned young woman in a sort of interior monologue that reminds one of Jean Cocteau's one-sided telephone conversation of *La Voix Humaine,* progressing from the initial joys of the affair to its unsatisfactory ending.[14] It should be noted that a series of rondeaux, perhaps dating from the same period, recounts a similarly disappointing affair from a young man's point of view. Even though these are not themselves dialogues, they would seem to serve as preparation for the sequence that follows in twenty-two poems (LXV to LXXXVI).

In this sequence Christine has a young woman begin by confessing that she has fallen in love with a man who has singled her out for his attentions. In her joy she praises love for this happy state of affairs and also praises her beloved. The young man is apparently a knight, for soon he lets it be known that he must go away to fight in the Holy Roman Empire. At the same time the development of their affair is threatened not only by a jealous husband but by gossips who spy on their meetings. Such gossips are a constant feature of this love poetry. In spite of these discouragements, however, the young woman eventually grants the lover the favor for which he has been begging. As he departs, she swears eternal fidelity to him, but she never sees him again, nor does she hear any word from him. Eventually she falls ill (Ballade XLIII), regretting her love and confessing that if she had ever suspected such an unhappy outcome, she would never have been so foolish. Her unhappiness is further increased by a rumor that her former lover is involved with another woman, so the sting of jealousy increases her chagrin. Finally, when two years have passed, she renounces love altogether:

Love, I will no longer serve you,
So farewell I now would say.
You enslave me when I'd be true,
Your reward is only punishment,
For trust you return but torment
Bringing me pain I never knew.
I can no more this love pursue.

The emotion revealed in these poems seems so authentic that in Ballade L Christine saw fit to make clear that she was not recounting a personal experience but merely creating a poetic fiction. It must be remembered, however, that Christine had indeed experienced both love and loss and so had some genuine understanding of both emotions. However, she insists:

But of love I now feel no torment,
Joy or grief, but some verses invent
To amuse, such as others devise;
In this I refer to poets wise.

The lover who speaks in the rondeaux is no more fortunate than the lady of the ballades. The lovers manage a reconciliation after an initial misunderstanding, but they are eventually separated by the return from travels of the lady's husband. The lover can only lament his bad fortune. This basic situation will be developed at greater length in *The Book of the Duke of True Lovers*.[15]

There is, however, a further sequence of ballades (LXV to LXXXVI) that develops a dialogue between two more lovers. In this second case the lady seems more experienced than in the first and indeed appears less hesitant about accepting the man's advances, although he complains bitterly that he has already admired her for several years without finding the courage to speak to her. Once more the development of the affair is inhibited by the presence of gossips who enjoy watching them, as well as by a jealous husband. In this case the woman is sufficiently sophisticated to dominate the relationship and to make the lover suffer. When he has been absent for a time, she reviles him, although when he proves to her that she has accused him falsely, she forgives him. As the problem of the gossips persists, however, he is eventually obliged to go away to avoid an open scandal. The final poem of the cycle finds him bitterly complaining of his loneliness so far from his lady.

The earliest collections of Christine's poetry include not only the *Hundred Ballades* and many of her other short poems, but also three longer poems that center on debates concerning the nature of love and the problems of lovers. These are the *Débat de Deux Amants* (*The Debate of Two Lovers*), the *Livre des Trois Jugemens* (*The Book of Three Judgments*) and the *Dit de Poissy* (*The Tale of Poissy*). [16] All three were undoubtedly written around 1400, although only *The Tale of Poissy* mentions a specific date. The time corresponds, of course, to the foundation in Paris of a Court of Love that tried to imitate early Provençal courts. This was to be devoted to poetry celebrating love and women, as well as discussions of love and poetic contests, favorite diversions of courtly society. Part of the game was to call on some nobleman in the group of participants to decide the merits of a given case.

In *The Debate of Two Lovers,* the Duke of Orleans is invited to decide the merits of the lovers' cases, whereas in *The Book of Three Judgments* the appeal is made to Jean de Werchin, Seneschal of Hainaut, whom Christine had compared favorably in the earlier poem to famous lovers of the past such as Tristan, Lancelot, or Arthur of Brittany. Werchin was himself a poet as well as a valiant knight, as can be seen from a *Songe de la Barge* that he composed in 1404 and an exchange of ballades on the subject of love with his squire, the future distinguished diplomat Guillebert de Lannoy.

It has been suggested that *The Tale of Poissy* was also directed to Werchin, but this is unlikely because the knight to whom it is dedicated was absent from Paris at the time the poem was written (April 1400), whereas there is no evidence that Werchin was not in France then. The pilgrimage to Santiago that has been mentioned in this connection did not take place until the summer of 1402. [17]

In any case, turning over the judgment of the plights of these lovers relieved Christine of having to give her own opinion of the merits of their cases. Although one suspects that she did not have a good opinion of the joys and sorrows of these love affairs, she was not yet ready to express her views.

The Tale of Poissy, of which some passages are included here, has an added interest because of its background, which describes a visit to the royal abbey of Poissy not far from Paris, where Christine's daughter had already been a nun for several years. This was an especially favored religious community where the king's aunt was abbess and his sister a nun. Christine's description of the abbey and the life there as well as her journey from Paris with a group of friends on a delightful spring day are both remarkable for the glimpse they provide of life in France at the beginning of the fifteenth century. It is on the return trip to Paris that the love debate occurs. Two of Christine's traveling companions, both quite obviously unhappy, discuss which of them is the more to be pitied, a young woman whose lover has been a prisoner of the Turks since the French defeat at Nicopolis in 1396, or a knight who, although continuing to love her in spite of her disdain, is rejected by his lady for another. There is also an interesting contrast here between the tranquility of life in the abbey and the unhappiness of the two disappointed lovers. One doubts that this is altogether accidental, for there is the suggestion that Christine may have thought that the life of the spirit might indeed have advantages over the worldly life. In any case, she agrees to seek the judgment of a well-known knight, and a member of the group offers to carry the request to the place where the knight is to be found.

The background that Christine provides for both *The Debate of Two Lovers* and *The Tale of Poissy* is a new feature of her writing. The scenes she evokes remind one of the miniatures that illustrate the texts in the two best manuscripts. The opening lines of *The Debate of Two Lovers* describe a gathering at a large Parisian house where the guests, the music, and the general decor present a scene of considerable elegance. As Christine, ever the sad widow, sits apart watching the other guests, she falls into conversation with a knight, who also chooses to be an onlooker. Presently they are joined by a lively young squire, and the three inevitably become involved in a discussion of the nature of love. They decide to go into the adjoining garden to continue their conversation more tranquilly. Christine very discreetly invites another woman, a young one, to join them. The debate takes place in a leafy and agreeable setting.

The Tale of Poissy opens with a charming description of the trip of a group of friends to Poissy on a spring day, a scene represented in one of the miniatures. Christine dwells on the pleasant ride through the forest. On their arrival at the abbey comes the accurate description of the abbey itself. After the debate during the return journey, Christine adds a charming domestic touch by inviting her two companions to dine with her at her house. One is struck, as often, by Christine's ability to collaborate with her illustrator in evoking these scenes of the world she knew so well.

This trait is developed even further in *The Book of the Duke of True Lovers*, in which the love story is enhanced by abundant descriptions of aristocratic country life. There are descriptions of hunting and boating and a marvelous description of an elaborate tournament. In this colorful setting a young nobleman falls in love with a married cousin. The affair, however, is impeded by a jealous husband and gossips who take an undue interest in the lovers' concerns. Here, Christine examines in detail the stages through which the relationship progresses, notably in the letters and poems that the pair exchange.

The story is set forth essentially by the young man, who feels an obligation to fall in love, but who speaks of the emotion as a malady from which he hopes the lady will cure him and make him brave, inspiring him to accomplish great deeds. The lady responds to his entreaties and arranges to evade her husband's watchful eye in order to meet with the young man. This conventional development of love, however, is opposed by an older friend and former governess of the lady, who refuses to help further the relationship. She suspects what is taking place and writes a letter to warn her young friend of the price she will inevitably pay for her indiscretions:

> Ah! dear Lady, when it happens that this love has subsided, can you conceive of how that lady who has been blinded by her envelopment in foolish pleasure bitterly repents when she realizes what she has done and reflects upon the follies and various perilous situations in which many a time she has found herself? Can you conceive of how much she might wish it had never happened, no matter what the cost might have been, and that such a reproach could not be said of her? You certainly could not imagine the enormous feeling of repentance and distasteful thoughts that remain in her heart.[18]

As it turns out, of course, the Dame de la Tour's advice is only too apt. The Duke is eventually driven by gossips to go away for some ten years; although after his return he sees the lady from time to time, they acknowledge their impossible situation. As long as the husband lives there is no honorable solution possible. Their sorrow gives rise to a final cycle of poems expressing their disillusionment. Christine finally states clearly the view of extramarital love she has been suggesting from the first introduction of the subject in her ballades.

A curious aspect of the tale is that at the beginning Christine explains that she had written down this love story at the request of a young nobleman whose own story it was. The first editor of the poem, Maurice Roy, thought that the person in question might have been

Jean de Bourbon, who had eventually married Marie de Berry.[19] This scarcely seems possible, for the tale was written after 1403, after the first collection of Christine's poetry. The couple in question had been married in 1400, at which time Marie de Berry had already been married and widowed twice. Her second husband was Philippe d'Artois, Count of Eu, who had been captured by the Turks at Nicopolis and had died in captivity. It is difficult to believe that Jean de Bourbon wished to suggest that he had loved Marie during the lifetime of her former husband, for that would certainly have been in questionable taste in view of the circumstances of his death. Furthermore, until 1399 he had been betrothed to Bonne of Burgundy, who had died before the marriage could take place. These circumstances scarcely provide a convincing background for a *roman à clef.*

It is equally difficult to believe, as Roy suggested, that it was Marie de Berry who commanded Christine to write *One Hundred Ballades of a Lover and His Lady.*[20] Christine explains in the opening lines that she has been ordered to write these poems as a sort of penance for having expressed the opinion that honorable ladies should not become involved in love affairs outside of marriage. This would appear to be a clear reference to the Dame de la Tour's letter, which Christine had seen fit to repeat in *The Treasury of the City of Ladies,* where she discusses quite clearly the price a woman might well pay for straying from the path of virtue. It should not be forgotten that no law protected a woman in these circumstances and that she was at the mercy of her husband if discovered. Christine did not like to see women victimized by the society in which they lived.

If *One Hundred Ballades of a Lover and His Lady* were composed between 1405 and 1410, which seems probable in view of the fact that they are to be found only in the third and final collection of Christine's poetry, Marie de Berry (born in 1375) would by then have been past thirty. She was a very capable mother of several children who, having rallied from the deaths of two husbands, would soon be obliged to manage the affairs of her third husband and try to ransom him from the English after his capture at Agincourt. She scarcely suggests the sort of woman who would dwell on the charms of illicit love.

Whoever may have requested it, Christine returned to a dialogue between two lovers, leading once more to an unhappy conclusion, especially for the woman. As Christine always enjoyed experimentation, she undertook to make the flow of the verse reflect the emotions of the lovers. In general, when they are uncertain or unhappy, they speak in longer verses than in moments of intense emotion, when the verses frequently shorten and the tempo quickens. Furthermore, these emotions are developed in a more complex pattern than in the earlier, shorter cycles. Although Christine claims at the beginning to have lost interest in writing love poetry, the evidence shows that her understanding of both human emotions and verse forms has continued to develop. Although she has been faulted for effacing herself so completely behind the voices of the two lovers, this could also be considered one of the charms of this love story. Although twentieth-century lovers would not be likely to communicate in poetry, it is intriguing to consider that both the situation and the psychology of the love affair are similar to Noël Coward's film, *Brief Encounter*. A happy outcome is no more possible there than at the beginning of the fifteenth century.

In Christine's brief encounter the young woman resists the man's advances at the start, but in Ballade VIII, the God of Love himself appears to remind her that youth and love can slip away all too rapidly. Although she protests, she wavers and finally succumbs, continuing to express some lingering doubts about the man's intentions (Ballade XXVI). Eventually she does give in to his pleas, and there follow several poems that are a sort of lovers' duet in which the pair converses rapturously in alternating voices. In spite of their joy, difficulties soon present themselves: the woman reproaches the man for making her wait so long for his arrival on one occasion; gossip inevitably begins to circulate about them. This gossip deters them from meeting as frequently as they would like, and the man eventually decides that he should go away until the rumors are quieted. After he takes his leave (XLVIII) there follows a series of poem-letters in which the lovers express their loneliness as well as their love. Eventually they are reunited (LVIII) and the next twelve poems give expression to their renewed joy. But soon after this, the lover begins to show signs of jealousy and to appear less frequently. Complaints on both sides are the result, and eventually the lovers quarrel. Here the story ends, with a long complaint from the lady, who now bitterly regrets her emotional adventure, especially as she recalls her initial misgivings. She admits that she should have known better than to fall into Love's trap.

Curiously, the "Mortel Lay," as it is called, is less appealing than the ballades, for Christine falls into the temptation of citing various classical lovers, which seems to falsify the lady's emotions. Christine must have been carried away here not only by her show of erudition, but by her virtuosity in employing a variety of verse forms.[21]

At the same time, her concern for the woman's fate is undoubtedly genuine, as she sees the woman as one of society's victims. She believed that women had a more constructive and useful role to play, as set forth in both *The Book of the City of Ladies* and *The Treasury of the City of Ladies.*

It must not be forgotten that Christine's earliest literary success was achieved at the Orleans court. The entourage of the Duke of Orleans, in particular, fueled a desire to revive courtly and chivalric traditions of an earlier age. Under the glamour of this atmosphere, however, lurked a more unpleasant truth. The duke was a notorious philanderer, and by the summer of 1405 his extramarital relations with the queen were causing a public scandal. The same summer a scandal broke out among the ladies of the queen's court, resulting in the dismissal of some of them. Christine was not merely a moralist but a keen observer of the society that surrounded her. Her disapproval of the traditional concept of courtly love was based not only on her disagreement with the popularity of *The Romance of the Rose,* the source of her own debate with Jean de Montreuil and the Col brothers, but also on her distress at seeing her contemporaries victimized by traditional attitudes towards women. At the same time, it is interesting to reflect that the situations that inspired this poetry were very similar to the one from which Madame de Lafayette would draw inspiration for *La Princesse de Clèves* more than two centuries later.

NOTES

1. *Oeuvres poétiques de Christine de Pisan,* II, pp. 295–301; E. Deschamps, *Oeuvres complètes,* VI, p. 251.
2. N. Wilkins, *One Hundred Ballades, Rondeaux and Virelais* (Cambridge, 1969), Introduction; also "Structure of Ballades, Rondeaux and Virelais in Froissart, and in Christine de Pisan," *French Studies* 23 (1969), 337–48.
3. Ballade IX, *Oeuvres,* I, p. 10.
4. Rondeau I, dated 1396, *Oeuvres,* I, p. 147; "Seulette suis," Ballade XI, *Oeuvres,* I, p. 12.
5. Ballade I, *Oeuvres,* I, p. 1.
6. The writings included in Paris, B.N. Ms. fr. 12779 and Chantilly, Musée Condé Ms. 492 point to this date. B.N. Ms. fr. 604 is possibly a later copy of this collection, or possibly a workshop model, for places are indicated for illustrations that were not painted.
7. K. Varty, ed., *Christine de Pisan: Ballades, Rondeaux and Virelais* (Leicester, 1965), p. xxvii.
8. Ballade XCVII, *Oeuvres,* I, p. 97. See also Glynnis M. Cropp, "Boèce et Christine de Pisan," *Moyen Age* 87 (1981), pp. 387–417.

9. *Oeuvres,* I, pp. 119–20.
10. *Oeuvres,* III, pp. 27–44.
11. *Oeuvres,* III, pp. 45–57. *The Morale Proverbes of Christyne* (Westminster, 1478).
12. *The Art of Courtly Love,* trans. with notes and Introduction by John Jay Parry (New York, 1959).
13. *L'Ere de Soupçon* (Paris, 1956); English trans. *The Age of Suspicion* (1963).
14. Paris, 1930.
15. *Oeuvres,* III, pp. 49–222. For an interesting discussion see *The Book of the Duke of True Lovers,* trans. with an Intro. by Thelma S. Fenster; lyric poetry trans. by Nadia Margolis (New York, 1991).
16. *Oeuvres,* II, pp. 49–222. For an interesting discussion of these poems, see Barbara K. Altman, "Reopening the Case: Machaut's *Judgment* Poems as a Source in Christine de Pizan," in *Reinterpreting Christine de Pizan,* ed. Earl Jeffrey Richards (Athens, Ga., 1992), pp. 137–56.
17. C. C. Willard, *Christine de Pizan,* pp. 66–67; also "Jean de Werchin, Seneschal de Hainaut: Reader and Writer of Courtly Literature," in *Courtly Literature: Culture and Context,* eds. Keith Busby and Erik Cooper (Amsterdam and Philadelphia, 1990), pp. 595–605.
18. *The Book of the Duke of True Lovers,* p. 118.
19. *Oeuvres,* II, p. xv.
20. *Oeuvres,* III, p. xvi. For the text, see pp. 209–317. Also *Cent Ballades d'Amant et de Dame,* ed. Jacqueline Cerquiglini (Paris, 1982).
21. C. C. Willard, "Christine de Pizan's *Cent Ballades d'Amant et de Dame:* Criticism of Courtly Love," in *Court and Poet,* ed. G. S. Burgess (Liverpool, 1981), pp. 357–64.
22. *Court and Poet,* pp. 362–63.

ONE HUNDRED BALLADES

XI. *Alone Am I*

Alone am I and alone would I be
Alone by my lover left suddenly.
Alone am I, no friend or master with me,
Alone am I, both sad and angrily,
Alone am I, in languor wretchedly,
Alone am I, completely lost doubtlessly,
Alone am I, friendless and so lonely.

Alone am I, at the door or window,
Alone am I, in a corner deposited,
Alone am I, with tears which freely flow,
Alone am I, whether sorrowful or comforted,
Alone am I, nevermore contented,
Alone am I, in my chamber closeted,
Alone am I, friendless and so lonely.

Alone am I, on any street or hearth,
Alone am I, whether moving or at rest,
Alone am I, more than any thing on earth,
Alone am I, by all others cast aside,
Alone am I, so cast down to abide,
Alone am I, who such hot tears have cried,
Alone am I, friendless and so lonely.

Prince, I can do little more than sigh,
Alone am I, with grief none can deny,
Alone am I, more blue than deepest dye,
Alone am I, friendless and so lonely.

CCW

XXI. *He Begs Me*

He begs me, oh, so sweetly,
As he knows so well to do;
He looks at me so neatly,
A handsome figure and visage, too.
He is so courteous and true,
Such great good of him I've heard said
That I could scarcely be misled.

He speaks to me so pleasantly—
Of misspeaking he should hesitate,
Swearing he loves me loyally,
To say it he could not wait
And nothing did he understate.
And then a sigh so gently did he shed
That I could scarcely be misled.

So I'm wondering most discreetly
About what I ought now to do,
For I fear I'm charmed completely;
Like it or not, Love gives a clue
That I know I should not pursue.
But my heart toward him is so sped
That I could scarcely be misled.

CCW

XXII. *The Gods and Goddesses*

The gods and goddesses, those great
Servants of Love, were diligent,
As Ovid tells, to celebrate
Love's rites—and suffered discontent
And woes of love. But true intent
And faith they kept, left none aggrieved,
If ancient fables be believed.

They left Olympus for some mate
Of lowly earth, in their descent
Impetuous to participate
In earthly joys, with quick consent

Embracing them, indifferent
To costs of all such zeal achieved
If ancient fables be believed.

Delights of love could subjugate
Enchantress and nymph; immortals spent
Time, strength, and wealth immoderate
On maids and shepherds, earthward went
Bestowing boons munificent
On those whose favor they received
If ancient fables be believed.

So ladies, lords, submit, assent
To love, nor seek to be reprieved
From service proved so excellent
If ancient fables be believed.

DWIGHT DURLING

XXIV. *My Sweet Love*

My sweet love, my dear darling,
My good friend, whom I love so much,
Your goodness keeps me from harm,
Truly I could cry out to you,
    Fountain from which all good comes,
You who sustain me with peace and joy,
Whose pleasures come to me so abundantly;
Oh, you alone give me joy.

This sorrow which has informed my heart
These many years, which has made me bitter,
Let your goodness, in every respect, abolish pain;
I cannot complain or blame
    Fortune who becomes
Good for me, if it comes at this time.
You have set me on this path and direction;
Oh, you alone give me joy.

Thus Love who, by his lordship,
With such pleasure wished to reclaim me;
For I can say truly, without flattery,

There is none better here, none more pure
Than you, my love, who keeps
My heart true, keeps it for you,
I have no other thought or care;
Oh, you alone give me joy.

REGINA DECORMIER

XXXIV. *The Joyous Month of May*

Now has come the joyous month of May,
So gay, with such sweet delights,
As these orchards, hedges, and these woods,
All decked with leaves and blossoms,
    And all things rejoice.
Among the fields all flowered and green,
Nothing is troubled or grieving,
In the sweet month of May.

Birds go joyfully singing,
Everywhere, all life rejoices
Except for me, alas! who grieves deeply,
For I am far from my love;
    I cannot feel joy,
The merrier the season, the more I sorrow,
As I well know since once I loved,
In the sweet month of May.

For him, whom I mourn, I weep often,
For him, from whom I have no help;
The painful grief of love I now more strongly
Feel, the stings, the blows, the tricks,
    In this sweet time than I have
Ever felt before; as all this destroys
The great desire I once so strongly felt,
In the sweet month of May.

REGINA DECORMIER

XLII. *There's a Messenger, Ovid Tells*

There's a messenger, Ovid tells
Who to sleepers curious news brings.
He makes them sleep, and then with dreams spells
Joy and sorrow and other such things.
Morpheus is this messenger's name,
Son of the god who sleeps, the fable says,
Possessing several forms, it is claimed.
He announces to folk things that amaze.

And may that god whose sleep so eases me
Be thanked, because of the sorrow I feel,
For now he brings such news to me
Of my friend whose love I can't conceal.
But when he says certain things that surprise
My heart like a maple leaf sways,
For never sad truth will he disguise,
He announces to folk things that amaze.

My grief he does much to assuage,
This god of sleep, for I'd be dead
If it were not so; though to weep with rage
He's sometimes made me, when he has said
To discomfort me, that another maid
Has my friend's heart, and that truth he conveys
I greatly fear, of such an escapade
He announces to folk things that amaze.

                                        CCW

LVIII. *Sir Knight, You Like Pretty Words*

Sir Knight, you like pretty words;
But I beg you to like fair deeds more.
It is a little late for you to begin,
But—better late than never.
You serve only as light entertainment:
In this court your ballads go singing;
The great deed is what you will never do.
Lord! Lord! What a valiant knight!

You are a good and bold knight,
But you love your ease a little too much,
If for you, as for cowards,
The heavy weight of arms causes grief.
Shame and defeat to such a knight
Who for honor's sake devotes himself to writing!
A life of ease will be yours henceforth.
Lord! Lord! What a valiant knight!

There is worse, by God in heaven.
The wretched fact is you can do more;
You defame, jongleur, you slander others,
This you do, and worse, but I will keep my peace
In the Court, in the Palace, everywhere
In the palace they say they can banish you;
What good are you? You write virelays.
Lord! Lord! What a valiant knight!

Desist from the slander of others,
Sir Knight, it is a thousand times worse
For you if the clergy and laymen say of you,
Lord! Lord! What a valiant knight!

REGINA DECORMIER

LXX. *Do You Want Then That I Should Die*

Do you want then that I should die
Fairest maid, from loving you?
Alas! wherever could I fly
If your sweetness makes me so blue?
For no protection now will do
Against love's unfeeling attack
For both strength and will now I lack.

For God's sake, don't love deny,
My very sweet star of the sea
On whose light I would rely;
To you alone I make this plea
That your true friend I still may be,
Though I will nothing answer back
For both strength and will I now lack.

On your good will I must rely
And in all ways myself subdue,
With nothing else can I comply
And all desires I must eschew
Without ever being untrue
To you despite every drawback,
For both strength and will I now lack.

CCW

LXXVIII. *The Jealous Husband*

What can we do with this jealous husband?
I pray to God someone can flay him.
He keeps us under such close guard
We cannot even approach one another.
May he be bound
With a rope, the dirty villain, faking gout,
How pained and weary he makes us!

May his body be thrown to the wolves,
As he serves only to hinder!
What good is this old one full of coughs,
Except for quarreling, sulking, and spitting?
The devil can love him and hold him dear,
I hate him, the cuckold, old and undone,
How pained and weary he makes us!

Hah! He deserves to be cuckolded,
The baboon who goes searching
His house! Hah! May a little
Chill take him to bed, or the stairs
Do him in,
This villain who is always suspicious,
How pained and weary he makes us!

REGINA DECORMIER

LXXXVIII. *If Mourning I Now Wear*

What can I do, if mourning I now wear
Because henceforth will all my pleasures fail,

As I must soon go far from the place where
The door of the manor will no more avail,
For which my heart is now in great travail
And with such grief is blackened to despair
So that my sad lot I only can bewail;
It is unlikely that I'll live for long.

Ah, lady, only think what grief I bear
That from this land I far away must sail,
Leaving you here, my love so fair,
With no power to let any hope prevail
Though any other love I would curtail
For from you comes all for which I could long;
But as Love with this burden does me assail
It is unlikely that I'll live for long.

Great suffering will nights and mornings share.
Cursed be the one who makes this state prevail
Through which I lose you, so I'd rather now prepare
For early death than long your loss bewail,
For compared to you all other loves would pale
In beauty and charms which to you belong
But I must leave, nothing else will now avail.
It is unlikely that I'll live for long.

CCW

(Translated from *Oeuvres Poétiques de Christine de Pisan,*
ed. Maurice Roy)

MORE BALLADES

❦

VII. *If Pallas I Could Only Know*

If Pallas I could only know
Joy and well-being would never be lacking
For through her the way I could go
Of comfort and could bear without slacking
Fortune's burden, which is never lacking.
But I am too weak to bear
So great a burden if she doesn't care
By her great power to help me to support
This burden (if God should me spare),
For from Juno I have no comfort.

Pallas, Juno, and Venus once wished to plead
Before Paris each her separate cares,
And each one said that she believed
That she was perfect, the most fair
In her own powers than were the others there.
From Paris they all wished to know,
Who when he judged them did bestow
The prize on Venus for beauty's report,
Saying: "Lady, I would have you know
That from Juno I have no comfort."

Then for the golden apple Venus's aid
Won for him Helen, though he paid a price
And death for it later; so by Venus dismayed,
Joy in my heart would suffice
If the valiant Pallas, by whom I've heard
Ills are vanquished and preserved
Are all good things. If she would be served
By me: then no further support

Would be needed by me or deserved,
But from Juno I have no comfort.

So by these three goddesses so mighty
The world endures in spite of ill report,
But of Pallas may God remind me,
For from Juno I have no comfort.

CCW

XIV. *Come, Pallas*

Come, Pallas, come, goddess most honorable
To comfort me in my distress,
For my pain and longing so intolerable
Will snuff out my life in great bitterness.
      For Fortune cuts me through
And my welfare devours and ruins, too,
Leaving me small hope in either nights or days,
For Juno hates me and Misfortune dismays.

I find no comfort at all meaningful
For my troubles, even when I press
Towards something somewhat more amenable
No remedy I find, but only endless stress
      In endless pain and trouble, too,
For Fortune destroys all that I renew
Wherever I might have hoped for blame or praise,
For Juno hates me and Misfortune dismays.

And so I pray to that great venerable
Daughter of a god, Pallas, who can redress
All those who stray, may she be approachable
To my pleas and, like a schoolmistress,
      Tell me what to do.
May Diana be with her the whole day through,
For long have I struggled in this maze,
Where Juno hates me and Misfortune dismays.

Prince, before death should overcome me,
Pray Pallas that my savior she'll be;
For always now as I follow my ways
Juno hates me and Misfortune dismays.

CCW

XXVI. *A Sweet Thing Is Marriage*

A sweet thing is marriage,
I can well prove it by my own experience.
It is true for one who has a good and wise husband
Like the one God helped me find.
Praised be He who wanted to save him for me,
For I can strongly vouch
For his great goodness,
And surely the gentle man loves me well.

On our wedding night
I was immediately able to recognize
His great worth, for he never did anything
To offend me or cause me pain.
But before the time had come to arise
He had kissed me a hundred times, I vow,
Without ever demanding any other base conduct.
And surely the gentle man loves me well.

And he said, with such sweet words:
"God guided me to you,
Sweet beloved, and I believe
He had me nurtured for your use."
Thus, he went on dreaming
Without otherwise losing control.
And surely the gentle man loves me well.

Prince, he makes me mad with desire for love
When he tells me he is completely mine.
He will make me die with sweetness,
And surely the gentle man loves me well.

JUNE HALL MCCASH

XXXV. *The Gentlest Man*

Ah, the gentlest man who was ever framed,
In talk and conversation ever glad,
The paragon by everyone acclaimed,
The best lover a woman ever had.
For my true heart, a repast to devour,
Most savory desire of any I hold dear,

My one beloved, my paradise, my bower,
Most perfect pleasure upon which eyes can peer—
Your sweetness only causes warlike havoc here.

Your sweetness truly in a havoc came
Upon my heart which never thought to be
In such a plight, but suddenly the flame
Of great desire lit it so recklessly
It would have died, had Sweet Thought not shown face.
Souvenir too upon heart's couch appears.
We lie and lock you round in thought's embrace;
But when I realize that not one kiss is near,
Your sweetness only causes warlike havoc here.

My sweet friend, whom I love with all my heart,
There's not one thought of ever throwing away
Your handsome look, which became a part
Enclosed within; nothing could ever efface
The sound of your voice or the gracious touch
Of those gentle hands which I hold dear,
That I like to feel and explore so much!
But when I can't see you, when you're not near,
Your sweetness only causes warlike havoc here.

Handsome and fine, who's come to make heart's seizure,
Never forget me; that one wish I hold dear;
For when I can't look upon you at my leisure,
Your sweetness only causes warlike havoc here.

JAMES J. WILHELM

RONDEAU I. *Like the Mourning Dove*

Like the mourning dove I'm now all alone,
And like a shepherdless sheep gone astray,
For death has long ago taken away
My loved one whom I constantly mourn.

It's now seven years that he's gone, alas
Better I'd been buried that same day,
Like a mourning dove I'm all forlorn.

For since I have such sorrow borne,
And grievous trouble and disarray,

For while I live I've not even one ray
Of hope of comfort, night or morn.
Like the mourning dove I'm now all forlorn.

CCW

RONDEAU III. *I Am a Widow Lone*

I am a widow lone, in black arrayed,
With sorrowful face and most simply clad;
In great distress and with manner so sad
I bear this sorrow that's now on me laid.

It's only right that I should be dismayed,
Full of hot tears and with tongue of lead,
I am a widow lone, in black arrayed.

Since I lost my love, by foul Death betrayed,
Grief has struck me, which has to perdition led
All my good days, and so my joy has fled.
In this bitter state have my fortunes stayed —
I am a widow lone, in black arrayed.

CCW

RONDEAU XLVI. *If I Often Go to Chapel*

If I often go to chapel,
It's to see the maiden who
Is as fresh as the rose that's new.

Why should those others babble?
Is it really some great news
If I often go to chapel?

There's no road that I will travel
Unless she will advise me;
They are fools to criticize me
If I often go to chapel.

JAMES J. WILHELM

Rondeau LV. *A Difficult Thing*

A difficult thing it is to endure
When the heart weeps while the mouth sings;

And from grief to rest secure
A difficult thing it is to endure.

In trying to do it one must be sure
To avoid the dishonor gossip brings,
A difficult thing this is to endure.

                                                    CCW

Rondeau LXVI. *Amorous Eye*

Amorous eye,
Agreeable marksman.

You I decry,
Amorous eye,

For to reply
Would cost me dear,
Amorous eye.

                                                    CCW

Rondeau. *My Good Lord*
(Inspired by the *Rose* debate and directed to the Provost of Paris,
Guillaume de Tignonville)

My good lord, please take my part
Against those who attack me and war propose—
Admirers of *The Romance of the Rose*—
Because on their views I don't repose.

So this cruel battle they would start
Thinking my frailty to expose,
My good lord, please take my part,

For their assaults I'll not depart
From my ideas. It's a common pose
To attack those who other ideas propose,

But from all that I'm quite apart,
My good lord, please take my part.

CCW

VIRELAY I. *This Mask No Grief Reveals*

This mask no grief reveals;
My eyes may overflow,
But none shall guess the woe
Which my poor heart conceals.

For I must mask the pain,
As nowhere is there pity;
Greater the cause to gain,
The less the amity.

So no plaint nor appeal
My aching heart can show
And mirth, not tears, bestow;
Those my gay rhymes conceal.
May this mask no grief reveal.

So it is I conceal
The true source of my ditty,
Instead I must be witty
To hide the wound that does not heal.
Let this mask no grief reveal.

CCW

VIRELAY X. *My Gentle Friend*

My gentle friend, you surely knew
That on this day I've chosen you
For my own friend, and so to you
I would give my heart entire and true.

For it's the style, as well you knew
Among true lovers all agreed
That on the spring's first day anew
A friend is for the year decreed.

And so to here one's love renew
A fine new chaplet of green hue
Each one must give
Until the year has passed from view
My gentle friend, you surely knew.

So I have chosen you and wait,
For my own love is pledged and true,
Great pain you've suffered, but with time
All that will be made up to you!
As now this custom I renew
The day of Saint Valentine retained
Must be my chaplet, for I have claimed
That I will love you sure and true,
My gentle friend, as you surely knew.

CCW

(Translated from *Oeuvres Poétiques de Christine de Pisan,*
ed. Maurice Roy)

SONGS FOR SALE

❧

1.

I sell you here the trembling leaf.
Some false lovers, by their belief
Make sheer falsehood resemble truth,
So do not all believe forsooth.

2.

I sell you now the popinjay,
For you are fair and good and gay,
Sire, and you're learned more than most,
But of Love's arts you cannot boast,
And will not learn, make no mistake,
So that by love you'll not me take.

3.

I sell you now Don Cupid's dart
Which easily has pierced my heart,
Lady fair, through your sweet eyes,
And to love you so fast me ties
That to die I'm now condemned
If by you I'm not avenged.

4.

I sell you here the harp and lyre,
For True Love does me now require
That for my love I choose but you,
Fair one. Now make this all come true
That we have joy, so to my verse
Agree straightaway. Don't be perverse.

I sell you here the turtledove.
Alone, apart, and far above
She flies on high without rein.
Like her alone so I remain;
Thus I will never find more pleasure
By any means or any measure.

6.

I sell you here the hawk that flies.
When a lover is full of lies,
And so falsehood is found to tell,
By love he should be scolded well,
For he should no such falsehood claim
Either for praises or for blame.

7.

I sell you now the lover's dream
Which joyful or sad will make seem
The one who dreams of love at night.
— My lady, an illusion that I might
Have in sleep can seem quite real
If I can only your love feel.

8.

I sell you now the fountain clear.
I can well see it will cost dear,
Lady, so much of you to see
When you so little care for me.
Cursed be the hour my eye on you fell;
I'm going now, and so farewell.

CCW

(Translated from *Oeuvres Poétiques de Christine de Pisan,*
ed. Maurice Roy)

CHRISTINE'S TEACHINGS FOR HER SON, JEAN DU CASTEL

Son, I have no great treasure
To make you rich, but a measure
Of good advice which you may need;
I give it hoping you'll take heed.

From your youth pure and aglow
You must learn the world to know,
So that you can by following this
In any case mishaps to miss.

Study seriously to inquire
How Prudence you can acquire,
For, mother of all virtues, she
Can from ill Fortune make you free.

Whatever then may be your state,
By Fortune who controls your fate
Govern yourself in such a way
That good sense will there hold sway.

If you knowledge would pursue
A life of books is then for you
So make sure that by your hard work
You're not inferior to any clerk.

Never serve an evil master,
For you would only court disaster
By wickedness to gain his aid,
So avoid such service like the plague.

Would you long life and victory lure?
Teach your heart it must endure;
It's by endurance that one gains
Rewards and comfort for one's pains.

If Fortune gives you as reward
That over others you are lord
Among your subjects then be not
Dangerous nor too proud thought.

Always be truthful in your word;
Speak little, to the point be heard,
For too much talk in any guise
Makes others think one far from wise.

Another's wealth do not envy,
The envious in this life may see
The flames of Hell and feel its pains,
A burden heavier than chains.

Never believe all the false blame
Of women that some books proclaim,
For women can be good and sweet;
May it be your fortune such to meet.
                                        CCW

(Translated from *Oeuvres Poétiques de Christine de Pisan,*
ed. Maurice Roy)

THE TALE OF POISSY

❦

vv. 1 – 112

Good Sir Knight, valiant, full of wisdom,
Since it pleases you to have one of my tales,
And you have so informed me in a letter
4   By your courtesy,
No matter that my poor weak self
Is unworthy that your graciousness
Condescend to notice me, I will keep the promise
8   That I made
To the messenger that you sent to me
From far away from here, and as a true friend
I commend myself to you, with a submissive heart.
12   Thus at your command—
I send to you to make this judgment
Concerning which two lovers contend in hard-fought debate;
So they have prayed and begged me dearly
16   That I seek for them
A loyal judge, and that I inquire well for one
To judge rightly their discord in such a manner
That he gives them an equitable judgment
20   According to reason.
And no matter that in France there is an abundance
Of the good and the beautiful, who in every season
Would know how to judge aright, for the excellent selection
24   Of the good in you
I have chosen you above all others as judge,
No matter that you are far away from us,
So may you accept, if it pleases you, sweet Sir,
28   To judge the right of it.
And, if it pleases you to take charge of the matter,

I will tell you the case as briefly as possible;
How it came about, you will hear without delay,
32   And in what time,
There where it was will be told you betimes,
For it was not a thousand years ago nor a hundred,
Not even a month past, but it was in the frolicsome
36   Gracious month
Of April the gay, when the woods grow green again,
This present year of 1400, before
The end of the month. It happened once
40   That I had a desire
To go out to play, so I wished to go see
A daughter that I have, to speak truly,
Beautiful and refined, young and well-schooled,
44   And gracious,
As everyone says; she is a religious
At an abbey rich and precious,
Noble, royal, and most delicious,
48   And the site is
Six leagues from Paris; this church
Is very well built in gracious guise;
Poissy is the name of the town where it is
52   And of this convent.
So I prepared my journey for a Monday,
I sent for pleasing companions
Who would want to do my pleasure
56   Without delay,
So there were many handsome squires
Who of their good will came to accompany me
To have a frolic, not for any other pay.
60   Then with great joy
We departed from Paris, taking our way
On horseback, and I rejoiced very much;
So did those gentlemen I brought with me
64   And all those ladies,
For there were with us some noble damsels,
Sweet, agreeable, gracious, and beautiful.
Then happily we talked of the latest news and gossip
68   And of the witty contentions
That very often arrive in love affairs;

While riding gaily, of many topics
We spoke, and there was no one mute or deaf
72 Or silent,
But each went along conversing
Of whatever seemed best to him;
There no hurtful word was sounded
76 But all were joyous.
So sang there whoever knew how to sing the best,
So high, so well, that often all the lands around
Echoed, and thus everyone did his best
80 To rejoice,
Each in his own way; and everyone took much joy
In the spring weather that was then beginning,
And the sun was clearly shining
84 On the green grass.
All the pathway there was full of and covered
With little flowers, each had opened its eye
To the sun which was shining in a cloudless sky.
Never in the year
Had there been before so sweet a morning,
And all the earth was illuminated
By the dew that the sky had given,
92 Which sparkled
On the green grass to gladden our hearts,
There was nothing there to make earth ugly,
All was beautiful to embolden lovers
96 To love well.
Through these meadows Nature had sown
Daisies and the flowers we call
Spring blossoms; everywhere we saw growing up
100 Many diverse
Grasses and flowers that were not yet mown down—
Green, red, and Persian blue,
Yellow, indigo, which muddy-hued or garish
104 Never were.
There was the flower of forget-me-not,
Remember-me, which is not pallid
But vermilion, of which lover and beloved
108 Make chaplets
And that they often make into rings

For love tokens and other ornaments
Which they exchange as pretty novelties
112   In pledging their love.

KITTYE DELLE ROBBINS-HERRING

∞

vv. 185–273

The dense forest, which greatly pleased me,
Was turning green again, so that the trees
That showed new growth were caught above
     in one another,
188   And the oaks,
Tall, large, and beautiful, stood very close together,
Not singly, but in great numbers,
As know those who have frequented the place;
192   And consequently the sun
Could not strike the ground at any spot.
And underneath lay the green grass,
Fresh and lovely to my liking. One cannot behold
196   A more beautiful place,
In my opinion; and I do not think that
     he who can see
His loved one there, face to face, or embrace her,
Would be displeased;
200   For it is a diversion
Most appealing, to be in this retreat
In the sweet spring, when birds are wont
To demonstrate their joy and their song
204   In the summery season.
And I believe in truth that the god of Love
Provided all decorous entertainments that day;
So, too, think those who were
208   With me then,
For we never stopped making merry,
Laughing and playing, and singing without pause,
Or recounting some tale of love.
212   And through the forest
We passed quickly and came without stopping

Directly to Poissy, where we soon found ready
All the necessities and amenities required
216   To satisfy our needs.
When we had dismounted, everyone dressed
In his best garments and checked his appearance
So that no fault could be found with our attire.
220   And then, at the abbey,
We went together to the ladies
In the locutory, and then we entered,
Despite the very solid, heavily barred doors
224   That are there;
But by permission, the doors had been opened.
There we found women of high condition,
For none of them was affected or unseemly,
228   But rather, most correct
In their apparel and their headgear,
Modest, proper, and ready to serve God.
There our friends welcomed us with great warmth
232   And smiling countenance.
Then she whom I love greatly and hold dear
Came towards me, and very humbly
Knelt, and I kissed her face
236   Sweet and tender,
And then hand in hand, without delay, we went
Into the church to pay reverence to God;
We heard mass, and wanted to take
240   Our leave thereafter,
But the ladies pressed us strongly
To take refreshment and led us
To a cool, bright, and lovely spot nearby
244   To have lunch,
For it was not yet dinnertime.
But we had not had time to stay
There long, or to converse at length
248   When the diligent
And most worthy, noble nun,
My formidable, gracious lady
Marie of Bourbon, who is prioress
252   Of that place,
Aunt to the king of France, in whom is gathered

All goodness and who dispels all vice,
Asked us, then, with her benevolent grace
256 To go
To her; nor did we fail to do so;
We were glad of this, and would not have wanted
To leave the premises without
260 Seeing her.
So we set out, two by two,
And went to the worthy lady;
By way of the stone stairs, which greatly pleased me,
264 We climbed up
To the lovely royal residence, which we found
Very well appointed, and we entered
Her beautiful chamber; then we knelt
268 Before her
And the most humble lady called us
Closer to her, and on many topics
Spoke to us sweetly, like one
272 In whom there is modesty
And goodness, intelligence and nobility.

⌒

vv. 947–1056

When I saw my dear friend
948 In tears,
It caused me great distress; I then, without delay,
Drew close to her, for I very much wanted to try
To discover what was causing the unhappy lady
952 To suffer so intensely.
And so I begged her with all my heart
To tell me at once what
Troubled her and why she was
956 So very disturbed.
She then began to sigh more deeply
And to weep softly.
When the squire noticed her crying,
960 It made him so unhappy
That tears came to his eyes

And like a man in whom all goodness can be found,
He said to her gently and with good will:

964 "Dear lady,
Sweet, agreeable, most gracious and beautiful,
Do not hide from us the misfortune or news
That troubles you, for I swear to you, by

968 The Virgin Mary
Who gave birth to God, that you will be relieved of
The grievous sorrow by which I see you so afflicted
If it is something that can be remedied

972 By my efforts.
I ask and beg of you, for friendship's sake,
Do not hide your great grief from us
For you know well that we wish above all

976 To safeguard your honour.
Tell us your story without delay
And then may it please you to speak and tell your
    bidding:
If in any way it can be set right,

980 I will do it,
You may be sure, and I will keep your secret."
And I said to her: "My loyal friend,
Do not hide your troubles from us, or I shall be

984 Very angry
For do not think that it pleases or suits me
To see you so perturbed;
I beg of you, calm yourself

988 And tell us
Why you feel such sorrow at the moment."
And then the squire once again turned
To her and said: "Rest assured,

992 Sweet, noble lady,
That whatever the situation, I wish to improve it."
And then the lady replied, in a quiet voice:
"I thank you, but there is nothing that can ease

996 My dreadful grief
Which certainly did not start just today or yesterday.
Let me weep: I am harming no one
And you should not concern yourselves with the business
    of others.

1000	Let me be,
	For you would not be able to relieve my grave sorrow.
	I am sorry that you hear me lament,
	But I cannot stop the sad tears now
1004	That make me suffer so;
	This weeping displeases me, for it is unseemly,
	But I have been in this state, you should know, for some
	time,
	Even though I do not wish
1008	To show it
	In front of people, no matter how much I often tremble
	From the pain that so troubles
	My unhappy heart; instead I often
1012	Flee
	The company of others and then give vent to my grief."
	Then the noble squire replied:
	"Alas, gracious, golden-haired lady, for God's sake
1016	Tell us your troubles,
	Do not hide them from us, if you please;
	I think truly that you are suffering for love,
	But no one is more tormented by it,
1020	Unhappy man! than I am,
	No matter what impression I give; I can find
	No rest and I am devoid of joy,
	Which makes me surmise that Love has opened the door
1024	To my sad death;
	I am sure that your grief is not nearly as great
	As the pain that I suffer,
	For no one could feel greater pangs
1028	Of distress
	Without dying, for I often want to consign
	Myself to death like a true martyr to love
	And I am often obliged to withdraw from company
1032	To express my grief.
	So please put an end to your sad weeping,
	Let me suffer this great misery,
	I who bear more of it and will have to endure it
1036	My whole life."
	Then the lady, who wanted nothing
	Other than to cry, of which she had not yet tired,

	Collected herself somewhat as though revived
1040	And said: "Alas!
	How can a heart have less comfort
	Than my poor heart, sorrowful and unhappy!
	Because I must disclose the bonds
1044	That bind me,
	I will tell you why I am so melancholy
	That I could die of grief, be it wise or foolish,
	And why I am not happy
1048	I will tell you
	In every detail, without lying about it,
	And what I once desired most
	And why I endure more pain and have endured it
1052	For a long time.
	For according to you, as I understand it, you suffer
	More pain than I do, but I do not agree
	To believe that anyone suffers worse and soon
1056	You will know the truth.

BARBARA K. ALTMANN

(Translated from *Oeuvres Poétiques de Christine de Pisan,*
ed. Maurice Roy)

THE BOOK OF THE DUKE OF TRUE LOVERS

❧

Here the Book of the Duke of True Lovers Begins

Although my desire and inclination may not have been to compose tales of love right away, since I was pursuing another interest which gave me more pleasure, I want to begin a new poem now, in consideration of others' concerns. For someone who can easily command a far more important person than myself has asked me to do so. He is a lord I am bound to obey, who has graciously confessed to me the pain he has had for a long time, many a summer and winter, whether rightly or foolishly, because of Love, to whose service his heart remains pledged. But he does not want me to state his name: he is content to be called the Duke of True Lovers, the person who relates this tale for them. He is pleased to have me recount, just as he tells me, his woeful troubles and his joys, the things he has done, and the strange roads he has traveled for many years now. He asks that in this season of renewal a new story be told by me, and I agree. For I know him to be of good sense—the sort of person whose humility will take in good part the frailty of my small understanding. With his approval, I shall in his stead recount the facts of the matter as he expresses them. (41)

The Duke of True Lovers

I was young and much the child when I first set my efforts toward becoming a lover. Because I had heard lovers praised more than other people and considered more gracious and better-taught, I wanted to be one. Toward that end I was often drawn to places where I might find a lady to serve. But I remained thus without a sweetheart for a long time because—upon my soul!—I lacked the sense to choose one; though I was certainly disposed to finding someone, I couldn't determine how. My desire caused me to frequent many a lovely group, where I saw many a lady and maiden whose every beauty was manifest. But Childhood still held me in its grip, so that I could not alight in any one place, no matter whom I might have chosen. For a long time I remained happy, carefree, and cheerful. In that sweet state I cried out often to Love, speaking in the following manner, because the time seemed long to me: (70)

Rondeau

True God of Love, who are to lovers lord,
And you, Venus, goddess most amorous,
Please take my heart and make it over as
Fit to love, then I desire nothing more.

So that to bravery I'm drawn forward,
Provide me a lady and a mistress,
True God of Love, who are to lovers lord.

And grant me the grace my choice to accord
To one, given my youth and callowness,
Who'd repay me and my honor address,
For my desire for this brings these words for'rd;
True God of Love, who are to lovers lord,
And you, Venus, goddess most amorous.

I often spoke thus, because of the desire I held in view, so that True Love heard me, and was gladdened by my wish. I'll relate how Love first seized and took hold of my heart, and how he has not released it since.

∞

I undertook to have a festival prepared in which I could learn to joust—or so I said, but I had something else in mind. And thus the celebration was held to which many an estimable lady was bidden. But well before I knew whether my Lady would come to our festival, I made request of an appropriate person, someone distantly related to me, who indeed granted it gladly and received me at his residence. There I saw my Lady at my leisure but did not tell her how I loved her with body and soul, and cherished her. I think my face made it sufficiently plain though, for Love, who was using all his tricks on me—the better to smite me—made me grow pale and then regain my color, changing completely. But my fair one said nothing about this, as if she had not noticed. I don't think she knew so little, though, that she failed to understand the reason for everything happening to me: that it came entirely from love, of which she was the cause and source of the loving spark that struck my heart, which hardly complained! I lived in happiness, however, and saw her often.

∞

Preparations for the grand and lovely festival, at which many people amused themselves, were hurried along. The jousts were proclaimed: he who won the jousting would receive a jewel of great worth, and thus the prize, and there would be twenty capable knights who would joust with all those from afar. The day for the gathering was set, and it would take place in a fair meadow, where there is a castle with six towers overlooking a pond. In the fields tents were set up, and high and wide scaffolding and pavilions were erected, and all the arrangements were made for the festival and the jousting. Now, without adding further detail, I tell you that when the day came that we had planned, my Lady arrived toward evening. I set out to meet her with a fine company of noble people. There were, to be sure, more than three pairs of minstrels, trumpets, and drums; they blew so loudly that the hills and valleys resounded. (669)

You understand that I was filled with joy when I saw my goddess come to my house. Nothing else could have happened to me that would have given me such joy. As I met her along the way with a very noble retinue, I approached her litter and greeted her, and she me. My beautiful Lady said to me: "You are giving yourself a great deal of trouble, my friend, coming here now. There is no need to." Thus with me talking happily to my sweet, dear Lady of one thing and another, we approached the castle. Riding next to her litter I certainly had enough of a reward for my trouble, I thought, because my great joy doubled when I perceived her behaving toward me in a friendlier fashion than ever before. We arrived at the castle where we found a fine group of ladies who curtsied before her in the manner due her station. She entered the courtyard, alighted from the litter, and was received with great joy. At her side, I guided her through the house into the changing rooms. My father, upon whom I depended and whose property I would inherit, had had all the lodgings decorated. (707)

Then the wine and sweets were brought by the bearers and the fair one invited me to partake of them with her. After that, my party withdrew and went elsewhere, allowing the Lady her privacy. I went off to another room on the right, where I dressed, attiring myself to dance the Allemande. So that the festival would lack nothing to make it perfect, I had had a hundred rich liveries made to my design. I believe that twenty-five of them—the knights wore them—were made of green velvet with appliqués in hammered gold cloth. The next day, after the joust, the squires and gentlemen (certainly not the servitors) put on satin that had been embroidered in silver with no thought to cost. When we were dressed, we went to my Lady. There we found a great throng of noble ladies and married women and maidens from the countryside, who had come to the festival. Immediately I greeted my Lady, as well as all the others, and I'm sure I blushed. I said: "My Lady, it is time for the evening meal." Then, without waiting, I took her arm and led her into the dining hall. The others followed. Knights escorted ladies, and those minstrels trumpeted so that the sound rang out, lending luster to the festival, which was very lovely to see! I seated my Lady in a prominent position at the high table; I don't think it displeased her! Next I seated my mother, quite near to her. Four countesses sat after her, who took their places rightfully. And in order, throughout the hall, each according to her rank, the noble ladies were seated, and the gentlemen sat alongside. In sum, I believe that all were copiously served with meats and wines at supper—I'm not guessing at that. Now without lingering here on the details, I'll simply tell you that when we had finished eating, after the sweets, we drank, and then minstrels came forward and began to trumpet in gracious harmony. Soon the latest dance began, joyful and gay, and every man was happy, looking at the handsome celebration. (776)

At that I hung back no longer, instead going straightaway to invite my Lady to dance. She demurred a bit but did not refuse me. I took her by the arm and led her to the dance, then back to her place—and there can be no doubt I was so head over heels in love that I felt transported by joy at being near her. I would have abandoned heavenly Paradise for this, I believe, nor could I have asked for better. What charmed and gladdened me more was her very sweet face which bore no sign of reticence or refusal, but was so pleasant, and appeared so favorable toward me through the amiable offices of Sweet Look, that I believed she viewed with approval all that I said and did. I saw it in her actions, and I cried out for the great joy I felt, so that it seemed I would fly! It was fitting for me to approach her gaily. (806)

And thus, pleasurably, we had danced a great part of the night away when the party ended. It was time to retire and the beds were readied.

Then I escorted the Lady, blond as amber, to her room. We exchanged many a gracious word and, after her eyes had gazed on me—the better to set me aflame—and after partaking of the sweets, I took leave of her and of all the ladies. In fine beds, under rich covers, we retired in our various places. But I didn't stop thinking all night about the beauty that was hers! I pronounced these words, which I read in my thoughts: (825)

Rondeau

My heart rejoices at your coming here
So much that for you in pure joy it leaps;
Flow'r of beauty, Rose that in freshness steeps,
To whom I'm a serf, and sweetly adhere.

Lovely Lady and one whom all revere
As best of all, for her beauty so deep;
My heart rejoices at your coming here.

Because of you the feast will persevere
In great revelry; no one such joy reaps
Within me but you, who alone appear
The one for whom life all joy in me keeps;
My heart rejoices at your coming here
So much that for you in pure joy it leaps.

∞

Then we went out to the fields where the jousts were to take place. We proceeded over the field to the handsome pavilions that were erected. The equipment was already there, the lances were being readied, and the chargers were being put through their paces. You would have seen high saddles with stirrups, white, red, and green, and covered with devices, shields of many colors, and painted lances. There was a great deal of equipment, much noise, and the sound of many voices. There were people in many a selion. In my tent I armed and readied myself, but I lingered there a while since it was not appropriate for me to lead off the jousting. We were twenty in our unit and all outfitted alike, and we were all knights, who would joust with those from outside. (947)

My cousin, about whom I spoke above, who had abundant goodness, was the first on the field. He was quite accustomed to that. He entered in such magnificent pomp, in complete regalia, that he seemed kin to a king: his helmet laced on, he himself outfitted beautifully, with banner and painted lances, and with a very handsome company. You could have seen and heard many a piper around there spreading cheer about. But we'll talk no more of that. I had had many tents set up there awaiting those from outside, where they could stay and shelter themselves. Believe me that before the day was out many valorous gentlemen came there, who gave us a good match in the joust. Others, who came to observe, sat on horseback. (973)

Without waiting long my cousin found his joust with a knight who aimed his lance at him, but my cousin didn't turn away. He met him and in the encounter knocked him from his horse so soundly that blood must have been spilled. We had won the opening joust! At that you would have heard the heralds cry and loudly call out his name, which was known in England and many a land. Then from the tent five of our men issued forth; they did not fail to find a challenger. Each one of them, in truth, did his duty so very well that he should be renowned for his deeds. The jousting over the fields began now high and low. In double file and strongly reinforced, our men went forth and, as they should, they jousted boldly. Then the minstrels trumpeted gaily and the heralds cried out, and those knights jousted enthusiastically and energetically, on great and eager chargers. (1003)

My Lady and many another, pictures of beauty, were in the richly draped spectators' galleries, graduated by many steps, the high-born ladies wearing crowns. They were twenty ladies with blond tresses whose sovereign and mistress was the Lady on my mind. All twenty ladies, for sure, were garbed in white silk with a device embroidered in gold—they seemed like goddesses come from Heaven, or fairies, made exactly as one might wish, all perfect. You may be sure that they inspired many clear exploits during that day. The scene could not have given only small pleasure to those who looked upon such creatures, so the combattants made great efforts to increase their worth and to outshine one another to earn the ladies' favor. There you might have seen many blows struck in different ways, and how one struck and unseated the other, and how the next, with another sort of stroke, aimed at the visor eye slits, or struck shield or helmet, the one unhelmeting the other, or bringing him down in a heap, and then another came along who removed him from the field. Lances broke, blows resounded, and those minstrels trumpeted loudly, so that God thundering might not have been heard. And thus, one against the other, they delivered great blows on both sides. (1042)

At that point I left my tent, my lance at rest, happier than a merlin, firmly in the stirrups, armed all in white on a white-caparisoned charger, with no other color—no red, no green—but fine gold. All who were in the pavilion issued forth and struck many a fine blow. Our men were armed all in white, and the lances they bore were of no color but white. I had ordered the richly designed sleeve given me by my Lady to be attached securely to my crest so that no one might tear it off, and on my helmet the green chaplet. With a good company of men, I set out, for I was yearning to see my very winsome goddess. I arrived where the jousting was, filled with joy. I raised my eyes to where she was and received her sweet look, and so had no thought of any harm. I passed in review before her, then quickly helmeted myself and withdrew to the ranks. (1074)

At once, in my Lady's view, a noble count gave me my lance, saying that it would be a great dishonor if I didn't joust well when I had such a noble crest! With my lance lowered, and wishing it to be well-positioned, I spurred my charger without restraint against another. You could have seen him come toward me, and we didn't falter in the encounter! But since it's embarrassing to tell of one's own deeds, I would not like to continue in this vein, except to say that my noble Lady thought my feats that day so well done that she gave me very great praise (thanks be to her!) and in the end she gave me the prize for those from within. I took it, with the kind agreement of her ladies, and I was thoroughly jubilant. Know surely that all day long, to my ability, I did my duty as my young years allowed. If I performed deeds of prowess there, no praise is mine, for it can be said that Love did it all, not I, and one mustn't make too much of it. There's no doubt that Love had found many experienced knights in that group, much better than me, for men of high and lesser station had come from everywhere and had better earned the prize—they knew it well. But I believe that the ladies chose me because they saw how fervent I was. That's why I think that in giving me the prize they took good will for accomplished fact, so that I would more willingly enter jousts. The prize announced for those from outside was given to a skillful German, a powerful jouster among a thousand. (1125)

Thus the jousting lasted all that day. New challengers appeared continuously and our men jousted against all comers. What should I say, in sum? All did fine and well, but there is no need for me to describe all the blows they struck—who, what, how, and in what style—for that's beside my point, nor is it what I propose to report. Night came, the jousting subsided. All the men and women left and returned to the castle, where the cooks were hurrying supper. (1142)

I sent my gentlemen to the outside lodgings, on behalf of the worthy ladies and myself, to beseech both the foreign gentlemen and those of my acquaintance, as I would friends, and as many as I could, to come and join us in celebrating. Thus I had a Round Table announced all about so that whoever wished would come and keep the feast. From the greatest to the least they came, with none remaining outside. And so barons from many countries were there—no need to ask whether the assembly was large, for so many people were welcomed with enormous joy that the castle was filled. I received them gladly. There was a great throng of knights and of gentlemen from many a land, and I honored each expressly and according to his rank. The meal was copious and memorable. When we arose from the table, minstrels trumpeted and noble partners drew themselves up for dancing. There wasn't one who didn't have on clothing richly embroidered with gold and silver work in great bands, and you would have seen ladies all dressed alike, in the same liveried attire. They readied themselves to dance elegantly. You would have seen a joyous ball begin happily, where many a gracious, noble lady and demoiselle courteously sought out the foreign guests and invited them to dance, leading them away. You would have seen round dances progressing through the hall, each guest striving to dance gaily. (1192)

And I, in whom Love had kindled the flame of desire, had no thought, glance, or wish but for my Lady. I delayed dancing a bit so that no one would perceive or know my thoughts. Rather, I remained with the knights who were not dancing until messengers came to tell me that I should go into the ballroom without delay, for my Lady was sending for me, asking for me in great earnest. I was certainly happy about that! With a fine company of gentlemen I entered the room, where no one was sad but rather all were vying with each other at dancing. When I reached my Lady, she said, "Fair cousin, why aren't you dancing?" I replied, "Come, my Lady, and dance with me, and show me the way!" (1215)

She said that I should dance first with another. And so to begin, I led a pretty lady cheerfully onto the floor. I danced her around once or twice, then escorted her back to her place. Then I took my Lady by the hand and led her to the dance happily, with her consent. The dancing lasted thus the greater part of that night and later was dispersed. Each guest retired, to lie down between fine white linens. (1229)

But I, who had a lady and mistress, and who felt in my breast the distress of my desire to be loved by her, by which I was pierced through, said to myself:

Rondeau

Laughing gray eyes, whose impression I bear
Within my heart in pleasant memory,
How this flash of memory gladdens me
About you, sweet one, who hold me in fear.

Love's sickness caused my life to disappear,
And yet you sustain the vigor in me,
Laughing gray eyes, whose impression I bear.

To me you're the goal of all that's dear,
Hence I'll come to where I desire to be:
'Tis retained as her serf Madame wants me
To be; I'll be held by you so near,
Laughing gray eyes, whose impression I bear
Within my heart in pleasant memory.

At the end of the month my Lady, for whom I lived in a state of urgent desire, was required to leave the aforementioned manor; she could not stay longer, so she departed. I was in a bad way about that because I was losing the sight of the very exquisite, beautiful woman without whom I could not live. I was entirely deprived of joy, since for a long time I had been used to seeing her and being with her. But now it would be necessary to go without hearing news of her or seeing her for three or four months (the possibility of such a long separation loomed ahead), which was a very harsh thing for me to endure. I was nostalgic for the time we'd spent together and felt such sadness at this departure that I lost color, reason, composure, and countenance. I believe (it could well have been) that many people noticed the state I was in, about which they exchanged gossip that was taken seriously. My chagrin was so great at hearing the rumor fly, about how I loved my beautiful Lady, that I thought I would die of grief. My pain grew worse, for I feared the talk would put an end to the great friendship between myself and her friends. That sad thought gave me very disagreeable pain, for I feared she was being made to leave because of the gossip. So displeased was I that I couldn't express it. Nevertheless I hid my painful anguish to the best of my ability and even better than was my wont, and sighing, burdened with grief, I uttered these words: (1475)

Ballade

Now from all things my joy's but nothingness,
And my solace to bitterness changed face.
My sweetest flower, since our separateness
I've gone far from you, and your gentle ways
    That used to be —
When I'd see you every day, you whose glee
Sustained me — exchanged for raw misery.
Alas! How can I now bid you good-bye?

My sweet love, my Lady, my share in bliss,
The one for whom my inner desires blaze,
What shall I do when in neither all nor less
I receive from Love naught but froth and haze?
    Where'er I be
I'll have neither comfort nor gaiety
From your beauty afar, no more close by.
Alas! How can I now bid you good-bye?

Vile gossips! You've wrought this work from malice,
And my death you've forged on an anvil's space.
Fortune's consented to my cruel duress,
Yields neither my body nor pen a place.
    No way is free
Save for death. I pray God for company,
Since without you none other would I try.
Alas! How can I now bid you good-bye?

    Ah, plainly, calmly,
Standing there; at least deign my tears to see
As you depart, which I'm tormented by.
Alas! How can I now bid you good-bye?

The day of leave-taking came and my Lady departed. I believe that she would have refrained from going had she dared, but she had to obey. And so, as was befitting her noble and well-bred disposition, she thanked everyone, begged her leave, and set out. And I, who escorted her, rode next to her litter. The fair one, who could wholly perceive that I loved her truly without deception, looked at me in serious concern, with such sweet demeanor that I believe she wanted to comfort my weak and grieving heart. She might have said more to me, but on her left rode another who came so close that we hadn't the chance to say anything for which he could have reproached us, because of which I hated him profoundly. But I saw that I would have to suffer many dangers; that would happen often. Thus we rode until, in a day and a half, we reached her dwelling. The trip did not seem long to me, however — rather, it seemed to pass quickly — for I hadn't tired of it, though I was truly suffering. I thought to take leave of her, but the master, feigning welcome, endeavored to keep me there, and I knew, from his behavior, that he was frantic because of me. Someone who was at our revel had put this jealousy in his mind. (I have since given that man his due, but I waited until no one was paying attention.) Thus this evil man watched the fair one, whom I adored, and because of that, I was dying of grief. I took my leave and set off, dissimulating and hiding my misery, nor did I raise my eyes to look at my sovereign Lady, which was a tormenting pain. My heart could barely restrain itself, as it had to, for fear of the scandalmonger. And so I said: (1565)

Ballade

Farewell, my Lady I dread;
Farewell, queen of all who reign;
Farewell, perfect in blameless stead,
Farewell, noblest, of honor plain;
Farewell, faithful to ascertain;
Farewell, flow'r cherished everywhere;
Farewell not farewell, blond and fair.

Farewell, wise one on whom none tread;
Farewell, stream with joy in its train;
Farewell, noble fame's watershed;
Farewell, songbird of sweet refrain;
Farewell, sweet payment for my pain;
Farewell, you who all graces bear;
Farewell not farewell, blond and fair.

Farewell, sweet eyes that through me read;
Farewell, looks Helen can't attain;
Farewell, by soul and senses led;
Farewell, most gracious in demesne;
Farewell, North Star, our joyous vane;
Farewell, wave of valuable fare;
Farewell not farewell, blond and fair.

Farewell, princess of high domain;
Farewell, whose smile brings fear in train;
Farewell, you who all vice forswear;
    Farewell not farewell, blond and fair.
              THELMA S. FENSTER
with lyric poetry translated by NADIA MARGOLIS

(Translated from Brit. Lib. Harley Ms. 4431)

ONE HUNDRED BALLADES OF A LOVER AND HIS LADY

❦

Neither Intention Nor Thought

Though I had neither intention nor thought
At this present time love poems to write,
For elsewhere now inspiration I've sought,
By the command of someone whose great might
All would please, I've thought it would be right
To try to comply with a love-story appealing
To offer here, as of course I ought,
A hundred ballades of amorous feeling.

All about how these lovers spent their days
In loving, which brought them many an ill,
But many joys also, intermingled always
With grief, and of boredom they had their fill.
I must tell it all, even though it dismays,
In this little book it all revealing,
Where I will write of joy but love unfulfilled
A hundred ballades of amorous feeling.

And now I pray God that I not become tired,
Though I'd rather be pursuing another affair
Of much greater seriousness, but required
I have been by a sweet person debonair
As a fine for what to say I did dare
In telling of love, the truth revealing
To all noble ladies, so I must prepare
A hundred ballades of amorous feeling.

Prince, I see that to this I must resign,
Not speaking willingly nor appealing

My sentence, so I freely pay my fine:
A hundred ballades of amorous feeling.
                                    CCW

I. *The Lover Speaks*

No longer, lady, can it be
Concealed from you, the love sublime
I have borne, without self-pity,
Without complaint, for such a time
Until my strength began to decline,
For death will come to me today
Unless you love me without delay.

Constraint has been my destiny
And forces me to speak in fear,
My lifeblood now is failing me
To end the suffering of many a year;
And death will carry me away
Unless you love me without delay.

My heart could live in captivity
If you, my lady, might grant this boon
And quickly give me your mercy;
Neither 'til evening nor afternoon
Can I endure, so end it soon;
My heart will grieve in every way
Unless you love me without delay.

Oh, how sweet! What generosity
If you would give your love to me;
My heart will never see the day
Unless you love me without delay.
                              SANDRA SIDER

IX. *The Lover's Complaint to Love*

Lord Love, please grant me revenge
Against my lady's loveless pride,
She who'd not deign to assuage
Anguished pains which in me writhe.
On you, sole recourse, I've relied

Against ills that are my curse.
My life in doom will subside,
Since the fair one stands averse.

She provokes in me such rage,
For the more she sees I've cried,
The less she cares: disengaged
Is she; so the other side
Of pleasure I must abide
From friendship — a paltry purse.
Shall I without aid have died
Since the fair one stands averse?

But may it please you to change
Your ways soon; set them aside,
For you might all of these engage,
Both foolish and wise; then stride
Quickly to succor my side.
At least your half you'd disburse,
My life partly justified,
Since the fair one stands averse.

God and my prince, never hide
From the message of my verse;
See the trouble in which I reside
Since the fair one stands averse.

NADIA MARGOLIS

X. *Love Speaks to the Lady*

Your vanity's most unwise,
My girl lovely and slender,
Who presumes that in such guise,
Love to you youth would tender,
So that a thoughless offender
You'd be with pleasures amorous —
From Him, the frequent sender —
Now joyous, then dolorous.

When, 'twas not you who decides —
Love's the sole recommender —

So you must now, I advise,
Your young, gay heart surrender
To Love's arrow; he'll render
You then quite desirous
Thoughts by diverse agenda:
Now joyous, then dolorous.

If he then from you requires
Good deeds, he's no pretender—
Of frank gaze with gentle eyes
May you be the ready lender.
What gain do you portend here
By keeping him languorous?
Thirty-plus sighs he'd render,
Now joyous, then dolorous.

Darling, of songs so tender,
Would you flee as onerous
Good times that impend here,
Now joyous, then dolorous?

NADIA MARGOLIS

XXXII. *The Lady and the Lover*

My gentle beloved, come speak to me.
—Of course, Madame, with a smile I appear.
—Now tell me, my friend, without secrecy.
—What should I tell you, my sweet lady dear?
　—Whether your heart's within me placed?
　—All yours, Madame, your doubt's erased.
　—Certainly so in you is mine.
　—Thank you, fair one, now our love's fine.

Now you no longer need love painfully.
—True, since I have your complete love so near.
—Would you like to embrace, honorably?
—Oho! Madame, for naught else have I care.
　—Mind you don't boast of it in haste.
　—I'd sooner out to sea be chased.
　—My own heart I give you for thine.
　—Thank you, fair one, now our love's fine.

So this will please you, but not cloyingly?
—What? Mistress, light of all that I revere!
—May you have a kiss—no more errantry.
—'Tis enough for me, your wishes most sincere.
   —Friend, my trust in you I place.
   —As such I swear I'll not disgrace.
   —And in you much good I'll define.
   —Thank you, fair one, now our love's fine.

All that I wish for, you embrace?
—I do, you're my one special case.
—To you o'er all else my love I'll confine.
—Thank you, fair one, now our love's fine.

NADIA MARGOLIS

XXXIX. *The Lover and the Lady*

Now it is to you I've turned,
My sweet and loyal mistress;
For whom else would I have yearned
To come, beloved blond tress?
You alone are my bounteousness,
I've no other, by my soul!
For me, make a happy face.
Lady, how is it, all told?
My sweet, let us now embrace.

—Friend, has your memory spurned
Me so? Would you say it's less
And more quickly, you've discerned,
I've seen you? Have you said yes
To another? Or why? Confess!
Or is it for fear that I'll scold?
Let's yield to luminous rays
And hug me—no one's around,
My sweet, let us now embrace.

—Lady, I have not returned
Sooner to you, though regrets
Plagued me; I was more concerned
To avert the rabidness

Of gossips' tongues, which distress
Me; their slurs I'd not uphold.
Thus did I withdraw a ways;
To you, my worth I extoll,
My sweet, let us now embrace.

—Friend, my swooning heart you hold
In your arms; You breathe sachets
Soothing me a thousandfold;
My sweet, let us now embrace.

NADIA MARGOLIS

XLVII. *The Lover and Lady*

Madame, I've come to bid farewell,
A kiss to me please avail,
And embrace me; may God well
Reward your worth; do not quail
At loving me, mistress and friend,
I leave my heart in your retreat.
Ne'er forget me, my godsend,
My true love loyal and sweet.

—Ah! Sweet friend, in truth I tell,
How worse grief ne'er did assail
Another, for my heart's hell
All but marks my parting trail.
Leaving, I toward pallor tend,
In fear of death soon to meet.
Ne'er forget me, my godsend,
My true love loyal and sweet.

—This should do, my demoiselle,
This suff'ring I'll let prevail
No more; you must now dispel
The ire causing you to ail
And, sadly trembling, descend.
In returning, I'll be fleet.
Ne'er forget me, my godsend,
My true love loyal and sweet.

—Half-dead, I say "Bye"; my end,
Not your return, I'll first greet.
Ne'er forget me, my godsend,
My true love loyal and sweet.

NADIA MARGOLIS

XCIX. *The Lover*

Anger makes me intolerant
Of her who treats me so harshly,
Bitterly spurned, I bear the brunt
Of loving, until finally
I am at a loss, and then she
Makes light of the situation,
But I doubt this disaffection.

To her eyes I am nonchalant,
But bitterness often grieves me;
Of her I will be negligent
Only when my body leaves me,
Or she loves me and believes me;
Her honor restrains my action,
But I doubt this disaffection.

A man is viewed as excellent
By valorous acts of prowess,
Even Roland, brave and gallant,
By love was reduced to sadness;
She discusses this in excess
And speaks without provocation,
But I doubt this disaffection.

Love denies me satisfaction,
But I doubt this disaffection.

SANDRA SIDER

(Translated from *Oeuvres Poétiques de Christine de Pisan,*
ed. Maurice Roy)

III

ALLEGORICAL POETRY

❧

CHRISTINE explains in her *Vision* that during the early years of her widowhood she sought comfort not only in writing courtly poetry but also in pursuing a program of self-education: "I turned to the path of study towards which I was inclined by nature and constellation." Apparently this began with a study of the history of the world as it was understood at the end of the Middle Ages, but soon included such books as Boccaccio's *De Genealogia Deorum* (*Of the Genealogy of the Gods*). Although it had not yet been translated into French, there is evidence that manuscripts of the Latin original were being copied and circulating in France during the later years of the fourteenth century. It would appear that Christine knew enough Latin to read it, for her understanding of allegory seems to be largely based on it. She claims: "I was glad to find . . . a style that seemed natural to me, and took pleasure in its subtle allegories and lovely material hidden beneath delightful moral fictions." It also seems certain that she early became acquainted with the *Moralized Ovid* and knew well *The Romance of the Rose*, as demonstrated in her participation in the debate over the popularity of Jean de Meun's part of the poem. She was one of the first in France to read Dante and to introduce him to a French audience, and she spoke on numerous occasions of her reading of Boethius' *Consolation of Philosophy*. These writers and their works form the basis for her taste for allegory.

It is scarcely surprising that she should have been attracted to allegory, for it was one of the most important poetic forms of her day. Indeed, there were two distinct approaches: allegorical interpretation, which sought to uncover a hidden truth beneath an existing text, and creative allegory, undertaken to personify abstract concepts and fashion a narrative around them. Christine was to try her hand at both sorts. *The Letter of Othea*, her first long allegory, belongs to the tradition of allegorical interpretation, whereas *The Book of the Long Road to Learning*, *The Book of the Mutation of Fortune*, as well as the later *Vision* and *The Book of the City of Ladies,* are examples of creative allegory. It should not be overlooked, however, that her first long poem, *The Letter of the God of Love,* written in 1399, was also her initial attempt at writing allegorical poetry.

Three of these allegorical poems, *The Letter of Othea, The Long Road to Learning,* and *The Mutation of Fortune,* are particularly interesting for the way in which they reflect Christine's program of study and her transformation from courtly poet to a writer concerned with the essential problems of her day.

The first of these works, *The Letter of Othea,* written around 1400, was apparently one of her most popular, to judge by some forty-five manuscripts that still exist along with imprints in both French and English. It is, however, one of the most difficult for modern readers to understand.[1] It is a proposed education, both social and spiritual, for a young man who has reached the age of preparation for knighthood. The one hundred chapters are based on quatrains similar to the ones composed for Christine's son Jean in the *Moral Teachings,* but in this case each is accompanied by an extended commentary, a gloss including a quotation from an ancient sage, and an allegory based on a reference to one of the Church Fathers, ending with a quotation from the Scriptures. The point is that the young man's education should not be limited to worldly concerns, for as the Prologue to the Allegory points out, Scripture is for "the edification of the soul residing in this miserable world."

The advice to a young Hector is provided by Othea, who represents "woman's wisdom." The Trojan prince was traditionally considered the ancestor of the French royal family. The text is clearly intended as an effort to reconcile ancient wisdom with Christian teachings, for early chapters are based on the Cardinal Virtues, the Theological Virtues, the Seven Gifts of the Holy Spirit, and the Seven Deadly Sins, all basic to the religious training of the day. It should not be overlooked that medieval children often learned to read from Books of Hours. But to these moral precepts are added the mythology and wisdom of the past, largely based on the *Moralized Ovid,* which Christine obviously considered a more suitable text than the Ovid that was popular in the schools. Christine had already found fault with *The Art of Love* for such a purpose in *The Letter of the God of Love.* For Trojan history she made use of a compilation of ancient history that provided a detailed account of the Trojan War.

The importance of Othea's womanly advice is underscored by the final chapter of the book, which recounts the prophecy of the Cumaean sibyl to Caesar Augustus concerning the coming of Christ, with the admonition that he had something of importance to learn from a woman and that neither he nor anyone else should resist hearing the truth from whomever might have it to offer.

Another interesting aspect of Othea's advice is the place it gives to examples of women, some of whom would reappear in *The Book of the City of Ladies*. Almost a third of the examples offered in this earlier work are devoted to women, with evidence that Christine already intended to give versions of their stories that would present them in a better light than was traditionally the case. Cassandra and Medea are good examples of this technique. As Christine had already pointed out in *The Letter of the God of Love*, if women had written these stories in the first place they would have been different from the usual misogynistic ones.[2] With this in mind, it is interesting to reflect on the fact that *The Letter of Othea* would have been completed shortly before Christine became involved in the debate over the merits of *The Romance of the Rose*.[3]

The debate had not yet ended when she began to write *The Long Road to Learning* on October 5, 1402. Indeed, she had written a final letter to her most offensive opponent, Pierre Col, only a few days earlier, insisting that her mind had turned to more serious matters.[4] In this long poem (nearly 6,400 verses) she not only describes an imaginary voyage across Europe and the Middle East and then up into the heavens to the Court of Reason, but she also gives a further glimpse of the studies she was continuing to undertake on this journey.

It is evident that her primary inspiration for the poem comes from Dante's voyage in the *Divine Comedy*.[5] Like Dante, Christine, now approaching forty, finds herself in the middle of life's journey. As Dante had had Virgil for his guide, Christine is conducted on her travels by the Cumaean sibyl. However, it was Boethius' *Consolation of Philosophy* that she had been reading on that October evening before she fell asleep, although she had also been reflecting on the sorry state of the world.

Upon the appearance of the sibyl in a vision, Christine eagerly accepts her proposal for a voyage. First they go to the Fountain of Wisdom on Mount Parnassus, where the nine Muses can be seen bathing in its waters. They then proceed to the Holy Land and Jerusalem, where Christine gives evidence of an impressive knowledge of geography, suggesting that she had been reading reports of travelers in the region beyond the imaginary accounts of Sir John Mandeville. Then they leave the Earth behind and mount into the skies. The passage chosen for inclusion here is of particular interest because it reflects astrological knowledge, which Christine would inevitably have learned from her father, and it provides an idea of how she understood the nature of the universe. In spite of echoes of Dante in the poem, her view of the world and the heavens is her own.[6]

Christine and her guide eventually arrive at the Court of Reason in the Heavens, where Queen Reason and four companions, Wisdom, Nobility, Chivalry, and Wealth, govern the destiny of the world. There the travelers listen to a discussion of the qualities required of a prince capable of being a universal ruler and setting the troubled world on a better course. The discussion of the queens reflects in an interesting fashion the extent of the reading Christine had already accomplished in her program of self-education. The conclusion of this debate is that a French prince alone would be capable of such a task. Christine is then charged by the queens to carry back to Earth a message to all the French princes, reminding them of their responsibilities to the world beyond their own selfish ambitions. This conclusion should be understood as Christine's self-justification for offering advice to these powerful men, reflecting the idea of Italian humanists of the day that study prepares one to offer advice to princes on their duties to society.

The poem is dedicated to the French king, Charles VI, and echoes the idea already proposed in *The Letter of Othea* that the merit of such advice should not be judged by the worldly status of the one offering it:

> So pray do not disdain advice
> Because it is in such guise
> Sent to you, for a simple soul
> Can pure reason to you extol.
> Great princes, do not disregard
> This little poem from a slight bard.
> (vv. 51–56)

Some of these same ideas are developed further in the longer allegorical poem (23,636 verses) that Christine composed the following year, presenting a copy to the Duke of Burgundy on January 1, 1404.[7] This was entitled *The Book of the Mutation of Fortune*.

Christine had shown an interest in the role of Fortune in human affairs from her earliest poetry. Indeed, she considered herself one of Fortune's victims in losing her husband after a happy marriage. She had devoted further attention to the subject in both *The Letter of Othea* and *The Long Road to Learning.* In this new poem, divided into seven books, Fortune's role in human affairs and in history is the central issue.

The first part of the poem is devoted to an allegorical account of her own misfortunes. After having lost her husband, "the captain of her ship," in a storm, she finds herself transformed into a man in order to take charge of her own fortunes. This primary mutation is reflected in Christine's advice to widows in *The Treasury of the City of Ladies,* where she admonishes them to "take on the heart of a man."[8]

Having described her own problems with Fortune, Christine then turns to a description of Fortune's dwelling place. This was a favorite theme for medieval writers who dwelt on the vagaries of Fortune. A basic idea was suggested by Boethius, who describes the sort of place that should be avoided by anyone seeking security in life. He speaks of an exposed spot on a high mountain surrounded by a sea. These details are later developed by Alain of Lille in his twelfth-century treatise, the *Anticlaudianus,* in a description of Fortune's abode. Jean de Meun took over this description in *The Romance of the Rose,* which was an important source for Christine, the principal ideas being the dangerous site of this dwelling and its inaccessibility. But as is so often the case, Christine added her own variants.[9] She describes Fortune's dwelling as being situated on a rock in a sea called "Great Peril." It is held in place by four chains, but nevertheless it rocks and turns perpetually. The castle has four entrances, which Christine describes along with those who dwell there. When she comes to the fourth she makes use of the portrait gallery in the castle's donjon to set forth her understanding of Fortune's role in world history as it has developed from her reading from the creation to her own times. She ends by mentioning the fates of Richard II of England and John of France. It is interesting to recall that Boccaccio's *Fates of Illustrious Men* ended with a description of King John being borne away into captivity after the French defeat at Poitiers. Christine was one of the early readers of Boccaccio's text in France.

At the end of the long poem she returns to her own efforts to cope with Fortune. It then becomes evident that she has come, some fifteen years after her husband's death, to view the world across her study of the past and to draw profit from the lessons of history, a thoroughly humanistic concept.[10] This not only encourages her to remake her life, but it prepares the way for even more important writing ventures. It was because of her presentation of the first copy of *The Mutation of Fortune* to the Duke of Burgundy, Philip the Bold, that he commissioned her to write the biography of his late brother, Charles V, initiating a new chapter in Christine's career as a writer.

NOTES

1. For helpful discussions of this work see Rosemond Tuve, *Allegorical Imagery* (Princeton, 1966) and Judith L. Kellogg, "Christine de Pizan as Chivalric Mythographer," in *The Mythographic Art*, ed. J. Chance (Gainesville, Fl., 1990), pp. 100–124.
2. Christine Reno, "Feminist Aspects of Christine de Pizan's 'Epistre d'Othéa à Hector,' *Studi Francesi* 71 (1980), 271–76. Christine had written in 1399:

   > Should it be said that books are filled with tales
   > Of just such women (I deplore that charge!)
   > To this I say that books were not composed
   > By women nor did they record such things
   > That we may read against them and their ways . . .
   > If women, though, had written all those books,
   > I know that they would read quite differently,
   > For well do women know the blame is wrong.
   > *(Poems of Cupid, God of Love,*
   > eds. T. S. Fenster and M.C. Erler
   > [Leiden, New York, 1990], p. 55.)

3. For a chronology of the affair, see Eric Hicks and Ezio Ornato, "Jean de Montreuil et le débat sur le *Roman de la Rose*," *Romania* 98 (1977), 216–19.
4. *Romania*, 115–16.
5.

   > But the name of that pleasant spot
   > At first moment I knew not
   > Until at last came to my mind
   > What in Dante of Florence one can find
   > In that book that he wrote
   > With a style of such great note . . .
   > (vv. 1125–30)

   C. C. Willard, "Christine de Pizan: the Astrologer's Daughter," in *Mélanges à la mémoire de Franco Simone*, I (Geneva, 1980), pp. 95–111, and "Une source oubliée du voyage imaginaire de Christine de Pizan," in *Et c'est la fin pourquoi sommes ensemble: Hommage à Jean Dufournet* (Paris, 1993), pp. 321–26.
7. This presentation copy is now Brussels, Bibl. Roy. Ms. 9508.
8. *A Medieval Woman's Mirror of Honor: The Treasury of the City of Ladies*, trans. C. C. Willard; ed. M. P. Cosman (New York, 1989), p. 199.
9. For a discussion of medieval descriptions of Fortune's dwelling-place, see Howard

R. Patch, *The Goddess Fortuna in Mediaeval Literature* (Cambridge, Ma., 1927; reprint, New York, 1967), pp. 123–46.

10. Myron P. Gilmore, "The Renaissance Conception of the Lessons of History," in *Humanists and Jurists: Six Studies in the Renaissance* (Cambridge, Ma., 1963), pp. 1–31.

THE LETTER OF OTHEA TO HECTOR

Othea in Greek can be taken to mean "woman's wisdom." Now, whereas the ancients, under whose religion the greatest empires arose that have ever existed in the world — such as the kingdoms of Assyria and Persia, the Greeks, the Trojans, Alexander, the Romans and many others, not to mention the greatest philosophers, did not yet possess the light of true faith and worshiped many gods, since God had not yet opened the door of His mercy — at present, we Christians, illuminated with true faith by the grace of God, are able to deduce the moral sense in the ancients' opinions, concerning which many fine allegories can be conceived. And as the ancients were wont to worship everything that had a claim to some grace beyond the ordinary course of things, they called many wise women who lived in their time goddesses. It is true, following historical accounts, that in the time when great Troy flourished with such high renown a very wise woman named Othea, considering the fair youth of Hector of Troy, who abounded in virtue (which could be proof of the grace which in the future would be manifested in him), sent him several fine and notable gifts, including the fair charger named Galatea, unequaled in the world.[1] And because all worldly graces that the good man must possess were found in Hector, we can say regarding the moral sense that he had received them from the admonishment of Othea who sent him this letter. We will take Othea to mean the virtue of prudence and wisdom with which he himself was adorned. As the four cardinal virtues are necessary for wise rule, we will speak of them afterwards. We have given a name to this first virtue and assumed a rather poetic manner of speech that harmonizes with the true history in order to pursue our argument better, and for our purposes we shall cite several ancient philosophers as authorities. Thus we shall say that the same lady dispatched or sent to the valiant Hector this present letter, which may function similarly for all others who desire goodness and wisdom. And as the virtue of prudence is very much to be recommended, Aristotle, the prince of philosophers, noted, "Because wisdom is the most noble of all things, it must be demonstrated with the best argument and in the most fitting manner."[2]

Prologue to the Allegory

In order to allegorize the import of our subject matter, we will apply Holy Scripture to our writings for the edification of the soul residing in this miserable world.

Just as all things were created by the supreme wisdom and mighty power of God, rationally they must gravitate toward Him, and because our soul, created by God in His image, is the most noble thing created in the world after the angels, it is fitting and necessary that it be adorned with virtues that may convey it toward that end for which it was made. Since it can be impeded by the ambushes and assaults of its infernal enemy, its mortal adversary, who can divert it from reaching blessedness, we may call human life "true chivalry," as Scripture says in several places. Inasmuch as all earthly things are fallible, we must keep the future that is without end constantly in mind. Because this is the supreme and perfect chivalry, to which all others are nothing in comparison, and with which the victorious will be crowned in glory, we will assume a manner of speaking about the chivalrous spirit and may this be accomplished primarily to the glory of God and for the benefit of all who will read the present work.

XXXII: Cassandra[3]

TEXT
Frequent the holy temple all hours of the day,
And to the gods of heaven fitting honor pay;
Moreover, be sure to assume Cassandra's guise,
That is, if you want all to consider you wise.

GLOSS
Cassandra was the daughter of King Priam and was a very good lady and devout in their religion. She served the gods and revered the temple and rarely ever spoke without need. When it suited her to speak, she never said anything that was not true, nor was she ever

found to be lying. Cassandra possessed great learning; for this reason Othea advises the good knight to resemble her, since foolish behavior and lying words are deeply reproachable in a knight. Thus he must serve God and honor the temple, by which is understood the Church and her ministers. Pythagoras has remarked, "It is a most praiseworthy thing to serve God and to sanctify His saints."[4]

ALLEGORY
The authority says that the good knight should frequent the temple; the good spirit, likewise, should do the same, and hold in singular devotion the Holy Catholic Church and the communion of saints, just as in the article of faith found in the Apostles' Creed spoken by Saint Peter, "one holy and apostolic Church and the communion of saints."

⬭

LVIII: Medea[5]

TEXT
Do not allow your sense to be devastated
By foolish pleasure, nor your belongings wasted
Or carried off, in case they are required of you,
And see your own reflection in Medea too.

GLOSS
Medea was one of the most learned women in fortune telling who have ever lived and had the most knowledge, according to what various accounts relate. Nevertheless she allowed her mind to be seduced by self-will in order to fulfill her desire when she let herself be mastered by foolish love and set her heart on Jason, honoring him, giving him her body and bestowing upon him wealth, for which he later so shabbily repaid her. For this reason Othea tells the good knight not to let his reason be conquered by foolish pleasure for whatever cause if he wishes to make use of the virtue of strength. Plato has said, "A light-hearted man is destroyed as soon as he loves."

ALLEGORY
The phrase "he should not let his sense be devastated" should be taken to mean that the good spirit should not allow his self-will to rule, for if the rule of self-will ceased, then there would be no Hell, nor would hellfire have any dominion except over whoever let his self-will rule, for self-will fights against God and leads to arro-

gance, which despoils Paradise and populates Hell and voids the value of the blood of Jesus Christ and delivers the world into the servitude of the Devil. The wise man has said on this subject, "The rod and reproof give wisdom, but a child left to himself bringeth his mother to shame" (Proverbs 29:15).

∞

LXXIII: The Judgment of Paris [6]

TEXT
Do not pass judgment in the manner Paris favored
Which gives but a harsh sustenance to be savored;
There are many who must take suffering in trade
For every single decision poorly made.

GLOSS
The fable recounts that three very powerful goddesses—that is, Pallas, goddess of wisdom; Juno, goddess of wealth; and Venus, goddess of love—appeared before Paris holding a golden apple which bore the inscription, "This should be given to the most beautiful and powerful." A great controversy arose from this apple, for each of the goddesses said she should have it, and when they came to Paris regarding this dispute, Paris sought diligently to investigate the strength and power of each goddess individually. First Pallas spoke: "I am the goddess of warfare and wisdom, and I dispense arms to warriors and learning to scholars. If you will give me the apple, I will make you valiant and you will surpass all in learning." Then Juno, goddess of wealth and dominion, said, "I distribute vast treasures in the world, and if you will give me the apple, I will make you richer and more powerful than anyone else." Finally Venus spoke many erotically charged words and said: "I am the one who gives lessons in love and sensuality, who makes the fools wise and the wise foolish, who makes the rich beggars and the exiles rich. Nor is there any power that compares with mine. If you will give me the apple, I will give you the love of the fair Helen of Greece, which will be worth more to you than any riches." Then Paris pronounced sentence, forsaking warfare, wisdom, and wealth for Venus, to whom he gave the apple. Troy was destroyed for this reason. It should be understood that Paris gave Venus the golden apple because he was not valorous, nor cared much for riches, but thought only about love. Therefore Othea tells the good knight that he should not act in

a similar fashion. Pythagoras maintained, "The judge who does not judge justly deserves every evil."

ALLEGORY
Paris, who judged foolishly, shows that the good spirit should refrain from passing judgment on others. Speaking against the Manichaeans on this topic, Saint Augustine noted that there are two reasons why we must especially avoid judging others: first, because we do not know the intention with which acts are carried out, which to condemn is a great presumption, so that we should interpret them positively; and second, because we are not sure what those who are now good or evil will turn out to be. To this end Our Lord says in the Gospel, "Judge not that ye be not judged, for with what judgment ye judge, ye shall be judged" (Matthew 7:1).

∞

LXXIV: Fortune[7]

TEXT
Do not confide in Fortune, the mighty goddess,
And do not trust too much in what she might promise
Because she is fickle and changes in no time,
Even toppling down the finest into the slime.

GLOSS
Fortune, according to the manner of speaking of the poets, may well be called the great goddess, for we see that the course of worldly things is governed by her. And because she promises to many considerable prosperity, and indeed bestows it on some and then overthrows them in a short time when it pleases her, Othea tells the good knight not to trust in Fortune's promises nor to be desolated by adversities. Socrates says, "The deeds of Fortune are like tricks."

ALLEGORY
That the good knight should not trust in Fortune, we should interpret to mean that the good spirit must flee and despise the pleasures of this world. Concerning this, Boethius says in the third book of his *Consolation of Philosophy* that the happiness of the Epicureans should be called unhappiness, for it is true, full, and perfect happiness that can make man important, powerful, devout, solemn, and joyous. These extra benefits do not accrue from the things in which the worldly place their

happiness. For this reason God says through the Prophet, "O my people, those who call you happy are deceiving you" (Isaiah 3:12).

∞

XCIII: Achilles[8]

TEXT
Do not grow foolish with strange love of any kind,
Remember Achilles' actions, keep them in mind:
For he foolishly thought to make his foe his friend,
And in this mistake found his undoing and end.

GLOSS
Achilles became foolishly enamored of Polyxena, the fair maiden who was the sister of Hector, when during a truce he saw her on the first anniversary of Hector's funeral, when several Greeks went to Troy to see the nobility of the city and the sumptuous funeral rites for Hector, the most impressive honors ever paid to the body of a knight. Achilles saw Polyxena there, and he was so overtaken with love for her that he could hardly bear it. For this reason he notified Queen Hecuba that he wished to negotiate a marriage, that he would end the war and lift the siege and that they would be friends forever. For a long time Achilles refused to fight the Trojans because of this love. He endeavored with great difficulty to send the army home, but he could not accomplish this and so the marriage never came about. Afterwards Achilles killed Troilus, who was so filled with valor that in spite of his youth he resembled his brother Hector. Hecuba was so saddened on this account that she sent for Achilles to come to Troy to contract the marriage. And so he went there and was killed. For this reason Othea tells the good knight not to become foolishly enamored, for many evils have come about through such far-off loves. With this in mind a wise man observed, "When your enemies are unable to avenge themselves, then you need to pay close attention to yourself."

ALLEGORY
That the good spirit should not become foolishly enamored means that it should not love anything that does not start and finish in God. It should avoid all strange things, such as this world. In explaining the Epistle of Saint John, Saint Augustine notes that the soul should hate the world: "The world and its lust shall pass. So what do you prefer, as a reasonable man: to love the temporal world and pass away with it, or to love Jesus Christ and to live forever with Him?" To this end

Saint John says in his first Epistle, "Love not the world, neither the things that are in the world" (1 John 2:15).

EARL JEFFREY RICHARDS

(Translated from the critical edition prepared by H. D. Loukopoulos[9])

NOTES

1. The name of Hector's horse is not to be confused with that of the nymph of the same name mentioned in Chapter 56. The horse was mentioned in the second account of the two versions of the *Ancient History* that were among Christine's principal sources. There, however, Galatea was said to have been given to Hector by Morgan the Fairy. (B.N. Ms. fr. 301, fol. 62).

2. Christine repeats this attribution of the concept of Wisdom to Aristotle again in *The Long Road to Learning:*

> Because Wisdom is the mother
> Of virtues more than any other,
> By all the best of reasons shown
> She should be universally known . . .
>
> (vv. 5415–18)

3. Christine's version of Cassandra's story differs from Boccaccio's. He says that it is not certain whether Cassandra acquired the art of prophecy by study, by God's gift, or the Devil's trickery. He mentions that Apollo may have given her the art in the hope that she would become his mistress, but she did not keep a promise that she made to him. It was for this reason that he arranged for her words not to be believed. Christine obviously considered this pure misogyny.

   The tradition of Cassandra's prophetic gifts first appears in Pindar and the *Agamemnon* of Aeschylus, which includes the account of Apollo's gift of prophecy.

   Christine includes a revised version of Cassandra's story in *The Book of the City of Ladies,* describing her as "a woman prophet in addition to being a great scholar who knew all the sciences. Her father and brother shut her up in a room so that they could not hear her predictions, but later regretted not having listened to her." In the *Vision,* the allegorical figure who recounts the history of France to Christine, including a discussion of contemporary problems, fears that her warnings about these will not be heeded more than were Cassandra's about the fall of Troy. Her fears were only too apt, for 1405 marked the beginning of serious troubles for France.

4. Christine's quotations from ancient philosophers generally come from a collection known as the *Dicta Philosophorum,* which had recently been translated into French by the Provost of Paris, Guillaume de Tignonville, to whom Christine would give a copy of the earliest group of letters exchanged in the debate over *The Romance of the Rose.*

5. Medea's story was of particular concern to Christine from this text to *The Book of the City of Ladies.* It is evident that she saw Medea's treatment as a prime example of misogyny, one of Christine's particular concerns, and as one of the tales that would have been different if told by a woman. Here it is shown that Medea was the victim of unwise love, the very sort about which Christine would warn her contemporaries in *The Treasury of the City of Ladies.* Medea's story also figures in

The Mutation of Fortune, where there are further details of her infatuation with Jason. In *The Book of the City of Ladies* (II. 56) Medea's abilities in the magic arts are emphasized along with her help to Jason in obtaining the Golden Fleece. His deception is also pointed out, but her evil doing, which is emphasized by Boccaccio's version of the tale, is not mentioned, suggesting that it is the sort of accusation made by men against capable women. In *The Letter of the God of Love* one reads:

> To Jason, what a friend Medea was
> In the procuring of the fleece of gold;
> How falsely he repaid her tenderness
> Whose help permitted him the fleece to hold.
> How may this man (shame on him) be so bold
> To lie and cheat her, who from death and shame
> Kept him, and got him everlasting fame.
>
> *(Poems of Cupid, God of Love,*
> trans. T. S. Fenster, p. 193)

6. Christine made use of the Judgment of Paris three different times: first in a ballade in which she herself chooses the guidance of Pallas over Juno; then in the *Letter of Othea to Hector,* where the contest among the three goddesses is recounted in Chapter 60 along with the wedding of Peleus and Thetis. There the good knight is advised to avoid contention. This chapter continues the fable. It is interesting to note that whereas the ballade was evidently inspired by the story as told in Guillaume de Machaut's *Fontaine amoureuse,* this second version shows the influence of the *Moralized Ovid.* In the third instance, a somewhat modified episode is recounted in *The Book of the Long Road to Learning,* where it figures in the debate among the four queens concerning the sort of prince capable of ruling the world. An interesting discussion of these variations is to be found in Margaret J. Ehrhart's "Christine de Pizan and the Judgment of Paris," in *The Mythographic Art,* ed. J. Chance, (Gainesville, Fl., 1990), pp. 125–56.

7. Fortune was a favorite theme of Christine's from her earliest poetry to the elaborate treatment in *The Mutation of Fortune,* and it was one that inspired many poets from classical times onward. An early influence on Christine's thought is found in Boethius' *Consolation of Philosophy,* one of Christine's favorite books, as she explains in the *Vision.* The uniting of pagan and Christian traditions likewise appears in Dante, another of Christine's sources. Among French works known to Christine are the *Roman de Fauvel* and Nicole de Margival's *Les Echecs Amoureux,* not to mention the poetry of Guillaume de Machaut. For a detailed discussion see H. R. Patch, *The Goddess Fortuna in Medieval Literature.*

8. Mention has already been made of episodes in this work inspired by the history of the Trojan War. Both P.G.C. Campbell, in *L'Epître d'Othéa: étude sur les sources de Christine de Pisan* (Paris, 1924), and S. Solente note that Christine's principal source for this material was a compilation known as *L'Histoire Ancienne jusqu'à César (Ancient History to the Time of Caesar),* which would have been available to her in the Royal Library. It seems evident that this is the history she referred to in the *Vision* (p. 17). Achilles is mentioned in some ten chapters of *The Letter of Othea* as well as in *The Mutation of Fortune.*

9. The translation is based upon H. D. Loukopoulos, "Classical Mythology in the Works of Christine de Pisan, with an edition of *L'Epistre Othea* from the Manuscript Harley 4431." (Ph.D. Wayne State University, 1977.) *L'Epistre Othea* is Appendix A.

CCW

THE BOOK OF THE LONG ROAD TO LEARNING

2100 It's sure the heavens have no star,
  Nor any planet, sun, or moon,
  Nor any one intelligence
  Who lacks a dwelling in that place,
  And all are charged with tasks for her.
2105 And do you know the names of those
  Residing there? They have the name
  Of influences, destinies,
  Predestined to the following:
  The moment that a man is born,
2110 Or woman, humble or high-placed,
  They organize their life's events,
  Assigning what will come to them,
  The good or bad, according to
  The planets and the course they're on
2115 The very hour a child is born. [1]
  But God, however, who's conferred
  Their might on them, remains above
  And oversees what pleases him. [2]
  They give the world its ordering,
2120 Its good and evil, joy and woe,
  In just the way they're told to do,
  Commanded by high heaven's course
  From which (I tell no falsehoods here)
  They get particular commands,
2125 Which they in turn send to the world.
  They vex the world, disturb its course,
  In measure as the planets who've
  A nature to encourage strife
  Are in their house of greatest strength.
2130 They also give out happy fates

When planets whose effect is good
Are in their most auspicious house.
And so these people do not lack
For things to do; accomplished in
2135 Their offices, they never cease
Arranging, nor do they refrain
From bringing what the world's to get.
I saw, indeed I well recall,
The plans that they were fashioning,
2140 And some distressed me quite to tears;
If I had been but capable,
I would have freely changed their course
Away from certain focuses,
If God would not have disapproved;
2145 But I cannot disturb their course.
I saw prepared there mighty wars
And famines and great massacres,
And the vicissitudes of will,
And divers people in revolt,
2150 And loss of lands and earthly goods
And tottering of seignories,
And towns destroyed and wiped away,
And earthquakes and ferocious winds,
And government by ignorance,
2155 And princes lost by treachery
Covertly done, their ruin clear,
And lightning and destructive storms,
With pestilence unthinkable,
And swelling of enormous waves.
2160 From every corner of the world
I saw events that were to come,
And she who knew it all exposed
It all to me, those things I saw— [3]
No other way could I have known.
2165 I saw the time when it would be,
When what I'd learned would come to pass,
To whom, and how, and in what place,
But God would not be pleased if I
Repeated it, for silence was
2170 Enjoined on me; it will be kept,

For it's not fitting to reveal
God's secrets, nor to speak of this,
Except to those who are among
The ones ordained of God as friends.
2175 I learned the reason clearly then,
The why and how, the origin,
The details of the comet which
Appeared aflame, as could be seen
Quite clearly and by all of us,
2180 (The year was fourteen hundred one),[4]
Which did not come without great cause,
And twenty years or more will spend
In bearing its significance;
But let our faith reside in God.
2185   And other comets yet to come
I saw, the moment they'll arrive,
For whom and why they will appear,
And how much time they will remain;
Eclipses of the sun and moon
2190 Saw I, so awe-provoking; one
Of them portends calamities
Which won't be quickly laid to rest.
The Sybils ten who knew so much,
Of Merlin and of those who were[5]
2195 The future prophets, with, as well,
Their years, effect, and where and how—
All that made manifest to me,
No gloss obscured their text at all.
     Yet then I watched more carefully,
2200 For very subtle were those most
Peculiar influences at
Manoeuvering and ordering.
I hadn't been there very long
When I perceived quite visibly
2205 The queen of all untoward events,
Whose movement, unpredictable,
Brings great chagrin to all the world.
That's Fortune, who thwarts harmony;[6]
I recognized her instantly,
2210 For elsewhere had I seen that one!
That false one with the double face,

That one of fickle influence,
Made ready as she organized
The damage she would bring the world,
2215 And insecurity of wealth;
Although just then she was above
To draw her influences there,
She can't diminish or remove,
Or give, or take, or cause a gain
2220 In any place but on the earth;
Her principal domain is here,
Despite her presence there that time.
    I saw alarming figures there
Quite hideous and frightening,
2225 And such that merely seeing them
Reduced me to a quaking state.
I saw there death so hideous —
Its somber image never since
Has given up its hold upon
2230 My heart. And I'm in such a state
So often, when I think of it,
That heart and body, arms and legs,
I tremble at its frightfulness
And at its very ugliness.
2235 I saw there famine, poverty,
Misfortune, and unhappiness.
I also saw there much that's good,
Good fortune, peace — they pleased me well —
Abundance, friendship, birth and life,
2240 Beginning and accomplished end,
Dissension, concord; plenty, war;
And pleasure, power, bitterness;
Increasing honor; love and hate;
Subjection, liberty; and shame,
2245 And Cupid, Jocus, gods of love, [7]
And other such, a thousand so,
Purveyors there of good and ill.

                            THELMA S. FENSTER

(Translated from *Le Livre du Chemin de Long Etude*,
ed. Robert Püschel)

NOTES

1. Christine is reflecting here her father's astrological knowledge. In her day belief in the influence of the stars on human destiny was widespread. See Maxime Préaud, *Les Astrologues à la fin du Moyen Age* (Paris, 1984), especially chap. 1, "L'Omniprésence des Astrologues," pp. 21–50. The horoscopes prepared for Charles V and the future Charles VI are still preserved at the end of a treatise concerning the influence of the planets on human destiny by a certain Pèlerin de Prusse (Oxford, St. John's College, Ms. 164).

2. In order to avoid any suspicion of heresy, Christine, along with others, points to God's ultimate supervision of the universe.

3. This is a reference to the Cumaean sibyl who was Christine's guide and who explained to her the sights Christine saw.

4. Christine refers here to a comet that appeared in January 1402, causing great concern about the future, especially the year 1405 — with good reason, as it turned out. Préaud, *Les Astrologues,* pp. 111–30.

5. On several occasions Christine expressed admiration for the sibyls, whom she considered the equivalents of the biblical prophets, notably in *The Mutation of Fortune* and in *The City of Ladies,* where she devotes the first three chapters of Book II to them, saying: "[T]hey were so called because they prophesied such marvelous things that what they said must have come to them from the pure thinking of God. Thus 'sibyl' is a title of office rather than a proper name." (Richards trans., p. 100). Merlin was the creation of Geoffrey of Monmouth, who wrote the *Prophetiae Merlini* (c. 1130), which he later included in his *Historia Regum Britanniae.* Christine undoubtedly knew Merlin through a thirteenth-century French translation, the *Prophécies de Merlin,* attributed to Master Richard of Ireland. See *The New Arthurian Encyclopedia,* ed. N. J. Lacy (New York, 1991), pp. 319–22).

6. Christine here depicts Fortune with her double face, an image that she would develop at length in *The Mutation of Fortune.* She is evidently influenced here by *The Consolation of Philosophy,* Book II, in which Philosophy addresses Boethius: "You are wrong if you think that Fortune has changed toward you. This is her nature, the way she always behaves. She is changeable, and so in her relations with you she has merely done what she always does . . . You have merely discovered the two-faced nature of this blind goddess." (Trans. Richard Green, The Library of Liberal Arts [Indianapolis and New York, 1962], pp. 21–22.)

7. According to Alain de Lille in *De Planctu Naturae,* Cupid and Jocus were both sons of Venus. Venus, unfaithful to Hymen, the god of weddings, produced Jocus through an adulterous affair with Antigamus. Cupid thus comes to represent sexual normality and Jocus sexual abnormality. See *The Plaint of Nature,* trans. J. J. Sheridan (Toronto, 1980). Christine may have known this work primarily by way of Jean de Meun, for whom it is an important source.

CCW

THE BOOK OF THE
MUTATION OF FORTUNE

❧

Here Begins the Book of the Mutation of Fortune (I)

However is it possible
That I, of wit just passable,
Shall appropriately relate
4   What we cannot estimate
Nor understand well. No—
For all that we try to know
We can never conceive it all
8   In spite of the Muse's call.
So great are the diversities
So real are the adversities,
So difficult are great events
12   To comprehend in any sense
Because of Fortune's changing ways:
Incertitude which plagues our days,[1]
Caused by her reflection
16   Defying our perception
As behooves the deepest abyss.
So how can I claim not to miss,
As I describe her jealousy,
20   Not falling for her spell, you see,
And hope to extirpate her ruse?
'Tis difficult, but I shall use
The finest language I can find;
A lofty task, a little mind
That I possess; where others failed—
Better writers, whose talents paled,
As they tried for all-inclusion,

28   Only ending in confusion.
There, however, I'll not lose nerve
For often did Dame Fortune serve
Me generously her own gruel:
A cup of joy, a fate so cruel.
I've seen it all, it must be told
As my memory must unfold
My understanding now discerns
The filaments of past concerns
That wind and twist at her behest
My wiser sense now meets the quest
That previously I could not face:
Whatever happened, I could not trace.
Sometimes only evil teaches
Causality, as reason reaches, [2]
Shaping our experiences
Molding them from our five senses.
I therefore think to speak no falsehood
To whomever it befalls, should
They care to listen, to the end;
My discourse I shall not extend
Beyond the limits of the truth:
50   As I instruct, I hope to soothe.

Here Is Told of the Person Who Compiled Said Book, How She Served Fortune, as She Will Tell Later (II)

I wish to tell my history,
'Twill seem to some pure mystery.
But even though they won't believe,
56   I'll tell the truth and won't deceive.
It all happened to me, really;
I was twenty-five, or nearly,
It was no dream when it occured,
60   No need to evoke the absurd
When one has seen what I have seen,
These wonders that have really been,
That we do not see every day
Because of Fortune's clever way

64   Of disguising her mutations,
      Those deceptive situations
      Which I hope to unveil here.
      For though she seems to sneer
      At our efforts as mere mortals
      As we grovel at the portals
      Of her kingdom and command,
      She fears our understanding
73   Of her vanity unending;
      That we'll see how her strange glory
      Tawdry is, and transitory.
      She deals in victory and loss
      As men pursue the shallow gloss
      Of honor, wealth, and property,
      While killing life and liberty,
      True happiness and so much more;
      We'd rather languish at her door
      As she blindly contradicts us
      Warmly welcomes, then evicts us.
86   This is strange, yet all too common.
      It is up to us to summon
      All our powers of perception
      In pursuit of her deception:
      She appears to one, then to a brother,
      In one form and then another.
      Although she is invisible,
      Rendering our senses risible,
92   I did see her, this mighty queen,
      Such as she has never been,
      By just looking at her plainly.
      She behaved to me quite tamely
      As I sojourned at her court.
      I learned quickly, as her cohort,
      That one must take with good the evil
      To effect one's self retrieval,
      And by serving, says the Bible,[3]
103   One can triumph, one is liable,
      Provided that the heart is true,
      To have honor and trust accrue.
      To those who sagely wish to rule,[4]

107   Wise servitude is the finest school.
It's not tyranny I've in mind,
But self-mastery, that you will find.
Virtue, friendship, all good things,
Outlasting jewels and golden rings.

112   It doesn't happen overnight
So don't be angry with your plight;
You may suffer for weeks and years
Before your faith's fruition nears:
If you've served well, you'll be rewarded,
Her servants she has never thwarted.
I'll tell you now all that I know
Of her courtiers, high and low,
About her castle and her court
Where events occur of every sort,
And especially what she did for me:

136   In my time of need she kept me
Out of danger; fear that swept me,
She assuaged and calmed my woes.

139   But, lest I'm caught up in the throes
Of my narration, 'twould be wise
Before my discourse grows in size,
Let me summarize, this moment,
Just who I am, what all this meant.
How I, a woman, became a man
By a flick of Fortune's hand

144   How she changed my body's form
To the perfect masculine norm.
I'm a man, no truth I'm hiding,

148   You can tell by how I'm striding
And if I was female before—
It's the truth and nothing more—
It seems I'll have to re-create
Just how I did transmutate
From a woman to a male:
I think the title of my tale
Is, if I'm not being importune,
"The Mutation of Fortune."

157 For the sake of presentation,
One should first state from what nation
Comes the family, who they were,
Whether they're noble, rich, or poor.
A family having wealth and fame
Deserves to be evoked by name;
For this reason, I'll feel free
To cite my birth near Lombardy
In a city so well known[5]

168 That many pilgrims call it home!
In ancient times, the Trojan race
Here built a city, full of grace.
Myself, I am of noble lines;
My father doubly blessed: for science
Was his calling, and he was known
For his wisdom, and his name shone
Like the jewels of his domain.
To gauge his worth, they count in vain.
It happens that, with many men
As rich as he, that thieves will then
Make off with some, or all, of it,
Leaving perhaps a little bit.
But Father's wealth could not be taken;
It was unique; he was unshaken

184 By any threat of larceny
So great was his security
In its abundance, like a spring
That fresh supply would always bring.[6]
The more one took the more it yielded
Oh the wondrous wealth he wielded!
So boundless was my father's treasure,

210 He gave to others with great pleasure.

This Tells of the Precious Stones Her Father Had (IV)

211 Within the priceless magnitude
That characterized the plenitude
Of father's riches are contained

Especially jewels he retained
Of virtue and of noble worth.
For Mount Parnassus gave them birth;
215   Father dug them from the fountain
Pegasus made in the mountain;
Where once struck his equine hoof
Now the Nine Muses dance, aloof,
Causing would-be poets anguish
Lest their verses tire and languish.
Father did not dally, either:
He worked hard to gather by there
More treasures than mere words can tell
The splendid fountain served him well.
Within this sumptuous treasure chest
228   Lay two jewels he valued best:
No bright red garnet, however dear,
Nor rich ruby, can compare
To them in value. One alone
Contains the virtues we condone.
234   Ever since the time of Arthur;
No emperor's worth transcends farther;
Its brilliant luster knows no equal,
No star can ever, as a sequel,
Shine in heaven high above.
As in every labor of love,
The time and toil involved in finding
Are compensated for by binding
Grace and happiness. For to those
Who strive, as the Muses propose,
For virtue, through pain, at the source—
The Fountain—comes, without remorse,
Eternal Happiness and strength.
Having told you all this at length,
I shall ask you if you've known
The function of this precious stone.
To celestial knowledge 'tis the key;
261   Enabling my learned father to see
So that he was in great demand
Advising princes, at whose command
He'd foretell battles, plagues, and famine,

The course of planets he'd examine:
Symbols of the zodiac could
To him reveal just how one should
React to avoid catastrophe
Rather than suffer atrophy
Before the unknown fate was done.
He also knew, each and every one,
279   The names of all created things
In the universe. Therefore came
To my father wide acclaim
For his goodness and common sense;
285   Kings showered on him benevolence.

More on this Same Subject

289   And now I'll tell you all about
The other stone that wields great clout.
This one too worth more than gold
For it keeps you from growing old,
Or falling ill; as it can cure
Any malady we endure.

∽

335   Over Octavian's power and wealth,
Galen, doctor to mankind's health,
My father chose to emulate;
His science to perpetuate.

Here Is Told of Her Mother (V)[7]

339   My mother's expansivity,
Not prone to inactivity,
Enabled her to excell in
Whatever Penthesilea did well in.
Her power only God can measure,
And despite his wondrous treasure,
She surpassed my father's mental
Capabilities. In gentle
Majesty she reigned since birth,
Of virtuousness she knew no dearth.

One sees her presence everywhere,
In all her works she is there;
Things of beauty she makes with care.
359 She is ageless, not senescent
All immortal, luminescent;
God has granted life eternal
To her, so she may act as vernal
Continuity: restore life,
And heal the earth's incessant strife,
Preserve from Fate's inanity
The life of all humanity.
She's the mother of all mankind,
Brother and sister all combined
We are, to one another.
So, about my father and mother
I've told you the essential,
And thus, to remain sequential,
My tale permits you now to learn
372 Whether or not you truly yearn
To know my name, of which part one
Bears the name of Our Lord's Son,
The most perfect man there ever was;
Adding to it I N E does
Provide you with my name,
No extra letters does it claim.

Here Is Told How She Collected Only the Shards of Her Father's Treasure (VI)

My father, whom I've aforementioned,
Had one wish in his great ascension:
To have a male child—unfulfilled.
To him he could have safely willed
His mighty fortune and his land.
Between my parents there did stand
A duplicitous agreement,
Or so it seems: my father meant
Something different from my mother,
For instead of male, the other

396 Sex was I born, though otherwise
I had my father's looks: his eyes,
His hair, his build. She had tricked him.
But despite the original dictum,
I was a loved and cherished child;
My father's doubts I had beguiled.
Mother, nurturing me as her best,
Lovingly nursed me at her breast.
And I thus grew up without fear
Of the injustice all too near:
Among infant playmates equality
Reigns, whereas adult polity,
Riddled with prejudice, reacts
In the interest of male contracts.
How little I knew, a woman destined
To have, by this menace, lessened
Her fortune, as sole legatee,
Stolen by legal repartee.

∞

I'd overcome this bitter pill
432 Only by talent and sheer will.
So angry was I that I cursed
God, out of anger that coerced
Me into sheer desperation.
But my undeserved privation
Taught me things more valuable:
The need to remain malleable
In light of changing circumstance
And all the vagaries of chance.
My loss became a different gain
So I no longer suffer pain
From materialistic loss
All of which is merely gloss,
By Fortune given and stolen
Just as our hopes become swollen
With vanity and shallowness.
Now I've outgrown my callowness
468 And Fortune's servant have become.

Here Is Said How She Came to Serve Fortune (V)

My beautiful mother, Nature,
Who nurtured me to full stature,
472   Began to think of my advancement
And education. What her stance meant
Was that I enter the service
Of a high-ranking mistress
Equal to my mother's level.
There's only one fit to revel
In that lofty, noble sphere,
479   Though unlike Mother she appeared;
Similarly yet differently,
Never, ever regularly,
Did they exist. This other, known
As Fortune, came from strange lands
And she's a weaver of many strands
Intricate and inscrutable.
And thus into her mutable
Way of life I entered, received
Graciously by Fortune, deceived
Thus far by my lack of need:
508   Her commands I learned to heed.

∞

Here Is Told of the Headdress That Her Mother Sent to Her (VIII)

535   She whose generosity
Would help me on immeasurably
Began to equip me, head first.
A noble headdress of great worth
In her workshop she had made,
Of stuff more valuable than jade.

∞

553   This special crown by its jewels
Gleamed. More than decor, the tools
For success it provided me;
Against that which could have divided me

In strength. It befits a maiden
Not only to parade in
But for its many virtues it
Is unique; I would choose it
For the four magic stones it bears
Which in quality, each compares
To no other in its value,
For each has its separate virtue.

This Tells of the Properties of the Stones in the Headdress (IX)

567 The first stone, placed in front, confers
Serenity: Its wearer demurs
Graciously, with sagacity,
For the stone gives perspicacity,
While restraining from stupidity,
Awkwardness and cupidity.
It keeps its wearer on the path
Of reason: no emperor hath
Such a valuable possession;
This noble jewel is named Discretion.
After it comes Consideration.
Mid-crown is its situation,
Appropriately, for, like its mate
It causes me to moderate
At all times between rash extremes.
To have both qualities combined
So that they function intertwined.
Not all people have them both
And for this reason they are loath
To act wisely, for having one
Exclusively, though often done,
Is not enough. Both are needed,
So that reason's call is heeded.
In front of Consideration
After much deliberation,
Mother placed another in front
Whose virtues one can never vaunt
Excessively. Lavish praise is
Heaped upon it; for it fazes

All other powers. Whosoever
Owns it remembers forever
All that is felt and said,
617   Heard and done, and expressed instead.
Their stone is named Retentiveness,
Target of much inventiveness.
And cannot be obtained by haste
Lest its talents be laid to waste.
Another jewel resides in back
Of the crown; it doesn't lack
For great beauty. It enables
One to recall facts and fables,
No matter how long past in time;
Science, history, all sublime.
629   Memory is the name of this stone
In which great secrets find their home,
Waiting there to be ordered and sorted
Until the time comes to be reported.
With Retentiveness, Memory works;
If by one of those fortunate quirks,
A person with both in syncopation,
She fulfills all obligations,
With the help of honor and sense
640   Can produce great accomplishments.

∽

This crown that gives me great gifts,
I make sure to say that it lifts
Me not to the grandeur of Nature
Nor above all other creatures.
I'm not as talented as I
Would like, but my crown of quasi-
Divinity contents me well.
660   Unlike Sibyl, I can't foretell
The future, but give thanks to God
For giving me the virtues named
Above. Indeed they are famed
But not possessed, in all the world;
Only by God's grace are they unfurled.
For even Nature cannot grant them:

She, too, born of God, must live, then,
By his commands, as she commands us.
Through our souls, He understands us;
While she governs corporeally
Over us, hyperboreally.
Therefore the body casts its lot
With material power. It is not
Like the soul, of celestial dust,
Which, elevated above all, must
Be ordered by God, who also gave
Us, within ourselves, nothing, save
Memory and Discretion,
Such a wondrous concession.

∞

729 Mother gave me the crown to wear
Upon my pretty, curly hair.
Its ownership by me was fateful
For such an honor was I grateful
On my head it sat not lightly,
736 'Twas difficult to wear politely
As I grew up, so did the crown,
The marvelous jewels weighed me down.
But the adventure was worth it
And nothing could coerce it
As it governed and protected me,
My own world, it eternally
Revolved upon my head.
Most importantly, I should note,
That virtues reversed can promote
Vice. God gave virtues to us all,
We should ensure that they not fall
Into the realm of evil, so
763 Upon ourselves the blame should go.
From infancy I found myself
Separated, as though from pelf.
Once I'd placed upon my head
The magic crown in such good stead.
Just as I was becoming used
To womanhood, tho' a bit confused,

Reason set about her ways
To educate my maturing days.

∞

(Christine enters Fortune's household service. Nature puts her on a ship to the land of Hymeneus, en route to Fortune's castle.)

823   Hymeneus,[8] or so he's called,
Is very old and very bald.
I was en route to his domain,
Where as a god he knew to reign,
According to many a poet,
In numerous ways he did show it:
Through his servants, of all estates:
Princes, kings, and potentates,
As well as serfs and peasantry.
Of his service, some speak pleasantly,
While others scorn the high price —
Usually because of bad advice —
That service chanced to have cost them.
Hymeneus has surely lost them;
'Tis the subject of many a harsh debate,
This game of finding the right mate.
Fortune has not helped them, either,
843   And churchmen rightly despise her.

∞

(Christine and the perfect young man are married by Hymeneus in a colorful, elaborate ceremony. They are very happy as they embark upon their marital voyage, leaving the land of Hymeneus for the open sea.)

Here Is Told of Some Miracles of the Gods, as Reported by Ovid (XI) [9]

1025   The time has come for me to tell
Of strange, diverse cases all pell-mell,
As I had promised, early on
In this book which my name's upon,
How from woman to man I'm turned,
When I to Dame Fortune returned;
An event all too marvelous

Without being fabulous:
It is no lie, no dishonesty
To relate metaphorically
The true meaning of an event,
As Fortune likes to circumvent
Our notion of reality
By her strange theatricality:
At will she can transform bold knights
Into beasts, as when alights

1044   Ulysses[10] at fair Circe's port.
She deceived his men as a retort,
Feigning amorous emotion,
She slipped them a sleeping potion;
And by Ulysses, unforeseen,
Such were the ways of Circe

1056   Who to many showed no mercy!
More great marvels every day
Without resting, in any way.
Such things Fortune does without strain;
There's little she doesn't retain
Or influence in her travail;
One thinks often of Ovid's tale,
In which a man, finding two snakes
Intertwined, wielding a pole, breaks
Them apart at their sinful game.
As punishment he then became

1076   A woman in all that counted.
The young man's name was Tiresias,[11]
And seven years he was to pass
Laboring at what women do
After this duration was through,
He returned to those woods, and there
By chance rediscovered just where
Those frolicking snakes he'd smitten;
According to what's been written,
He found those same snakes together,
Struck them again, to see whether

1088   He could to his male form return.
By repetition did he earn
Rights to his original form—

So said Ovid, seeking to inform
Us of this, and then of a king,
Lygdus[12] by name, who sought to bring
His queen to kill their newborn, were
It a girl; for women incurred
In him such hatred and ire
That King Lygdus ordered that fire
Should return a daughter to ash,
Because a female heir would dash
His hopes of dynasty. A boy
However, would create much joy
And the queen must preserve him well.
The queen bore a girl, but did not tell;
Rather than kill her child by fire,
1108   Her powerful motherly desire
Saved her child, which she raised as male
So that everywhere ran the tale
That the queen had borne a handsome son.
The king believed, as did everyone,
That this was true. Iphis, she was called:
A boy's or girl's name — she enthralled
By her lovely body and face,
Hidden under men's clothes, not lace.
Her mother feared discovery
As time went by. Recovery
Could be guaranteed by marriage
To someone of noble carriage.

∞

(Continuation of the story of Iphis, who meets her bride, and by the intervention of Isis ("Vestis), Iphis is changed into a man [vv. 1122–58].)[13]

How She Lost the Captain of Her Ship (XII)

(Christine now introduces the story of her own mutation as she sails from the
land of Hymeneus with her husband, thus leaving her life of "great repose"
to continue her mission as ordered by Fortune. During the voyage, a storm
occurs, and she and her husband are caught in its midst. A great wave sweeps
away her husband, and she is left to grieve and suffer, as well as to survive the

storm—alone. There is a lengthy allusion to Ovid's story of Ceyx and Alcyone (vv. 1256–60). We then return to the narrator-heroine as she seems to be doomed to die in the tempest.)

1314   So moving were my desperate cries
       That even before her cold eyes
       My plight caused Fortune to amend
       Her fiendish ways and be my friend.
       She wanted, as a good friend should,
       To succor me in my widowhood.
       And oh, how marvelous her aid!
1320   All aware, I'd have been afraid
       But, fatigued was I from crying;
       Near-paralyzed, there lying
1324   I fell asleep toward suppertime
       Then, descending from her clime,
       My mistress came to me distressed—
       Though many by her were oppressed—
       She had arrived to help me, there,
       And touched my body everywhere:
1328   She felt each member, one by one,
       Massaging it 'til she was done
       And went away. There I remained
       Aloft; ocean waves waxed and waned,
1332   Finally, with one mighty crash,
       Our ship against the rocks was smashed,
       Awakening me. I felt all strange:
       My body undergoing change
       All over I felt transmutated:
       No longer weak and subjugated.
1337   Each limb of mine did feel much stronger,
       I, discomfited no longer,
       Felt no further need for crying
       As I'd done before, just lying
       Helpless. I was now astonished
       Never had I been admonished
       Of such rapid transformation,
       So sudden a salvation,
       From grim loneliness and fear,
       Perils, dangers, hovering so near;

But Dame Fortune would not leave me,
Though she'd set out to bereave me.
All over I felt myself afresh,

1348 As I touched muscle—a man's flesh!
And my voice took on assurance
As my body gained endurance;
But there from my once fragile hand,
From my finger, my own wedding band
Had fallen, this gift of Hymeneus
That, like eternal love, should weigh us
Down, but blissfully, for I love
Him whose soul now soars above.

1356 And so I buoyantly arise,
My shroud of sorrow now complies:
Sloughed off, freeing me from chagrin
As I endeavor to begin
Bravely so that I still wonder
At this change; as if by thunder,
I, now made a man, must censure

1363 Any urge to shirk adventure.
So I raised my eyes all around,
At the mangled ship all dashed aground
Sail and mast I saw in tatters;
To angry storms, nothing matters.
The tops and rigging were in pieces,
While the hull, through ravaged creases,
Took in water by vast swallows,

1374 Drinking down to Neptune's hollows.
When I'd seen this devastation,
I prepared for reparation.
Hammer in hand, with mortar and nails,
I rejoined the planks; then where snails
Dwell, under rocks, I gathered moss
To cover leaks, I spread it across,
And made the hull watertight, then
I drained the bilge: she floats again!

1384 In no time at all, I could sail,
For I learned to pilot, to prevail
Over oceans at my command,
I and my crew knew to withstand

Danger and fend off death. Now see,
Like a real man; I have to be.
1392   Fortune kindly taught me the way
To do manly deeds, to this day.
As you can tell, men are my peers
As they have been for thirteen years.
Though 'twould please me more than a third,
To return as woman and be heard.

∞

(After the end of Part I, Christine describes Fortune's castle throughout Part II: the Portal of Wealth; Fortune's two brothers, Eur and Meseur [Good and Bad Fortune] and how they influence those under their power; the Portal of Hope and her followers; the Portal of Poverty and her victims; and finally the guardian of the Fourth Portal, Atropos [Death].) [14]

This Tells of the Fourth Wall of the Castle and Its Portal and Its Guardian (XIIII)

2731   Now I will tell of the fourth side,
Whose very sight gives cause to hide.
To explain properly defies
The viewer. So much it horrifies
One, beyond all human senses,
Mortal fears are its main defenses,
Not its walls, which have fallen low,
Nor its shadowy depths below.
Its facade crumbles, brick by brick;
With naked souls its gates are thick.
Nature repairs it dutifully
2760   But when the wind blows fitfully,
This side's walls go tumbling down.
Away from glorious renown
This wall leans from the Castle's weight,
In its midst, its own groaning gate,
Echoing the laments of those
Who, all distraught, find no repose.
2771   And if this place is horrible,
Its guardian is terrible;
Ne'er was there a ghastlier sight

'Tis hard to believe Nature might
Have created this condition,
Countenancing such affliction.

∞

2791   All earthen-colored is her face [15]
Her gaping mouth her teeth displays
Some teeth push in, others outside,
Encircled by lips pale and dried.
Pained and troubled roll her eyes,
Her nose, discolored, breathes crosswise.
2798   The suffering face is twisted 'round
Revealing how she's beaten down;
All of her is dark and blackened,
She's so thin her skin has slackened
Over its carapace of bone.
This pelt's so thin it appears sewn,
The ventral side onto the spine,
As every day, further decline
Occurs; incredibly enough—
For it would seem she could not slough
Off more. Even her clothing,
Sparse and torn, brings one to loathing,
Upon seeing her lying there
At the gate, covered everywhere
With twisting branches, sinewy plants.
She's so pathetic, it seems she grants
Free entry to all those who pass.
2819   Atropos, this keeper's known as,
Speaking properly in those terms,
The ones the Poet so confirms, [16]
Respecting arts of metaphor.
This is the way to nevermore;
The last door, to him who checks it:
It's the Castle's major exit.
Furthermore, no one can enter
For to penetrate the center
Of the fortress. No supplies come;
Beasts of burden are not welcome;
No people, be they dressed or nude,

2832   Come; this gate will only exude.
But each and every issuant,
However great his wealth pursuant,
Leaves it here. Each social station
Finds enforced normalization
Within this grim democracy.
Thus, though the aristocracy
And poor believe they needn't pay,
Their tribute's due the final day.
That length of time we strive to make
Longer by ways designed to slake
Her tireless appetite for souls
Heedless of eternal goals
Conceived by them. No remission
Exists, for Death's decision
Is fixed; though we always strive in vain
To defy her and remain
Immortal; that's what some believe
Hoping that they might retrieve
2860   That day, that extra we treasure
Before we must obey her pleasure.
Whatever we've in life acquired,
We find Atropos has aspired,
To make us leave it all behind,
Except our deeds which can remind
Successors in this earthly life
Of our triumphs gained in strife,
After we pass on, denuded,
For truly have we been deluded
Up to coming to this gate.
2864   Yet after seeing her sad fate
Of moribund eternity,
Meeting death, not mere infirmity,
With God's love only, easing pain
Of this departure, does remain,
The better prospect, you'll agree:
As met by all humanity.

Here Is Told of the Highest Throne (I)

Just as I have done describing
The Castle, all the while ascribing
To it qualities, such as how
It rotates on its track and now
4276   How its lofty tower, shining
Houses all the floors, entwining
Personalities and stations
According to their elevations
On which their forms are lodged and housed;
As for the routines they've espoused,
The inhabitants of this place,
4284   From the highest to lowest space,
I'll describe each situation
Rank to rank in syncopation
Beginning with the highest throne,
4292   From God inherited and known
Via the Path of Righteous Life
St. Peter's throne, now rent by strife:[17]
Occupied by two, not one,
Men of power; neither had won,
But both did covet, this throne on high;
Their struggle shook things all awry,
As power passed from one of them
To the other and back again.[18]
Common sense is neither's forte
And each attack meets with retort.
The Castle vibrates with their game
4300   As each man fights to be the same—
Or not really—rather, unique,
While the other he would seek
To topple down forevermore.
Fraud advised them both to ignore
The ways of Reason and Good Sense,
But rather to act as malcontents,

Dishonest men: rapaciously,
Appealing so capaciously
At the gate of Lady Wealth
Whose goods are gotten more by stealth.
This precious throne—contested prize—
Is, however, of narrow size
Having been built for only one
4312   Not for two, let these men be done.

∞

PART IV.

(Christine has outlined the entire social hierarchy in Part III and now, in Part
IV, describes the Gallery of Historical Portraiture in Fortune's Castle, providing a vehicle for recounting all of world history as it was then known in verse.
Then something curious happens when illness strikes her as she comes to
writing the history of the Jews. No doubt a real illness, it is alluded to in some
of her other works composed or in process at this time.) [19]

Rhyming is no trivial task
'Tis for me now too much to ask
As I relate the great events
8748   Abridged in words of truest sense.

(Christine recounts the history of the Jews in prose, after which she begins
Part V, on the Babylonians and Greeks, continuing in verse.)

PART V. THE BABYLONIANS AND THE GREEKS

Here Is Told of Semiramis (III)

After Ninus was laid to rest, [20]
His widow reigned, among the best,
9088   Semiramis the powerful; [21]
The queen whose every hour, full
Of glory—never of decline—
Reigned in seigneury sublime.
With prowess and great chivalry

She vanquished every rivalry,
Bringing rulers to their knees,
Surpassing her husband's deeds.
9096   The dignity that came to lordship
While she ruled, dispelled all hardship
As her kingdom flourished wholly,
Ethiopia she boldly
Conquered, then she entered
India, in which she countered
Mighty armies, which she routed;
No man more than she was touted,
No man's feats were ever grander,
Not even those of Alexander,
Of whom I shall later write,
Than this queen's, whose royal right,
She exercised with sense and strength
And forcefulness, so that, at length
By the hundreds, her great legions
9110   Dominated many regions.

∞

Part VI.

The Meeting of Jason and Medea [22] (V)

14357   Love, whose diverse obligations
Chose Medea's situation,
Allowed that Jason come before
Her, by misadventure; what's more,
Fortune's hand was in this, too;
She had Jason's fate in view:
Difficulties she'd contrive
As long as he would be alive.
"What brings them here?" Medea asks
Of Jason, the leader, "and what tasks
Do they seek to accomplish here?"
14365   Came the answer, "The occasion
For this voyage, without evasion,
Is to conquer the Fleece of Gold

Just as he has vowed and told
His men as they will bear the brunt
Of obstacles he shall confront
To finish what he's undertaken:
14372   The Golden Fleece to have taken.
While Medea upon Jason gazed
He pleased her greatly; left her dazed
As she heard his explanation,
Winning by infatuation
So that she would do his will.
As she stared, her heart did fill
With admiration for his grace,
His courtliness, his handsome face,
Intelligence and charming speech.
Oh how Medea yearned to reach
Out to touch him as did her eyes.
At which time Love's sharp arrow flies
And penetrates Medea's heart,
14383   Gravely wounding from the start.

∞

Part VII.

Here Is Told of the Book's Conclusion (LVII)

23595   Now I've written sufficiently
Of what, I hope, omnisciently,
I've found and seen and known
As every day to me has shown
Up to today where I am now
Just as before, when I did vow
Dame Fortune faithfully to serve
23602   Despite her anger's bitter verve.
My salary for suffering her
And her ways, so hard to endure
Is the knowledge that I must not
Acquire those things She'll cause to rot,
Or disappear, or be stolen:
The gold with which a purse is swollen.

No one escapes Her harsh embrace;
Sooner or later, face to face.
Goods She'll bring and then reclaim
Even from those of wealth and fame.
You, princes of imposing towers,
Reflect on this, forget your powers—
Against Her they are vanity!
Constraining Her inanity
Is hopeless, isn't it? Instead,
Considering all that's been said,
23616   Are mutations like this so slight?
What good is it to strive for gain
When Her caprice will make it wane?
There's no escape nor surety,
23620   Just pain and insecurity,
Saint Paul said, in his epistle,[23]
For different reasons, of Her Castle,
Regardless of what state one's in,
The risk of peril stretches thin
Our happiness, whether we be
Inside or out, on land or sea,
In company or solitude,
There is but one certitude:
The banners of Peril will rise,
And Bad Fortune will realize[24]
Another victory, again,
23632   For nothing goes beyond his ken.
Because of this, I have decided
So that no more I should be chided
And discarded, like some old toy,
I've discovered an inner joy,
Possessed by others—though too few—
Of which Bad Fortune never knew
To steal from me. There's nothing shrewd
In choosing peace and solitude
23636   Disdaining things material
For abstract and ethereal.

NADIA MARGOLIS

(Translated from *Le Livre de la Mutacion de Fortune*,
ed. Suzanne Solente)

NOTES

1. As has been noted, Christine had concerned herself with Fortune since her early poetry. In her *Moral Proverbs* (Roy, *Oeuvres,* III, p. 48) she had written:

   > Who does not fear Fortune is not wise,
   > For perils she often will devise.

   It is, however, possible to confront Fortune with Prudence as she points out in the *Moral Teachings* (*Oeuvres,* III, p. 28):

   > Through study sufficiently inquire
   > That Prudence you may thus acquire,
   > For Virtue's mother can force display
   > To drive bitter Fortune away.

2. A reference to the French proverb: *A quelque chose est malheurté bonne* (Misfortune can be good for something). Le Roux de Lincy, *Le Livre des proverbes français* (Paris, 1842), p. 229.

3. Psalms 101:23.

4. This sentiment echoes the proverb *Car celuy qui bien sert/Par droit son louier en desert.* (Who serves well need not ask for wages). Le Roux de Lincy, II, p. 102

5. Christine is obviously referring here to her birth in Venice.

6. This is a reference to her father's knowledge.

7. Christine's representation of Nature as her mother is probably inspired by *The Romance of the Rose,* but perhaps also by Alain de Lille's *De Planctu Naturae (The Complaint of Nature).*

8. Hymeneus, or Hymen, also recalls *The Romance of the Rose.* In the course of retelling the story of Pygmalion, he says:

   > With this ring I thee wed, and thus become
   > All thine, as you all mine, let Hymen hear
   > And Juno heed my vows, and present be
   > At this our marriage.
   > (Trans. H. W. Robbins, p. 447).

   He is also spoken of in the *Ovide Moralisé:* See the *Ovide moralisé, poème du commencement du quatorzième siècle,* ed. C. de Boer, 5 vols. (Amsterdam, 1915–36), Bk. IV, vv. 2232–33.

9. Christine's knowledge of Ovid comes primarily from this *Moralized Ovid,* of which she had already made considerable use in *The Letter of Othea.*

10. *Ovide Moralisé,* IV, vv. 2362–2562. These references are from the notes of Suzanne Solente's edition of *La Mutacion de Fortune,* 3 vols. (Paris, 1959–60).

11. *Ovide Moralisé,* III, vv. 1023–49.

12. Christine refers to him as King of Lydia.

13. *Ovide Moralisé* IX, vv. 2763–3112, where the goddess who performs the transformation is Isis rather than Vesta.

14. Christine had already spoken of Atropos in *The Letter of Othea,* chap. 34:

    > In every hour have regard
    > For Atropos and his dard
    > Which strikes and spares none of mankind,
    > So you should keep your soul in mind.

    In the gloss she explains: "The poets call death Atropos." For an interesting discussion of this figure, see M. Meiss, *French Painting in the Time of Jean de Berry: The Limbourgs and Their Contemporaries* (New York, 1974), pp. 30–33.

15. This passage, like the illustration of Atropos in the *Epître d'Othéa* (B.N. Ms. fr. 606), recalls the description of the Siren in Dante's *Purgatorio,* XIX:

> There came to me in a dream, a stuttering woman,
> With eyes asquint, and crooked on her feet,
> With maimed hands, and of sallow hue.
> (Trans. Thomas Okey, Temple Classics [London, 1901], p. 229)

16. Reference to the *Ovide Moralisé,* VI, v. 2246.
17. This is one of the paths described in Part I. The others are Pride, Ruse, and Great Learning.
18. A reference to the Great Schism in the Catholic Church. Christine had already spoken of it in *The Long Road to Learning* and would do so again in later writings. The two popes referred to here are Boniface IX and Benedict XIII (Pedro de Luna).
19. *Avision,* ed. Towner, p. 155, and Margolis, Nadia, "Christine de Pizan and the Jews: Political and Poetic Implications," in *Politics, Gender, and Genre,* ed. Margaret Brabant (Boulder, Co., 1992, pp. 53–73).
20. The reign of Ninus, king of Babylonia and Assyria, is recounted following the *Histoire Ancienne jusqu'à César.*
21. Semiramis conquered Ethiopia and India and fortified Babylonia. She married her son and reigned for forty-two years, as recounted in the *Histoire Ancienne.* Christine had already spoken of both Ninus and Semiramis in the *Chemin de Long Estude* (vv. 3763–72) and would tell of the exploits of Semiramis again in *The Book of the City of Ladies.* See L. Dulac, "Un mythe didactique chez Christine de Pisan: Sémiramis ou la veuve héroïque (Du *De mulieribus claris* de Boccace à la *Cité des Dames*)," in *Mélanges de philologie romane offerts à Charles Camproux* (Montpellier, 1978, pp. 315–43).
22. Medea also appears in *The Letter of Othea* (54 and 58) as well as in *The Book of the City of Ladies* where she is discussed twice (I.32 and II.56). In both cases she is presented in a more favorable light than in either the *Moralized Ovid* or Boccaccio.
23. Corinthians XI: 26–27.
24. Christine is referring here to Fortune's brother, Meseur, described in Part II of the poem.

CCW

IV

THE DEFENSE OF
WOMEN

❦

NO ASPECT of Christine de Piza̅   evoked such
great interest in recent years as her i̅   the importance
of women in society, especially her attack o̅   misogyny that was
an all too pervasive characteristic of the writing popular in her day. A
discussion has developed around the question of whether or not
Christine should be considered a feminist, and there has even been a
complaint that Christine's feminism has never been properly defined.

This debate, however, is not as recent as might be supposed, for in
the 1920s Blanche Hinman Dow and Lula McDowell Richardson
were already characterizing her as a "forerunner" of feminism,
whereas Léon Abensour attributed to her the first expression of modern feminism.[1] Of course, the definition of feminism sixty years ago
was not precisely what it is today.

As for Christine's position, it should be evident that her views on
women's situation in society must be considered in relation to the
society she herself knew. It could scarcely be expected, for instance,
that she would undertake to change the nature of a society that was
generally believed to have been ordained by divine will. It must also
be recognized that the Paris in which she lived was not similar, except
in the most general way, to cities such as London or Venice, for
example. She claimed the authority of experience in setting forth her
views, and fortunately she is a very good witness of her society. It is
therefore unwise to consider her writings about women apart from her
other works. It then becomes evident that the most she could be
expected to envisage would be the reform of others living in the
society with which she was familiar. Women, to be sure, were all too
often its victims, although they were not the only victims. Since their
lot could obviously be improved by a change in men's attitudes and
behavior towards them, one of Christine's aims was to educate these

men. She also advocated a more constructive attitude on the part of women towards their own lives.

To begin with, Christine had been understandably horrified by the treatment she experienced at the hands of both public officials and acquaintances after her husband's death. Having led the sheltered life of a privileged young woman, she had been utterly unprepared to deal with either the material or the psychological problems of widowhood. People she had considered her friends shunned her, and her efforts to settle her husband's financial affairs resulted in a series of lawsuits. Even worse, she had been cheated by the merchant with whom money had been invested for her children's future. She bitterly resented the fact that women such as she were so completely unprepared to deal with the problems imposed on them by a society that was all too indifferent to their situation. This resentment is clearly expressed in some of her early poetry and is still evident in the advice she offers widows in *The Treasury of the City of Ladies.*

Her personal situation undoubtedly also fueled her resentment of the long literary tradition of speaking ill of women, dating from both classical and biblical times. Certain misogynistic writings such as Ovid's *Art of Love* were even used as school texts, where they had every opportunity to set a bad example in forming attitudes in schoolboys.[2] Christine's views on the education of the young were by no means theoretical, for she was now entirely responsible for the education of her own children. Her disapproval of Ovid was exacerbated by the great popularity of *The Romance of the Rose.* The long poem detailing Guillaume de Lorris's allegorical quest for a beloved rose had been composed in the thirteenth century and its erudite continuation written by Jean de Meun towards the end of the same century. It was still enjoying great popularity at the end of the fourteenth century, especially in Parisian society surrounding the royal court and among young intellectuals of the day, who claimed to admire Jean de Meun for his erudition.[3] However, among the array of characters who advise Jean de Meun's Lover on his conquest of the symbolic flower, some of them recommend deceit and few show any real respect for the object of the Lover's desires. There was indeed good reason to suspect ulterior motives in the minds of these men who spoke approvingly of the Duenna's advice concerning the advantages of deceiving rather than being deceived. There were also suggestive illustrations in some manuscripts of the poem, expressly mentioned in a sermon by Jean Gerson, especially some illustrating the final episode of the poem, where the Rose in the Ivory Tower is taken by force.[4]

Christine, for her part, believed that women should be protected from this sort of slander and that their positive contributions to society should be recognized. She expressed these ideas for the first time as early as 1399, when she wrote a poem entitled *The Letter of the God of Love*. It seems possible that she composed this poem for some sort of poetic contest, a form of entertainment popular at the court of the king's younger brother, Louis of Orleans. Christine's idea of presenting herself as Cupid's secretary is clever and the general tone of the poem is witty in spite of some rather sharp barbs.

The particular object of her attack is the sort of stylish young courtier who flatters a woman to her face, but then speaks disparagingly of her behind her back, notably while carousing in a tavern with his friends. The poem, moreover, is nearly contemporary with the founding in Paris of the so-called Court of Love, modelled after the earlier Provençal courts where troubadours honored women with their poetry. Christine could not resist exposing the hypocrisy of some of the men who frequented these gatherings.

It was once assumed that it was Christine's poem that stirred up the literary debate known as the Quarrel of the Rose, concerning the merits of Jean de Meun's poem, but the publication of the correspondence of Jean de Montreuil, one of Christine's opponents in the debate, has given a more accurate idea of how the affair came about.[5] As a matter of fact, the debate did not begin until May 1401, some two years after Christine had written her poem.

It is now evident that the controversy was initiated by Jean de Montreuil, royal secretary and Provost of Lille. He read *The Romance of the Rose* in the spring of 1401 and wrote an enthusiastic treatise on Jean de Meun, a document now unfortunately lost.[6] Christine was moved to write a response to this treatise, the first document preserved in the debate. An exchange of letters followed involving two other royal secretaries, Pierre and Gontier Col, and Jean Gerson, chancellor of the University of Paris, who supported Christine. Pierre Col's letters are especially vituperative, to the point where he was finally taken to task by Gerson with the threat that he could be accused of heresy. Gerson had already preached a sermon against Jean de Meun, "Consider the Lilies of the Field," in August 1401 and he wrote a treatise against the poem in the form of a vision in May 1402.[7]

In the meantime, in February 1402, Christine had presented copies of the letters that had been exchanged up to this point to the Queen of France, Isabeau of Bavaria, inviting her to judge the affair, and to the Provost of Paris, Guillaume de Tignonville, a man of some literary pretensions, asking for his support. These acts angered Christine's learned opponents, perhaps because they were mildly embarrassed at having their involvement in a rather frivolous debate made public, perhaps also because they were not prepared to have a woman dispute their claims so eloquently. Christine, of course, was entirely serious in her defense of women against the sort of slander represented by Jean de Meun's poetry, and she may well have thought that if the discussion had an audience beyond the young intellectuals of the royal chancellory there might be some more support for her point of view. As she wrote in the Envoi of one of her ballades:

> Princes, speaking the truth may indeed give pain
> To those of whose wish to deceive there's proof,
> As sons may lie to their fathers, we claim
> One is often chastised for speaking the truth.[8]

In spite of Christine's earlier reservations about the Court of Love, it may have inspired another poem that she composed at this point in the debate, in February 1402. This poem opens with the description of an elegant gathering at the Parisian residence of the Duke of Orleans. *Le Dit de la Rose* (*The Tale of the Rose*) then describes the foundation of a new chivalric order, the Order of the Rose, in celebration of Saint Valentine's Day. In the midst of the festivities a supernatural creature appears, who introduces herself as Lady and Goddess of Loyalty. She is accompanied by attendants, maidens who distribute roses to the guests and entertain them by singing charming motets. Lady Loyalty then explains that those who accept roses are expected to make a vow of loyalty to the opposite sex. As all the guests willingly make this vow, the goddess promises to take the good news to Cupid, the God of Love, who has sent her there to offer support to his true servants against their enemies, presumably admirers of Jean de Meun. Although she then vanishes, her companions remain to entertain the guests for the rest of the evening.

Later, after Christine has retired for the night, Loyalty reappears to her in a vision, explaining how greatly the God of Love has been disturbed by the behavior of the so-called courtly society, where disrespect for women and a general lack of honorable behavior are all too prevalent. Loyalty then charges Christine to make known wherever possible the new Order of the Rose with its ideal of loyalty between lovers. Then, as the goddess disappears, she leaves behind her on the pillow the charter of the new Order, written in blue letters on golden parchment. This inspires Christine to seek the support of all true lovers everywhere on their special day, the Feast of Saint Valentine. Although there is no evidence that such an order ever existed, the poem is a charming formulation of Christine's ideal of love and her argument against Jean de Meun's overly erudite doctrines. The poem reflects the problems posed by Charles VI's Court of Love, and celebrates the foundation of the Marshal Boucicaut's Order of the White Lady on the Green Shield established at the same time for the defense of women. It is evident from the poem that Christine expected from these courtly gentlemen some evidence of their willingness to fit their actions to their theories.

Curiously, this poem does not appear in any but the first collection of Christine's poetry and there is no explanation for this. It is true that only a year or two after it was composed, the Duke of Orleans's reputation for philandering went from bad to worse. Not only did he force his duchess, Valentina Visconti, to raise with her own children his illegitimate son (the one who would be known to history as Joan of Arc's captain, Dunois), but by 1405 his equivocal relationship with the queen was causing an open scandal. His court was scarcely the place to find Lady Loyalty. Furthermore, Christine's admiration for the duke may have diminished somewhat after he failed to respond to her request for a place in his household for her son, Jean du Castel. It was the Duke of Burgundy who provided a situation for Jean in his own establishment.

As for the Rose debate, it came to its end in the winter of 1402–3 with the reproving letter addressed to Pierre Col by Gerson and a series of Lenten sermons that Gerson preached during the spring, especially one on chastity in which he made references to the evil influence of *The Romance of the Rose.*[9] Even before this, however, Christine had lost interest in the whole affair, for she was already engaged in the composition of *The Long Road to Learning.*

It has been claimed that little came of this debate, but this is not entirely true. The debate encouraged Christine to continue her defense of women in *The Book of the City of Ladies,* in which she undertakes to show women's contribution to history, as well as in *The Treasury of the City of Ladies* (or *The Book of the Three Virtues*), an attempt to show contemporary women how they might deal with the problems confronting them in society and how to make their lives more significant.

The Book of the City of Ladies was inspired in large measure by

Boccaccio's *De Claris Mulieribus* (*Concerning Famous Women*), which had only recently been translated into French for the first time. Although many of Christine's examples of famous women from antiquity were inspired by this book, she added to these biblical heroines, saints, and some contemporary women. In contrast to Boccaccio's chronological presentation, moreover, she grouped her stories so as to refute traditional criticism of women, organizing them in a series of interesting conversations with three supernatural creatures, Reason, Rectitude, and Justice who, like Loyalty, appear to her in a vision. It is at their direction that she undertakes to build the ideal city to provide a refuge for women against a society that does not appreciate them for their true value. As the stories unfold, often in quite a different manner from previous versions, one should recall that in her *Letter of the God of Love,* Christine had protested that if certain misogynistic books had been written by women they would have been quite different. At the beginning of this new book, she is obviously concerned with the misogyny of Jean de Meun and other such writers, but by the end she calls upon women of all classes in society to take advantage of the city constructed in their honor and make something better of their lives.

Thus, having rewritten the history of women to their advantage, Christine set herself the task of offering women advice on how they might achieve this improvement in their lives in the real world. The opportunity to write such a book presented itself soon after she had finished *The Book of the City of Ladies.* The marriage of the heir to the French throne, Louis of Guyenne, to the Duke of Burgundy's daughter, Marguerite of Nevers, took place in August 1404. *The Treasury of the City of Ladies* was therefore dedicated to the princess who would one day presumably be queen of France. It is possible that the young woman's parents encouraged Christine to write this book; in any case, they rewarded Christine for some of her writings shortly after the book was completed.[10]

Once again her mentors from *The Book of the City of Ladies* appear, this time to organize a school for women from all ranks of society based on the principle of Worldly Prudence. This stands in interesting contrast to all earlier books for women, which had been devoted, for the most part, to spiritual guidance. The first half of Christine's book is devoted to practical advice for queens and princesses for dealing with various problems they might encounter, from the organization of daily life and the apportionment of personal and household expenses to the demands of serving as regent for a prince too young to rule. As it turned out, Marguerite would never be queen of France, but she must surely have profited from Christine's advice to widowed princesses after the untimely death of Louis at the end of 1415. She would later lead a rather momentous life as the wife of Joan of Arc's lieutenant, Arthur of Richmont. She lived up to the high standards set for princesses in Christine's book.

The second half is devoted to the problems of women from other sectors of society, from ladies living at court to the wives of agricultural workers, and even to prostitutes, whom Christine believed could be encouraged to reform their ways in time to save their souls from damnation. The ideal of Worldly Prudence dominates throughout. It is not, however, so much the advice that is interesting to modern readers as the depiction of the society that Christine considered in need of correction, with the rivalries and petty jealousies of women at court, the pretensions of wives of wealthy merchants, or the unscrupulous behavior of certain servingwomen who did not hesitate to take advantage of inexperienced mistresses. Few writers have provided such a vivid picture of daily domestic life at the end of the Middle Ages.

At the same time, the advice that Christine offers to these women is not to be underestimated, for she constantly warns all of them, regardless of their individual situations in society, against allowing themselves to be victimized by the social system. Especially interesting is her advice, undoubtedly from the heart, to widows who must sometimes go to court to get what is rightfully theirs. She is quite obviously speaking from experience when she admonishes them not to cower in a corner like some poor, abused dog, but rather "to take on the heart of a man." Such advice quite clearly reflects her own determination to overcome the obstacles in her path and not to be a victim herself.

Was Christine then a feminist? Modern feminists have sometimes insisted that she has little to say to modern women, but it has also been noted that she represents the first example, with *The Book of the City of Ladies*, of what are now called "women's studies" by attempting to reorganize knowledge from a feminist point of view.[11] She also reoriented the medieval clerical debate on marriage into a debate on women. Above all, *The Book of the City of Ladies* provided subsequent writers of both sexes with a model for the defense of women. As for *The Treasury of the City of Ladies*, it was read by a whole generation of important women who made their mark on history: Anne of France;

Louise of Savoy and her daughter Marguerite of Navarre; Margaret of Austria; Mary of Hungary; and perhaps unexpectedly, Diane of Poitiers. It must also have been read by countless unknown women; three editions were printed between 1497 and 1536. Those who insist on the importance of rewriting the history of women should not underestimate the contribution of Christine de Pizan.

NOTES

1. Blanche Hinman Dow, *The Varying Attitude toward Women in French Literature of the Fifteenth Century* (New York, 1936), p. 128; Lula McDowell Richardson, *The Fore-runners of Feminism in French Literature of the Renaissance from Christine de Pisan to Marie de Gournay* (Baltimore, 1929), p. 34; Léon Abensour, *La femme et le féminisme avant la Révolution* (Paris, 1923), pp. v−vi.
2. Giovanni Dominici, who wrote his *Regola del governo di cura familiare* between 1400 and 1405, complained of the bad effect on children of reading Ovid's *Art of Love*. See W. W. Woodward, *Vittorino da Feltre and Other Humanist Educators* (New York, 1963), pp. 212−13.
3. Its popularity is discussed in detail by Pierre-Yves Badel in *Le Roman de la Rose au XIVe siècle; Étude de la réception de l'oeuvre* (Geneva, 1980).
4. Valencia, Biblioteca Universitaria Ms. 1327, which appears to be contemporary with early manuscripts of Christine's works, is a case in point. See illustrations reproduced in J. F. Fleming, *The Roman de la Rose: A Study in Allegory and Iconography* (Princeton, 1969) and F. Avril, "La Peinture française au temps du Jean de Berry," *Revue de l'Art* 28 (1975), especially p. 50 and p. 52, note 22. Fleming gives the manuscript number as 387 and dates it incorrectly, but he and Avril are clearly referring to the same manuscript.
5. E. Hicks and E. Ornato, "Jean de Montreuil et le débat sur le *Roman de la Rose*," *Romania* 98 (1977), 34−64.
6. See also the chronology of the debate in E. Hicks, *Le Débat sur le Roman de la Rose* (Paris, 1977), pp. iii−liv.
7. The importance of the sermon is pointed out by M. Lieberman in "Chronologie gersonienne," *Romania* 83 (1962), 71−73; Gerson's *Vision* is included by E. Hicks in *Le Débat*, pp. 59−87.
8. *Oeuvres poétiques*, III, pp. 250−51.
9. The relevant passages are in Hicks, *Le Débat*, pp. 179−85.
10. The Duke of Burgundy recompensed Christine for two books in February 1405 and for others in November 1407. Unfortunately, the only title specified is the biography of Charles V. See Pinet, *Christine de Pisan*, p. 101.
11. Joan Kelly, "Early Feminist Theory and the *Querelle des Femmes*, 1400−1789," in *Women, History and Theory* (Chicago, 1984), p. 83.

THE LETTER OF
THE GOD OF LOVE

Above all other lands their plaint's of France,
24   Defense and shield to them in former days,
Protecting them from harm on every side;
That's right, that's what a noble land must do,
A country in which gentle breeding rules.[1]
28   But now in France, the place where in the past
Women were honored so, those men who're false
Dishonor them, more than in other lands,
Especially — and here they grieve the more —
32   The noblemen, who used to champion them.
For such are many knights these days, and squires
Who've less experience and training at
Betraying them through pretty flatteries.
36   The loyal lovers' pose they strike is false.
Hiding behind their myriad deceits,
They go declaring that a woman's love
Inflames them sorely, keeps their hearts locked up;
40   The first laments, the second's heart is wrenched,
The next pretends to fill with tears, and sighs;
Another claims to sicken horribly:
Because of love's travail he's grown quite pale,
44   Now perishing, now very nearly dead.
Swearing their fervent oaths, they lie and vow
To be discreet and true, and then they crow.
Sparing themselves no pain to come and go,
48   They promenade in church and peer about,
Bending their knees upon the altar steps
In fake devotion: many are like that!
They spur their horses up and down the streets
52   Jaunty and handsome, jingling as they go.
They make a show of great activity,

And spare no horse or mule. Then ever so
Attentively they tender their requests,
56   Inquiring for the weddings and the feasts
At which those polished, ardent, gallant swains,
Display how much they feel our arrows' cut,
So much that they can barely stand the pain!²
60   Still other would-be lovers strive and strain,
Sending their messengers or coming 'round,
To get the thing their faking hearts intend.
Maintaining thus a thousand masquerades
64   These suitors hide behind their false parades;
That is to say, those traitors who detest
Fidelity or faith, who aim to trick.
The loyal aren't numbered in that count,
68   It's those one ought to love and count upon;
In no case would they want to practise fraud,
For I forbid it. So I grant to them
Good portion of our sweet and tasty store,
72   Because I give abundantly to those
Who're mine, and they uphold my true commands,
My just, sincere, and worthy tutelage.
Thus I forbid them evil or misdeed,
76   Ordering them to strive for real esteem,
To be sincere, discreet, speak truthfully,
Be giving, courtly, flee from gossipers;
Be humble, gentle, loving, and refined.
80   Be steady, noble, seek to be well-loved,
And let all those deserving of acclaim
Take weapons up. Whoever holds to that,
Let him know surely I won't fail to grant
84   A beautiful, sweet lady-love to him,
For when I'm served by someone in such wise,
I render him reward as he's deserved.
If good, though, comes by chance to those who're false,
88   It's not a good that's true, although I may
Put up with it; indeed, there's paltry gain
When one partakes with little appetite.

∞

The ladies mentioned here above complain
260   Of many clerks who lay much blame to them,

Composing tales in rhyme, in prose, in verse,
In which they scorn their ways with words diverse;
They give these texts out to their youngest lads,
264 To schoolboys who are young and new in class,
Examples given to indoctrinate
So they'll retain such doctrine when they're grown. [3]
    Thus, "Adam, David, Samson, Solomon,"
268 They say in verse, "a score of other men,
Were all deceived by women morn and night;
So who will be the man who can escape?" [4]
"They're treacherous," another clerk opines,
272 "And false and cunning; they're no good at all."
    "They're dreadful liars," other men pronounce,
"They're faithless, fickle, they are low and loose."
Of many other wrongs they stand accused
276 And blamed, in nothing can they be excused.
And that's what clerks are up to noon and night,
With verses now in Latin, now in French,
They base their words on I don't know what books
280 Which tell more lies than any drunkard does.
Now Ovid, in a book he wrote, sets down
Profuse affronts; I say that he did wrong.
He titled it *The Remedy for Love,*
284 And there he lays to women nasty ways,
Repulsive, sordid, filled with wickedness. [5]
That women have such vices I deny;
I take my arms up in defense of them
288 Against all those who'd throw the challenge down.
It's honorable women I'd defend;
I put no worthless women in my tales.
Now since their childhood days the clerks have read
292 That book in grammar class, the subject that
One studies first. They teach it to the rest
In hopes they'll not seek out a woman's love.
They're foolish, though, their effort's thrown away.
296 Such obstacles are but a vain attempt:
Between my lady Nature and myself,
We'll not accept, as long as life endures,
That women not be cherished well and loved,
300 In spite of all who'd censure them; nor will
We hinder women who would steal the hearts

Of just those very men who blame them most.
Engaging in no fraud or fakery,
304 But simply through persuasion on our part,
No more will men be taught as they have been
By learnèd clerks, nor by all of their verse,
Regardless of the many books that talk
308 Of women, blaming them: their value's slim.

      ∞

Now Ovid speaks of men like that in his
The Art of Love; the pity that he felt
For them encouraged him to write a book
368 In which he teaches them and openly
Elucidates the way to trick the girls
By means of subterfuge, and have their love.
And then he called the book *The Art of Love,*
372 Although it doesn't teach the terms or ways
Of loving well, but quite the opposite.⁶
The man who would behave as in that book
Will never love, however he is loved.
376 Because of that its title's misconceived,
Its subject is *The Art of Great Deceit,*
Of False Appearances—I dub it that!
  But now, if women are such easy marks,
380 If they're the fickle, foolish, faithless lot
That certain clerks maintain they are, then why
Must men pursuing them resort to schemes,
To clever subterfuge and trickery?
384 And why don't women yield more readily,
Without the need for guile to capture them?
A castle taken needs no further war,
And surely not from such a learnèd bard
388 As Ovid, later exiled from his land.
  And Jean de Meun's *The Romance of the Rose,*
Oh, what a long affair! How difficult!
The erudition clear and murky both
392 That he put there, with those great escapades!
So many people called upon, implored,
So many efforts made and ruses found
To trick a virgin—that, and nothing more!

396 And that's the aim of it, through fraud and schemes!
     A great assault for such a feeble place?
     How can one leap so far so near the mark?
     I can't imagine or make sense of it,
400 Such force applied against so frail a place,
     Such ingenuity and subtlety.
     Then necessarily it must be thus:
     Since craft is needed, cleverness and toil,
404 To gull a peasant or a noble born,
     Then women mustn't have such fickle wills
     As some declare, nor waver in their deeds.[7]
        Should it be said that books are filled with tales
408 Of just such women (I deplore that charge!),
     To this I say that books were not composed
     By women, nor did they record the things
     That we may read against them and their ways.
412 Yet men write on, quite to their heart's content,
     The ones who plead their case without debate.
     They give no quarter, take the winner's part
     Themselves, for readily do quarrelers
416 Attack all those who don't defend themselves.
     If women, though, had written all those books,[8]
     I know that they would read quite differently,
     For well do women know the blame is wrong.
420 The parts are not apportioned equally,
     Because the strongest take the largest cut
     And he who slices it can keep the best.

                                        THELMA S. FENSTER

(Translated from Brit. Lib. Harley Ms. 4431)

NOTES

1. Christine is referring here to the decline in behavior from the days of Charles V. It is a historical fact that the pleasure-loving Charles VI and his brother, Louis of Orleans, favored rather wild entertainment of the sort that led to disaster. On one occasion, at a ball, the costumes of some courtiers dressed as savages were accidently set on fire by a torch. The king nearly lost his life.
2. This passage recalls the Duenna's advice to the Lover in the *Romance of the Rose* (vv.

12987–13172) and Ovid's advice to would-be seducers in his *Art of Love*, which presents love as a science in mockery of serious textbooks on other subjects. It was not intended to describe serious love with respectable women.

3. Here Christine is referring, of course, to the misogynistic character of much traditional literature, from the Bible to Boccaccio. The clerics who particularly admired this sort of literature were also often schoolmasters.

4. Christine appears to be referring to a Latin proverb: *Adam, Samsonem, si David, si Salomonem Femina decepit, quis modo tutus erit?* (If woman deceived Adam, Samson, David and Solomon, who will then be safe?)

5. Christine is referring here to Ovid's *Remedia Amoris* (*Remedies for Love*) which he composed as a mock-penance for his *Art of Love*, which had inspired disapproval because of its facetious tone. Ovid's claim was that erotic poetry brings renown and that he had been successful in his original ambition.

6. Christine was not alone in objecting to Ovid's *Art of Love* being read by schoolboys. Her Italian contemporary Giovanni Dominici in his *Regola del governo di cura familiare* (*Rule Governing the Care of the Family*) complained even more specifically about the same practice. See W. H. Woodward, *Vittorino da Feltre and Other Humanist Educators*, pp. 212–13.

7. These lines are a good example of Christine's irony. She was fond of pointing out inconsistencies in the claims made by men, a technique she would develop further in *The Book of the City of Ladies*.

8. Chaucer's Wife of Bath expresses a similar opinion of books written by men.

> By God, if women had but written stories
> Like those the clergy keep in oratories,
> More had been written of man's wickedness
> Than all the sons of Adam could redress.
> (*The Canterbury Tales*,
> trans. Neville Coghill [London, 1951])

This idea would furnish the basis for rewriting the history of women in *The Book of the City of Ladies*.

CCW

LESSER TREATISE
ON THE
ROMANCE OF THE ROSE
JUNE – JULY, 1401

To that most worthy and learned personage, master Jean Johannes,[1] secretary to our lord the king:

Reverence, honor, and all commendation to you, lord provost of Lille, most precious lord and scholar, sage in conduct, lover of knowledge, soundly erudite, well versed in rhetoric, your humble Christine de Pizan,[2] an unlearned woman of small understanding and penetration, with hopes that your wisdom will not despise my arguments withal but make due allowances in consideration of female weakness.

Since it has pleased you to send me freely of your wealth (for which good thanks) a short treatise set forth in fine rhetoric with persuasive argumentation, in which, as I gather, you have given your own opinions reproaching certain critics of certain passages of that compendious *Romance of the Rose*, vigorously defending this work and its authors, more specifically [Jean de] Meun; as I have read and considered your aforesaid prose and grasped its meaning so far as my slight intelligence would permit, though it be neither addressed to me nor require any answer, yet moved by a persuasion contrary to yours and in accordance with that renowned fine scholar to whom your aforesaid epistle is addressed, I wish to hold, proclaim, and sustain publicly that, with all due respect, you are entirely in error and without justification in giving such accomplished praise to the aforesaid work, which were better called utter frivolity than any profitable book, in my opinion. And although you strongly criticize its adversaries, saying that it is "an admirable thing to understand so fully what is held in another text," that he has "better composed and assembled through profound study and diligent application," let it not be accounted presumption on my part to dare repudiate and criticize so august and penetrating an author; consider, rather, the sound and formal judgment which leads me to oppose certain particular aspects of the work, notwithstanding that such matters as are held by opinion and not prescribed by law may be freely argued without prejudice. And although I am neither instructed in erudite matters nor skilled in subtleties of language (the better to employ elegant constructions and polished expression for the embellishment of my arguments), still I will not refrain from stating grossly and in the common vernacular the opinion that I hold, though I be incapable of explaining it in the manner of decorous speech.

But why was it said above that it "were better called utter frivolity?" Clearly it seems to me that anything lacking valid use, even if composed, constructed, and elaborated by diligent work and effort, may be called frivolous or worse than frivolous to the degree that harm can come of it. And since for some time now, because of its universally great fame, I have desired to look at the said romance, having acquired through study some ability in understanding difficult matters, I read and considered it up and down so far as my understanding would permit. True it is that since the subject matter was not to my liking in several passages, I jumped over them like a cat on hot bricks, and hence have not examined them thoroughly. Nonetheless, there lodged in my memory certain items treated therein which my judgment strongly condemned, nor can the opposing praise of others bring me to approve them. True it is that my humble understanding deems it fine artistry to have spoken so eloquently, in certain passages, on the chosen subject: the terms are full of beauty and the verse is gracious, with polished rhyme, and it were impossible to speak with greater sophistication or in more fitting traits on the matter he wished to treat. But to agree with the opinion you contradict, it is beyond a doubt, as I see it, that his manner is completely indecent in certain passages, particularly in the case of the character he calls Reason, who baldly mentions the private parts by name.[3] And to answer your defense of his opinion, when you assert that it were reasonable to do so, alleging that there is nothing shameful in that which has been created by God and that the names should therefore not be eschewed, I hold and affirm that truly all things were clean and pure as God first created them, and that therefore in the state of innocence it would not have been shameful to name them; yet by corruption of sin has man been made foul, so that original sin still remains in us (such is the witness of Holy Scripture). And I may therefore argue by analogy that God made Lucifer handsome above all the other angels, giving him a name most resplendent and fine, which through his sin thence became a horror of ugliness, so that the name, though in itself most beautiful, does horrify all those who hear it, as their minds are deeply affected by the thought of the individual concerned.

Again, you set forth that Jesus Christ, "speaking of sinful women, called them *meretrix*,"[4] and so on. But I can answer to His having used this word in speaking of them that the word *meretrix* is not as indecent as the deed is repugnant, and it were possible to speak more offensively even in Latin. As for dispensing with modesty in speaking publicly about things where nature herself shows modesty, I hold that, with all due respect for you and the author, you do commit a most grievous offense against the noble virtue of modesty, which naturally restrains debauchery and indecency in word and deed, while it is plain from many passages in the Holy Scriptures[5] that such is thoroughly immoral and beyond the pale of decent conduct. And that the word were no more shameful "than if they were called relics,"[6] I grant you that the word does not create the indecency of the thing: it is the thing which makes the word indecent. Which is why, in my humble opinion, we should observe discretion in speaking about these things, and only where it is unavoidable, for the ends of some special case, such as illness or any other decent necessity. For just as our primal parents naturally hid them from view, so should we, in word and in deed.

Furthermore, I cannot remain silent about the following, for I find it most offensive that the character of Reason, whom he himself calls the daughter of God,[7] should put forth such a statement as I note in the aforesaid chapter, where she says by way of a proverb that "in the war of Love it is better to deceive than be deceived."[8] And indeed I dare say that in making that statement Jean de Meun's Reason denied her Father, for the doctrine He gave was altogether different. And to say that one is better than the other would imply that both are good: which is impossible. And to consider the truth of the matter, I hold the opposite opinion, that it is better to be deceived than to deceive.

But let us go on in considering the material or manner of speech which, in the sound opinion of many people, is subject to reproach. Good Lord in Heaven! What an abomination! What indecency! He has surely set down a variety of reprehensible teachings in the Duenna's chapter![9] Who, in Heaven's name, could find anything therein but sophistical exhortations, rotten to the core and of the vilest repute? Oh ho! Those of you who have fine daughters and wish to instruct them in decent living, give them, then, go out and get *The Romance of the Rose* to learn to distinguish right from wrong—indeed!—rather wrong from right! For what good is it and what profit can come to listeners from hearing so much filth? As for the chapter of the Jealous Husband,[10] in Heaven's name, what sound instruction can be retained therein? What good is it to have set down such improprieties and foul speech as are surely common in the mouths of those so unfortunate as to suffer from this disease? What good example or instruction can this serve? And as to the filth written there about women, some say to excuse him that it's only a jealous man speaking, and that it is at bottom no different from God speaking through the mouth of Jeremiah.[11] But doubtless whatever lying overstatements he may have heaped on, they cannot, thank heavens, diminish in any way or worsen the true conduct of women. Oh ho! When I recall the scheming, the hypocrisy, and all the things concealed in marriage or in other institutions that can be retained from this treatise, surely I must judge that here are written sound and profitable lessons to be heard!

But truly astonishing are the things said by the character he calls the priest Genius.[12] Doubtless some time ago the works of Nature would have ceased had he not so vehemently ordered them accomplished. But for God's sake, can anyone explain to me or answer what benefit there can be in that great indictment, so full of vituperation, which as if to deride holy preaching he calls a sermon, given as he says by the aforesaid Genius? Wherein there is gross indecency in words and sophistical terms contrived to incite to Nature's secret acts, which should be kept silent and not be spoken of, since we do not see interrupted a work which the general order of things will not allow to cease—for if it were otherwise, it would be well for the use of human generation to find enticing and arousing words to hearten man in pursuing his work.

The author did not stop at that, if my memory is correct, and to what end I am at a loss to comprehend: for he has mixed in figuratively with this sermon, paradise and the joys it holds.[13] He says indeed that there will go the just, and then concludes that all must apply themselves—men and women alike, sparing none—in accomplishing and performing the works of Nature. Nor does he make any exception of law, as if he intended to say—nay, plainly does say—that they will all be saved. And in this it would seem that he desires to maintain that the sin of lechery is nil, or rather a virtue, which is heresy and contrary to the law of God. Ah, such teachings! Such excellent doctrine! How great the good to come of it! I do believe that many have left the secular life and taken orders or have become hermits thanks to this holy script, or have lain off evildoing and ill ways, saved by such fine admonishment, which in truth could only come—I dare say so whomever it displease—from a corrupt will given over to dissolution and vice, which can give occasion to grave prejudice and sin.

And again—good Lord!—to go on a bit further: how can it be of any value or to any good purpose that he accuse, blame, and defame women so much, so excessively, impetuously, and certainly most falsely, for several extremely grave vices, holding that their behavior is full of all perversity, as if so many speeches, and in some measure all his characters, were not sufficient to slake his thirst? For if I am told that the Jealous Husband speaks out of passion, I cannot see how it is in character for Genius, who so strongly commands and advises that women constantly be bedded, without ever interrupting the work he so stringently commands, when he himself, more so than any other character, speaks so strongly in vituperation of them, saying in fact: "Flee, flee, flee the venomous snake"[14]—and then goes on to say that the work should be pursued without interruption. It is a blatantly grievous contradiction to order avoiding what he wants one to follow and following what he wants one to avoid. For if women are so perverse, he should not have ordered them to be approached in the slightest, since those who fear trouble ought to eschew it.

And since he so strongly prohibits telling secrets to wives[15]—who are so avid to learn them, so he says (and I wonder where by all the devils he found all that bilge and all those empty words he assembled in composing that weary indictment)—I beg all those who claim him as their authority and lend him their faith to please inform me how many men they have seen accused, killed, or hanged, or blamed in the streets on accusation by their wives. I think they will find them few and far between. Notwithstanding it were good and praiseworthy advice for everyone to consider it surer to keep one's secret for one's self, for there are corrupt people in every way of life, and I recently heard of a man who was accused and then hanged for having confided in one of his fellows who had his trust. Still I believe that before the face of justice there go few complaints or petitions on these horrifying evils, these great betrayals and diabolical acts that women are said to have learned to perpetrate so maliciously and so furtively. (All the same, a secret is a secret when no one knows it.) And as I said on this matter in one of my poems called *The Letter of the God of Love*,[16] where are the lands and countries which were lost through their great misdeeds? To speak dispassionately, can we hear what great crimes can be blamed on even the worst among them, and who have deceived the most? For what can they do? And how can they deceive you? If they ask for money from your purse, then they neither steal it nor carry it off: don't give it to them if that is what you want. And if you say that you are besotted by them, then you need not be so stupid. Do they go looking for you in your homes, begging your favor or taking you by force? It would be nice to know just how it happens you are deceived.

And again, he has spoken quite superfluously and basely of women in marriage — an institution of which he could know nothing from experience, and yet made such sweeping generalizations: what just cause can this serve or what good come of it? I can see none, other than an impediment to peace and harmony, or to make husbands hearing such silliness and bilge, should they take any stock in it, suspicious of their wives and less affectionate to them. And to tell the truth, since he has condemned them all generally, this very reason leads me to believe that he never knew or frequented a virtuous woman, but having consorted with several dissolute women of ill repute — as the lecherous are wont to do — he believed or pretended to have learned that they were all of a kind, since he had no experience of the others. And had he only blamed dishonorable women and recommended that they be shunned, it would have been right and just instruction. But no! Rather he accuses them all without exception. Still if the author, beyond all reasonable limits, took it upon himself to accuse them or judge them with no regard for the truth, it is not to them that any blame should be imputed, but to the one who told such a lie so obviously untrue that none can believe it, for the opposite is manifestly clear. And no matter what he and all his accomplices in this matter may have sworn, and let none take offense, there have been, still are, and will be many more worthy women, more honorable, better bred, and even more learned, who have done more good for the world than he ever did personally, particularly in matters of ordinary civil conduct and the proper exercise of good morals. And there are many who have set aright their husbands' businesses, bearing the weight of their affairs and secrets, gently and discreetly — despite crudeness and lack of love on the part of their husbands. Many illustrations to the point can be found in the Bible and in ancient history: for example, Sarah, Rebecca, Esther, Judith, and many others;[17] and in our own time we have seen many worthy women in France: Queen Jeanne, pious and devout; Queen Blanche, the Duchess of Orleans and daughter of the King of France; the Duchess of Anjou who now bears the title of Queen of Sicily,[18] all women of beauty, modesty, honor, and wisdom—and there are many others; among good women of lesser state, there is Lady de la Ferté, wife of Lord Pierre de Craon,[19] much deserving of our praise,—and many others, so that it were too long a tale to say more.

And believe not, my fair lord, nor let any hold the opinion that I have made and put together this defense because, being a woman, I am prejudiced in women's behalf, for indeed my sole intent is to sustain the very truth, since I know by certain knowledge that it is just the opposite of those things I have here refuted. Yet precisely because I am a woman I can bear truer witness in this dispute than someone who had no direct experience, but instead spoke aimlessly and through conjecture.

But in addition to all this—good Lord!—let us consider what kind of an end there is to this treatise, for as the saying goes, "it all comes out in the end."[20] Thus let it be seen and noted how there can be any good in that horrifying and shameful conclusion[21]—nay, not shameful, but so very indecent that I dare say no one who loves virtue and decency could hear it without being embarrassed for shame, and outraged to hear suggested, transposed, and couched in indecent imagery things the very thought of which must be refrained, in temperate persons, by reason or modesty. And indeed I dare say that even the debauched would be ashamed to read or listen to it in public, in polite society, or before people they would consider decent. On what grounds then can a text be praised which no one would dare read or quote, as it is, at the tables of queens, princesses, or worthy decent women, who perforce would blush and hide their faces for shame? And should you reply in his defense that he found it pleasing to describe in novel merriment the act of love in such metaphor, I can answer that he has told us nothing unfamiliar here. Do we not know full well how men and women cohabit together? Had he told us how it is with bears or lions or some other exotic beast, such a figure might have offered some amusement, but nothing new is said here. And surely he could have brought it off more pleasantly, more properly, and in more courteous terms, which even light-hearted and right lovers would have found more pleasing, not to mention other decent folk.

And thus to my small mind and judgment, with no further prolixity of words—although much more could be said and better—I cannot consider any use in the said treatise; what I do seem to understand is that much work went into it for no good. For I must admit that master Jean de Meun was, in my own judgment, a very great scholar and a master of language; and had he applied himself, he could well have given us a much better and more useful work, of more worthy inspiration—and it is a great pity; but I assume that profound lust, to which perhaps he fell prey, made him tend to his own desires rather than anything worthwhile, since our inclinations are generally known by the works we perform. Nonetheless, I cannot condemn *The Romance of the Rose* in all its parts, for it surely contains much good and many things well said. But the danger is only the greater: for the more authentic the good, the more credible the evil, and thus have many subtle minds sowed the seeds of heresy by mixing and tempering them with some measure of truth and virtue. But just as his priest Genius says: "Flee, flee woman, the evil snake lurking in the grass," so can I say: "Flee, flee hidden malice, under cover of good and virtue!" [22]

And so I say in conclusion to you, my lord most fair, and all your allies and confederates who bestow such great praise upon this work and seek to glorify it so highly as to well nigh intend and make bold to disparage all others by comparison, that with all due respect it is unworthy of receiving such praise, and you do great prejudice to those which are worthwhile. For a work which serves no purpose or public or private good, although it be agreeable, painstakingly written, and of great material worth, can merit no praise. And as in ancient times the Romans in their triumphal marches [23] allowed no praise or honor to such things as did not serve the good of the republic, let us look to their example in determining whether or not this romance is deserving of a crown. Thus, as I see it, considering the above and a host of other reasons, I find that it were better condemned to the flames than crowned by laurel. And despite your proclaiming it a "mirror for right conduct, a model for all walks of life in public affairs or in living religiously or prudently," I hold on the contrary that it is, with all due respect, an exhortation to vice giving comfort to dissolute ways, an indoctrination in deceit, a road to damnation, a universal libel, a cause for suspicion and mistrust, of disgrace to sundry individuals, and perhaps of heresy.

Yet I know full well that you will defend it on this score by replying that the good it contains is given to be followed and the evil to be eschewed. My refutation is, however, that it were sounder to argue that human nature, which is of itself inclined to sin, need not be told which leg is lame in order to walk a straighter path. And as for all the good that can be gotten out of that book, surely many more virtuous teachings can be found, better written, of higher authority, and more useful ones, even in matters of public affairs and morals, in a host of other volumes written by philosophers and doctors in our faith, such as Aristotle, Seneca, Saint Paul, Saint Augustine and others—as you well know, whose witness and teachings concerning virtue and eschewing vice are more valid and clear than any Jean de Meun could ever have given: they are, however, commonly not readily sought out or retained by profane sensualists, since a sick man suffering from great thirst is mightily pleased when the doctor allows him a hearty drink, and convinces himself quite readily, to gratify his lust to drink, that it will never do him any harm.

And I am finally persuaded that you—may it please the Lord!—and all the others to whom the grace of God restore clarity and purity of clean conscience, without taint or corruption of sin or the intent to sin, cleansed by compunction of remorse (which penetrates and reveals the depths of conscience and condemns self-will as a standard of truth), will give a new judgment on *The Romance of the Rose,* wishing, perhaps, that you had never read it.

Let this then suffice. And may it not be laid to folly, arrogance, or presumption that I, a woman, do upbraid and refute so difficult an author, diminishing the good fame of his work, when he, a sole and solitary man, dared take it upon himself to defame and condemn without exception an entire sex.

ERIC HICKS

(Translated from Paris B.N. Ms. fr. 12779)

N O T E S

1. Jean de Montreuil was probably appointed as a royal secretary while Christine's husband was still alive. His birthplace, usually believe to be Montreuil-sur-Mer, has now been identified by Gilbert Ouy as the town of Monthureux-le-Sec, in the Département des Vosges (see *Mélanges à la mémoire de Franco Simone,* Geneva: Slatkine, 1980, p. 46–55, 591–593).

2. The insistence on humility was a frequent formula used by letter-writers; it is probably not meant to be taken too seriously.
3. Christine's accusation refers to vv. 5507–8, 7081–82, and 7086–87 (Lecoy ed.) of the poem.
4. Harlots.
5. Christine is referring to the words of Saint Paul in 1 Cor. 25:33: "Be not deceived; evil communications corrupt good manners." She cites this again in the biography of Charles V (Solente ed., I, p. 85).
6. *The Romance of the Rose,* vv. 7078–86.
7. *The Romance of the Rose,* vv. 5783–87.
8. *The Romance of the Rose,* vv. 4369–71.
9. *The Romance of the Rose,* vv. 12710–14516.
10. *The Romance of the Rose,* vv. 8437–9330.
11. Jeremiah was often cited by the debaters of the poem, but it has never been possible to identify this reference.
12. Genius appears in vv. 19475–20637.
13. The life of the blessed in Paradise is described in vv. 19907–20036.
14. This reference to the snake in the grass is in vv. 16548–86.
15. The matter of telling secrets to wives is discussed in vv. 16347–16706.
16. Christine is referring to vv. 641–48 of her *Letter of the God of Love:*

> She doesn't kill or wound or mutilate
> . . . Nor does she bring harm
> To empires or to duchies or to realms.
> (Trans., Fenster p. 65)

17. These same exemplary women will all appear again in *The Book of the City of Ladies;* Judith will be cited in *The Mutation of Fortune, The Book of Peace,* and the poem on Joan of Arc.
18. Queen Jeanne is Jeanne d'Evreux (1310–1371), second wife of King Charles IV. Christine mentions in *The Book of the City of Ladies* having seen her during her early years in Paris; she also praises her in *The Treasury of the City of Ladies.* Queen Blanche of Navarre (1331–1398), the second wife of Philip VI, is also mentioned in *The Book of the City of Ladies* and *The Treasury of the City of Ladies.* Blanche of France was the posthumous daughter of Charles IV and Jeanne d'Evreux and wife of Philip of Orleans, son of Philip VI. The Queen of Sicily refers to Marie de Châtillon, daughter of Charles de Blois, Duke of Brittany, who was married in 1360 to Louis I of Anjou, younger brother of Charles V. Chosen as heir by Jeanne of Naples and crowned king by Pope Clement VII, Louis' rights to the throne were contested by Charles de Durazzo. After his death in 1384, his wife and his son continued the struggle. Marie is praised by Christine in her biography of Charles V, as well as *The Mutation of Fortune* and *The Long Road to Learning.*
19. Jeanne de Châtillon was the wife of Pierre de Craon, Lord of Sablé and La Ferté-Bernard in Brittany.
20. Christine was fond of proverbs and used a variant of this same one in the biography of Charles V (Solente ed. II, p. 180) and also in her *Moral Teachings* (*Oeuvres* III, pp. 43–44).
21. Reference to the Lover's attack on the tower that ends *The Romance of the Rose,* vv. 20676–20780; 21553–21712.
22.

> Fair sirs, of womankind beware;
> If you for soul or body care,
> Speak not, nor act you in such wise
> As layeth bare to women's eyes

The things your hearts hold secretly.
Fly! fly! I bid you, fly! fly! fly!
(Trans. F. S. Ellis vv. 17391–
17396 [London, 1900] III, p. 68)

23. Roman triumphs are described by Christine in both the *Long Road to Learning* (vv. 4950–63) and in the *The Book of the Body of Policy* (I.29, Lucas ed. pp 90–92). It is probable that she knew of the custom by way of the translation of Valerius Maximus undertaken for Charles V by Simon de Hesdin and later finished by Nicolas de Gonesse.

CCW

THE TALE OF THE ROSE

The goddess, though, who loved me well [1]
272 (All praise to her!) and called me her
Sister in sensibility,
Had made a lovely bed for me,
As white as snow and richly draped,
276 Arranged so carefully and placed
Amidst a splendid chamber, white
As snow that lies upon the branch.
She'd done it thus, I have no doubt,
280 Because I am Diana's friend,
The greatly honored deity,
Always appareled all in white. [2]
    Alone, unclad, I went to bed
284 And fell asleep. But then a cloud
Appeared before me as I slept, [3]
Brilliant and glowing. Greatly did
I wonder what, indeed, it was!
288 Then from the cloud, upon the right
Beside the bed, shining and bright,
Like lightning in the summertime,
There issued forth a charming voice,
292 Pleasurable and filled with love.
    Not heeding if I slept or not,
The voice addressed me by my name,
And thus it spoke to me: "Dear friend,
296 Who've loved me well and cherished me
For all your life, as well I know,
For I have often tested you:
I am the faithful goddess of
300 The high and royal lineage
Of God, who formed and fashioned me,
And inculcated his commands.
So hear me out, devoted friend,

304   I'll tell you what has brought me here.
        "You know that just before, I came
       With greatest pleasure where you were,
       There to present the roses fair
308   That in no season lose their bloom.
       I represented Love, who guides[4]
       All those who're skilled in doing good,
       Who sends me once again to you
312   (It pleases him my service be
       As messenger upon this route)
       And willingly I bring this word.
        "Love so profoundly grieves and sighs
316   About a custom that's maintained
       Too well and in so many parts.
       He would indeed prefer it changed,
       For it is evil, ugly, low,
320   And vulgar, I can certify,
       Especially when found in those
       Who shouldn't spare an effort toward
       Acquiring fine, well-mannered ways
324   So that their honor may increase.
       The word is meant for gentlemen
       And nobles, who should set their minds
       Toward being better than the rest:
328   Good suits them more than silver or
       Than gold. My care's not common folk,
       Whose good's accomplished through sheer force,
       Who can't be altered either through
332   One's exhortation or command,
       Because the common circumstance
       (Which smells much worse than breath that's foul)
       Is much too hard to rectify,
336   A vice that's just too strong to purge.
       I call those common who commit
       Vulgarities which bring them low.
       By common I don't mean low birth,
340   But rather lowly heart and mind.[5]
        "A man who claims nobility
       Through lineage undoes that claim
       Should he reduce his noble state

344 To commonness, I don't deny.
A man like that earns more reproof
If he is caught at lowly deeds.
That's why I say, nor is it false,
Each noble, if he cares for worth,
Must guard himself against reproach
For ugly deed or vulgar word.
He'd be a much less worthy man,
352 However great his battle skill.
For valor isn't found alone[6]
Residing in the bravery
To make assaults and mount defense
356 Against some foe who'd bring attack,
For those are but the body's feats.
Now certainly of greater worth
Is goodness coming from the soul;
360 No one can tell me otherwise.
It's valor and great bravery
When noble heart directs itself
To favor virtue, all the while
364 Fleeing from vice, avoiding it,
So no one may discover there
Something to slur, unless it be
In error or through jealousy.
368 For in this mortal life there's not
A man who might be loved by all,
Nor one whom all consider good.
That's Envy's doing, who attempts
372 To harm high fame; a worthy man
Should pay no heed, but just do good.
For honor will win out, I say.
And if a man who's learned those things
376 Can also have esteem at arms,
So much that his renown attests
He cares to do all that is right,
In nothing is he cowardly,
380 A man like that, I promise you,
Deserves indeed to win high praise,
If he is good in peace and war,
And fair and true in every case.

384   And with him may his counselor
Be Courtesy, who'd teach him so
He'd bear the mark of noble style
In deed, in word, and in his speech,
388   Avoiding pride, so often man's
Demise. Thus let his thoughts aim high,
And his endeavors; pride like that
Is not the kind one scorns—having
392   A mind so high that it won't stoop
To vile pursuits, a mind that loves
The lofty things and not the low.
Indeed, such qualities belong
396   To noblemen; and may they keep
The cause of justice everywhere,
And goodness; that's their rightful task.
    "Returning to my subject, though,
400   The reason I've disturbed your sleep,
Upon command of Love, my lord,
Whom God has brought into the world,
To say just why he grieves and mourns,
404   And thus through me laments to you—
That tiresome habit is the cause,
By which so many people lose
Their honor—it's that slandering[7]
408   (God curse it!) which dishonors scores
Of women, wrongly, senselessly,
And many worthy men as well,
More so now than ever before.
412   That's Envy's work, who brings that dish
From Hell to serve it up above,
To poison everything about,
And bring a double death to him
416   Who's drawn to such malevolence.
For slander, when one ponders it,
Is like a lance or javelin
That kills the man who launches it
420   As well as him at whom it's aimed.
For sometimes he who's thrown the jab
Is left more wounded than the man
At whom the damage has been aimed,

424   Behind closed doors or on the street.
He wounds his soul more grievously,
His honor, his nobility,
More often than the man who's blamed.
428   Many a time has he accused
Another, one of greater worth:
How hard to bear the other's wealth!
And often, too, the man who slurs
432   Some other man is guiltier
Of just the same misdeed, I'm sure,
Than he maintains the other is.
The fault is one of judgment, and
436   In Envy lies its origin.
For no one wants capricious things
Said of himself, whatever he
Deserves. But we may feel assured
440   That there exists a judge so sure
He knows the inside and the out,
He knows it all and sees it all,
He'll render up what each deserves
444   Of good or ill, that's sure to be.
     "Detestable are gossipers,[8]
Their company the more to flee
Even than that of warring folk.
448   More evil and more dangerous
And harmful is the company
Of gossip-hawking, smirching men.
Whoever spends his time with bad
452   Companions can't avoid their stench:
In company with wolves one howls
And wears their skin. And when I say
A man, I mean a woman, too,
456   Should she spread gossip and untruth;
For nothing is more poisonous,
Nor should be less beloved than
An evil woman's wagging tongue,
Which slurs, insults, or ridicules,
460   In fun or with intent to harm.
If ill results, that's alms to her
Who makes a habit of such ways.

464 An ugly and a vile pursuit,
Misspeaking ill suits womankind.
Instead, whenever women hear
Some word that harms another's name,
468 They must extinguish all such talk
As they can, or themselves be still,
If nothing else is possible.
For women must, in truth, possess
472 A gentleness and charity;
If they do else, it's not their way;
A well-bred silence suits their style.
Because that custom, though, runs through
476 The many places set aflame
By Envy, Love would like to pluck
Away the ones he cherishes.
It's nobles who are suited least
480 To being blamed for such a stain.
For none's so fine, I dare to say,
That if he's known to spread untruth,
He won't be loved the less by all,
484 Less prized and called a slanderer.
Above all other calumny
It's talk of women basely done,
Defaming them, that Love hates most.
488 He doesn't want the ones who try
To act with dignity to earn
Esteem and worth in many lands,
To have this stain attach to them;
492 For that's a sin, and wrongly done.
To stop those acid-dripping tongues
The God of Love has sent me down
To bring the Order, fine and new,[9]
496 The one whose news I publicized
Before you not so long ago.
And further, as I understand,
The God of Love would like that this
500 Be broadcast, in whatever way,
Made known about, in many lands,
So slandering will be disliked
In every place where noblemen

504   Apply themselves to earning praise.
To you he gives the mission of
Ordaining ladies, deputies
In every realm, and they would be
508   Empowered, should they wish it so,
To give the charming Order out,
The Order of the pleasing Rose,
Hearing the vow that goes with it.
512   But Love desires, I well recall,
That none be named to give the high
And joyful Order lest she be
An honored lady or a maid
516   Of breeding, fair, and courteous.
For women all are beautiful
When goodness passes loveliness.
    "By reason of this covenant,
520   You'll have this charge forevermore.
Thus send it out to every land
Where noble people war against
The ladies, whose renown is spread
524   By virtue of the good they do.
To them good Love commands and wants
And orders you, through me, to give
The lovely Order to their care,
528   Where none, with right, can challenge it.
And though I brought a fine supply
Of roses which the good will wear,
To whom I proffered them just now,
532   (And though I've got enough of them,
For in my orchard's where they're plucked)
Yet Love desires that roses not
Be lacking in the other lands
536   Where such as these cannot be found.
If men who'll wear the Order's badge,
Bestowed by ladies you've ordained
So that the Order may exist,
Would wear their roses worked in gold,
In silver, or embroidered silk,
Provided they've been rendered in
The rose's shape, that would suffice.

544   And so, in order to complete
Your task, I give the bull to you;[10]
There's nothing like it in the world,
The mandate testifies to that.

548   May God who knew the passion now
Sustain you at that studying
Which brings great learning in its wake.
And grant you reach His Paradise.

552   I'm leaving now, and say adieu."
    At that she disappeared. I woke
In great astonishment. Seeing
No door or window left ajar,

556   I wondered what that could have been;
At first I thought it was a dream,
But then I knew it for no lie:
I found the letter next to me,

560   The one the sceptered goddess placed
Upon my bed, quite near my head,
Who then departed through the air.

THELMA S. FENSTER

(Translated from Chantilly Musée Condé Ms. 492)

NOTES

1. This is the second part of the poem, where Loyalty, who has already appeared in the midst of the guests at the evening gathering, now appears to Christine alone.
2. White is the symbol of Diana's chastity.
3. The dream vision was a popular literary form in Christine's day and would be used by her again, notably in *The Long Road to Learning*. See A.C. Spearing, *Medieval Dream Poetry* (Cambridge, 1976).
4. Love here is Cupid, the God of Love, who is also the central figure in *The Letter of the God of Love*.
5. Although Christine believed in the structured society which existed in her day, she did not condone the moral shortcomings of the aristocratic, or privileged, classes.
6. Christine would develop similar views of valor later in *The Book of the Deeds of Arms and of Chivalry*.
7. Christine is probably referring here to certain members of the recently founded Court of Love, whose behavior had caused scandal.
8. The damage caused by idle gossip is a constant theme in Christine's poetry. She makes it clear here that her strictures apply to both men and women gossips.
9. This Order is similar in many respects to the Marshal Boucicaut's Order of the

White Lady on the Green Shield, although there is no evidence that Christine's Order of the Rose ever really existed.

10. This bull or charter would have been usual in the establishment of such an Order, as was the case when Philip the Good established the well-known Order of the Golden Fleece in 1430.

CCW

THE BOOK OF
THE CITY OF LADIES

❧

Here Begins the Book of the City of Ladies, Whose First Chapter Tells Why and for What Purpose this Book Was Written (I.1)

One day as I was sitting alone in my study surrounded by books on all kinds of subjects, devoting myself to literary studies, my usual habit, my mind dwelt at length on the weighty opinions of various authors whom I had studied for a long time. I looked up from my book, having decided to leave such subtle questions in peace and to relax by reading some light poetry. With this in mind, I searched for some small book. By chance a strange volume came into my hands, not one of my own, but one which had been given to me along with some others. When I held it open and saw from its title page that it was by Mathéolus,[1] I smiled, for though I had never seen it before, I had often heard that like other books it discussed respect for women. I thought I would browse through it to amuse myself. I had not been reading for very long when my good mother called me to refresh myself with some supper, for it was evening. Intending to look at it the next day, I put it down. The next morning, again seated in my study as was my habit, I remembered wanting to examine this book by Mathéolus. I started to read it and went on for a little while. Because the subject seemed to me not very pleasant for people who do not enjoy lies, and of no use in developing virtue or manners, given its lack of integrity in diction and theme, and after browsing here and there and reading the end, I put it down in order to turn my attention to more elevated and useful study. But just the sight of this book, even though it was of no authority, made me wonder how it happened that so many different men — and learned men among them — have been and are so inclined to express both in speaking and in their treatises and writings so many wicked insults about women and their behavior. Not only one or two and not even just this Mathéolus (for this book had a bad name anyway and was intended as a satire) but, more generally, judging from the treatises of all philosophers and poets and from all the orators—it would take too long to mention their names—it seems that they all speak from one and the same mouth. They all concur in one conclusion: that the behavior of women is inclined to and full of every vice. Thinking deeply about these matters, I began to examine my character and conduct as a natural woman and, similarly, I considered other women whose company I frequently kept, princesses, great ladies, women of the middle and lower classes, who had graciously told me of their most private and intimate thoughts, hoping that I could judge impartially and in good conscience whether the testimony of so many notable men could be true. To the best of my knowledge, no matter how long I confronted or dissected the problem, I could not see or realize how their claims could be true when compared to the natural behavior and character of women. Yet I still argued vehemently against women, saying that it would be impossible that so many famous men—such solemn scholars, possessed of such deep and great understanding, so clear-sighted in all things, as it seemed—could have spoken falsely on so many occasions that I could hardly find a book on morals where, even before I had read it in its entirety, I did not find several chapters or certain sections attacking women, no matter who the author was. This reason alone, in short, made me conclude that, although my intellect did not perceive my own great faults and, likewise, those of other women because of its simpleness and ignorance, it was however truly fitting that such was the case. And so I relied more on the judgment of others than on what I myself felt and knew. I was so transfixed in this line of thinking for such a long time that it seemed as if I were in a stupor. Like a gushing fountain, a series of authorities, whom I recalled one after another, came to mind, along with their opinions on this topic. And I finally decided that God formed a vile creature when He made woman, and I wondered how such a worthy artisan could have deigned to make such an abominable work which, from what they say, is the vessel as well as the refuge and abode of every evil and vice. As I was thinking this, a great unhappiness and sadness welled up in my heart, for I detested myself and the entire feminine sex, as though we were monstrosities in nature.[2] And in my lament I spoke these words:

"Oh, God, how can this be? For unless I stray from my faith, I must never doubt that Your infinite wisdom and most perfect goodness ever created anything which was not good. Did You yourself not create woman in a very special way and since that time did You not give her all those inclinations which it pleased You for her to have? And how could it be that You could go wrong in anything? Yet look at all these accusations which have been judged, decided, and concluded against women.[3] I do not know how to understand this repugnance. If it is so, fair Lord God, that in fact so many abominations abound in the female sex, for You Yourself say that the testimony of two or three witnesses lends credence, why shall I not doubt that this is true? Alas, God, why did You not let me be born in the world as a man, so that all my inclinations would be to serve You better, and so that I would not stray in anything and would be as perfect as a man is said to be? But since Your kindness has not been extended to me, then forgive my negligence in Your service, most fair Lord God, and may it not displease You, for the servant who receives fewer gifts from his lord is less obliged in his service." I spoke these words to God in my lament and a great deal more for a very long time in sad reflection, and in my folly I considered myself most unfortunate because God had made me inhabit a female body in this world.

Here Christine Describes How Three Ladies Appeared to Her and How the One Who Was in Front Spoke First and Comforted Her in Her Pain (I.2)

So occupied with these painful thoughts, my head bowed in shame, my eyes filled with tears, leaning on the pommel of my chair's armrest, I suddenly saw a ray of light fall on my lap, as though it were the sun. I shuddered then, as if wakened from sleep, for I was sitting in a shadow where the sun could not have shone at that hour. And as I lifted my head to see where this light was coming from, I saw three crowned ladies standing before me, and the splendor of their bright faces shone on me and throughout the entire room.[4] Now no one would ask whether I was surprised, for my doors were shut and they had still entered. Fearing that some phantom had come to tempt me and filled with great fright, I made the Sign of the Cross on my forehead.

Then she who was the first of the three smiled and began to speak, "Dear daughter, do not be afraid, for we have not come here to harm or trouble you but to console you, for we have taken pity on your distress, and we have come to bring you out of the ignorance which so blinds your own intellect that you shun what you know for a certainty and believe what you do not know or see or recognize except by virtue of many strange opinions. You resemble the fool in the prank who was dressed in women's clothes while he slept; because those who were making fun of him repeatedly told him he was a woman, he believed their false testimony more readily than the certainty of his own identity. Fair daughter, have you lost all sense? Have you forgotten that when fine gold is tested in the furnace, it does not change or vary in strength but becomes purer the more it is hammered and handled in different ways? Do you not know that the best things are the most debated and the most discussed? If you wish to consider the question of the highest form of reality, which consists in ideas or celestial substances, consider whether the greatest philosophers who have lived and whom you support against your own sex have ever resolved whether ideas are false and contrary to the truth. Notice how these same philosophers contradict and criticize one another, just as you have seen in the *Metaphysics*[5] where Aristotle takes their opinions to task and speaks similarly of Plato and other philosophers. And note, moreover, how even Saint Augustine and the Doctors of the Church have criticized Aristotle in certain passages, although he is known as the prince of philosophers in whom both natural and moral philosophy attained their highest level. It also seems that you think that all the words of the philosophers are articles of faith, that they could never be wrong. As far as the poets of whom you speak are concerned, do you not know that they spoke on many subjects in a fictional way and that often they mean the contrary of what their words openly say? One can interpret them according to the grammatical figure of *antiphrasis,* which means, as you know, that if you call something bad, in fact, it is good, and also vice versa. Thus I advise you to profit from their works and to interpret them in the manner in which they are intended in those passages where they attack women. Perhaps this man, who called himself Mathéolus in his own book, intended it in such a way, for there are many things which, if taken literally, would be pure heresy. As for the attack against the estate of marriage—which is a holy estate, worthy and ordained by God—made not only by Mathéolus but also by others and even by the *Romance of the Rose* where greater credibility is averred because of the authority of its author, it is evident and proven by experience that the contrary of the evil which they posit and claim to be found in this estate through the obligation and fault of women is true. For where has the husband ever been found who would allow his wife to have authority to abuse and insult him as a matter of course, as these authorities maintain? I believe that, regardless of what you might have read, you will never see such a husband with your own eyes, so badly colored are these lies. Thus, in conclusion, I tell you, dear friend, that simplemindedness has prompted you to hold such an opinion. Come back to yourself, recover your senses, and do not trouble yourself anymore over such absurdities. For you know that any evil spoken of women so generally only hurts those who say it, not women themselves."

Here Christine Tells How the Lady Who Had Said This Showed Her Who She Was and What Her Character and Function Were and Told Her How She Would Construct a City with the Help of These Same Three Ladies (I.3)

The famous lady spoke these words to me, in whose presence I do not know which one of my senses was more overwhelmed: my hearing from having listened to such worthy words or my sight from having seen her radiant beauty, her attire, her reverent comportment, and her most honored countenance. The same was true of the others, so that I did not know which one to look at, for the three ladies resembled each other so much that they could be told apart only with difficulty, except for the last one, for although she was of no less authority than the others, she had so fierce a visage that whoever, no matter how daring, looked in her eyes would be afraid to commit a crime, for it seemed that she threatened criminals unceasingly. Having stood up out of respect, I looked at them without saying a word, like someone too overwhelmed to utter a syllable. Reflecting on who these beings could be, I felt much admiration in my heart and, if I could have dared, I would have immediately asked their names and identities and what was the meaning of the different scepters which each one carried in her right hand, which were of fabulous richness, and why they had come here. But since I considered myself unworthy to address these questions to such high ladies as they appeared to me, I did not dare to, but continued to keep my gaze fixed on them, half-afraid and half-reassured by the words which I had heard, which had made me reject my first impression. But the most wise lady who had spoken to me and who knew in her mind what I was thinking, as one who has insight into everything, addressed my reflections, saying:

"Dear daughter, know that God's providence, which leaves nothing void or empty, has ordained that we, though celestial beings, remain and circulate among the people of the world here below, in order to bring order and maintain in balance those institutions we created according to the will of God in the fulfillment of various offices, that God whose daughters we three all are and from whom we were born. Thus it is my duty to straighten out men and women when they go astray and to put them back on the right path. And when they stray, if they have enough understanding to see me, I come to them quietly in spirit and preach to them, showing them their error and how they have failed, I assign them the causes, and then I teach them what to do and what to avoid. Since I serve to demonstrate clearly and to show both in thought and deed to each man and woman his or her own special qualities and faults, you see me holding this shiny mirror which I carry in my right hand in place of a scepter. I would thus have you know truly that no one can look into this mirror, no matter what kind of creature, without achieving clear self-knowledge. My mirror has such great dignity that not without reason is it surrounded by rich and precious gems, so that you see, thanks to this mirror, the essences, qualities, proportions, and measures of all things are known, nor can anything be done well without it. And because, similarly, you wish to know what are the offices of my other sisters whom you see here, each will reply in her own person about her name and character, and this way our testimony will be all the more certain to you.[6] But now I myself will declare the reason for our coming. I must assure you, as we do nothing without good cause, that our appearance here is not at all in vain. For, although we are not common to many places and our knowledge does not come to all people, nevertheless you, for your great love of investigating the truth through long and continual study, for which you come here, solitary and separated from the world, you have deserved and deserve, our devoted friend, to be visited and consoled by us in your agitation and sadness, so that you might also see clearly, in the midst of the darkness of your thoughts, those things which taint and trouble your heart.[7]

"There is another greater and even more special reason for our coming which you will learn from our speeches: in fact we have come to vanquish from the world the same error into which you had fallen, so that from now on, ladies and all valiant women may have a refuge and defense against the various assailants, those ladies who have been abandoned for so long, exposed like a field without a surrounding hedge, without finding a champion to afford them an adequate defense, notwithstanding those noble men who are required by order of law to protect them, who by negligence and apathy have allowed them to be mistreated. It is no wonder then that their jealous enemies, those outrageous villains who have assailed them with various weapons, have been victorious in a war in which women have had no defense. Where is there a city so strong which could not be taken immediately if no resistance were forthcoming, or the law case, no matter how unjust, which was not won through the obstinance of someone pleading without opposition? And the simple, noble ladies, following the example of suffering which God commands, have cheerfully suffered the great attacks which, both in the spoken and the written word, have been wrongfully and sinfully perpetrated against women by men who all the while appealed to God for the right to do so. Now it is time for their just cause to be taken from Pharaoh's hands, and for this reason, we three ladies whom you see here, moved by pity, have come to you to announce a particular edifice built like a city wall, strongly constructed and well founded, which has been predestined and established by our aid and counsel for you to build, where no one will reside except all ladies of fame and women worthy of praise, for the walls of the city will be closed to those women who lack virtue."[8]

Here the Lady Explains to Christine the City Which She Has Been Commissioned to Build and How She Was Charged to Help Christine Build the Wall and Enclosure, and Then Gives Her Name (I.4)

"Thus, fair daughter, the prerogative among women has been bestowed on you to establish and build the City of Ladies. For the foundation and completion of this City you will draw fresh waters from us as from clear fountains, and we will bring you sufficient building stone, stronger and more durable than any marble with cement could be. Thus your City will be extremely beautiful, without equal, and of perpetual duration in the world.

"Have you not read that King Tros founded the great city of Troy with the aid of Apollo, Minerva, and Neptune, whom the people of that time considered gods,[9] and also how Cadmus founded the city of Thebes with the admonition of the gods?[10] And yet over time these cities fell and have fallen into ruin. But I prophesy to you, as a true sybil, that this City, which you will found with our help, will never be destroyed, nor will it ever fall, but will remain prosperous forever, regardless of all its jealous enemies. Although it will be stormed by numerous assaults, it will never be taken or conquered.

"Long ago the Amazon kingdom[11] was begun through the arrangement and enterprise of several ladies of great courage who despised servitude, just as history books have testified. For a long time afterward they maintained it under the rule of several queens, very noble ladies whom they elected themselves, who governed them well and maintained their dominion with great strength. Yet, although they were strong and powerful and had conquered a large part of the entire Orient in the course of their rule and terrified all the neighboring lands (even the Greeks, who were then the flower of all countries in the world, feared them), nevertheless, after a time, the power of this kingdom declined, so that as with all earthly kingdoms, nothing but its name has survived to the present. But the edifice erected by you in this City which you must construct will be far stronger, and for its founding I was commissioned, in the course of our common deliberation, to supply you with durable and pure mortar to lay the sturdy foundations and to raise the lofty walls all around, high and thick, with mighty towers and strong bastions, surrounded by moats with firm blockhouses, just as is fitting for a city with a strong and lasting defense. Following our plan, you will set the foundations deep to last all the longer, and then you will raise the walls so high that they will not fear anyone. Daughter, now that I have told you the reason for our coming and so that you will more certainly believe my words, I want you to learn my name, by whose sound alone you will be able to learn and know that, if you wish to follow my commands, you have in me an administrator so that you may do your work flawlessly. I am called Lady Reason; you see that you are in good hands. For the time being then, I will say no more."

Here Christine Tells How the Second Lady Told Her Name and What She Served as and How She Would Aid Her in Building the City of Ladies (I.5)

When the lady above finished her speech, before I could resume, the second lady began as follows: "I am called Rectitude[12] and reside more in Heaven than on Earth, but as the radiance and splendor of God and messenger of His goodness, I often visit the just and exhort them to do what is right, to give to each person what is his according to his capacity, to say and uphold the truth, to defend the rights of the poor and the innocent, not to hurt anyone through usurpation, to uphold the reputation of those unjustly accused. I am the shield and defense of the servants of God. I resist the power and might of evil-doers. I give rest to workers and reward those who act well. Through me, God reveals to His friends His secrets; I am their advocate in Heaven. This shining ruler which you see me carry in my right hand instead of a scepter is the straight ruler which separates right from wrong and shows the difference between good and evil: who follows it does not go astray. It is the rod of peace which reconciles the good and where they find support and which beats and strikes down evil. What should I tell you about this? All things are measured by this ruler, for its powers are infinite. It will serve you to measure the edifice of the City which you have been commissioned to build, and you will need it for constructing the façade, for erecting the high temples, for measuring the palaces, houses, and all public buildings, the streets and squares, and all things proper to help populate the City. I have come as your assistant, and this will be my duty. Do not be uneasy about the breadth and long circuit of the walls, for with God's help and our assistance you will build fair and sturdy mansions and inns without leaving anything vague, and you will people the City with no trouble."

Here Christine Tells How the Third Lady Told Her Who She Was and Her Function and How She Would Help Build the High Roofs of the Towers and Palaces and Would Bring to Her the Queen, Accompanied by Noble Ladies (I.6)

Afterward, the third lady spoke and said, "My friend Christine, I am Justice, [13] the most singular daughter of God, and my nature proceeds purely from His person. My residence is found in Heaven, on Earth, or in Hell: in Heaven, for the glory of the saints and blessed souls; on Earth, for the apportionment to each man of the good or evil which he has deserved; in Hell, for the punishment of the evil. I do not bend anywhere, for I have not friend nor enemy nor changeable will; pity cannot persuade me nor cruelty move me. My duty is only to judge, to decide, and to dispense according to each man's just deserts. I sustain all things in their condition, nothing could be stable without me. I am in God and God is in me, and we are as one and the same. Who follows me cannot fail, and my way is sure. I teach men and women of sound mind who want to believe in me to chastise, know, and correct themselves, and to do to others what they wish to have done to themselves, to distribute wealth without favor, to speak the truth, to flee and hate lies, to reject all viciousness. This vessel of fine gold which you see me hold in my right hand, made like a generous measure, God, my Father, gave me, and it serves to measure out to each his rightful portion. It carries the sign of the fleur-de-lis of the Trinity, and in all portions it measures true, nor can any man complain about my measure. Yet the men of the Earth have other measures which they claim depend upon and derive from mine, but they are mistaken. Often they measure in my shadow, and their measure is not always true but sometimes too much for some and too little for others. I could give a rather long account of the duties of my office, but, put briefly, I have a special place among the Virtues, for they are all based on me.[14] And of the three noble ladies whom you see here, we are as one and the same, we could not exist without one another; and what the first disposes, the second orders and initiates, and then I, the third, finish and terminate it. Thus I have been appointed by the will of us three ladies to perfect and complete your City, and my job will be to construct the high roofs of the towers and of the lofty mansions and inns which will all be made of fine shining gold. Then I will populate the City for you with worthy ladies and the mighty Queen whom I will bring to you. Hers will be the honor and prerogative among all other women, as well as among the most excellent women. And in this condition I will turn the City over to you, completed with your help, fortified and closed off with strong gates which I will search for in Heaven, and then I will place the keys in your hands."

Here Christine Tells How She Spoke to the Three Ladies (I.7)

When the speeches of all three ladies were over—to which I had listened intently and which had completely taken away the unhappiness which I had felt before their coming—I threw myself at their feet, not just on my knees but completely prostrate because of their great excellence. Kissing the earth around their feet, adoring them as goddesses of glory, I began my prayer to them:

"Oh ladies of supreme dignity, radiance of the heavens and light of the earth, fountains of Paradise and joy of the blessed, where did such humility come from to Your Highnesses that you have deigned to come down from your pontifical seats and shining thrones to visit the troubled and dark tabernacle of this simple and ignorant student? Who could give fitting thanks for such a boon? With the rain and dew of your sweet words, you have penetrated and moistened the dryness of my mind, so that it now feels ready to germinate and send forth new branches capable of bearing fruits of profitable virtue and sweet savor. How will such grace be bestowed on me that I will receive the boon, as you have said, to build and construct in the world from now on a new city? I am not Saint Thomas the Apostle, who through divine grace built a rich palace in Heaven for the king of India,[15] and my feeble sense does not know the craft, or the measures, or the study, or the science, or the practice of construction. And if, thanks to learning, these things were within my ken, where would I find enough physical strength in my weak feminine body to realize such an enormous task? But nevertheless, my most respected ladies, although the awesomeness of this news seems strange to me, I know well that nothing is impossible for God. Nor do I doubt that anything undertaken with your counsel and help will not be completed well. Thus, with all my strength, I praise God and you, my ladies, who have so honored me by assigning me such a noble commission, which I most happily accept. Behold your handmaiden ready to serve. Command and I will obey, and may it be unto me according to your words."[16]

Here Christine Tells How, Under Reason's Command and Assistance, She Began to Excavate the Earth and Lay the Foundation (I.8)

Then Lady Reason responded and said, "Get up, daughter! Without waiting any longer, let us go to the Field of Letters. There the City of Ladies will be founded on a flat and fertile plain, where all fruits and freshwater rivers are found and where the earth abounds in all good things. Take the pick of your inquiring mind and dig and clear out a great ditch wherever you see the marks of my ruler, and I will help you carry away the earth on my own shoulders."

I immediately stood up to obey her commands and, thanks to these three ladies, I felt stronger and lighter than before. She went ahead, and I followed behind, and after we had arrived at this field I began to excavate and dig, following her marks with the pick of cross-examination. And this was my first work:

"Lady, I remember well what you told me before, dealing with the subject of how so many men have attacked and continue to attack the behavior of women, that gold becomes more refined the longer it stays in the furnace, [17] which means the more women have been wrongfully attacked, the greater waxes the merit of their glory. But please tell me why and for what reason different authors have spoken against women in their books, since I already know from you that this is wrong; tell me if Nature makes man so inclined or whether they do it out of hatred and where does this behavior come from?"

Then she replied, "Daughter, to give you a way of entering into the question more deeply, I will carry away this first basketful of dirt. [18] This behavior most certainly does not come from Nature, [19] but rather is contrary to Nature, for no connection in the world is as great or as strong as the great love which, through the will of God, Nature places between a man and a woman. The causes which have moved and which still move men to attack women, even those authors in those books, are diverse and varied, just as you have discovered. [20] For some have attacked women with good intentions, that is, in order to draw men who have gone astray away from the company of vicious and dissolute women, with whom they might be infatuated, or in order to keep these men from going mad on account of such women, and also so that every man might avoid an obscene and lustful life. They have attacked all women in general because they believe that women are made up of every abomination."

"My lady," I said then, "excuse me for interrupting you here, but have such authors acted well, since they were prompted by a laudable intention? For intention, the saying goes, judges the man."

"That is a misleading position, my good daughter," she said, "for such sweeping ignorance never provides an excuse. If someone killed you with good intention but out of foolishness, would this then be justified? Rather, those who did this, whoever they might be, would have invoked the wrong law; causing any damage or harm to one party in order to help another party is not justice, and likewise attacking all feminine conduct is contrary to the truth, just as I will show you with a hypothetical case. Let us suppose they did this intending to draw fools away from foolishness. It would be as if I attacked fire—a very good and necessary element nevertheless—because some people burnt themselves, or water because someone drowned. The same can be said of all good things which can be used well or used badly. But one must not attack them if fools abuse them, and you have yourself touched on this point quite well elsewhere in your writings. But those who have spoken like this so abundantly—whatever their intentions might be—have formulated their arguments rather loosely only to make their point. Just like someone who has a long and wide robe cut from a very large piece of cloth when the material costs him nothing and when no one opposes him, they exploit the rights of others. But just as you have said elsewhere, if these writers had only looked for the ways in which men can be led away from foolishness and could have been kept from tiring themselves in attacking the life and behavior of immoral and dissolute women—for to tell the straight truth, there is nothing which should be avoided more than an evil, dissolute, and perverted woman, who is like a monster in nature, a counterfeit estranged from her natural condition, which must be simple, tranquil, and upright—then I would grant you that they would have built a supremely excellent work. But I can assure you that these attacks on all women—when in fact there are so many excellent women—have never originated with me, Reason, [21] and that all who subscribe to them have failed totally and will continue to fail. So now throw aside these black, dirty, and uneven stones from your work, for they will never be fitted into the fair edifice of your City.

"Other men have attacked women for other reasons: such reproach has occurred to some men because of their own vices and others have been moved by the defects of their own bodies, others through pure jealousy, still others by the pleasure they derive in their own personalities from slander. Others, in order to show they have read many authors, base their own writings on what they have found in books and repeat what other writers have said and cite different authors.

"Those who attack women because of their own vices are men who spent their youths in dissolution and enjoyed the love of many different women, used deception in many of their encounters, and have grown old in their sins without repenting, and now regret their past follies and the dissolute life they led. But Nature, which allows the will of the heart to put into effect what the powerful appetite desires, has grown cold in them. Therefore, they are pained when they see that their 'good times' have now passed them by, and it seems to them that the young, who are now what they once were, are on top of the world. They do not know how to overcome their sadness except by attacking women, hoping to make women less attractive to other men. Everywhere one sees such old men speak obscenely and dishonestly, just as you can fully see with Mathéolus, who himself confesses that he was an impotent old man filled with desire. You can thereby convincingly prove, with this one example, how what I tell you is true, and you can assuredly believe that it is the same with many others.

"But these corrupt old men, like an incurable leprosy, are not the upstanding men of old whom I made perfect in virtue and wisdom— for not all men share in such corrupt desire, and it would be a real shame if it were so. The mouths of these good men, following their hearts, are all filled with exemplary, honest, and discreet words. These same men detest misdeeds and slander, and neither attack nor defame men and women, and they counsel the avoidance of evil and the pursuit of virtue and the straight path.

"Those men who are moved by the defect of their own bodies have impotent and deformed limbs but sharp and malicious minds. They have found no other way to avenge the pain of their impotence except by attacking women who bring joy to many. Thus they have thought to divert others away from the pleasure which they cannot personally enjoy.

"Those men who have attacked women out of jealousy are those wicked ones who have seen and realized that many women have greater understanding and are more noble in conduct than they them-selves, and thus they are pained and disdainful. Because of this, their overweening jealousy has prompted them to attack all women, intend-ing to demean and diminish the glory and praise of such women, just like the man—I cannot remember which one—who tries to prove in his work, *De philosophia,* that it is not fitting that some men have revered women and says that those men who have made so much of women pervert the title of his book: they transform 'philosophy,' the love of wisdom, into 'philofolly,' the love of folly. But I promise and swear to you that he himself, all throughout the lie-filled deductions of his argument, transformed the content of his book into a true philofolly.

"As for those men who are naturally given to slander, it is not surprising that they slander women since they attack everyone any-way. Nevertheless, I assure you that any man who freely slanders does so out of a great wickedness of heart, for he is acting contrary to reason and contrary to Nature: contrary to reason insofar as he is most ungrateful and fails to recognize the good deeds which women have done for him, so great that he could never make up for them, no matter how much he try, and which he continuously needs women to perform for him; and contrary to Nature in that there is no naked beast anywhere, nor bird, which does not naturally love its female counterpart. It is thus quite unnatural when a reasonable man does the contrary.

"And just as there has never been any work so worthy, so skilled is the craftsman who made it, that there were not people who wanted, and want, to counterfeit it, there are many who wish to get involved in writing poetry. They believe they cannot go wrong, since others have written in books what they take the situation to be, or rather, *mis*-take the situation—as I well know! Some of them undertake to express themselves by writing poems of water without salt, such as these, or ballads without feeling, discussing the behavior of women or of princes or of other people, while they themselves do not know how to recognize or to correct their own servile conduct and inclinations. But simple people, as ignorant as they are, declare that such writing is the best in the world."

∞

Here She Speaks of Minerva, Who Invented Many Sciences and the Technique of Making Armor from Iron and Steel (I.34)[22]

"Minerva, just as you have written elsewhere, was a maiden of Greece and surnamed Pallas. This maiden was of such excellence of mind that the foolish people of that time, because they did not know who her parents were and saw her doing things which had never been done before, said she was a goddess descended from Heaven; for the less they knew about her ancestry, the more marvelous her great knowledge seemed to them, when compared to that of the women of her time. She had a subtle mind, of profound understanding, not only in one subject but also generally, in every subject. Through her ingenuity she invented a shorthand Greek script in which a long written narrative could be transcribed with far fewer letters, and which is still used by the Greeks today, a fine invention whose discovery demanded great subtlety. She invented numbers and a means of quickly counting and adding sums. Her mind was so enlightened with general knowledge that she devised various skills and designs which had never before been discovered. She developed the entire technique of gathering wool and making cloth and was the first who ever thought to shear sheep of their wool and then to pick, comb, and card it with iron spindles and finally to spin it with a distaff, and then she invented the tools needed to make the cloth and also the method by which the wool should finally be woven.

"Similarly she initiated the custom of extracting oil from different fruits of the earth, also from olives, and of squeezing and pressing juice from other fruits. At the same time she discovered how to make wagons and carts to transport things easily from one place to another.

"This lady, in a similar manner, did even more, and it seems all the more remarkable because it is far removed from a woman's nature to conceive of such things; for she invented the art and technique of making harnesses and armor from iron and steel, which knights and armed soldiers employ in battle and with which they cover their bodies, and which she first gave to the Athenians whom she taught how to deploy an army and battalions and how to fight in organized ranks.

"Similarly she was the first to invent flutes and fifes, trumpets and wind instruments. With her considerable force of mind, this lady remained a virgin her entire life. Because of her outstanding chastity, the poets claimed in their fictions that Vulcan, the god of fire, wrestled with her for a long time and that finally she won and overcame him, which is to say that she overcame the ardor and lusts of the flesh which so strongly assail the young. The Athenians held this maiden in such high reverence that they worshiped her as a goddess and called her the goddess of arms and chivalry because she was the first to devise their use, and they also called her the goddess of knowledge because of her learnedness.

"After her death they erected a temple in Athens dedicated to her, and there they placed a statue of her, portraying a maiden, as a representation of wisdom and chivalry. This statue had terrible and cruel eyes because chivalry has been instituted to carry out rigorous justice; they also signified that one seldom knows toward what end the meditation of the wise man tends. She wore a helmet on her head which signified that a knight must have strength, endurance, and constant courage in the deeds of arms, and further signified that the counsels of the wise are concealed, secret, and hidden. She was dressed in a coat of mail which stood for the power of the estate of chivalry and also taught that the wise man is always armed against the whims of Fortune, whether good or bad. She held some kind of spear or very long lance, which meant that the knight must be the rod of justice and also signified that the wise man casts his spears from great distances. A buckler or shield of crystal hung at her neck, which meant that the knight must always be alert and oversee everywhere the defense of his country and people and further signified that things are open and evident to the wise man. She had portrayed in the middle of this shield the head of a serpent called Gorgon, which teaches that the knight must always be wary and watchful over his enemies like the serpent, and furthermore, that the wise man is aware of all the malice which can hurt him. Next to this image they also placed a bird that flies by night, named the owl, as if to watch over her, which signified that the knight must be ready by night as well as by day for civil defense, when necessary, and also that the wise man should take care at all times to do what is profitable and fitting for him. For a long time this lady was held in such high regard and her great fame spread so far that in many places temples were founded to praise her. Even long afterward, when the Romans were at the height of their power, they included her image among their gods."[23]

∞

Christine Asks Reason Where Prudence Is Found in the Natural Sensibility of Women; and Reason's Answer to Her (I.43)

Then I, Christine, said to her, "My lady, I can truly and clearly see that God—may He be praised for it—has granted that the mind of an intelligent woman can conceive, know, and retain all perceptible things. Even though there are so many people who have such subtle minds that they understand and learn everything which they are shown and who are so ingenious and quick to conceptualize everything that every field of learning is open to them, with the result that they have acquired extraordinary knowledge through devotion to study, I am baffled when eminent scholars—including some of the most famous and learned—exhibit so little prudence in their morals and conduct in the world. Certainly scholarship teaches and provides an introduction to morals. If you please, my lady, I would gladly learn from you whether a woman's mind (which, as it seems to me from your proofs as well as from what I myself see, is quite understanding and retentive in subtle questions of scholarship and other subjects) is equally prompt and clever in those matters which prudence teaches, that is, whether women can reflect on what is best to do and what is better to be avoided, and whether they remember past events and become learned from the examples they have seen, and, as a result, are wise in managing current affairs, and whether they have foresight into the future. Prudence, it seems to me, teaches those lessons." [24]

"You speak correctly, my daughter," she replied, "but this prudence of which you speak is bestowed by Nature upon men and women, and some possess more, others less. But Nature does not impart knowledge of everything, as much as it simultaneously perfects in those who are naturally prudent, for you realize that two forces together are stronger and more resistant than one force alone. For this reason I say that the person who, from Nature, possesses prudence (which is called 'natural sense'), as well as acquired knowledge along with this prudence, deserves special praise for remarkable excellence. Yet just as you yourself have said, some who possess the one do not possess the other, for the one is the gift of God thanks to the influence of Nature, and the other is acquired through long study, though both are good. But some people prefer natural sense without acquired knowledge rather than a great deal of acquired knowledge with little natural sense. All the same, many opinions can be based upon this proposition, from which many questions can arise. For one could say that one achieves more good by choosing what is more useful for the profit and the utility of the general public. Therefore, one person's knowing the different fields of learning is more profitable for everyone than all the natural sense which he might possess which he could demonstrate to all: for this natural sense can only last as long as the lifetime of the person who has it, and when he dies, his sense dies with him. Acquired learning, on the other hand, lasts forever for those who have it, because of their fame, and it is useful for many people insofar as it can be taught to others and recorded in books for the sake of future generations. In this way their learning does not die with them, and therefore I can show you, using the example of Aristotle and others through whom learning has been transmitted to the world, that their acquired knowledge was more useful to the world than all the prudence without acquired knowledge possessed by all men, past and present, although thanks to the prudence of many, several kingdoms and empires have been well-governed and directed. All of these things are transitory, however, and disappear with time, while learning endures forever.

"Nevertheless, I will leave these questions unanswered and for others to solve, for they do not pertain to the problem of building our City, and I will come back to the question you raised, that is, whether women possess natural prudence. Of course they do. You know this already from what I have said to you before, just as, in general, you can see from women's conduct in those duties assigned to them to perform. But be careful if you find this good, for you will see that all women, or the vast majority, are so very attentive, careful, and diligent in governing their households and in providing everything for them, according to their capacities, that sometimes some of their negligent husbands are annoyed; they think their wives are pushing and pressuring them too much to do what they are supposed to and they say their wives want to run everything and be smarter than they are. In this way, what many women tell their husbands with good intentions turns out to their disadvantage. The proverbs of Solomon discuss such prudent women [25] and what follows gives you the gist of this book for the purposes of our argument here."

∞

Christine Speaks to Rectitude (II.7)

"My lady, because I understand and clearly see that women are overwhelmingly innocent of what they are so frequently accused, now make me better acquainted than ever with their accusers' great guilt. Once more I cannot remain quiet regarding a practice with widespread currency among men — and even among some women — that when women are pregnant and then give birth to daughters, their husbands are upset and grumble because their wives did not give birth to sons. And their silly wives, who should be supremely joyful that God has delivered them to safety and, similarly, should heartily thank Him, are unhappy because they see their husbands upset. Why does it happen, my lady, that they grieve so? Are daughters a greater liability to their parents than sons, or less loving and more indifferent toward their parents than sons are?"

"Dear friend," she replied, "because you ask me the cause from which this springs, I can assure you that it comes from the excessive simplemindedness and ignorance of those who become so upset. Yet the principal reason which moves them is the cost which they fear the marriage of their daughters will force them to pay. Also, some are upset because they are afraid of the danger that, by bad advice, their daughters could be deceived when they are young and naive. But all of these reasons are nothing when examined with common sense. For, as regards their fear that their daughters might do something foolish, one need only instruct them in wisdom when they are young, making sure that the mother herself sets a good example of integrity and learnedness, for if the mother lives foolishly, she will hardly be an example for the daughter. The daughter should also be protected from bad company and raised in accordance with strict rules which she respects, for the discipline exercised over children and young people prepares them to live upright lives for their whole lifetime.[26] Similarly, as far as cost is concerned, I believe that if the parents looked closely at that incurred on account of their sons—whether in teaching them knowledge or skills, or in simple upkeep, and even in superfluous expenses, whether on a large, middle, or small scale, for silly companions or for a lot of frivolities—they will hardly find a greater financial advantage in having sons rather than daughters. And if you consider the anger and worry which many sons cause their parents—for they often get involved in harsh and bitter riots and brawls or pursue a dissolute life, all to the grief and expense of their parents—I think that this anguish can easily exceed the worries which they have because of their daughters. See how many sons you will find who gently and humbly care for their parents and mothers in their old age, as they are supposed to. I insist that they are few and far between, although there are and have been many who have helped when it was too late. Thus, after a father and mother have made gods out of their sons and the sons are grown and have become rich and affluent—either because of their father's own efforts or because he had them learn some skill or trade or even by some good fortune—and the father has become poor and ruined through misfortune, they despise him and are annoyed and ashamed when they see him. But if the father is rich, they only wish for his death so that they can inherit his wealth. Oh! God knows how many sons of great lords and rich men long for their parents' deaths so that they can inherit their lands and wealth. Petrarch observed the situation accurately when he remarked, "Oh foolish men, you desire children, but you could not have such mortal enemies; for, if you are poor, they will be annoyed with you and will wish for your death, in order to be rid of you; and if you are rich, they will wish for your death no less, in order to have your possessions.'[27] I certainly do not mean that all sons are like this, but there are many who are. And if they are married, God knows their enormous greed to sap their fathers and mothers. It hardly matters to them whether these miserable old people die of hunger, provided, of course, that they inherit everything. Some sustenance indeed! Nor does it matter to them when their mothers are widowed, then—when they ought to comfort them and be the support and aid in their old age—those same mothers, who so cherished and so lovingly and tenderly nourished their children, are well rewarded for all their trouble! For these evil offspring think that everything should be theirs, and if their widowed mothers do not give them everything they want, they do not hesitate to vent their displeasure on them. God knows how much reverence is shown there! Moreover, what is worse, they have no pangs of conscience about bringing lawsuits and court proceedings against their mothers. This is the reward which many parents have after having spent all their lives trying to acquire some wealth or put their children ahead. There are many sons like this, and there may well be daughters like this, too. But if you are very attentive, you will find more sons than daughters who are so corrupt. And let us suppose that all sons were good, nevertheless one usually sees the daughters keep their fathers and mothers company more often than the sons, and the daughters visit them more, comfort them more, and take care of them in sickness and old age more frequently.[28] The reason is that the sons wander through the world in every direction and the daughters are calmer and stay closer to home, just as you can see from your own experiences; for even though your brothers are quite normal, very loving, and virtuous, they went out into the world and you alone remained to give your mother a little company, which is her greatest comfort in old age. For this reason, I tell you in conclusion that those who are troubled and upset when daughters are born to them are exceedingly foolish. And since you have gotten me onto this topic, let me tell you about several women mentioned among others in various writings who were quite natural and most loving toward their parents."

∽

Here Rectitude Announces That She Has Finished Building the Houses of the City and That It Is Time That It Be Peopled (II.12)

"It seems to me at this point, most dear friend, that our construction is quite well advanced, for the houses of the City of Ladies stand completed all along the wide streets, its royal palaces are well constructed, and its towers and defense turrets have been raised so high and straight that one can see them from far away. It is therefore right that we start to people this noble City now, so that it does not remain vacant or empty, but instead is wholly populated with ladies of great excellence, for we do not want any others here. How happy will be the citizens of our edifice, for they will not need to fear or worry about being evicted by foreign armies, for this work has the special property that its owners cannot be expelled. Now a New Kingdom of Femininity is begun, and it is far better than the earlier kingdom of the Amazons, for the ladies residing here will not need to leave their land in order to conceive or give birth to new heirs to maintain their possessions throughout the different ages, from one generation to another, for those whom we now place here will suffice quite adequately forever more.

"And after we have populated it with noble citizens, my sister, Lady Justice, will come and lead the Queen,[29] outstanding over all, and accompanied by princesses of the highest dignity who will reside in the uppermost apartments and in the lofty towers. It is fitting that on her arrival the Queen find her City supplied and peopled with noble ladies who will receive her with honors as their sovereign lady, empress of all their sex. But what citizens will we place here? Will they be dissolute or dishonored women? Certainly not, rather they shall all be women of integrity, of great beauty and authority, for there could be no fairer populace nor any greater adornment in the City than women of good character. Now let us go, dear friend, for now I am putting you to work, and I will go ahead so that we can go look for them."

Christine Asks Lady Rectitude Whether What the Books and Men Say Is True, That Married Life Is So Hard to Endure Because of Women and the Wrong They Cause;[30] *Rectitude Answers and Begins to Speak of the Great Love Shown by Women for Their Husbands* (II. 13)

Then, as we were searching for these women by order of Lady Rectitude, I spoke these words as we went along, "My lady, truly you and Reason have solved and settled all the problems and questions which I could not answer, and I consider myself very well informed about what I asked. I have learned a great deal from you: how all things which are feasible and knowable, whether in the area of physical strength or in the wisdom of the mind and every virtue, are possible and easy for women to accomplish. But could you now please confirm for me whether what men claim, and what so many authors testify, is true—a topic about which I am thinking very deeply—that life within the institution of marriage is filled and occupied with such great unhappiness for men because of women's faults and impetuosity, and because of their rancorous ill-humor, as is written in so many books? Many assert that these women care so little for their husbands and their company that nothing else annoys them as much? For this reason, in order to escape and avoid such inconveniences, many authorities have advised wise men not to marry, affirming that no women—or very few—are loyal to their mates. Valerius wrote to Rufus along similar lines, and Theophrastus[31] remarked in his book that no wise man should take a wife, because there are too many worries with women, too little love, and too much gossip, and that, if a man marries in order to be better taken care of and nursed in sickness, a loyal servant could better and more loyally care for him and serve him and would not cost him nearly as much, and that if the wife becomes sick, the languishing husband does not dare budge from her side. But enough of such things, which would take too long to recite in full, therefore I say to you, dear lady, that if these remarks are true, so evil are these faults that all the other graces and virtues which women could possess are wiped out and canceled by them."

"Certainly, friend," she replied, "just as you yourself once said regarding this question, whoever goes to court without an opponent pleads very much at his ease.[32] I assure you that women have never done what these books say. Indeed, I have not the slightest doubt that whoever cared to investigate the debate on marriage in order to write a new book in accordance with the truth would uncover other data. How many women are there actually, dear friend—and you yourself know—who because of their husbands' harshness spend their weary lives in the bond of marriage in greater suffering than if they were slaves among the Saracens? My God! How many harsh beatings—without cause and without reason—how many injuries, how many cruelties, insults, humiliations, and outrages have so many upright women suffered, none of whom cried out for help? And consider all the women who die of hunger and grief with a home full of children, while their husbands carouse dissolutely or go on binges in every tavern all over town, and still the poor women are beaten by their husbands when they return, and *that* is their supper! What do you say to that? Am I lying? Have you ever seen any of your women neighbors so decked out?"

And I said to her, "Certainly, my lady, I have seen many, and I feel very sorry for them."

"I believe you, and to say that these husbands are so unhappy with their wives' illnesses! Please, my friend, where are they? Without my having to say any more to you, you can easily see that such foolishness spoken and written against women was and is an arbitrary fabrication which flies in the face of the truth. For men are masters over their wives, and not the wives mistresses over their husbands, who would never allow their wives to have such authority. But let me hasten to assure you that not all marriages are conducted with such spite, for there are those who live together in great peacefulness, love, and loyalty because the partners are virtuous, considerate, and reasonable. And although there are bad husbands, there are also very good ones, truly valiant and wise, and the women who meet them were born in a lucky hour, as far as the glory of the world is concerned, for what God has bestowed upon them. You know this perfectly well from your own experience, for you had such a good husband that, given a choice, you could not have asked for better, whom no other man in your judgment could surpass in kindness, peacefulness, loyalty, and true love, and for whose sake the remorse over Fate's having taken him from you will never leave your heart. In spite of what I have told you — and it is true that there are many women greatly mistreated by their husbands — realize, however, that there are very different kinds of women, and some unreasonable, for if I claimed that they were all good, I could easily be proven a liar, but that is the least part. I will not meddle with evil women, for such women are like creatures alienated from their own nature.

"But to speak of good women, as for this Theophrastus, whom you have mentioned, and who says that a man can be cared for by his servant as loyally and as carefully as by his wife — ha! How many good women there are who are so conscientious in caring for their husbands, healthy or sick, with a loyal love as though their husbands were gods! I do not think that you will ever find such a servant. And since we have taken up this question, let me give you numerous examples of the great love and loyalty shown by women for their husbands. Now we have come back to our City, thank God, with all the noble company of fair and upright women whom we will lodge there. Here is the noble queen Hypsicratea,[33] long ago the wife of the rich king Mithridates. We will lodge her first of all in the noble residence and palace which has been readied for her because she is from such an ancient time and of such worthiness."

∽

Against Those Men Who Claim It Is Not Good for Women to Be Educated (II.36)

Following these remarks, I, Christine, spoke, "My lady, I realize that women have accomplished many good things and that even if evil women have done evil, it seems to me, nevertheless, that the benefits accrued and still accruing because of good women—particularly the wise and literary ones and those educated in the natural sciences whom I mentioned above—outweigh the evil. Therefore, I am amazed by the opinion of some men who claim that they do not want their daughters, wives, or kinswomen to be educated because their mores would be ruined as a result."

She responded, "Here you can clearly see that not all opinions of men are based on reason and that these men are wrong. For it must not be presumed that mores necessarily grow worse from knowing the moral sciences, which teach the virtues, indeed, there is not the slightest doubt that moral education amends and ennobles them. How could anyone think or believe that whoever follows good teaching or doctrine is the worse for it? Such an opinion cannot be expressed or maintained. I do not mean that it would be good for a man or a woman to study the art of divination or those fields of learning which are forbidden—for the holy Church did not remove them from common use without good reason—but it should not be believed that women are the worse for knowing what is good.

"Quintus Hortensius, a great rhetorician and consummately skilled orator in Rome, did not share this opinion. He had a daughter, named Hortensia, [34] whom he greatly loved for the subtlety of her wit. He had her learn letters and study the science of rhetoric, which she mastered so thoroughly that she resembled her father Hortensius not only in wit and lively memory but also in her excellent delivery and order of speech—in fact, he surpassed her in nothing. As for the subject discussed above, concerning the good which comes about through women, the benefits realized by this woman and her learning were, among others, exceptionally remarkable. That is, during the time when Rome was governed by three men, this Hortensia began to support the cause of women and to undertake what no man dared to undertake. There was a question whether certain taxes should be levied on women and on their jewelry during a needy period in Rome. This woman's eloquence was so compelling that she was listened to, no less readily than her father would have been, and she won her case.

"Similarly, to speak of more recent times, without searching for examples in ancient history, Giovanni Andrea, a solemn law professor in Bologna not quite sixty years ago, was not of the opinion that it was bad for women to be educated. He had a fair and good daughter, named Novella,[35] who was educated in the law to such an advanced degree that when he was occupied by some task and not at leisure to present his lectures to his students, he would send Novella, his daughter, in his place to lecture to the students from his chair. And to prevent her beauty from distracting the concentration of her audience, she had a little curtain drawn in front of her. In this manner she could on occasion supplement and lighten her father's occupation. He loved her so much that, to commemorate her name, he wrote a book of remarkable lectures on the law which he entitled *Novella super Decretalium,* after his daughter's name.

"Thus, not all men (and especially the wisest) share the opinion that it is bad for women to be educated. But it is very true that many foolish men have claimed this because it displeased them that women knew more than they did. Your father, who was a great scientist and philosopher, did not believe that women were worth less by knowing science; rather, as you know, he took great pleasure from seeing your inclination to learning. The feminine opinion of your mother, however, who wished to keep you busy with spinning and silly girlishness, following the common custom of women, was the major obstacle to your being more involved in the sciences. But just as the proverb already mentioned above says, 'No one can take away what Nature has given,'[36] your mother could not hinder in you the feeling for the sciences which you, through natural inclination, had nevertheless gathered together in little droplets. I am sure that, on account of these things, you do not think you are worth less but rather that you consider it a great treasure for yourself; and you doubtless have reason to."

And I, Christine, replied to all of this, "Indeed, my lady, what you say is as true as the Lord's Prayer."

∽

"Just as is written in the *Miracles de Nostre Dame,*[37] the noble Florence, empress of Rome, endured great adversity with amazing patience and greatly resembled Griselda, marquise of Saluces, in strength and constancy of character.[38] This lady was overwhelmingly beautiful and even more chaste and virtuous. Her husband once had to go off on a very long voyage to a distant war and so left the care of his land and wife to a brother of his who, tempted by the devil after the emperor's departure, foolishly desired his sister-in-law Florence. Put briefly, he imposed severe restrictions on her to compel her to do his will either out of fear or, if his entreaties were of no avail, forcibly. The lady had him imprisoned in a tower, and he remained there until the emperor's return. When the news came of the emperor's return, the lady, never imagining her brother-in-law would slander her, had him released so that the emperor would not learn of his brother's treachery and so that he could go out to meet him. But when he arrived before the emperor, he accused the lady of every possible evil, as though she were the most immoral woman ever, and he claimed she had held him in prison in order to carry out her own evil will rather than to follow the emperor's command. Believing his brother's story and without mentioning any of this, the emperor ordered his servants to kill her before he arrived, for he did not wish to see her nor find her alive. However, while astounded by these reports, she managed to beg the servants who had been commissioned to kill her to let her live incognito. Through a strange twist of fate this noble lady came to be entrusted with watching over the child of a great prince. It happened that the prince's brother was so smitten with love for her that, when she would not consent to his numerous petitions, in his spite and in order to destroy her, he killed the little child next to her while she slept. This noble lady endured with great patience and strong, unfailing courage all of these not inconsiderable adversities. After she had been led to the place where she was to be executed as the child's presumed murderer, the lord and lady were overwhelmed with such pity that, for the sake of her fair life and outstanding virtues which they had noted, they did not have the heart to put her to death and instead sent her into exile. Once, during her exile, in all her poverty, long suffering, and devotion to God and His gentle mother, she fell asleep in a garden after saying her prayers. There she beheld a vision of the Virgin who told her to pick a certain plant which grew under her head, so that she could earn her living by curing every illness with this plant.[39] After a time, thanks to this very plant, the lady, who had already healed so many illnesses, became famous everywhere. Then it happened that God willed that the prince's brother, who had killed the child, should fall ill with a most horrible sickness, and Florence was summoned to heal him. After coming into his presence, she told him that he should know that God was punishing him with His scourges and that if he publicly acknowledged his sin, then he would be cured, but otherwise she could not heal him. Then, moved by great contrition, he confessed his horrible misdeed and told how he himself had killed the child, although he had blamed the good lady who had cared for the child. The prince was furious and wanted to exact justice from his brother at all costs. The noble lady interceded and calmed the prince and cured his brother. In this way she returned good for evil to him, according to God's commandment. Likewise, not long afterward, it happened that the emperor's brother, on whose account Florence had first been exiled, fell sick with such horrible leprosy that his body was almost completely putrid. But, since the news that there was a woman who could cure every sickness had spread everywhere in the world, Florence was summoned by the emperor without his knowing who she was, for he thought that his wife was long dead. When she appeared before the emperor's brother, she told him he must confess publicly, otherwise she could not cure him. Finally, after refusing for a long time, he confessed the entire evil deed which he had without reason or cause perpetrated against the empress, and it was for this sin, he knew, that God was punishing him. Upon hearing this, the emperor flew into a rage because he thought on this account that he had had his beloved wife put to death. He wanted to kill his brother, but the good lady appeared and pacified the emperor. And so Florence regained her standing and good fortune by virtue of her patience, to the great joy of the emperor and all the people."[40]

∽

Concerning Ghismonda, Daughter of the Prince of Salerno (II.59)

"Boccaccio tells in his *Decameron*[41] that there was a prince of Salerno, named Tancredi, who had a most beautiful daughter, well-bred, wise, and courteous, named Ghismonda. This father loved his daughter with such devotion that he could not live unless he saw her, and only with the greatest reluctance and under great pressure did he consent to have her married. Nevertheless, she was given in marriage to the count of Campania, but she did not remain married for long, for this count died shortly afterward, and her father took her back into his household, intending never to let her marry again. The lady, who was the complete joy of her father's old age, was well aware of her own beauty, youth, and fine upbringing, and thought that it was not particularly pleasant to spend her youth without a husband, though she did not dare to contradict her father's will. During the time which she spent in court at her father's side, this lady happened to see a squire among the nobles at court who seemed to her more handsome than all the others — although there were a great many knights and noblemen there — and even better mannered and, in all, quite worthy of being loved. To put the matter briefly, she had studied his behavior so closely that she decided to take her pleasure in this squire in order to pass her youth more joyfully and to satisfy the gaiety of her pretty heart. Every day, even for a long time before she revealed her love, while she sat at the table she watched the behavior and deportment of this young man who was named Guiscardo. The more attention she paid to him, the more he seemed to her from day to day to be perfect in everything. For this reason, after having observed him a great deal, she summoned him one day and said to him: [42] 'Guiscardo, dear friend, my trust in your goodness and loyalty and integrity moves me and urges me to reveal myself to you regarding several extremely secret matters which concern me and which I would not tell any other. But before I tell you, I want your pledge that they will never be revealed or made known by you.' Guiscardo replied, 'My lady, you must not be afraid that I will ever reveal anything you tell me.' Thereupon Ghismonda said to him, 'Guiscardo, I want you to know that my pleasure lies in a noble man whom I love and wish to love. And because I cannot speak to him, nor do I have anyone who could convey my wishes, I want you to be the messenger for our love. You see, Guiscardo, I trust you so much more than any other that I wish to place my honor in your hands.' Then he knelt down and said, 'My lady, I know that you possess so much good sense and valiance that you would never do anything unseemly; therefore I thank you most humbly for having so much confidence in me, more than in anyone else, that you wish to reveal to me your secret thoughts. So, my dear lady, without having the slightest fear, you may command me to carry out all your good pleasures, as you would command someone who had offered body and soul to obey all your commands to the best of his ability. Moreover, I offer myself as the most humble servant to whomever is so lucky to possess the love of a lady so worthy as you, for truly, he has not been without a lofty and most noble love.' When Ghismonda, who had wanted to test Guiscardo, heard him speak so wisely, she took him by the hand and said to him, 'Guiscardo, my love, you are the one whom I have chosen for my only love and in whom I wish to take all my pleasure, for it seems to me that the nobility of your heart and the good manners with which you are filled make you worthy of such a lofty love.' The young man rejoiced at this and humbly thanked her. And, put briefly, their love flourished for a long time, unknown to all. But Fortune, jealous of their happiness, did not want the two lovers to live in joy and so changed their happiness into the most bitter sorrow. By extraordinary chance one summer day it happened that, while Ghismonda was relaxing in the garden with her maids, her father—whose only wealth was in seeing her—went all alone to her bedroom to chat with her and to relax in her company. But finding the windows closed, the bed-curtains drawn, and not a soul there, he thought she was taking a nap. Not wanting to awaken her he lay down on a couch and fell sound asleep. Ghismonda, thinking she had been in the garden long enough, retired to her bedroom, lay down on her bed as if to sleep, and had her maids leave. She shut the door without noticing her sleeping father. When she saw she was alone, she got up and went to look for Guiscardo, who was hiding in one of her closets, and she led him to her bedroom. While they were speaking with one another behind the bed curtains like a couple who believed they were alone, the prince woke up and heard a man speaking with his daughter. He suffered such enormous grief over this that the consideration that he might be dishonoring his daughter barely prevented him from rushing upon the stranger. Nevertheless, he kept himself under control and listened carefully for who it was. Then he managed to slip out of the bedroom without being heard. After the two lovers had been together for a while, Guiscardo left. But the prince, who had prepared an ambush for him, had him captured and imprisoned immediately. He then went to his daughter and, speaking alone to her in her bedroom with a sad face and tear-filled eyes, he said:

" 'Ghismonda, I used to think that I had in you a daughter more beautiful, chaste, and wise than all other women, but now I am more convinced of the opposite in my anger than I would be if I had thought the contrary in spite of myself—for if I had not seen it with my own eyes, there would have been nothing that could make me believe that you could be seduced by the love of any man unless he were your husband. What aggravates my anger even more is that I believed you had the noblest heart of any woman ever born. And I see that the contrary is true because you were taken with one of the lowliest members of my household. For, if you wanted to do such a thing, you could have found in my court an overabundance of nobler men, without having to be smitten with Guiscardo, who, I think, will pay dearly for the grief which I have suffered on his account. I want you to know that I will put him to death and I would do the same to you if I could undo the foolish love I have for you in my heart, a far greater love than any other father ever had for his daughter, which keeps me from doing this.'

"No one need wonder whether Ghismonda was grief-stricken when she realized that her father knew about the one thing she had most wanted to hide, and yet, above all, the greatest grief wrung her heart because he threatened to kill the one man whom she loved so much. She wanted to die at that very moment, but with an unwavering heart and composed countenance and without shedding a tear—although she had prepared herself to die—she replied, 'Father, since Fortune has consented that you discover what I had so wished to keep secret, I do not need to make any request of you, except that, if I intended to beg for your forgiveness and for the life of the man whom you threaten to kill by offering myself in his place, I would beg you to take my life and spare his. And as for my asking pardon from you, in case you do with him what you say, I will not ask for pardon, for I do not wish to live any longer; I assure you that with his death you end my life. And concerning the cause of your anger against us, you have only yourself to blame, for you are a creature of the flesh and did you ever stop to think that you fathered a daughter from the flesh and not from stone or iron? You should remember, even though you have grown old, what terrible ennui afflicts youth living in luxury and ease and what pricks of temptation must be overcome. Since I saw you had decided never to let me marry again, and feeling young and urged on by my own prettiness, I fell in love with this young man, and not without discussion or long deliberation I granted to my heart what it desired. First I observed his behavior—more perfect in every virtue than any other in your court. This you should realize yourself, for you brought him up. And what is nobility except virtue? It never comes from flesh or blood.[43] Therefore you have no right to say that I was taken in by the least noble of your court, and you have no cause for the great anger which you have expressed against us, considering your own fault. But, most of all, if you wish to exact punishment for this deed, it is not right to take it out on his person, for that would be wrong and sinful. Rather, it would be more fitting that I be punished, for I urged him on to this deed which he himself did not think of at all. What was he supposed to do? Indeed, he would have had a base heart to refuse a lady of such high standing. So you must forgive him this misdeed but not me.' The prince immediately took leave of Ghismonda but was not in the least pacified toward Guiscardo because of this, and on the following day had him killed and ordered his heart torn out of his body. The father placed Guiscardo's heart in a gold goblet and had one of his secret messengers take it to his daughter and inform her that he was sending her this present to give her joy in the one thing which she loved most, just as she had made him joyful in the one thing he had held most dear. The messenger came to Ghismonda, presented his gift, and said what he had been charged. She took the goblet, opened it, and immediately realized what had been done. But in spite of the inestimable grief she felt, nothing could shake her lofty heart and she replied without any change of expression, 'My friend, tell the prince that I perceive that he is wise in one matter, that is, he has given such a noble heart a fitting sepulcher, for it ought not to have any but of gold and precious stones.' Then she leaned over the goblet and kissed the heart, saying piteously, 'Oh most sweet heart, vessel of all my pleasure, cursed be the cruelty of him who has shown you to my eyes, you who were always visible to my mind's eye. Now, through a bizarre turn of events, you have passed the course of your noble life. Yet in spite of such misfortune you have received from your own enemy a sepulcher worthy of your merit. Thus it is most fitting, my sweet heart, that for the last rites you be bathed and washed in the tears of her whom you loved so much, for you will never beat again. Besides, your soul will not be bereft of hers, since that would not be right, for she will shortly join you. And yet, in spite of this treacherous Fortune, which has harmed you so much, it has still turned out well for you, insofar as my cruel father sent you to me so that you could be honored all the more and so that I could speak to you before I leave this world and so that my soul could go with yours whose company I desire, for I know that your spirit is asking and longing for mine.' Ghismonda spoke these words and many others as well, so pitiful that no one who heard her could not collapse in tears. She wept so much that it seemed as if she had two fountains in her head which poured without stop into this goblet. She made no uproar or cry, but with a low voice kept kissing the heart. The ladies and maids who stood around her were quite amazed at this, for they knew nothing of what had happened nor the possible cause of her sorrow; they wept out of pity for their mistress and tried to comfort her, but nothing was of any use. Her intimates could only ask in vain about the cause of her sorrow. After Ghismonda, overcome with incredible grief, had wept for a long time, she said, 'Oh most beloved heart, I have carried out my duties on your behalf, nothing remains but to send my soul to keep your soul company.' Having said these words, she stood up, went to open a cupboard, and removed a small flask where she had placed poisonous herbs in water to dissolve to be ready should need ever arise. She poured this water into the goblet containing the heart and, without the slightest fear, drank it all. She lay down on her bed to wait for death, still clutching the goblet tightly in her arms. When her maids saw her body change with the signs of death, in their terrible grief they summoned the father, who had gone out to amuse himself in order to forget his melancholy. The poison had already spread through her veins by this time. Filled with grief for what had happened and remorse for what he had done, he began to speak to her sweetly, mourning greatly, and he thought he was comforting her. His daughter, speaking as best as she could, replied, 'Tancredi, save your tears for something else, for they have no place here, nor do I desire or want them. You are like the serpent which kills a man and then weeps for him. Would it not have been better for your daughter to have lived as she pleased, secretly loving a good man, than to watch such a horrible death—to your own grief but caused by your own cruelty—a death which makes what had been secret public knowledge.' With that she could speak no more; her heart burst as she held the goblet. And the poor man of a father died of grief.[44] So died Ghismonda, daughter of the prince of Salerno."

∞

Justice Speaks of Many Noble Women Who Waited on and Lodged the Apostles and Other Saints (III.18)

"What more do you want me to tell you, my fair friend, Christine? I could recall other similar examples to you without stop. But because

I see that you are surprised—for you said earlier, that every classical author attacked women [45]—I tell you that, in spite of what you may have found in the writings of pagan authors on the subject of criticizing women, you will find little said against them in the holy legends of Jesus Christ and His Apostles; instead, even in the histories of all the saints, just as you can see yourself, you will find through God's grace many cases of extraordinary firmness and strength in women. [46] Oh, the beautiful service, the outstanding charity which they have performed with great care and solicitude, unflinchingly, for the servants of God! Should not such hospitality and favors be considered? And even if some foolish men deem them frivolous, no one can deny that such works in accordance with our Faith are the ladders leading to Heaven. So it is written regarding Drusiana, [47] an honest widow who received Saint John the Evangelist in her home and waited on him and served him meals. It happened when this same Saint John returned from exile that the city dwellers held a large feast for him just as Drusiana was being led to burial, for she had died from grief over his long absence. And the neighbors said, 'John, here is Drusiana, your good hostess, who died from sorrow at your absence. She will never wait on you again.' Whereupon Saint John addressed her, 'Drusiana, get up and go home and prepare my meal for me.' And she came back to life.

"Likewise, a valiant and noble lady from the city of Limoges, named Susanna, was the first to give lodging to Saint Martial, who had been sent there by Saint Peter in order to convert the country. And this lady did many good things for him.

"Similarly, the good lady Maximilla removed Saint Andrew from the cross and buried him and in so doing risked death.

"The holy virgin Ephigenia in like manner followed Saint Matthew the Evangelist with great devotion and waited upon him. And after his death she had a church built in his honor.

"Similarly, another good lady was so taken with holy love for Saint Paul that she followed him everywhere and served him diligently.

"Likewise, during the time of the Apostles, a noble queen named Helen (not the mother of Constantine but the queen of Adiabene, in Assyria) went to Jerusalem, where there was a terrible shortage of foodstuffs because of the famine there. And when she learned that the saints of our Lord, who were in the city to preach to the people and to convert them, were dying of hunger, she had enough food purchased to provide them food as long as the famine lasted.

"Similarly, when Saint Paul was led to be beheaded at Nero's command, a good lady named Plautilla, who had customarily waited on him, walked ahead of him, weeping profoundly. And Saint Paul asked her for the scarf which she had on her head. And she gave it to him, whereupon the evil men who were there taunted her, saying that it was a fine thing for her to forfeit such a beautiful scarf. Saint Paul himself tied it around his eyes, and when he was dead, the angels gave it back to the woman, and it was completely smeared with blood, for which she cherished it dearly. And Saint Paul appeared to her and told her that because she had served him on Earth, he would serve her in Heaven by praying for her. I will tell you many more similar cases.

"Basilissa[48] was a noble lady by virtue of her chastity. She was married to Saint Julian, and both of them took a vow of virginity on their wedding night. No one could conceive of the holy way of life of this virgin, nor the multitude of women and maidens who were saved and drawn to a holy life through her sacred preaching. And, in short, she was so deserving of grace because of her great chastity that our Lord spoke to her as she was dying.

"I do not know what more I could tell you, Christine, my friend. I could tell of countless ladies of different social backgrounds, maidens, married women, and widows, in whom God manifested His virtues with amazing force and constancy. But let this suffice for you, for it seems to me that I have acquitted myself well of my office in completing the high roofs of your City and in populating it for you with outstanding ladies, just as I promised. These last examples will serve as the doorways and gates into our City. And even though I have not named all the holy ladies who have lived, who are living, and who will live—for I could name only a handful!—they can all be included in this City of Ladies. Of it may be said, 'Gloriosa dicta sunt de te, civitas Dei.'[49] So I turn it over to you, finished perfectly and well enclosed, just as I promised. Farewell and may the peace of the Lord be always with you."[50]

The End of the Book: Christine Addresses the Ladies (III.19)[51]

My most honored ladies, may God be praised, for now our City is entirely finished and completed, where all of you who love glory, virtue, and praise may be lodged in great honor, ladies from the past as well as from the present and future, for it has been built and established for every honorable lady. And my most dear ladies, it is natural for the human heart to rejoice when it finds itself victorious in any enterprise and its enemies confounded. Therefore you are right, my ladies, to rejoice greatly in God and in honest mores upon seeing this new City completed, which can be not only the refuge for you all, that is, for virtuous women, but also the defense and guard against your enemies and assailants, if you guard it well. For you can see that the substance with which it is made is entirely of virtue, so resplendent that you may see yourselves mirrored in it, especially in the roofs built in the last part as well as in the other parts which concern you. And my dear ladies, do not misuse this new inheritance like the arrogant who turn proud when their prosperity grows and their wealth multiplies, but rather follow the example of your Queen, the sovereign Virgin, who, after the extraordinary honor of being chosen Mother of the Son of God was announced to her, humbled herself all the more by calling herself the handmaiden of God. Thus, my ladies, just as it is true that a creature's humility and kindness wax with the increase of its virtues, may this City be an occasion for you to conduct yourselves honestly and with integrity and to be all the more virtuous and humble.

And you ladies who are married, do not scorn being subject to your husbands, for sometimes it is not the best thing for a creature to be independent. This is attested by what the angel said to Ezra:[52] Those, he said, who take advantage of their free will can fall into sin and despise our Lord and deceive the just, and for this they perish. Those women with peaceful, good, and discreet husbands who are devoted to them, praise God for this boon, which is not inconsiderable, for a greater boon in the world could not be given them. And may they be diligent in serving, loving, and cherishing their husbands in the loyalty of their heart, as they should, keeping their peace and praying to God to uphold and save them. And those women who have husbands neither completely good nor completely bad should still praise God for not having the worst and should strive to moderate their vices and pacify them, according to their conditions. And those women who have husbands who are cruel, mean, and savage should strive to endure them while trying to overcome their vices and lead them back, if they can, to a reasonable and seemly life. And if they are so obstinate that their wives are unable to do anything, at least they will acquire great merit for their souls through the virtue of patience. And everyone will bless them and support them.

So, my ladies, be humble and patient, and God's grace will grow in you, and praise will be given to you as well as the Kingdom of Heaven. For Saint Gregory[53] has said that patience is the entrance to Paradise and the way of Jesus Christ. And may none of you be forced into holding frivolous opinions nor be hardened in them, lacking all basis in reason, nor be jealous or disturbed in mind, nor haughty in speech, nor outrageous in your acts, for these things disturb the mind and lead to madness. Such behavior is unbecoming and unfitting for women.

And you, virgin maidens, be pure, simple, and serene, without vagueness, for the snares of evil men are set for you. Keep your eyes lowered, with few words in your mouths, and act respectfully. Be armed with the strength of virtue against the tricks of the deceptive and avoid their company.

And widows, may there be integrity in your dress, conduct, and speech; piety in your deeds and way of life; prudence in your bearing; patience (so necessary!), strength, and resistance in tribulations and difficult affairs; humility in your heart, countenance, and speech; and charity in your works.

In brief, all women—whether noble, bourgeois, or lower-class—be well-informed in all things and cautious in defending your honor and chastity against your enemies! My ladies, see how these men accuse you of so many vices in everything. Make liars of them all by showing forth your virtue, and prove their attacks false by acting well, so that you can say with the Psalmist, "the vices of the evil will fall on their heads."[54] Repel the deceptive flatterers who, using different charms, seek with various tricks to steal that which you must consummately guard, that is, your honor and the beauty of your praise. Oh my ladies, flee, flee the foolish love they urge on you! Flee it, for God's sake, flee! For no good can come to you from it.[55] Rather, rest assured that however deceptive their lures, their end is always to your detriment. And do not believe the contrary, for it cannot be otherwise. Remember, dear ladies, how these men call you frail, unserious, and easily influenced but yet try hard, using all kinds of strange and deceptive tricks, to catch you, just as one lays traps for wild animals. Flee, flee, my ladies, and avoid their company—under these smiles are hidden deadly and painful poisons. And so may it please you, my most respected ladies, to cultivate virtue, to flee vice, to increase and multiply our City, and to rejoice and act well. And may I, your servant, commend myself to you, praying to God who by His grace has granted me to live in this world and to persevere in His holy service. May He

in the end have mercy on my great sins and grant to me the joy
which lasts forever, which I may, by His grace, afford to you.
Amen.

Here Ends the Third and Last Part of the Book of the City of Ladies.

Earl Jeffrey Richards

(Translated from Brit. Lib. Harley Ms. 4431)

N O T E S

1. Mathéolus wrote his *Lamentation* at the end of the thirteenth century. For him,
    marriage was merely a trial to make a man worthy of Paradise, since women existed
    only to make men suffer. The original Latin text was translated into French around
    1370 by Jean LeFèvre des Ressons, a professional translator who was moved to
    refute Mathéolus in a *Livre de Leesce* (*A Book of Pleasure*). It was presumably the
    translation of Mathéolus that Christine had in her study. Its popularity in her day
    is attested to by references in the contemporary *Quinze Joies de Mariage* (*The Fifteen
    Joys of Marriage*), noted for its satire of marriage. See A. G. Van Hamel, ed., *Les
    Lamentations de Mathéolus et le Livre de Leesce de Jean LeFèvre des Ressons*, 2 vols. (Paris,
    1905).
2. It is important to recognize the satiric intent of this passage. There is no real
    evidence from any of Christine's writings that she seriously regretted not being a
    man, and the whole point of *The Book of the City of Ladies* is to show women that
    they have no real reason for any such regret.
3. The medieval attitude towards women to which Christine is referring is well
    summarized in the section entitled "Les Normes de Contrôle" in the *Histoire des
    Femmes en Occident*, II: *Le Moyen Age*, edited by Christiane Klapisch-Zuber (Paris,
    1990), pp. 31–168. See also Glenda McLeod's *Virtue and Venom: Catalogues of Women
    from Antiquity to the Renaissance* (Ann Arbor, 1991).
4. As Glenda McLeod has pointed out (pp. 120–21), these three ladies, sent by God,
    represent the inner character of the narrator Christine, who would not only make
    use of her own experience and personal judgment in opposing misogyny, but also
    the authority of Christian texts as well as the pagan texts to be found in her
    principal source, Boccaccio's *De Mulieribus Claris*.
5. In writing her biography of Charles V, as well as her *Vision*, Christine had made
    use of a commentary on Aristotle's *Metaphysics* by Saint Thomas Aquinas. As no
    known translation of this text existed at the time, it must be assumed that Christine
    was able to read the original Latin. See Pinet, pp. 383–84 and 422 and *Fais et Bonnes
    Meurs*, Solente ed. I, p. 1xvii.
6. These three Virtues are secular in concept, and so quite different from the tradi-
    tional Theological Virtues (Faith, Hope, and Charity) and with only a slight
    resemblance to the Cardinal Virtues (Prudence, Magnanimity, Fortitude, and
    Justice). As the mirror Reason carries is intended to show, those who look into it
    are able to see their true selves. This was probably inspired by Vincent of Beauvais
    who, in his *Historical Mirror*, recommended holding the mirror up to nature, long
    before the idea was popularized by the theater of Molière.

7. As Richards suggests in his translation of the complete text (p. 260) the appearance of these three ladies recalls the opening of Dante's *Divine Comedy,* where "three blessed ladies" appear (*Inferno* 2.124). As has been noted, Christine had already been inspired by Dante at the beginning of *The Long Road to Learning.*

8. A detailed and interesting interpretation of these first chapters is provided by Maureen Quilligan, *The Allegory of Female Authority: Christine de Pizan's Cité des Dames* (Ithaca, N.Y., 1991), pp. 45–68.

9. Christine had already written of the founding of Troy in *The Mutation of Fortune* (Solente ed. III, p. 25ff.). Her sources were the compilation of ancient history known as the *Histoire ancienne jusqu'à Cesar* (B.N. ms. fr. 301) and the *Historical Mirror* of Vincent de Beauvais.

10. Christine had already referred to Cadmus as the founder of Thebes in *The Letter of Othea* (XXVIII). Her source here could have been either Ovid or the compilation of ancient history.

11. The Amazon kingdom had already been mentioned in *The Mutation of Fortune* (Solente ed. III, pp. 141 ff.) She would develop the history of the Amazons in greater detail in *The Book of the City of Ladies,* Book I, chapters 16–19. For an interesting modern discussion of the Amazons, see Elizabeth Constantinides, "Amazons and Other Female Warriors," in *The Classical Outlook* (October–November, 1988), 3–6.

12. Rectitude had made an earlier appearance in Philippe de Mézières' *Songe du Vieil Pèlerin* (Dream of the Old Pilgrim) written in 1387. Christine presumably knew Philippe de Mézière personally for after the death of her husband she sold him some family property.

13. Justice, one of the traditional Cardinal Virtues, was usually represented carrying a sword, or scales, or sometimes both. Christine's representation of Justice here is not, however, entirely new, for in *The Letter of Othea to Hector,* she is presented as receiving her measuring vessel from God. The accompanying gloss quotes Aristotle as saying that "Justice is a measure established by God to limit all things." Curt Bühler, in his edition of Stephen Scrope's English translation of this work, thinks that her source for this was a compilation entitled *Les Fleurs de Toutes Vertus* (Flowers of All the Virtues). See his article, "The *Fleurs de Toutes Vertus* and Christine de Pisan's *L'Epître d'Othéa,*" PMLA 62 (1947), 32–44.

14. In another of her favorite sources, the *Manipulus Florum,* Christine would have found this line attributed to Tullius (Cicero) in his *De Officiis:* "Tullius says that Justice is the mother and leader of all other Virtues; nothing can endure in the world without Justice."

15. Christine is recalling here a passage in Vincent of Beauvais's *Speculum Historiale,* X, chap. 65.

16. Christine's acceptance of the task laid upon her recalls Mary's response in the Annunciation. It is, of course, the three superhuman ladies, of whom Christine is merely the willing servant, who provide eternal authority for her book.

17. Proverbs 27:21.

18. This first basketful of dirt is clearly a reference to the examples of misogynistic writing that will be the subject of the following passage.

19. This would appear to be a correction of what is said about Dame Nature in *The Romance of the Rose.*

20. Undoubtedly a reference to *The Letter of the God of Love* and also to Christine's letter to Jean de Montreuil in the Rose debate. See Hicks, pp. 18 and 232.

21. As Richards points out (p. 260), Christine is taking exception to the representation of Reason by Jean de Meun in *The Romance of the Rose.*

22. Minerva was one of Christine's favorite figures. She appears in *The Letter of Othea, The Long Road to Learning, The Mutation of Fortune,* and *The Deeds of Arms and of Chivalry.* In *The Long Road to Learning* she indicates that her source for her knowledge of Minerva is the *Moralized Ovid,* as she explains when she first encounters the Sibyl who will be her guide:

> That lady . . . made me here recall
> The goddess of such great knowing
> Of whom Ovid is one showing
> That Pallas she is often named,
> For whom great knowledge can be claimed.
> (vv. 475–80)

In *The Deeds of Arms and of Chivalry,* however, she cites Boccaccio as her source for information about Minerva, and elsewhere she included details from the *Ancient History.* As P.G.C. Campbell points out (p. 151), this goddess provides a clue to the complexity of Christine's sources.

23. Although Boccaccio mentions most of the attributes associated with Minerva by Christine, he ends the chapter he devotes to the goddess by saying: "There are, however, some very serious men who assert that the things mentioned were not done by one Minerva, but by many. I shall gladly agree with them so that there may be a number of famous women." (*Concerning Famous Women,* p. 15). In the *Genealogy of the Gods,* Boccaccio does indeed refer to several Minervas.

24. Prudence, according to the *Manipulus Florums,* is as follows: "Prudence, discretion with wisdom, is in three manners, according to Tullius. The first is memory, which is to say, of things past; the second is recognizing good from evil by reason, and truth from falsehood; the third is foresight as in foreseeing for future time what man should do." See the *Livre de Prudence,* (B.N. Ms. fr. 605 fol. 20v⁰–21r⁰), the *Livre de la Paix,* ed. Willard, p. 66, and the *Epistre de la prison de vie humaine,* ed. A. J. Kennedy (Glasgow, 1984), pp. 34–35.

25. Book of Solomon, 31:10–13.

26. Education of young women is an important aspect of Christine's next work, *The Treasury of the City of Ladies.*

27. This is interesting evidence of Christine's knowledge of the writings of Petrarch, who lived in Venice at the same time as Christine's father and around the time of Christine's birth there. It was Petrarch's version of the Griselda story that Christine used in *The Book of the City of Ladies,* although she probably knew it through its retelling by Philippe de Mézières. Here, however, she appears to be referring to Petrarch's *Remedies for Fortune* as translated for Charles V's library by Jean Daudin.

28. Christine is speaking from her own experience here, for it was she who looked after her mother in old age after her two brothers went back to Italy to claim family property there.

29. The queen who would eventually preside over the city was, of course, the Virgin Mary, who is introduced at the beginning of Book III.

30. Christine undoubtedly had in mind here such books as the satirical *Fifteen Joys of Marriage* and Eustache Deschamp's *Mirror of Marriage,* both of which had been written shortly before this. See C. C. Willard, "Women and Marriage around 1400: Three Views," *Fifteenth Century Studies* 7 (1990), 475–84.

31. The letter of Valerius to Rufinus refers to Walter Map's *Dissuasio Valerii ad Rufinum de non ducat uxorum* (The Dissuasion of Valerius to Rufinus against taking a wife), c. 1190). See Walter Map, *De Nugis Curialum* (Oxford, 1983) and G. McLeod, *Virtue and Venom,* pp. 48–50. This medieval bestseller is referred to in the Prologue to the *Fifteen Joys of Marriage.* Theophrastus was the source of many

popular misogynistic attitudes. His *Aureolus* was known to medieval readers primarily through Saint Jerome's *Adversus Jovanianum,* also a treatise against matrimony.

32. Christine had written in *The Letter of the God of Love:*

> To this I say that books were not composed
> By women, nor did they record the things
> That we may read against them and their ways
> Yet men write on, quite to their heart's content,
> The ones who plead their case without debate.
> They give no quarter, take the winner's part
> Themselves, for readily do quarrelers
> Attack those who don't defend themselves.
> (Fenster trans., vv. 408–416, p. 55)

33. The following chapter is devoted to Hypsicratea as a model of wifely devotion, even following her husband to his wars. Although Christine's source is Boccaccio, she omits certain details in her account of the queen: that her husband, Mithridates, was polygamous and that he eventually poisoned her, so that she would not outlive him. Christine thus presents him as a much more worthy and appreciative husband than does Boccaccio.

34. Hortensia comes from Boccaccio's *Concerning Famous Women,* chapter 82.

35. Novella was the daughter of Giovanni Andrea, a Bolognese professor who must have been known to Christine's father during the years he was a student and teacher there. In *The Deeds of Arms and of Chivalry,* parts III and IV, Christine made use of the *Tractatus de Bello* of John of Legnano, who had married into this same family, so all of this must have been known to Christine directly.

36. This proverb had already been quoted by Christine in *The Book of the City of Ladies* (I.10). Christine frequently repeated herself in citing proverbs she admired.

37. This story was known throughout Europe during the Middle Ages in several versions with slightly differing details. Although Christine cites as her source a collection of *Miracles of Nostre Dame,* possibly the one by Gautier de Coincy (ed. V. F. Koenig, Geneva-Lille, 1955), she would have found the same version in one of her other favorite sources, the *Historical Mirror* of Vincent of Beauvais. The story was dramatized at the end of the fourteenth or beginning of the fifteenth century. See *Florence de Rome, chanson d'aventure du premier quart du XIIIe siècle,* ed. A. Wollen-sköld (Paris, 1909), pp. 105–29.

38. The story of Griselda immediately precedes this one. It was undoubtedly a conscious aspect of Christine's refutation of misogynistic literature that she made use of such widely popular tales for her own purposes.

39. The Virgin appears in only one version to explain Florence's discovery of the miraculous plant.

40. In other versions of the story Florence retires to a convent after curing the wicked brother and exonerating herself. Christine preferred this more worldly solution to the story.

41. This tale as well as the one of Florence of Rome calls attention to the variety of Christine's sources. This is one of three tales taken from Boccaccio's *Decameron* which, it should be noted, had not yet been translated into French. Christine, as was her custom, did not hesitate to modify her source somewhat. In this case she centers the story on the daughter, whereas in the original, the major attention is given to the father. Here it is introduced as an example of fidelity in love.

42. It has been pointed out that Christine introduced this conversation into this version of the story to idealize the situation and relate it more closely to the traditions of courtly literature. See Carla Bozzolo, "Il 'Decameron' come fonte del 'Livre de la

Cité des Dames' di Christine de Pizan," in *Miscellanea di Studi e Recerche sul Quattrocento Francese*, ed. Franco Simone (Turin, 1967), pp. 8–9.

43. It is noteworthy that Christine repeats Boccaccio's idea that nobility is more dependent on virtue than on birth, a rather advanced idea at the French court in the early years of the fifteenth century.

44. Whereas in Boccaccio's original version the father, repenting his cruelty, has a fine tomb built for the lovers, Christine chooses to have him die of grief.

45. In speaking of the attacks of classical authors, Christine is perhaps calling attention to the difference between her intent and Boccaccio's, which tells the stories only of pagan women. She has just devoted the third part of her book to tales of saints.

46. As Glenda McLeod points out (p. 133) the emphasis has not been on the saints' ascent to Heaven but on their resistance to oppression on Earth.

47. The source for these examples, as it was for the saints' tales, is Vincent of Beauvais's *Historical Mirror*. The examples of Christian women come from books IX and X.

48. It is undoubtedly significant that this last example is of a woman priest, the ecclesiastical counterpart of the pagan women rulers, who appear at the beginning of the first part, and to the Virgin Mary, who opens Book III. (McLeod, p. 134). Perhaps Christine's choice of Vincent of Beauvais as the source for her saints' legends stems from her desire to make this very contrast. The source for the case of Basilissa is XIII, chapters 106–108.

49. Psalms 86: 3. This is also quoted in *The Letter of Othea* (LXXXVI—Allegory) and in the dedication of *The Book of Peace* to the dauphin, Louis of Guyenne (Willard ed., p. 61).

50. This sentence figures in the Holy Mass, after the Confession and Absolution of Sins.

51. It is surprising that Maureen Quilligan sees this final chapter as an "advice-giving prayer" (p. 244). It would rather seem to be an admonition to Christine's contemporaries to be worthy to dwell in the City of Ladies. In doing this she suggests ideas that would be elaborated in her next work, *The Treasury of the City of Ladies*.

Her idea that women should accept and endure unpleasant situations, notably difficult marriages, is scarcely to modern tastes, but it must be remembered that during the Middle Ages women's legal situation was extremely limited. Christine's point here would seem to be that women should make every effort to avoid becoming victims of society's limitation. If the saints could endure martyrdom, earthly women should be capable of dealing with lesser problems. Since society was thought to be ordained by God, it could scarcely be expected to change radically.

52. The apocryphal Books of Ezra report a series of conversations between the prophet and an angel, but given Christine's habit of quoting from memory, it has been impossible to identify the exact quotation. It might also have come from some secondary source, such as one of the compilations of quotations of which she sometimes made use.

53. This quotation from Saint Gregory apparently comes from the *Manipulus Florum*, where he is quoted under the entry *Patience*.

54. Psalms 7:16 says of the wicked: "His mischief shall return upon his own head, and his violent dealing shall come down upon his own pate."

55. Christine returns here once more to *The Romance of the Rose*, reversing the advice of Genius to Nature as she had already done in her letter to Jean de Montreuil (see p. 158).

CCW

THE TREASURY OF
THE CITY OF LADIES

❦

*The First Chapter, Which Tells How the Virtues, by Whose
Command Christine Had Composed and Compiled the Book of the
City of Ladies, Appeared Once More and Commissioned Her to
Write this Present Book (I.1)*

After I built the City of Ladies with the aid and instruction of the three
lady Virtues: Reason, Rectitude, and Justice, as I described in my book
called *The City of Ladies,* I was worn out by that strenuous labor. My
body was exhausted by such long and sustained effort, and I was
resting, idly, when suddenly the three radiant creatures appeared to
me once more, saying: "Studious daughter! Have you spurned and
silenced the instrument of your intellect? Have you let your pen and
ink dry out? Have you given up the labor of your hand which usually
delights you? Are you willing to listen to the seductive song which
Idleness sings to you? Surely you will hear it if you are willing to
listen: 'You have done enough; you have earned your time for rest.'
But remember what Seneca says: 'Although the wise one's intellect
deserves repose after great effort, still a good mind should not neglect
further good work.'[1] Do not be distracted in the middle of your long
journey! Shame on the knight who leaves the battle before victory!
Only those who persist deserve the laurel crown. Now up, up! Lend
a hand! Get ready! Stop crouching on this dustheap of fatigue! Obey
our words, and your work will prosper.

"We are not fully satisfied with your labors as our handmaiden in
the furthering of our grand scheme. Therefore, we deliberated and
decided in the Council of Virtues to follow God's example: At the
beginning of the world, God saw that His work was good, blessed it,
and then went on to create man, woman, and the animals. So may our
preceding work, *The City of Ladies,* which is fine and useful, not only

be blessed and praised throughout the world—but now may it grow further. Just as the wise birdman prepared his cage before trying to catch birds,[2] we have prepared the bower of ladies. Now, with your help, we will devise and fabricate benevolent snares tied with knots of love to cover the ground where honored ladies and all sorts of women will walk. Even the shy and unwilling will be caught in our nets. None will be able to resist or escape, and all will be taken within the beneficent boundaries of our glorious city. They will learn to sing the sweet song that those who live there already sing in splendor, perpetually chanting *Alleluia* with the blessed angels."

Hearing those harmonious voices, I, Christine, began to tremble with joy. Kneeling before the three, I vowed to carry out their desires. So, they commanded me: "Take up your pen and write. Blessed be those who will inhabit our city and swell the number of its virtuous citizens. May all of this College of Women[3] learn Wisdom's lesson. Our first students must be those whose royal or noble blood raises them above others in this world. Inevitably, the women, as well as the men, whom God establishes in the high seats of power and domination must be better educated than others. Their reputations will lead to great worthiness in themselves and in others. They are the mirror and example of virtue for their subjects and companions. The first lesson, therefore, will be directed at them—the queens, princesses, and other great ladies. Then, step by step, we will begin to set forth our doctrine for women of the lower degrees, so that the discipline of our College may be useful to all."

∽

Wherein It Is Explained How the Good and Wise Princess Will Attempt to Make Peace Between the Prince and His Barons if There Is Any Difficulty Between Them (I.9)[4]

If any neighboring or foreign prince wars for any grievance against her lord, or if her lord wages war against another, the good lady will weigh the odds carefully. She will balance the great ills, infinite cruelties, losses, deaths, and destruction to property and people against the war's outcome, which is usually unpredictable. She will seriously consider whether she can preserve the honor of her lord and yet prevent the war. Working wisely and calling on God's aid, she will strive to maintain peace. So also, if any prince of the realm or the country, or any baron, knight, or powerful subject should hold a grudge against her lord, or if he is involved in any such quarrel and she foresees that for her lord to take a prisoner or make a battle would lead to trouble in the land, she will strive toward peace. In France the discontent of an insignificant baron (named Bouchard) against the King of France, the great prince, has recently resulted in great trouble and damage to the kingdom.[5] The *Chronicles of France* recount the tale of many such misadventures. Again, not long ago, in the case of Lord Robert of Artois,[6] a disagreement with the king harmed the French realm and gave comfort to the English.

Mindful of such terrible possibilities, the good lady will strive to avoid destruction of her people, making peace and urging her lord (the prince) and his council to consider the potential harm inherent in any martial adventure. Furthermore, she must remind him that every good prince should avoid shedding blood, especially that of his subjects. Since making a new war is a grave matter, only long thought and mature deliberation will devise the better way toward the desired result. Thus, always saving both her own honor and her lord's, the good lady will not rest until she has spoken, or has had someone else speak to those who have committed the misdeed in question, alternately soothing and reproving them. While their error is great and the prince's displeasure reasonable, and though he ought to punish them, she would always prefer peace. Therefore, if they would be willing to correct their ways or make suitable amends, she gladly would try to restore them to her lord's good graces.

With such words as these, the good princess will be peacemaker. In such manner, Good Queen Blanche,[7] mother of Saint Louis, always strove to reconcile the king with his barons, and, among others, the Count of Champagne.[8] The proper role of a good, wise queen or princess is to maintain peace and concord and to avoid wars and their resulting disasters. Women particularly should concern themselves with peace because men by nature are more foolhardy and headstrong, and their overwhelming desire to avenge themselves prevents them from foreseeing the resulting dangers and terrors of war. But woman by nature is more gentle and circumspect. Therefore, if she has sufficient will and wisdom she can provide the best possible means to pacify man. Solomon speaks of peace in the twenty-fifth chapter of the *Book of Proverbs*. Gentleness and humility assuage the prince. The gentle tongue (which means the soft word) bends and breaks harshness. So water extinguishes fire's heat by its moisture and chill.[9]

Queens and princesses have greatly benefitted this world by bringing about peace between enemies, between princes and their barons, or between rebellious subjects and their lords. The Scriptures are full of examples. The world has no greater benevolence than a good and wise princess. Fortunate is that land which has one. I have listed as examples many of these wondrous women in *The Book of the City of Ladies.*[10]

What results from the presence of such a princess? All her subjects who recognize her wisdom and kindness come to her for refuge, not only as their mistress but almost as the goddess on earth in whom they have infinite hope and confidence. Keeping the land in peace and tranquility, she and her works radiate charity.

⊚

Wherein It Speaks of the Supervision Which Should Be Provided for the Newly Married Young Princess (I.24)[11]

Earlier I explained how the wise princess will arrange for her daughter's instruction during infancy and childhood. Now we can proceed to consider arrangements suitable for a young princess who wants to live properly after she has married, away from her parents' protection.[12] A young, newly married princess ought to have her own household of men and women organized in the manner appropriate to the importance of the lord or prince she has married. Those selected for her service will be gentlemen who are not too young, nor too talkative, nor too handsome; rather, they should be wise, discreet, and virtuous. If they are married, so much the better, especially those who will serve her at table and be around her and her servingwomen most frequently. And if it can be arranged, it is useful for their wives also to live at court.

Her major-domos particularly should be mature, experienced men. To teach and train the young princess the better for the salvation of her soul and her conscience, a good priest ought to be appointed for her, one knowledgeable in theology, prudent in habits, and inherently dependable in judgment—in short, an admirable man of impeccable character. Her servingwomen properly should include both older and younger women. Before they are appointed it is essential that they prove themselves suitable in judgment, background, and style of life. More attention must be given to their character than would be necessary for women selected for the household of an older princess. For, despite the fact that women attendants should be virtuous in any court, nevertheless, inappropriate courtiers chosen for a young princess would place her in greater peril than they would an older woman. Two reasons for this are significant. First, the standard of behavior observed by a household commonly leads to a judgment concerning the character and condition of the lord or lady. If the attendant women are not all particularly well-behaved, some might possibly suppose that neither is their mistress. That certainly could damage her honor.

Second, a young mistress, even a mere infant, could learn or see something among her women which would provide quite an unsuitable example for her. Hence, one particular woman must be entrusted with the upbringing of the young lady, even if there reside at court many more distinguished ladies, among them her own relatives, who would be pleased to honor her and bear her company. This one governess must be sufficiently old, prudent, good, and devout. She must have principal responsibility for the princess's care. If this lady performs her duty well, she will have no minor undertaking, no trivial, perfunctory job. She must keep two major considerations ever in mind. First, she must instruct her mistress in prudent behavior and courteous conduct, and always so supervise her that no talk or gossip will prove detrimental to her honor. Second, she must cherish her young charge, always keeping her affection and maintaining her good graces. These two, that is, giving correction and instruction to the young while at the same time retaining their love and devotion, often are difficult to achieve simultaneously.

Therefore, the governess must act with great discretion. Just as it is far more difficult to extinguish a fire when it already has spread and is burning down the house than it is to keep it from starting in the first place; and just as the wise housekeeper, always on guard to avoid peril which might threaten her, often must search through the house, especially in the evening, lest some careless servant has left a candle or torch or any other dangerous thing unattended which might cause damage; just so, this wise instructor will be prepared for whatever must be done to bend the twig in the desired direction while it is young. She will direct her mistress into such a desirable shape that henceforth the young lady will retain it. But she will direct that force gradually, rather than all at once, lest the twig break.

Starting their association in the manner appropriate to attaining her desired ends, the governess will begin immediately to direct her charge with a pleasant and courteous manner, giving her mistress inconsequential gifts of the sort which please young people. Thereby she will gain her young mistress's confidence and affection. Presupposing that the governess is not too old, she will sometimes indulge in games and diversions when she and the young princess are alone. Or she might tell fables or stories of the type customarily told to young children or young girls. This will attract her mistress to her so that the child will take it better when it is necessary to reprove or correct her. For if the governess were to appear serious every day, without humor or playfulness, youth's inclination to gaiety and pleasure could not abide it. The young princess would be so afraid of the governess she would take offence at her admonitions and thus behave badly.

When the governess has won the confidence of her mistress and has her well in hand, then, depending upon the child's age or the level of judgment she observes in her, she will begin telling her stories when they are talking together in their rooms, relating histories of ladies and maidens who have governed themselves intelligently, thus having turned out well and gained much honor from good conduct. Contrariwise, she will tell how misfortune pursued those who behaved foolishly. She will say that she has seen all these things happen in her own time. Moreover, she will repeat all sorts of contemporary anecdotes bearing upon these matters. But she must not appear to be giving examples, only recounting adventures. By telling these stories well, she will touch her mistress's heart, as well as that of others who may be hearing her who have gathered around her to listen. Sometimes she will tell them stories of the saints, their lives, and their passions.[13] So that her tales won't become boring, she will interrupt them to tell some little jokes. Also she will encourage the others to tell stories and jests, so that each may have a turn at speaking. Such methods the wise lady will use to lure the young princess's affection.

As for specific correction and instruction, she will counsel with wise, benevolent words. First advice of all is to arise early. Then she will teach the young princess some good, short prayers which she will urge her to say upon getting up, hailing at the beginning of day Our Lord and the Virgin. She will tell the princess that she has always heard that the one who sincerely makes it habit to address the first words of the day to Our Lord upon arising in the morning will not suffer misfortune during that day. She will be telling her the truth; many good people believe this. Then she will have her mistress dress and array herself suitably, without devoting overmuch time to clothing, as some ladies do. That is a ridiculous waste of time and, furthermore, an unseemly custom. Then directing her to attend mass, she will have her say her Hours devoutly and attentively.

She will urge the young princess to maintain excellence in speaking, propriety in facial expression, suitability in ornaments and clothing for a highborn princess, and perfection in conduct, allowing nothing about her to be criticized. The instructor will accomplish all this in as few words as possible, offering wise commentary and counsel. So doing, she will train the young princess so well that everyone will say that they never saw a lady at such a young age with such charming manner nor better brought up. These same people will say of her: "How praiseworthy is the young heart, so mature and wise through benevolent habits."

Of course, we must assume that the young princess is already so well trained as to wish herself instructed, and to remember what she has learned. For she might well be so obstreperous that the governess must be excused if unable to do anything for her improvement. In such a case, the wise instructor will reprove her young mistress for the mistakes that young people tend to make. With such a wild one it is less effective for her to be kind, gentle, and have her mistress's control in hand, than it is to threaten that if she does not behave differently, or if she continues to do and say forbidden things, she, the governess, will no longer continue to serve her, and will return home. Further, such bad behavior is completely unsuitable for such a lady as her mistress. If the princess really is good, gentle, and fond of her governess, she will fear losing her and will reform with little further reproof. If, however, she is contrary, contemptuous, spiteful, and emotionally cold, the lady must speak severely to her in private. Whether the young one likes it or not, the governess necessarily will report her to her parents or to her lord if she does not conduct herself better.

Nevertheless, the lady responsible for teaching good behavior to her young mistress wisely will understand that young people sometimes must play and laugh. So, she will arrange for this at particular times and in the company of the younger ones among the ladies, particularly when no strangers are present, and according to her mistress's temperament. One cannot, and indeed should not, deny young people pleasures unless they are harmful or unsuitable. Concerning these morals and good behaviors necessary for the princess we will speak no further here, but will discuss them presently in the letter which the governess may send to her mistress.

Which Speaks of Widows Young and Old (III.4) [14]

In order for this work to be more completely profitable to women of all classes, we will speak now to widows among the more common people, having already discussed the case of widowed princesses.

Dear friends, we pity each one of you in the state of widowhood because death has deprived you of your husbands, whoever they may have been. Moreover, much anguish and many trying problems afflict you, affecting the rich in one manner and those not rich in another. The rich are troubled because unscrupulous people commonly try to despoil them of their inheritance. The poor, or at least, those not at all rich, are distressed because they find no pity from anyone for their problems. Along with the grief of having lost your mate, which is quite enough, you also must suffer three trials in particular, which assault you whether you are rich or poor.

First is that, undoubtedly, you will find harshness and lack of consideration or sympathy everywhere. Those who honored you during the lifetime of your husbands, who may well have been officials or men of importance, now will pay little attention to you and barely even bother to be friendly. The second distress facing you is the variety of lawsuits and demands of certain people regarding debts, claims on your property, and income. Third is the evil talk of people who are all too willing to attack you, so that you hardly know what you can do that will not be criticized. In order to arm you with the sensible advice to protect yourself against these, as well as other overpowering plagues, we wish to suggest some things you may find useful. Though some of them we have already spoken of elsewhere, nevertheless they also fit particularly well here.

Against the coldness you undoubtedly will find in everyone — the first of the three tribulations of widowhood — there are three possible remedies. Turn toward God, who was willing to suffer so much for human creatures. Reflecting on this will teach you patience, a quality you will need greatly. It will bring you to the point where you will place little value on the rewards and honors of this world. First of all, you will learn how undependable all earthly things are.

The second remedy is to turn your heart to gentleness and kindliness in word and courtesy to everyone. You will overcome the hard-hearted and bend them to your will by gentle prayers and humble requests.

Third, in spite of what we just said about quiet humility in words, apparel, and countenance, nevertheless you must learn the judgment and behavior necessary to protect yourself against those only too willing to get the better of you. You must avoid their company, having nothing to do with them if you can help it. Rather, stay quietly in your own house, not involving yourself in an argument with a neighbor, not even with a servingman or maid. By always speaking quietly while protecting your own interests, as well as by mingling little with miscellaneous people if you don't need to, you will avoid anyone taking advantage of you or ruining you.

Concerning the lawsuits which may stalk you, learn well how to avoid all sorts. They damage a widow in many ways.[15] First of all, if she is not informed, but on the contrary is ignorant in legal affairs, then it will be necessary for her to place herself in the power of someone else to solicit on behalf of her needs. Those others generally lack diligence in the affairs of women, willingly deceiving them and charging them eight crowns for six. Another problem is that women cannot always come and go at all hours, as a man would do,[16] and therefore, if it is not too damaging for her, it may be better to let go some part of what is her due rather than involve herself in contention. She should consider circumspectly any reasonable demands made against her; or if she finds herself obliged to be the plaintiff, she should pursue her rights courteously and should attempt alternatives for achieving her ends. If assailed by debts, she must inform herself of what rights her creditors have and make an appropriate plan of action. Even presupposing there is no official "owing" letter or witness, if her conscience tells her that something is owing, she must not keep anything that really belongs to another. That would burden her husband's soul as well as her own, and God indeed might send her so many additional, expensive misfortunes that her original losses would be doubled.

But if she protects herself wisely from deceitful people who make demands without cause, she is behaving as she should. If, in spite of all this, she is obliged to go to court, she should understand three things necessary for all who take action. One is to act on the advice of wise specialists in customary law and clerks who are well versed in legal sciences and in the law. Next is to prepare the case for trial with great care and diligence. Third is to have enough money to afford all this. Certainly if one of these things is lacking, no matter how worthy the cause, there is every danger the case will be lost.

Therefore, a widow in such a situation necessarily must look for older specialists in customary law, [17] those most experienced in various sorts of cases, rather than depending on younger men. She should explain her case to them, showing them her letters and her titles, listening carefully to what they say without concealing anything which pertains to the case, whether in her favor or against her. Counsel can utilize in her behalf only what she tells him. According to his advice, either she must plead steadfastly or accede to her adversaries. If ever she goes to court, she must plead diligently and pay well. Her case will so benefit.

If it is necessary for her to do these things, and if she wishes to avoid further trouble and bring her case to a successful conclusion, she must take on the heart of a man. [18] She must be constant, strong, and wise in judging and pursuing her advantage, not crouching in tears, defenseless, like some simple woman or like a poor dog who retreats into a corner while all the other dogs jump on him. If you do that, dear woman, you will find most people so lacking in pity that they would take the bread from your hand because they consider you either ignorant or simpleminded, nor would you find additional pity elsewhere because they took it. So do not work on your own or depend on your own judgment, but hire always the best advice, particularly on important matters you do not understand.

Thus your affairs should be well managed among those of you widows who have reached a certain age and do not intend to remarry. Young widows must be guided by their relatives or friends until they have married again, conducting themselves particularly gently and simply so as not to acquire a doubtful reputation that might cause them to lose their prospects and their advantage.

The remedy against the third of the three misfortunes pursuing a widow—being at the mercy of evil tongues—is that she must be careful in every way possible not to give anyone reason to talk against her because of appearance, bearing, or clothing. All these should be simple and seemly, and the woman's manners quiet and discreet regarding her body, thus giving no cause for gossip. Nor should the widow be too friendly or seemingly intimate with any man who may be observed frequenting her house, unless he is a relative. Even then discretion should be observed, including the presence of a father-in-law, brother, or priest, who should be permitted few visits or none at all. For no matter how devout a woman herself may be, the world is inclined to speak evil. She should also maintain a household where there is no suspicion of any great intimacy or familiarity, however fine she knows her staff to be and despite the innocence of her own thoughts. Nor should her household expenses give people opportunity for slandering her. Moreover, to protect her property better, she should make no ostentatious display of servants, clothing, or foods, for it better suits a widow to be inconspicuous and without any extravagance whatsoever.

Because widowhood truly provides so many hardships for women, some people might think it best for all widows to remarry. This argument can be answered by saying that if it were true that the married state consisted entirely of peace and repose, this indeed would be so. That one almost always sees the contrary in marriages should be a warning to all widows. However, it might be necessary or desirable for the young ones to remarry. But for all those who have passed their youth and who are sufficiently comfortable financially so that poverty does not oblige them, remarriage is complete folly.[19] Though some who want to remarry say there is nothing in life for a woman alone, they have so little confidence in their own good sense that they will claim that they don't know how to manage their own lives. But the height of folly and the greatest of all absurdities is the old woman who takes a young husband: There a joyful song rarely is heard for long. Although many pay dearly for their foolishness, nobody will sympathize with them—for good reason.

∞

Which Speaks of Artisans' Wives and How They Should Conduct Themselves (III.8)

Now we must speak of the lifestyle of women married to the artisans who live in the cities and good towns, both in Paris and elsewhere. Of course, these women will find valuable the good advice already given to others if they so wish. However, although certain trades are more highly regarded than others (for instance, goldsmiths, embroiderers, armorers, and tapestry weavers are thought more distinguished than masons and shoemakers), we address the wives of all craftsmen. All of them should be attentive and diligent.

If they wish to earn money honorably, they should urge their husbands and their workmen to take up their trade early in the morning and leave it late. No trade is so good that if one is not hardworking one barely lives from one crust of bread to the next.

Urging the others to action, she herself should put her hand to the task, making sure that she knows the craft so well that she can direct the workmen if her husband is not there and reprove them if they do not work well. She must admonish them against laziness; a master often is deserted by irresponsible, lethargic workmen. When her husband gets a commission for some difficult and unusual task, she firmly must convince him not to accept any work through which he might suffer a loss. If he does not personally know his client, she should advise him to produce as little work as possible on credit. Several already have been ruined by this.[20] Sometimes greed to earn more or the importance of the tendered offer tempts one to such risks.

The artisan's wife should keep her husband attracted to her by love, so that he will stay at home the more willingly, not tempted to join those foolish bands of young men in taverns[21] and not likely to dissipate his earnings with superfluous, outrageous expenses, as many young artisans do, especially in Paris. Rather, treating him with tenderness, she should keep him nearby. Common wisdom has it that three things drive a man from his home: a quarrelsome wife, a smoking hearth, and a leaking roof.[22]

Furthermore, she should be willing to stay home, not running here and there every day, gossiping in the neighborhood to find out what everybody else is doing, nor frequenting her cronies. All this makes for poor housekeeping. Neither is it good for her to go to so many gatherings across town, nor to go traveling off needlessly on pilgrimages, which invariably would cause unnecessary expense.

She also should encourage her husband to let them live within their income so that their expenses will not be greater than their earnings, which would force them into debt at the year's end. If she has children, she first should have them taught at school[23] so that they will better know how to serve God; then she ought to have them apprenticed to some trade so that they can earn their living. For a great gift to one's child is knowledge, a skill, or a trade. Beyond these, the mother above all must protect the child from affectation and indulgence. These greatly discredit children of the good towns — and reflect badly on their fathers and mothers, otherwise expected to be the source of virtue and good habits. Sometimes, however, parents so spoil their children by pampering them during their years of growing up that they cause their offspring's ultimate misfortune and ruination.

∞

Conclusion and End of this Present Book (III.14)

The three ladies stopped speaking and suddenly vanished. I, Christine, remained there, somewhat weary from writing for so long a time, but overjoyed at seeing the fine work which had come from their worthy lessons. Afterward, having summarized, reviewed, and revised it, I think it is better than ever now, and extremely useful for the improvement of virtuous habits intended to increase the honor of ladies and all women now living and to be born. This advice will endure wherever this work may circulate and be read.

I, their servant, though in no way adequate to the task, intend, as always has been my habit, to devote myself to promoting their welfare. Therefore, I thought I would multiply this work throughout the world in various copies, whatever the cost might be, and present it in particular places to queens, princesses, and noble ladies. Through their efforts, it will be the more honored and praised, as is fitting, and better circulated among other women. I already have started this process; so that this book will be examined, read, and published in all countries, although it is written in the French language.

Since French is a more common and universal language than any other, this work will not remain unknown and useless but will endure in its many copies throughout the world. Seen and heard by many valiant ladies and women of authority, both at the present time and in times to come, they will pray to God on behalf of their faithful servant, Christine, wishing that her life in this world had been at the same time as theirs so that they might have known her. May those who now see me and my work keep me in their grace and memory as long as I live, praying to God that in His mercy He will increasingly favor my understanding, granting me such light of knowledge and true wisdom that I may employ these to continue the noble labor of study, in behalf of the praise and promotion of virtue through good example to every human being. After my soul has left my body, may these good women recognizing and rewarding me for my services offer to God on my behalf *Pater Nosters,* oblations, and other devotions for alleviating such pains as I may suffer for my shortcomings, so that I may be presented before God in the World Without End, which reward also is promised to you. Amen. [24]

Here ends the Book of the Three Virtues for the instruction of women.

CCW

(Translated from Boston Public Library Ms. 1528)

NOTES

1. Christine probably knew this saying of Seneca's from the *Manipulus Florum,* which she used throughout her career. (Rouse, pp. 213–15).
2. This image inevitably calls to mind a well-known miniature from the *Livre de la chasse* (Book of the Hunt) written by Gaston Phebus. E. Panofsky in *Early Netherlandish Painting* (Cambridge, 1953, p. 52), was of the opinion that one of the most important manuscripts, B.N. Ms. fr. 616, was illustrated in a Paris workshop before early 1403, so it could have been known to Christine. She must also have known the work of Pietro Crecenzi, like her father a native of Bologna, whose work on agriculture, the *Liber Ruralium Commodorum* (Book of Rural Profits) was translated into French for Charles V in 1374. It includes a chapter entitled "How Birds are Taken" (B.N. Ms. fr. 12, 330, fol. 289).
3. *College* should be understood here as meaning community. Several manuscripts of the text show women of various social classes seated at the feet of Worldly Prudence and listening to her lessons.
4. Jeanne of Evreux, third wife of Charles VI, was well-known as a peace-maker. As she lived until March 1371 Christine had seen her as a child, praised her in the biography of Charles V (Solente ed., I, p. 54n) and in *The Book of the City of Ladies* (Richards trans., p. 34), and mentioned her in a letter in the Rose debate (Hicks ed., p. 19). At the end of the fifteenth century the Peace of Cambrai was negotiated by Louise of Savoie and Marguerite of Austria, both of whom owned copies of Christine's book.
5. Christine was alluding here to the rebellion of Bouchart, Count of Corbeil and three Montlhery brothers who succeeded each other as Viscount of Troyes during the reign of Philip I (1108–1137). It was Philip's son, Louis VI, who was finally able to put down this revolt of nobles. See *Les Grandes Chroniques de France,* ed. R. Delachenal (Paris, 1910–1920), V, pp. 103, 191.
6. Robert of Artois was a fourteenth-century nobleman who coveted the title of his aunt Mahaut, Countess of Artois, and even invented false documents to substantiate his claim. He was also suspected of trying to poison her. Banished in disgrace when his schemes failed, he took refuge at the court of the English king, Edward III, and was suspected of machinations encouraging the English invasion of France. *Les Grandes Chroniques,* IX, pp. 109–12; 123–33.
7. Queen Blanche of Castille (1188–1252) was Regent of France during the early years of Louis IX's reign, since he was only twelve at the time of his father's death. His youth inspired a revolt of some barons, including princes of the royal blood, but by taking advantage of dissension among these rebels, the queen was able, with the support of faithful townspeople, to overcome her opponents. See E. Berger, *Histoire de Blanche de Castille, Reine de France* (Paris, 1895).
8. This is a reference to Thibaud of Champagne (1201–1253), who spent a part of his youth at the court of Blanche's husband, Louis VIII, but in 1226 abandoned his king during the siege of Avignon. He was even suspected of having poisoned the king, who died shortly after this. Although he was one of the noblemen who subsequently conspired against Blanche and the young Louis IX, at a critical moment he had a sudden change of heart, for which he nearly paid with his life. In 1234 he became King of Navarre, and he was subsequently involved in another conspiracy against Louis IX, from which he again withdrew. An undependable friend and mediocre politician, he was nevertheless a good poet, although the claim that some of his poetry was inspired by love for Blanche of Castile is probably mere legend.

9. Proverbs 25:15: "By long forbearing is a prince persuaded, and a soft tongue breaketh the bone."

10. In *The Book of the City of Ladies* (Book I, chaps. 12 and 13) Christine cites the examples of the Empress Nicaula of Ethiopia, of Queen Fredegund of France, and then of several other queens and princesses, including Blanche of Castile; Jeanne of Evreux, queen of Charles IV; Blanche of Navarre, queen of Philip VI; as well as Blanche of France, Duchess of Orleans; and Marie of Châtillon, Duchess of Anjou. She had already praised several of them in the letters of the Rose debate.

11. Christine was always interested in the education of the young, and her ideas were more advanced than those of her French contemporaries, even such Italian educators as Guarino da Verona. This book is contemporary with the well-known ones of Giovanni Dominici and Petrus Paulus Vergerius. See W. H. Woodward, *Vittorino da Feltre and Other Humanist Educators*, pp. 247–50.

12. It was customary to send a young princess after her marriage to the court of her husband's family. Marguerite of Guyenne had recently been sent to the French court dominated by the frivolous Isabeau of Bavaria, which might have been a matter of some concern to her own family.

13. Book III of *The City of Ladies* is devoted to the lives of saints who rose above formidable oppression and suffering. One might suppose that these had been inspired by *The Golden Legend*, but Christine mentions that she found them in the *Speculum Historiale* (Historical Mirror) of Vincent of Beauvais (Book III, chap. ix).

14. Christine had already given advice to royal widows in Book I, chap. xxii, but this chapter undoubtedly reflects her reaction to her personal experiences, as described in the *Vision*.

15. In the *Vision*, which is more or less contemporary with this book, Christine dwells on the lawsuits that consumed the early years of her own widowhood. She also made some sharp comments on the miscarriage of Justice in *The Book of Man's Integrity* (see pp. 261–67).

16. A woman alone on Parisian streets at a late hour would scarcely have been safe, but her reasons for being there would certainly be open to question, for respectable women did not go about unattended.

17. Customary law, as opposed to canon or church law, was established by custom or usage. It was the basis of medieval civil law in France, varying from region to region. Christine would have more to say of law and legists in *The Deeds of Arms and of Chivalry*.

18. Christine repeatedly admonished women to stand on their own feet. This idea of taking on the heart of a man is undoubtedly related to her account of having been changed by Fortune into a man, as described in *The Mutation of Fortune*.

19. It is noteworthy that certain important women of a slightly later generation, Louise of Savoy, Margaret of Austria, and Mary of Hungary, all of whom numbered among Christine's readers, chose not to remarry.

20. The extravagance of some noblemen is well documented and was the source of considerable criticism in Christine's day. The prodigality of the Duke of Orleans was notable, and some of the Duke of Berry's manuscripts and works of art had to be sold at the time of his death in 1416 to satisfy his creditors.

21. The young artisans who gathered in taverns were the further object of Christine's disapproval in *The Book of the Body of Policy*, Book III, chap. 9. See Lucas ed., pp. 194–99.

22. This proverb is of biblical origin (Proverbs 27:15), but it had passed into common usage. See J. W. Hassell, Jr., *Middle French Proverbs, Sentences and Proverbial Phrases*, p. 76, no. 201.

23. From the fourteenth century there existed the organized school or *collegium*, where

children were taught to count and spell. They learned to read from the psalter in Latin, which they did not understand until they studied Latin grammar in the Donatus Minor and progressed to reading such standard texts as the *Disticha Catonis (The Distichs of Cato).*

24. Christine's concern for her future reputation is an excellent example of her humanistic concerns.

CCW

V

THE BIOGRAPHY OF
CHARLES V

❦

CHRISTINE'S first long work written entirely in prose was devoted to a life of the king who had brought her family from Italy to the French court. Although there is little evidence that *The Book of the Deeds and Good Character of King Charles V the Wise* was widely read at the time it was written (1404), as only six manuscripts of it are known as compared to some forty of her *Letter of Othea,* this biography played a significant role in preserving Christine's literary reputation as well as providing an account of Charles V's reign from the fifteenth century on, for it was the first of her writings to be rediscovered. The Abbé de Choisy published a part of it in the seventeenth century, excerpts were printed on several occasions during the eighteenth, and the complete text was published at the beginning of the nineteenth. Best of all, Suzanne Solente's excellent modern critical edition has become available in the twentieth century.[1] The editors have been unanimous in applauding Christine's value as an eyewitness of Charles V's court. Only recently has she been criticized for presenting an overly idealized account of the king.[2] We must consider her objectives in writing the biography.

It was probably neither Christine's intention, nor the idea of the king's brother, Philip of Burgundy, who commissioned Christine to write the account, to repeat the sort of information already available in official chronicles of the reign. The Duke of Burgundy, in common with Christine, had every reason to remember the late king with gratitude, for he owed him nearly everything he possessed: not only his extraordinarily advantageous marriage to Margaret of Flanders, whose hereditary lands had greatly extended his own territories, but even the Duchy of Burgundy itself with which he had been endowed by his brother. In 1404, moreover, there was ample reason for both Christine and the duke to remember with nostalgia the promises of

Charles V's reign, which contrasted so markedly with the inadequacies of the rule of his son, the mad Charles VI.

It should also be borne in mind that at the beginning of the fifteenth century in France, there was an almost complete lack of models for the biography of a lay person. Joinville's biography of Saint Louis was available, but there is no evidence that Christine made use of it. At the same time, early humanists in Italy were beginning to show an interest in secular biographies, making considerable use of the Roman history of Valerius Maximus. Yet nothing of this sort had been written in France. The only possible exception might have been the prose version of Jean Cuvelier's poem, which was inspired by the deeds of Charles V's constable, Bertrand DuGuesclin, a work mentioned by Christine.[3] It seems quite possible that the duke did indeed have in mind some sort of humanistic biography that would preserve his brother's memory. Clearly Christine wanted to depict Charles V as a "wise" king and to present his manner of ruling as worthy of emulation, most especially by his grandson, Louis of Guyenne, now heir to the French throne. She was, at the same time, interested in indicating parallels between the late king's moral qualities and those of ancient rulers, thus obeying Petrarch's dictum of using the past to inform the present. According to this idea, the role of the historian was primarily to arrange material in such a way as to save great men from the Triumph of Death and the ravages of time. It was perhaps with this in mind that Christine started to write about Charles V.

Having explained how she came to undertake the biography, Christine divides her material into three parts. The first discusses the manner in which a king should govern himself, especially by what she calls "nobility of heart," the quality she considers the basis for worldly renown. She also describes his daily schedule, a particularly interesting glimpse into the life of a medieval king. A rare picture of the king in action is to be found in the description of him riding through the streets of Paris, probably as Christine herself had seen him. She tells us:

> His accustomed manner of riding through the city was impressive, accompanied as he was by a large company of barons and gentlemen, all well-mounted and handsomely dressed. He himself would be seated on a well-chosen mount, always dressed in royal garments, riding among his people, who stayed at a certain distance from him but in such impressive array, that by the appearance of this arrangement any man, stranger or any other,

could easily recognize him and know for certain that he was the king. (I, xviii) [4]

The second part describes other members of the royal family in portraits that have been criticized as unduly flattering. Christine seems to have been troubled by this possibility; she justifies her treatment of the royal family by insisting that nobody has the right to pass judgment on the living. She also discusses the nature and purpose of chivalry, taking pains to show how the king, never noted for physical courage and increasingly plagued by ill health, could be considered a model knight. She does this, in part, by calling attention to the ways in which France benefited from Charles's efforts, especially through the victory of Cocherel and the abrogation of the Treaty of Brétigny, which had been imposed on the French by the English after the French defeat at Poitiers.

The third part of the biography is especially interesting; Christine describes the king's intellectual interests and accomplishments, especially his establishment of the royal library in a tower of the Louvre. It is here that she dwells on the qualities of a "wise" king, defining wisdom as the combination of learning and prudence with inherent seriousness.

Unfortunately, this impressive king's life was cut short; he died in 1380 at the age of forty-three. One of the most touching chapters in the biography has to do with his death. Christine had very possibly heard some of the details from her father, who was one of the royal physicians. She permits herself to elaborate on the known circumstances, however, by describing how the dying king had Christ's crown of thorns brought from the Sainte Chapelle, where it had been placed by Saint Louis, along with the crown used for his own coronation, which was brought from Saint Denis, where he had been crowned and would soon be buried. Charles's ceremonial comparison of the emblems of the spiritual and worldly frame is an impressive moment. It is one of Christine's most moving literary accomplishments, and worthy of the image the king wished to leave of himself.

On the whole, Christine's account of Charles V has been confirmed; certainly it is superior to that of the more famous historian, Froissart, whose knowledge of the French court was less direct than hers. Charles V had already indicated his own wishes for the preservation of his memory by ordering his tomb for Saint Denis and supervising the account of his reign in the official *Chronicles of France.* [5] It was

Christine's contribution to dramatize his personality, his way of life, and, above all, his intellectual vigor.

Historians have seldom spoken well of the fourteenth century; lately it has been regarded as a period of unmitigated disaster. Christine's ability to breathe life into some of the figures who frequented this royal court she had known as a child and to provide some notion of the milieu in which they lived illuminates the period for her readers.

NOTES

1. L'Abbé de Choisy, *Histoire de Charles cinquième roi de France* (Paris, 1689). Three extracts were published during the eighteenth century; a complete text was published by C. B. Petitot, *Collection complète de mémoires relatifs à l'histoire de France,* Vol. V (Paris, 1824) and Vol. VI (Paris, 1825), along with three other imprints from the nineteenth century; S. Solente, ed., *Le Livre des fais et bonnes meurs du sage roy Charles V,* Société de l'Histoire de France, Vol. I (Paris, 1936) and Vol. II (Paris, 1940).

2. J. B. Henneman, "The Age of Charles V" in *Froissart: Historian,* ed. J.J.N. Palmer (Woodbridge, England and Totowa, N.J., 1981), p. 45.

3. Solente is uncertain whether Christine made use of the poem by Cuvelier or a prose version made in 1379 for a military leader, Jean d'Estouteville (See Solente ed., I, p. lxi.).

4. Solente ed., I, p. 50.

5. R. Delachenal, *Histoire de Charles V* (Paris, 1909–1938), Vol. IV, pp. 541–42; P. Pradel, "Les Tombeaux de Charles V," *Bulletin Monumental* 109 (1951), 273–96.

THE BOOK OF THE DEEDS AND GOOD CHARACTER OF KING CHARLES V THE WISE

❦

Concerning the Origins of this Book, and the Manner of Its Commission (I.ii)

Since unknown or unexplained motives occasionally cause people to wonder at the reasons why things have been done, I shall recount faithfully, making no concession to flattery, how this modest composition came to be written, and what its origins were. It happened in the present year of the Grace of Our Lord, fourteen hundred and three, that I presented one of my volumes, called *The Mutation of Fortune*, to that most august prince, my Lord of Burgundy, as a gift for the first day of January, which we call New Year's Day. In his gracious humility he accepted it kindly and with great pleasure. Afterwards, Monbertaut, his treasurer, told and explained to me personally that the aforementioned lord would be pleased if I were to compose a treatise on a certain subject which the said prince would outline to me, so that I might understand exactly what it was he wanted. And thus I, desirous of fulfilling his kind wishes, so far as my modest intelligence would allow, betook myself with my servants to the Louvre palace in Paris, where he was then residing, and there, informed of my presence, by the goodness of his grace he bade me come before him, sending two of his squires to conduct me in his presence, men accomplished in all manner of courtesy, Jean de Chalon and Taupinet de Chantemerle by name. I found him in relative privacy, retired in the company of his noble son Antoine, Count of Rethel. Having made my reverence before him in the proper fashion, I explained why I had come and how the desire of his service and the pleasure of His Highness had brought me there, if only I were worthy of so high a cause, but that he needed to inform me what kind of treatise it pleased him to have me work upon. Then, having thanked me more profusely in his humility than befitted someone of my modest station, he told and explained to me how and on what subject it pleased him that I work. And having received of his goodness many considerable assurances I took my leave, content of my charge, holding this commission more honorable than myself able or worthy of its perfect accomplishment.

Concerning the Reason Why the Present Volume Will Be Treated in Three Distinct Parts (I.iii)

And thus it was the pleasure of the aforementioned revered lord that I apply the small understanding of my wits to recall to memory the virtues and deeds of that most exalted prince King Charles the Wise, a lover of wisdom and all manner of virtue. To fulfill this charge, I informed myself of his acts, consulting both chronicles and several distinguished persons still alive, who had served him in the past—his life and custom, habits and manner of living, as well as specific deeds. And since I found upon proper investigation that his qualities could be set forth under the heading of three merits, I said in my prologue that I would treat his excellence of character, knighthood, and wisdom, dividing my book in three parts, and bringing up as appropriate many notable additions.

ERIC HICKS

∞

Here Christine Tells How King Charles Established the Manner of His Life in Good Order (I.xv)

As it is proper and in accordance with the ancient and commendable custom for kings to be advised by the prelates of the realm—for which cause it would be good for the electors to have sole oversight of the elections of these men, and, in rejecting those unworthy, to assign promotions on the basis of true judgment, according to the teachings of their knowledge and their integrity, and not from arbitrary preference, etc.—the wise King, in order to distribute sagely and piously from on high the accounts of the revenues of his realm, drew to his council all the learned prelates of sound judgment and the integrity of a good and pious life.

Item, desirous that, by rendering to each his rights, justice and equality might be truly protected in his realm, the wise King also had a sufficient number of the most reputable jurists appointed to his court of parliament; these he instituted and established in the assembly of his noble council. He made other deserving, famous men the masters of requests at his palaces, and for all other offices, where advice appertained, he provided proper and suitable men, so that all his work might be conducted according to the order prescribed by rectitude and the law of justice.

Item, for the adornment of his conscience, it was pleasing to him, who was circumspect in all things, to hear often in his conferences the masters of theology and divinity from all the orders of the Church, to listen to their words and to have around him these men whom he honored so much. He also greatly rewarded his spiritual father, a wise, just person of salutary learning whom he held in great respect.

Item, for the preservation of bodily health, the most expert physicians and renowned masters trained in the medical sciences were sought.

Item, in the manner of the noble, ancient emperors, in order to plant the foundation of virtue within himself, he ordered that in all nations the celebrated clerks and philosophers grounded in the mathematical and speculative sciences be sought for, invoked, and summoned to him. Concerning this, experience teaches me the truth, because Reputation then gave witness throughout Christendom to the power of my natural father, the greatest of astronomers, in the speculative sciences. His Grace sent his messengers to seek for him all the way to Italy, in the city of Bologna. By this command and desire my father, and then my mother with her children and myself, her daughter, were transported to this realm, as is known by many still living. Thus, generally, because of the nobility of his spirit, which attracted to him the excellence of virtue, he wanted to have all honorable, valiant, wise and good men around him, as many as he could, and he wished to use their counsels and to be led and governed in all his affairs by these aforesaid masters. So it will hereafter be declared that he truly followed the proverb that says:

> If you trust in good counsel and for it fare
> Then good fortune and honor will be your share.[1]

GLENDA McLEOD

Here Reference Is Made to Examples of Virtuous Princes and the
Well-Ordered Life of King Charles as Recalled (I.xvi)

As remembering the virtues of the good and famous dead should be
an example for the living, and speaking further of the well-ordered life
of our king, it seems suitable to recall some who, in the past, have
governed themselves well. As it is written, for example, of the valiant
King Alfred of England, a wise and virtuous man, who translated from
Latin into his own language the *History of the World* of Orosius, Saint
Gregory's *Pastoral Care*, Bede's *Chronicles* and *The Consolation of Philosophy* of Boethius. This king kept in his chapel a lighted candle, which
was divided into twenty-four parts: eight of these the king devoted to
prayers and to study, eight more to tending the needs of his kingdom,
and the other eight to personal recreation. There were people appointed to tell him how far the candle had burned and what he should
be doing. This arrangement that he devised suggests that clocks were
not yet common. The king likewise divided his income into two parts.
One of these he divided further into three parts: the first to pay those
who served him at court; the second for his architectural projects, for
he built many fine buildings; the third part he put into his treasury.
The other half of his income he divided into four parts: one for the
poor, another for the churches, the third for poor scholars, and the
fourth for prisoners overseas.[2]

I find a comparable order in the case of our own wise King Charles,
so that it seems to me reasonable to recount his agreeable habit of
leading a life well-regulated in all respects, which should be an example to all who may follow be it in empires, kingdoms, or important
lordships for a well-ordered life.

The hour of his rising in the morning was normally six or seven
o'clock, and indeed anyone who wanted to make use here of the
language of poets might say that just as the goddess Aurora, by her
rising, rejoices the hearts of those who see her, so the king gives
pleasure to his chamberlains and other servants appointed to attend
his person at that hour, for, regardless of anything that might make it
otherwise, his face was joyous. Then, after making the sign of the cross,
and very devoutly addressing his first words to God in prayer, he
exchanged with his servants, in agreeable familiarity, some pleasant
and happy remarks, so that his kindness and gentleness would encourage even the least of them to joke and enjoy themselves with him,

however humble they might be. They all enjoyed these comments and exchanges. When he had been combed, dressed, and outfitted according to the demands of the day's program, his chaplain, a distinguished person and honorable priest, brought him his breviary and helped him to say his hours, according to the canonical day of the calendar. Around eight o'clock he would go to mass, which was celebrated each day with glorious, melodious, solemn singing. In the retirement of his oratory low masses were sung for him.

As he came out of the chapel, all sorts of people, rich or poor, ladies or maidens, widows or others who had problems, could make their petitions to him and he very kindly would pause to listen to their supplications, responding charitably to those that were reasonable or piteous. More doubtful cases he turned over to some master of requests to examine. After this, on appointed days, he would meet with his council, and then with some noblemen of his own blood or some clergymen who happened to be present. If some particular lengthy business did not prevent him, he would go to the table around ten o'clock. His meal was not long, for he did not favor elaborate food, saying that such food bothered his stomach and disturbed his memory. He drank clear and simple wine, light in color, well cut, and not much quantity nor great variety. Like David, to rejoice his spirits, he listened willingly at the end of his meals to stringed instruments playing the sweetest possible music. When he had risen from table after his light meal, all sorts of strangers and others who had come with requests could approach him. There one might find several kinds of foreign ambassadors, noblemen, and knights, of whom there was often such a crowd, both foreign and from his own realm, that one could scarcely turn around. Nevertheless, the very prudent king received them all and replied to them in such a civil manner and received each one so justly with the honor due him, that all considered themselves content and left his presence happily. There he received news from all sorts of places, perhaps incidents and details of his wars, or the battles of others, and all such matters; there he arranged what should be done according to what was proposed to him, or promised to solve some matter in council, forbade what was unreasonable, accorded favors, signed letters with his own hand, gave reasonable gifts, promised vacant offices, or answered reasonable requests. He occupied himself with such details as these for perhaps two hours, after which he withdrew and retired to rest for about an hour. After his rest period, he spent a time with his most intimate companions in pleasant diversions, perhaps looking at his jewels or other treasures. He took this recreation so that excessive demands on him would not damage his health, because of his delicate constitution, in view of the fact that he spent most of his time busy with demanding affairs. Then he went to vespers, after which, if it was summertime, he sometimes went into his gardens where, if he was in his Hôtel of Saint Paul,[3] sometimes the queen would join him with their children. There he spoke with the women of the court, asking news of their children. Sometimes he received curious gifts from various places, perhaps artillery or other armaments and a variety of other things, or merchants would come bringing velvet, cloth of gold, and all sorts of beautiful, exotic objects, or jewels, which he had them show to the connoisseurs of such things among members of his family.[4]

In winter, especially, he often occupied himself by having read aloud to him fine stories from the Holy Scriptures, or the *Deeds of the Romans,* or *Wise Sayings of the Philosophers*[5] and other such matters until the hour of supper, where he took his place rather early for a light meal. After this, he spent a short period in recreation with his barons and knights before retiring to rest. And thus in continual good order, this wise and well-bred king followed the course of his life.

ERIC HICKS

∽

Here Christine Tells How King Charles Could Be Said to Be a True Knight (II.v)

Now it is time to return to the main purpose of our material, so that by holding to our promise the truth will be made clear in the royal portrait—how our wise King Charles, notwithstanding that his person appeared most of the time to be in repose within his rich palaces, was in fact chivalrous in the manner that appertains to a true prince, and that the four aforementioned graces suitable to produce true chivalry were all found within him. Thus to draw to an end the form of our proofs, it is fitting to return to the time of his coronation, at which ceremony, it seems to me by what I find in the true chronicles of his time, two-faced Fortune truly wished to begin to show and shine upon France the sunbeams of her smiling and beautiful face, a face that had long been covered in this realm by black and misfortune-laden clouds.

For it is written that when Charles, the oldest son of King Jean of France, left Paris to go to Rheims to be crowned king of France, almost three thousand armed men, his strong and powerful enemies, then assembled. I do not mention the names of these captains and their nations, these being reported in the aforesaid chronicles.[6] They are there for those who wish to know them. These men left, making their way toward Vernon,[7] where they thought to cross the Seine and hinder and break up the coronation of the aforementioned Charles.

But as the French were advised of this, they hastily assembled the Count of Auxerre; Louis, his youngest brother, who died; the good Bertran de Claquin, constable of France; and many other valiant and virtuous knights in a sufficient company of armed men. The enemy were before them just as they came together for battle beside the mountain called Cocherel, where there was a fierce engagement of many men.[8] Many on both sides died, as is to be expected in such engagements, but in the end God gave the victory to the French. Their enemies were all dead or taken, and our king joyously went from the coronation to Paris, where he was received with great celebration, as was appropriate.

The good king, not being ungrateful, by taking the path of chivalrous princes and giving the knights an example of good conduct, gave Bertran de Claquin the county of Longueville in remuneration for the good deeds that he did in this aforesaid battle and at other times. This suffices in this passage for one of our proofs of the good fortune suitable for a good knight.

GLENDA MCLEOD

∞

Proving That King Charles Was a True Philosopher, and Defining Philosophy (III.iii)

As we have already explained, according to the Philosopher [Aristotle] the sciences and virtues of the soul and where they lead, we should now return to our subject, to see if we can apply these noble muses or sciences to the virtues of our King Charles, true disciple of knowledge, as we can well see by his habits and the terms described above. This king, with the other attributes with which he was endowed, and described in other parts of this book of mine, will be rightfully called once more a *true philosopher,* lover of wisdom. And as to how this name of philosopher was invented, Saint Augustine explains[9] that on an island named Samos, there flourished a wise man named Pythagoras and, as before his time such men were called wise men, when Pythagoras was asked his profession, he replied that he was a lover of knowledge, which in Greek means philosopher, for it seemed presumptuous to him for a man to call himself wise. And as for our King Charles being a true philosopher, which is to say a lover of knowledge, even imbued in it, it appears that he was a true investigator of genuine high causes, which is to say of theology, which represents the outer limit of knowledge, for it is nothing but knowing God and his heavenly virtues through natural science. And our good king demonstrated this, for he wished to be instructed and taught in these matters by wise masters, and because he may not have had sufficient Latin for such subtle matters that are more commonly explained in Latin than in French, he had translated several books on theology by Saint Augustine and other wise theologians, as will be explained presently in the chapter on the translations he commissioned. He often wished to have theology read to him, for he understood the technical points and was able to discuss them, comprehending by reason and study what theology sets forth, which is true knowledge.

∞

How King Charles Loved Books, and the Excellent Translations He Commissioned (III.xii)

Let us now speak further of the wisdom of King Charles, the great love he had for study and learning; the truth of this is shown by his collection of important books and his great library where he had all the most outstanding works compiled by great authors, whether of the Holy Scriptures, or theology, or the sciences, all very well written and richly decorated,[10] for always the best scribes who could be found were engaged to work for him. There is no need to ask if his fine study was well arranged, as he wanted everything to be handsome and neat, polished and well ordered, and it could not have been better. Even though he understood Latin well and there was no need of translating for him, he was so provident that because of the great love he had for those who would follow him in times to come, he wanted to provide them with teachings and knowledge leading to all sorts of virtue, and for this reason he had all the most important books translated from Latin into French by solemn masters highly competent in all the sciences and arts: the Bible in three ways, which is to say the text, then the text and the glosses together, and then in another allegorized fashion;[11] also *The City of God;*[12] likewise, *The Book of the Sky and the World*[13] and Saint Augustine's *Soliloquy;* the *Ethics* and *Politics* of Aristotle with the addition of new examples;[14] Vegetius' *On Chivalry;*[15] the nineteen books of *The Properties of Things;*[16] Valerius Maximus;[17] *The Policraticus;*[18] Titus Livius;[19] and a great many others as he unceasingly had scholars engaged in this work, who were well paid for their efforts.

This great love that he had for possessing many books and the pleasure he derived from them remind me of a king of Egypt named Ptolomy Philadelphius, a very studious man who loved books above everything else to the point where he could never have enough of them. Once when he asked his librarian how many books he had, he was told that he had fifty thousand. At that, Ptolomy had heard that the Jews possessed God's law written by His own hand, he wanted very much to have that law translated from Hebrew into Greek. When he was told that God would be displeased if any but a Jew were to translate it, and that if anyone else were to try it he would soon go mad, the king commanded Eleazer, the high priest of the Jews, to send to him wise men who knew both Hebrew and Greek so that they might translate this law for him. Because of the great desire he had to see this translation carried out, he relaxed the oppression of the Jews who were in Egypt, where there were many, and gave them many gifts. Eleazar rejoiced, thanked God, and chose seventy-two outstanding men to accomplish this task and sent them to King Ptolomy, who received them with great honor. Saint Augustine tells us that the king had each of them put into individual cells where they might study, and the translation was finished in seventy-two days. Although there was no collaboration among them while they were making the translation, it was discovered that one had done exactly what the others had done without a difference of word or syllable, which would not have been possible without God's miracle. The translation greatly pleased the king. That King Ptolomy was very wise. He was well versed in the science of astronomy and he measured the circumference of the earth.[20]

∽

What King Charles Said of the Pleasure of Kingship (III.xxx)

One time in the presence of King Charles there was talk of kingship, and one knight said that it was a wonderful thing to be a prince. The king replied: "Indeed, there is more burden to it than glory!"

When the other continued: "But Sire! Princes are so well off!"

"I know of only one pleasure in kingship," said the king.

"Pray tell us what it is," said the other.

The king then said: "Certainly it is in the power to do good for others."[21]

This remark well shows the affectionate desire that he always had to do good for others, and truly it could be said of him what is written about a good emperor, that nobody left his presence who was not pleased. And as for what he said about worldly kingship being more burden than glory, a valiant emperor replied to his senators, who begged him, because of his excellent qualities, to arrange for his son to reign after him. "Ha," he said, "you ask me to put on the shoulders of my son, who is free and happy, the weight of a very sorrowful and heavy burden, which is full of confusion."

CCW

∞

Here Christine Speaks of the Death and Good End of Wise King Charles (III.lxxi)[22]

Towards the end of the first half of September in the year 1380, King Charles went to his castle of Beauté, where, a few days later, he was taken by the illness from which he died in a very short time. However, I do not seek to give a long account of his illness; rather in accordance with the continuous procedure of the proceeding, I will speak of his fervent faith, piety, constancy, and sound understanding, that is, his virtues worthy of perpetual memory. As his frail constitution was powerless to support the state of so grievous a malady for long, in a very few days he was amazingly debilitated, and during this time his sound discretion, unhindered unto death, made him judge by all of the sufferings of his body that the term of his life would be brief.

Because of this, he wanted to arrange his last orders and attend to the salvation of his soul; thus, notwithstanding that he was always accustomed to confess every week, his spiritual father being continually with him, he, very carefully examining his conscience that nothing might remain to trouble him, confessed several times more in great piety, tears, and contrition. As he was already very hard pressed by his illness, he wanted to receive his Creator, who, after several masses, was administered to him. Before that act, he said these words in the presence of the sacrament with wondrous demonstration of piety: "O God! My Redeemer, to whom all things are manifest, realizing how many times I have offended before Your Majesty and worthy Holiness, I ask You to be favorable to me, a sinner, and as You have thus consented to approach the bed of a poor, languishing man, may it please You, by Your mercy, that I may reach You in the end!" Speaking such words with flowing tears and giving thanks to God, he received communion.

This wise king, manifesting his great constancy, notwithstanding the torments of his illness, requested each day to be gotten up and dressed and to eat at the table so that by forcing his strength, he might bring some respite of comfort to his servants, who he saw were greatly grieved for him and for whom he had great pity. Feeble though he was, he spoke words of comfort and virtuous advice to them, without any cry or complaint or sign of pain beyond calling on the names of God, of Our Lady, and of the saints. Two days before his death, he passed a very painful night. Having got up and been dressed, he went to see his chamberlains and all the other servants and physicians, who were all in tears. He took them aside to tell them with a most joyful face, and in semblance of a good convalescence, "Be happy, my good and loyal friends and servants, for in a brief time I will be out of your hands."

Because of the joy of his countenance, the people hearing these words did not understand in what sense he had said them, but soon afterwards events gave them clarity. The Saturday before his death, there appeared in him signs of approaching death, in which the sufferings were horrible. He showed no evidence of impatience, but, continuing his worship, always addressed his cries to God. Beside him, his aforementioned confessor admonished him in the words necessary at such a point, to which he responded like a most sincere Christian Catholic, and gave indications of a great faith in Our Lord.

When Sunday morning and the day of his death arrived, he had summoned before him all his barons, prelates, his council and chancellor. Then he said many pious words before them so that they all were constrained to tears. Among other things, concerning the work of the Church he said that, as he had been informed by all the college of cardinals and from making as complete an inquiry as he knew how and was able to make, presuming so many noble prelates would not have wanted to damn themselves for one man, he declared Pope Clement to be the true pope, and that which he had done in this matter he took upon his soul that he had done it in good faith.[23] *Item*, he wanted his testament and legacy, which he had made a long time before, to be respected in that form. After these things, he requested that Our Lord's crown of thorns be brought to him by the Bishop of Paris, and also the kings' coronation crown by the Abbot of Saint Denis. The one of thorns he received with great piety, tears, and respect and had it placed high above his head; that of the coronation he had placed at his feet.[24]

Then he began this prayer to the holy crown: "O precious crown, diadem of our salvation, so sweet and honeyed is the satisfaction that you give, from the mystery that was embodied within you at our redemption; in truth may that One, with whose blood you were sprinkled, be favorable to me, as my spirit rejoices in the visitation of your holy presence!" And he said a long prayer very devoutly.

Afterwards, turning his words to the crown of France, he said, "O crown! How inestimable you are and inestimably how very vile. Inestimable considering the mystery of justice, that you enclose within you and that you carry with such force, but vile and the vilest of all things considering the labors, deeds, anguishes, torments, and pains of heart, body, conscience, and the perils of the soul that you give to those who wear you on their shoulders, and he who might truly see these things would rather leave you lying in the mud than lift you to be placed on his head." There the king said many notable words, full of such great faith, devotion, and gratitude towards God, that all hearing them were moved to tears and great compunction.

After that, mass was sung and the king requested that lauds and benedictions be sung to God in melodious chants and with musical instruments. The king was carried from his couch to his bed and as he began to weaken considerably, his confessor went to him and said, "Sire! You commanded me that, without waiting for the last need, I was to say the last rites, although necessity may fail to pursue you and although after such unction many may return to good health. Do you wish for the comfort of your soul to receive it?"

The king responded that it would please him greatly. It was then made ready for him, and the king requested that all manner of people to whom it would be pleasing might enter within his chambers, which were full of barons, prelates, knights, celebrated clerks, and nobles, all crying with great sobs at the death of their good prince. Grief especially led there his loyal chamberlain, the Lord de la Rivière,[25] whose sorrow was so great that he seemed like a man entirely out of his senses. And as he came from outside, he went to kiss his king with such a countenance that it made all present feel great pity.

The king himself, in accordance with his weakness, helped to administer the last rites. When the cross was presented to him, he kissed it, and, while embracing it, began to speak, regarding the figure of Our Lord. "My most sweet Savior and Redeemer, who deigned to come into this world so that I and all the human race might be repurchased by the death that You consented to suffer, voluntarily and without constraint; who has instituted me, unworthy and unable to govern Your realm of France, as Your vicar, I have very grievously sinned against You, about which I say, *'Mea culpa, mea culpa, mea gravissima culpa, mea maxima culpa.'* Notwithstanding, my sweet God, that I have angered You by innumerable faults, I know that You are truly merciful and do not desire the death of a sinner; for this reason, to You, Father of mercy and of all consolation, on the threshold of my very great need, crying and calling unto You, I ask pardon."

This prayer finished, he turned his face towards his people and followers who were there, and he said, "I well know that in the government of this realm and in several things, big, medium, and small, I have offended, and I have also offended my servants, to whom I must be kind and not ungrateful for their loyal service, and for this also, I pray you have mercy upon me; I ask pardon from you."

And then he raised his arms and joined his hands; thus you can imagine the great pity and tears shed there by his loyal friends and servants. Still he said: "All know and God knew it first, that nothing of this world, nor prosperity of worldly vanity, would separate me from nor incline my will to any other thing except what God wished to command of me. He knows that there is no precious thing whatsoever for which I would have wanted or desired to be turned back from this illness."

A little later, while approaching the time of his end, in the manner of the ancient patriarchs of the Old Testament, he had his oldest son, the dauphin, led before him. Then, while blessing him, he began thus to speak: "Thus as Abraham blessed and established his son Isaac, in the dew of the heavens and in the fat of the earth, and in the abundance of wheat, wine, and oil, while adding that he who would bless him would be blessed, and he who would curse him would be filled with curses, thus may it please God to give to this Charles the dew of the heavens, and the fat of the earth, and the abundance of wheat, wine, and oil, and may all the races serve him, may he be lord of all his brothers, and may the sons of his mother bow before him. He who will bless him, let him be blessed, and he who will curse him, let him be filled with curses!"

This rite done, at the prayer of the Lord de la Rivière, he blessed all present, speaking thusly, *"Benedicio Dei, Patris et Filii et Spiritus sancti, descendat super vos et maneat semper";* which benediction all received on their knees with great devotion and tears; then the king said to them: "My friends, go from here and pray for me and leave me that my work may be finished in peace." Then turning himself on his other side, and soon afterwards sliding toward the anguish of death, he heard the whole story of the Passion and near the end of the Gospel of Saint John, began to work towards the final end. And, with a few cries and sobs, in the arms of La Rivière, whom he loved very dearly, he rendered his soul to Our Savior, which was, as is told, around noon on the twenty-sixth day of September in the reported year 1380, at forty-four years of age, and in the seventeenth year of his reign.[26] His death was bemoaned and mourned greatly by his brothers, family, and friends, and greatly regretted by his servants and by all other wise and noble men, and with good reason, because it is not surprising if the loss of so excellent a prince is devastating.

GLENDA MCLEOD

(Translated from *Le Livre des Fais et Bonnes Meurs du Sage Roy Charles V,* ed. Suzanne Solente)

NOTES

1. This proverb is listed in J. W. Hassell, Jr., *Middle French Proverbs, Sentences and Proverbial Phrases* (Toronto, 1982) and in B. J. and H. W. Whiting, *Proverbs, Sentences, and Proverbial Phrases from English Writings Mainly before 1400* (Cambridge, MA, 1968).

2. This account of Alfred the Great comes from the French translation of Bernard Gui's *Flores Chronicorum* (Flowers of the Chronicles). Charles V's copy of this translation, made by Jean Golein, is now in the Vatican Library (Ms. Reg. Lat. 697).

3. The Hotel of Saint Paul, between the modern Place de la Bastille and the Quai des Celestins, was a collection of buildings connected by a series of galleries that Charles had acquired while still dauphin. Because of civil unrest during his father's

captivity in England, he had unhappy associations with the old palace on the Ile de la Cité and he enjoyed the relative peace of the location outside the center of Paris. This palace was surrounded by gardens and orchards and even included a zoo, which housed exotic birds and the boars and lions fancied by the king, an installation recalled in the name of the still-existing Rue des Lions.

4. The most noted connoisseur in the family was, of course, his brother John, Duke of Berry, but the king also had extensive collections of jewels and other treasures.

5. Several copies of both of these works appear in the inventories of the king's library. See L. Delisle, *Recherches sur la librairies de Charles V* (Paris, 1907), 2 vols.

6. Christine is referring here to the *Chronique normande du XIVe siècle*, eds. A. and E. Molinier (Paris, 1882), p. 172.

7. Vernon is a town on the Seine River, north of Paris and just within the border of the Duchy of Normandy.

8. The Battle of Cocherel marked the triumph of Charles V over his brother-in-law and rival for the French throne, Charles (the Bad), King of Navarre. The latter's claim was through his mother, daughter of Louis X, and was even more direct than that of Edward III of England. In addition to being denied the crown, he had been despoiled of Champagne and Angoulême, to which he had inherited a title, and when he married John II's daughter (Charles V's sister), her dowry was never paid. At the beginning of 1364 he was in revolt, having just been deprived of another inheritance, Burgundy, which had been bestowed on the king's younger brother, Philip. Recruiting troops in Normandy and enlisting the help of the powerful Captal de Buch with Edward III's blessing, he attacked the French forces at Cocherel, not far from Vernon, in May, but was routed by the superior military prowess of the Breton captain Bertrand DuGuesclin, who would subsequently become Charles V's chief military leader in his reconquest of France.

9. Although it is possible to identify this detail in the writings of Saint Augustine (Migne, *Patr. lat.*, vol. XLV, col. 1432), it is probable that Christine is quoting one of her favorite sources, the *Manipulus Florum* attributed to Thomas Hibernicus, a collection of quotations from religious and secular classical texts much favored by preachers. Christine made use of it in several of her important works. See R. and M. A. Rouse, *Preachers, Florilegia and Sermons* (Toronto, 1979), pp. 213–15.

10. Charles V's library was installed in a tower of the palace of the Louvre, the official royal residence. Supervised until 1411 by Giles Malet, an especially trusted member of the royal household and a friend of Christine's husband's family, this collection of manuscripts had no equal in Europe except for the Visconti Library in Pavia. Above the principal room was another where visitors might come to consult the books. Desks and chairs were provided, as well as iron grilles at the windows to keep birds from flying in.

11. Christine is presumably speaking of the translation by Raoul de Presles, which does not seem to have been completed. The oldest known copy, with the translator's preface, is now London, British Library Ms. Lansdowne 1175. See S. Berger, *La Bible française au moyen âge* (Paris, 1884), pp. 244–45.

12. Likewise translated by Raoul de Presles, the manuscript presented by the translator to Charles V is now in Paris, Bibl. Nat. Ms. fr. 22912–22913. See *La Librairie de Charles V*, Bibliothèque Nationale (Paris, 1968), no. 177; C. C. Willard, "Raoul de Presles's Translation of Saint Augustine's *De Civitate Dei*" in *Medieval Translators and their Craft*, ed. J. Beer (Kalamazoo, 1989), pp. 329–46.

13. Nicolas Oresme translated Aristotle's *De Caelo et Mundo* around 1377.

14. Oresme also translated Aristotle's *Ethics* and *Politics*. The king's manuscript is now Brussels, Bibl. Roy. Ms. 11.201–11.202.

15. This is probably a reference to an anonymous translation made in 1380, although Charles V also had in his library a copy of the earlier translation by Jean de Meun.

16. This popular encyclopedia was translated into French in 1372 by the king's chaplain, Jean Corbechon.

17. The translation of the first four books was completed by Simon de Hesdin in 1375. The king's copy, with a miniature showing the translator presenting his work to Charles, is now B.N. Ms. fr. 9749.

18. The Franciscan Denis Foullechat completed this translation of John of Salisbury's twelfth-century political treatise for Charles V in 1372. The presentation copy, with its miniature depicting the king consulting the work, is now Paris, B.N. Ms. fr. 24287.

19. Christine was mistaken in thinking that this Roman history was translated at the request of Charles V. It was his father, John II, who commissioned Pierre Bersuire to translate it. Charles V's copy, bearing his signature, is now Paris, Bibl. Sainte-Geneviève Ms. 777.

20. Christine is obviously confusing here the king of Egypt with Claude Ptolomy, the celebrated astronomer and geographer. This confusion may, however, be accounted for by her sources, Bernard Gui's *Flower of the Chronicles* and Jean Golein's *Rational of Holy Offices,* of which the king's copy is now Paris, B.N. Ms. fr. 437. Either one would explain the error.

21. This anecdote about Charles V is repeated in both the *Livre de la Paix* (Willard ed., p. 157) and the *Epître de la Prison de Vie Humaine* (Kennedy ed., p. 36).

22. Although Christine claimed (chap. LXX) to have heard the details of the king's death from her father, who was in attendance, it appears that she could also have known an anonymous Latin account of the event (Paris, B.N. Ms. lat. 8299). Even so, she was mistaken about the date of Charles V's arrival at his Château of Beauté, which was actually around August 21st.

23. Christine chose to pass as lightly as possible over Charles V's role in the continuing schism of the Church.

24. This scene of the two crowns, and especially Charles V's words over the crown of thorns, is not known from any other account. It is possible that it was Christine's invention to heighten the drama of the scene.

25. Bureau de la Rivière was the king's First Chamberlain and one of the favorite members of his entourage. He and his wife were both friends of Christine; she would praise the wife in *The Book of the City of Ladies.* Bureau de la Rivière could also have given Christine details of the king's final hours.

26. Both Christine and the Latin chronicle were mistaken about the actual date of the king's death, which was Sunday, September 17th.

CCW

VI

THE FATE OF FRANCE

❦

AN ASPECT of Christine de Pizan's career that has been all too frequently overlooked is her concern for the fate of France. She was, in fact, a fascinating witness of the times in which she lived, concerned about the significance of the events she witnessed, as well as a telling observer of the life of women.

Her first organized comments on the state of France date from early in her career as a writer, shortly after she had written *The Letter of Othea*, it would appear, for in the *Prod'hommie de l'Homme (The Book of Man's Integrity)* she refers to what she had already said in the earlier work. This second work also belongs to the period when she was frequenting the Orleans court, for it is dedicated rather flamboyantly to the Duke of Orleans. Thus it might also have been more or less contemporary with *The Tale of the Rose,* which has as its setting this same court. It should also be recalled that at the end of *The Long Road to Learning,* Christine had presented herself as a messenger from the Court of Reason, directed to advise the French princes on their obligations to society. All these factors would explain the composition of a work intended to remind these princes of the need for uprightness and integrity in French society.

The Book of Man's Integrity presents itself as a translation of the popular *Book of the Four Virtues,* widely attributed to Seneca but really the work of Martin of Braga, a Portuguese bishop who lived in the sixth century.[1] The text, devoted to an exposition of the Cardinal Virtues, was popular throughout the Middle Ages, as numerous manuscripts of both the Latin original and translations into several other languages testify. A curious aspect of Christine's interest in the text is that another translation, presumably by Jean Courtecuisse, was presented to the Duke of Berry in 1403.[2] It is indeed surprising that Christine should have presented a translation and commentary of the same text to Louis of Orleans at so nearly the same time. One is inclined to think that hers was slightly earlier and that she was unaware of the other. Another curious aspect of Christine's translation is that when she later included the text in the principal collections of her works, it was entitled the *Livre de Prudence (The Book of Prudence)* with all reference to Louis of Orleans omitted.

Christine's authorship of the actual translation has been questioned, but it has already been noted that she was able to read Latin sufficiently well to use Latin sources for *The Letter of Othea* and *The Mutation of Fortune*. She would later translate and comment on Latin quotations at the beginning of each chapter of *The Book of Peace*. As she mentions in the *Vision*, she was falsely accused of having learned men write her books; she might indeed have been referring to this translation. It is not, however, the merit of the translation but rather the commentary that should interest Christine's readers.

There is no doubt that Christine was familiar with the translations commissioned by Charles V for his library. She mentions them in both her biography of the king and *The Book of Peace*. These translations were normally accompanied by commentaries by the translator, who intended to show, among other things, how the text in question had a message for contemporary readers. A notable case was Raoul de Presles's translation of Saint Augustine's *City of God*, where the original account of God's favors to Constantine as he built the city of Constantinople gives rise to the translator's discussion of the legendary Trojan origins of Paris, along with an important description of Charles V's rebuilding of the city. Another passage in the text inspired a commentary on the Salic law, for which there was no real foundation in the Latin original; while it was pure invention on the translator's part, the commentary provided an essential element in Charles V's claim to the French throne.[3] Commentaries on classical texts were, of course, a well-established method of instruction in universities of the day.

Nothing could reveal Christine's intentions in presenting her translation better than a comparison of her commentaries on the Four Virtues with those of Courtecuisse. His function was primarily a display of erudition, explanations of the meanings of certain expressions and comparisons with the ideas of other writers, notably of Cicero in the chapter devoted to Justice. Christine, on the other hand, seeks to apply the principles of Justice to the problems of the day. As she would later explain in the *Vision*, she had herself experienced the miscarriage of justice in the French legal system. She would dwell further on the importance of this quality in public life in both the *Body of Policy* and *The Book of Peace*.

She was by no means alone in her discussion of such problems, for they preoccupied a good many thinkers of the day, notably Philippe de Mézières in his advice to the youthful Charles VI in the *Songe du Vieil Pèlerin*, written around 1389, and the sermons preached by Jean Gerson at the French court.[4] One inevitably suspects that Christine's intent was to use this translation as a sort of cover for rather pointed criticisms of French society directed to the Duke of Orleans, who might be expected to have some influence in such matters. One is forced to conclude, however, that the duke was not pleased. In contrast with the multiple copies of *The Letter of Othea*, there are but two known copies of this translation, one of them in a compilation of texts dating from the middle of the fifteenth century. In the revised *Book of Prudence*, there is no mention whatsoever of the duke. Moreover, the Duke of Orleans was unable to find a place in his household for Christine's son, Jean. It was the Duke of Burgundy, Philip the Bold, who solved that problem for Christine, and shortly thereafter commissioned her to write the biography of his brother, Charles V.

Unfortunately, Philip the Bold did not live to see the biography completed, for he died in March 1404. The arrival of his son on the French political scene created serious new problems. Philip had been ambitious, but he was a sufficiently skilled politician to see to it that at least a superficial calm was maintained. His son, John the Fearless, was brash in addition to being ambitious, and he was a very unprepossessing man who would have been understandably jealous of his suave, handsome cousin, Louis of Orleans. Both were determined to dominate the government of the hopelessly incompetent king. John did enjoy the advantage of having just married his daughter, Marguerite, to the heir to the French throne, Louis of Guyenne. Arranging the marriage had been the old duke's last political accomplishment.

Serious trouble arose during the summer of 1405 when Burgundy proposed to come to Paris to do homage to the king for lands he had just inherited from his mother, who had been Countess of Flanders in her own right. In August, the Duke of Orleans learned that his rival was preparing to come to Paris at the head of a sizable army. Doubtful of his intentions, Orleans fled from the city with the queen, with whom he was now on terms of intimacy. The two of them took refuge in Melun, south of Paris, arranging for the Duke of Guyenne and his young wife to follow them, in order to avoid the Duke of Burgundy's influence.

When John the Fearless learned of this plot on his arrival in Paris, he lost no time in intercepting the royal children and bringing them back to Paris, where he had them well guarded in the Louvre. Since Louis of Orleans had also provided himself with an army, Paris was soon surrounded on all sides. The Parisians were understandably alarmed, fearing the outbreak of civil war. No solution to the crisis was achieved until the beginning of October; in the meantime, both sides waged a war of propaganda. However, several other members of the royal family, the kings of Sicily and Navarre, along with the dukes of Berry and Bourbon, worked to bring about a reconciliation of the conflicting parties. At the end of September the queen and the duke agreed to leave Melun; at the last moment, however, they refused to return to Paris, and went instead to the Château of Vincennes, just outside the city gates. It was at this time that the queen was reminded of her duty, established in 1402, to act in the king's place if he was incapacitated. So it was that the queen, at the beginning of October, wrote to the dukes of Berry and Bourbon and even Burgundy, commencing negotiations for a truce. A letter written by the King of Navarre to the King of Castille about the same time expressed confidence that the difficulties would soon be resolved. On October 5th, Christine addressed a letter to the queen begging her to heal the rift between the dukes of Burgundy and Orleans and to save the country from disaster, citing the example of queens of the past who had done as much for their people.

It seems doubtful that she would have done this entirely on her own initiative. Raimond Thomassy, who first published the text of this letter in 1838, assumed that it had been written at the request of Louis of Orleans, an opinion that has been repeated on several occasions. It must nevertheless be remembered that neither he nor the queen was in Paris. It would have been difficult for Christine to get a letter to the duke through the lines of military men who were still surrounding the city unless she had some sort of official authorization to do so. Two of three copies of Christine's letter are introduced with an explanation of the circumstances in which it was written. [6] Since Christine emphasizes the efforts of the royal princes to bring about a reconciliation, it seems reasonable to suppose that it was at the request of one of them that she wrote the letter. A good candidate would have been the King of Navarre, for whom she later composed the *Seven Allegorized Psalms*. It is interesting to note that in writing the letter she seems to be unaware that the queen and the duke were no longer at Melun. It is also interesting that the letter echoes those queenly achievements already praised in *The Book of the City of Ladies* and some exhortations to queenly responsibilities developed in *The Treasury of the City of Ladies,* or *The Book of the Three Virtues.*

The kidnapping of the dauphin underscores the importance of controlling him and dramatizes the struggle in progress since the onset of his father's insanity. In addition to the relatives who wanted to direct the destiny of the young prince and, therefore, the country, there were writers who wished to guide his education so that he would reign successfully on his own.

These works dedicated to Louis of Guyenne belong to the great body of medieval literature known as "mirrors of princes," aimed at the formation of the "perfect prince," capable of dealing successfully with all sorts of social ills. Although the concept goes back as far as Saint Augustine, of particular importance to the tradition was John of Salisbury's twelfth century *Polycraticus,* which had been translated for Charles V by Denis Foullechat in 1372.[7] It develops the concept of the state as a human body, an organic unity of which the prince is the head, the nobles and knights the hands and arms to defend it, the artisans and peasants the feet and stomach to support and nourish it. This concept inspired Christine's next book, the *Livre du Corps de Policie (The Book of the Body of Policy).* Although John of Salisbury was the most obvious source, Christine also made considerable use of the treatise on the education of princes entitled the *Livre du Gouvernement de Rois (The Book on the Government of Kings)* by Gilles of Rome (or Egidio Colonna, as he was also called). She also made use of the Roman history by Valerius Maximus, the translation of which had been commissioned by Charles V from Simon de Hesdin, although it was subsequently finished by Nicholas de Gonesse.[8] Furthermore, *The Book of the Body of Policy* is a sort of parallel work to *The Treasury of the City of Ladies,* which Christine had dedicated to the Duchess of Guyenne only a short time before. The organization of the two books is similar, and both are devoted to the education of all classes of society.

It is probable that *The Book of the Body of Policy* was written between 1405 and the end of 1407, for there is a reference to the Duke of Orleans as still alive; in November 1407 he would be murdered in the streets of Paris by the Duke of Burgundy's assassins. The book is full of other references to troubles that were endangering life in France: jealousies at court; the corruption of the clergy; the menace of soldiers plundering the countryside and the shocking treatment of civilian populations in towns captured by these marauding soldiers. It is quite evident that Christine shared with some contemporary writers the hope that a humane prince would be able to deal with some of these miseries.

Although the first section, by far the longest, is devoted to the education and duties of this ideal prince, the second part discusses the need of adequate training for knights and for a disciplined army, which should be properly paid so that members are not tempted to engage in unlawful activities; the third part emphasized the role of clerks, merchants, and the laboring classes in good government. Especially interesting is the emphasis Christine places on the importance of the middle class in maintaining governmental stability. Her confidence in the popular classes is limited.

The chapters included in this collection of translations outline the early education of the prince. Even more so than those contemporaries who gave advice on this subject, Christine insists on the importance of early education in the formation of a worthy person, whether prince or commoner. She therefore recommends that the prince, like the young princess described in *The Treasury of the City of Ladies,* should early be provided with a suitable tutor—in this case a man of excellent character—who will instruct the child in a kindly but firm manner to distinguish between good and evil. Then, if he shows any aptitude, he can be encouraged to seek out the pleasures that can be derived from learning.

Christine's ideas about the instruction of children with kindness in order to awaken their curiosity naturally have never been given the attention they deserve. Her books for the Duke and Duchess of Guyenne are contemporary with the earliest of the Italian humanistic treatises on education that advocate compassion in the early education of children. [9] It would be interesting to know more about the educational ideas of Christine's father and his generation in Italy in order to appreciate fully Christine's theories, which were rather advanced for her day.

Her next book, devoted to the training and duties of knights in defense of the country, would seem to have grown logically out of *The Body of Policy. Les Faits d'Armes et de Chevalerie (The Deeds of Arms and of Chivalry)* was written in 1410. At the end of 1409, John the Fearless had managed to become the virtual ruler of Paris, charged especially with the education of the dauphin, who had by now reached the traditional age for training for knighthood. Up to this time the young prince had shown neither interest in nor aptitude for such activity, which was indeed unfortunate in a country constantly threatened by civil war. The Duke of Burgundy, on the other hand, was an unusually competent military leader, as he had demonstrated not long before by a resounding victory over the rebellious citizens of the prince-archbishopric of Liège, an enclave between Brabant and Limbourg ruled by the duke's brother-in-law. He would therefore have been concerned about his son-in-law's shortcomings in this regard. Since Christine had already demonstrated her interest and skill in providing books for the education of his daughter and son-in-law, it seems quite possible that he should have encouraged Christine, if not actually commissioned her, to write a textbook on the art of warfare. A substantial gift paid to her by the royal treasury in May 1411, certainly under his control at that date, supports such a supposition.

Christine has been accused of "pilfering" Vegetius in writing her *Deeds of Arms and of Chivalry;* this is not only unjust but distorts the nature of her undertaking. The *De Re Militari* of the Roman Vegetius was the only book on military training that had been written in several centuries. It remained a standard text on the subject not only in the fifteenth century but as late as the nineteenth. Furthermore, the French military, which had been reasonably well organized during the reign of Charles V, had fallen into a sorry state of confusion. Many knights in Christine's day were more interested in personal glory than in the country it was their sworn duty to protect. The force of Roman example was much needed; in the Roman army soldiers fought collectively in units rather than for individual prowess.

Vegetius had indeed been translated into French several times during the Middle Ages, and most recently in 1380,[10] but warfare had changed in thirty years, especially with the development of gunpowder and artillery, and Christine's constant references to the differences between past and present necessities provide some of the most interesting moments in the book.

An important source for the second half of the book was the *Arbre des Batailles (Tree of Battles)* written for Charles VI in 1387 by Honoré Bouvet (or Bonet), prior of Salon in southern France.[11] Bouvet, in his turn, had been largely inspired by a treatise written by John of Legnano, a professor of law at the University of Bologna, entitled *De Bello, de Represaliis et de Duello (On War, on Reprisals and on Dueling)*. It is probable that Christine at least knew of this work of the Italian lawyer, for he had been a contemporary of her father's at the University of

Bologna. Legnano had married into the family of another famous Bolognese law professor, Giovanni Andrea, whose daughter Novella figures in *The Book of the City of Ladies.*[12] Christine also mentions on more than one occasion the civil strife in Bologna around 1350 that inspired Legnano's treatise. It was perhaps his support for the Roman pope during the papal schism that accounts for the fact that neither Christine nor Bouvet, who lived in a place that favored the Avignon pope, saw fit to mention Legnano by name.

Although Christine has been criticized for lack of originality in *The Deeds of Arms and of Chivalry,* it is important to remember that she was writing a military textbook, where fact supersedes inspiration. Furthermore, she had few models for her undertaking, although the number of manuscripts that remain indicate its success. Furthermore, she was writing not only for a young, inexperienced prince but for other military men, some of whom may have had little formal education if indeed they could read at all. She refers on several occasions to those who would hear the text read to them. She needed to simplify ideas from more learned treatises and to apply them to problems then existing in France. It is evident that she also had sought the advice of some experienced military men whom she knew personally, perhaps some who remembered the regime of Charles V when greater importance had been given to military training and to an organized army. Charles V had also concerned himself with the development of a useful navy, which perhaps accounts for Christine's vivid account of a sea battle. Much of this expertise had been lost in France by the time Christine was writing.

Although she was writing in an era when pacifism would have been futile, Christine sees warfare as always honorable and, insofar as possible, humane, especially for civilian populations that had so much to worry from undisciplined armies. Thus the second half of the book takes the form of conversations that Christine purports to hold with Honoré Bouvet, who is easily identifiable even if he is not specifically named. She joins him in attempting to outline a basic international law governing warfare, a concept that people in the modern world take for granted but that was then in its infancy. Discussions such as the ones in Christine's book made no small contribution to the theories later codified as international law.

The response to Christine's art of warfare shows that it achieved a considerable degree of success in other respects, too. In addition to the manuscripts that still exist, a number of them dating from the period when the French army was being reorganized under Charles VII, the text was printed in Paris by Antoine Vérard in 1488 and reprinted in 1527; an English translation was also prepared and printed by William Caxton at the direction of Henry VII in 1489. A curious aspect of one group of the manuscripts, as well as the French imprints, is that they suppress all mention of Christine, although the work is attributed to her in the Caxton edition. Possibly there was an assumption that a woman would have been incapable of writing such a book, but there is also the suggestion that her book continued to be useful long after she was forgotten. A modern military historian has commended her book as an example of the resumption of professionalism in the military, a quality that had been largely unknown since the time of Vegetius himself.[13] It should be added that Louis of Guyenne subsequently showed evidence of having developed some skill as a military leader; if he had not unexpectedly died at the age of eighteen, he might have improved the fortunes of his sorely tried country.

Just as Christine would probably have been finishing *The Deeds of Arms and of Chivalry,* however, France was suffering another crisis: a showdown between the Duke of Burgundy and supporters of the House of Orleans, now dominated by the young duke's father-in-law, the Count of Armagnac. This latter group of noblemen was determined to overthrow John the Fearless. The menace of these events led Christine to write another public letter, this one to the elderly Duke of Berry, the last member of Charles V's generation and the only one who seemed to have the required prestige and spirit of neutrality to resolve the situation.[14] At the same time, she appealed to all elements of French society to marshal the strength to combat the dangers facing them all. It is an eloquent letter from the pen of a writer who was by now well aware of her talents, but at the same time it reflects the mortal terror felt by Parisians at the prospect of civil war.

Fortunately, a truce achieved in 1412 spared them. This was due, at least in part, to the Duke of Guyenne's efforts. The treaty that was signed in November was brought about in large measure because both sides had exhausted provisions and money. The Treaty of Bicêtre, however, merely gave them breathing space: the following year civil war broke out in earnest. In order to obtain much needed help, the Armagnacs had felt obliged to make a compromise with the English. This gave the Duke of Burgundy, who had been unwilling to go so far, the opportunity to declare himself the defender of the realm and persuade Charles VI and Louis of Guyenne to join him in punishing the traitors. Another truce was achieved at the end of August, but with little good faith on either side. This lull in hostilities, however, inspired Christine to begin her *Livre de la Paix (Book of Peace),*[15] in which she pinned her hopes for a peaceful solution on the dauphin, who was indeed beginning to show some qualities of leadership. In it she repeated much of the advice on kingship she had already presented in *The Body of Policy,* although this time she was applying it to a specific situation.

Unfortunately, before anything constructive could be achieved, a new element appeared in the struggle. Merchants, artisans, and laborers, exhausted by the selfish and irresponsible behavior of their princes, voiced a strong demand for reform in the government. It was their misfortune to be headed by the corporation of butchers, a large and violent group that led the others to revolt in the spring of 1413.[16] On March 28th, they marched on the Bastille; a group of them even invaded the dauphin's private apartments in the Louvre, seizing fifteen members of his household. Eventually the prince was forced to appoint to official posts in the city government the leading butchers, notably Denis de Chaument and Simeon de Caboche, who gave his name to the revolt. It was a preview of revolutions to come, and Christine's comments on the events she witnessed confirmed the misgivings about the stability of the common people she had already expressed in *The Body of Policy.* Even the efforts of John the Fearless and university leaders to calm the rebels were of no avail. Terror reigned throughout the summer, and it was only on August 4th that the crowds were dispersed. The reforms that had been promised were then quickly annulled by Parliament. In the end, petty class jealousies had prevented the Parisians from working for their common benefit. Christine's account of these events not only gives a vivid impression of her horror at the violence in the streets, but reflects her upper-class disdain for mobs. More important, however, is the fact that she spoke for a new group of Parisians who were trying to make their voices heard, those who were neither Armagnac nor Burgundian sympathizers. These are the views that form the basis for *The Book of Peace,* along with Christine's attempt to urge the dauphin to his responsibility in his country's destiny.

It was, however, too late. The Armagnacs, now favored by the dauphin, gained the upper hand, and the Burgundians were expelled from Paris. New difficulties with England encouraged Henry V to undertake his invasion of France, leading to the French disaster at Agincourt in November 1415. This was followed only a few weeks later by Louis of Guyenne's unexpected death, leaving the country vulnerable to both invasion and civil war. It was one of France's darkest hours.

An interesting aspect of Christine's writings about France is that she shared ideas on the salvation of the country—and the need for a prince sufficiently well-educated to deal effectively with the country's problems—with other intellectuals of the day. One thinks not only of Jean Gerson, whose educational ideas for the prince are expressed in a letter to his tutor, Jean d'Arsonval, and the sermon *Vivat Rex (Long Live the King)* preached to the French court in November 1405, or *Veniat Pax (Let Peace Come)* of November 1408, but also the treatises of Jean de Montreuil, *A Toute la Chevalerie (To All Knighthood)* and *Contre les Anglais (Against the English)*.[17] Although he had been Christine's opponent in the debate over *The Romance of the Rose*, they were united in their concern for France, which was perhaps as important to Christine as her interest in the situation of women. Ultimately for her, the two would be combined.

NOTES

1. Saint Martin, bishop of the northern Portuguese city of Braga, died in 579. See C. W. Barlow, *Iberian Fathers: Martin of Braga, Paschasius of Duminium, Leander of Seville* (Washington, D.C., 1969).
2. *Sénèque des IIII vertus; la Formula Honestae Vitae de Martin de Braga (pseudo-Sénèque) traduite et glosée par Jean Courtecuisse (1403)*, ed. H. Haselbach (Berne-Frankfort, 1975).
3. C. C. Willard, "Raoul de Presles's Translation of Saint Augustine's *De Civitate Dei*," *Medieval Translators and their Craft*, ed. J. Beer (Kalamazoo, 1989), pp. 329–46.
4. J. Krynens, *Idéal du Prince et Pouvoir Royal en France à la fin du Moyen Age, 1380–1440* (Paris, 1981), especially pp. 184–99.
5. L. Mirot, "L'Enlèvement du dauphin et le premier conflit entre Jean sans Peur et Louis d'Orléans, Juillet-Octobre 1405," *Revue des Questions Historiques* 95 (1914), 329–55 and 96 (1914), 47–68 and 369–419; M. Nordberg, *Les Ducs et la Royauté* (Uppsala, 1964), pp. 185–204.
6. R. Thomassy, *Essai sur les écrits politiques de Christine de Pisan* (Paris, 1838), pp. 133–40; Chantilly, Musée Condé, Ms. 493, fol. 427v°–429v°.
7. John of Salisbury, *Policraticus; of the Frivolities of Courtiers and the Footprints of Philosophers*, ed. and trans. C. J. Nederman (Cambridge, 1990). The copy of the French translation presented to Charles V is B.N. ms. fr. 24287.
8. The translation of the first four books of Roman history by Valerius Maximus was dedicated to Charles V by Simon de Hesdin in 1375; it was completed by Nicolas de Gonesse for the Duke of Berry in 1401. Christine had already made use of it in *The Long Road to Learning* in 1403.
9. See W. H. Woodward, *Studies in Education during the Age of the Renaissance, 1400–1600* (New York, 1967). Also C. C. Willard, "Christine de Pizan as Teacher,"

Romance Languages Annual III (1991), (Purdue Research Foundation, 1992), pp. 132 – 36.

10. J. Camus, "Notice d'une traduction française de Végèce faite en 1380," *Romania* 24 (1896), 393 – 400. This translation is attributed, although without convincing evidence, to Eustache Deschamps.

11. G. W. Coopland, *The Tree of Battles of Honoré Bonet* (Liverpool, 1949). For the name of the author, see G. Ouy, "Honoré Bouvet (appelé à tort Bonet) prieur de Selonnet," *Romania* 35 (1959), 255 – 59; A. R. Wright, "The Tree of Battles of Honoré Bouvet and the Laws of War," in *War, Literature and Politics in the Late Middle Ages*, ed. C. T. Allmand (Liverpool, 1976), pp. 12 – 31.

12. John of Legnano, *Tractatus de Bello, de Represaliis et de Duello*, ed. T. E. Holland and trans. J. L. Brierly (Oxford, 1917). Christine's reference to Novella is in *The City of Ladies*, Book II, chap. 36 (Richards trans., p. 154).

13. R. E. and T. N. Dupuy, *The Encyclopedia of Military History from 3500 B.C. to the Present* (2nd ed.; New York, 1986), p. 400.

14. The best modern text of *La Lamentacion sur les Maux de la France* is edited by A. J. Kennedy in the *Mélanges . . . offerts à Charles Foulon*, I, (Rennes, 1980), pp. 177 – 85.

15. *Le Livre de la Paix*, ed. C. C. Willard (The Hague, 1958).

16. A. Coville, *Les Cabochiens et l'Ordonnance de 1413* (Paris, 1888).

17. Jean Gerson, *Oeuvres complètes*, Vol. VII (2), ed. Mgr. Glorieux (Paris, 1968), pp. 1137 – 85; 1100 – 23; Jean de Montreuil, *Opera*, II, ed. N. Grevy, E. Ornato, G. Ouy (Turin, 1975), pp. 89 – 149; 159 – 218.

THE BOOK OF MAN'S INTEGRITY[1]

❦

Here We Speak to Princes and Officers of Justice Concerning the Virtue of Justice, the Third Cardinal Virtue, with Reference to Showing Merit by Deeds

Speaking about what applies to the teaching of anyone who wishes to be virtuous and just and what is involved in this, and following what we have already said concerning the application of virtues, we come to the third cardinal virtue, which is called Justice. Even though it is necessary to all for their salvation to be just, still the application of this virtue, properly speaking, is especially significant for princes by whom others are governed, or for those who are responsible for administering justice, than it is for others.[2] So we will say, following our authority: TEXT: Justice after these other things. This is to say after the other virtues we have already discussed. TEXT: Justice is a silent composition of nature established for the benefit of the group. What is just except our constituted or divine law, the binding together of human company? GLOSS: Justice, according to Aristotle, is a measure that gives everyone his due.[3] It is what keeps the world in peace wherever it reigns, but where it is imperfectly kept confusion exists. O, how justice is beloved of God and how necessary it is to the world! It is a bond of equity that preserves peaceful order.

TEXT: Through it nobody should have doubts about what he ought to do, for whatever it orders is expedient. GLOSS: Honored worldly princes, may all of you who are guardians of Justice hear the wise authority who speaks to you and says that you should not hesitate to act justly, for what Justice recommends is proper and what it leads you to do is pleasing to God. O ministers of God, begin then with yourselves, and have concern for your souls that should be Heaven's heirs. Do not allow sensuality or vice to supress or remove them from their proper place, and take care that your judgment is not corrupted by undue greed, which might undermine the effect of reason and propriety. For your further instruction the text says: Those among you who would wish for this quality to be given to you, first of all you must fear and love God, so that you may be loved by Him. This text requires no explanation, for it is clear, but consider once more how it says that what is done should be for the good of your fellow man.

TEXT: Therefore you will love God, if you would follow Him, by concerning yourselves with the good of all without harm to anyone. Then all will call you just and follow you, honoring and loving you. GLOSS: Thus you can understand how loving God befits the one who wishes to be just. Heavens! What a great thing it is merely to love God, and surely nothing more is needed to do good. This is the first commandment, for who loves Him fears Him, and this fear is the beginning of wisdom, as the Psalmist says.[4] Therefore, anyone who puts his love before all actions cannot go astray. It is like the light that goes before to show the way. Who loves Him will follow Him in this respect and in all others and will wish for the good of all, for all virtues will flourish in him and he will provide an example to others in good works and true doctrine as well as by his acts of mercy. He will not injure anyone through bad advice or dishonest pretensions, or by any sort of extortion, and so all will call him a just man, will follow him, admire him and honor him; that is to say, all those who are just and virtuous.

The authority says further, describing the points of Justice: TEXT: In order to be just, not only will you not injure, but you will correct those who injure others, for justice is not merely in avoiding harm, but in protecting others from harm. GLOSS: Here you are told what you should do, lovers of Justice. This means that it is not sufficient for you, officers of Justice, merely not to cause harm, but you should punish those who do, for otherwise, as it is said, you will not be just. True justice is to protect people from harm, which is to say from criminals and others who would do them harm. The authority says further concerning these matters: TEXT: Begin then by these points: do not take what belongs to another, and do even more, restore what has been stolen, pursue and punish the thieves so that they cannot threaten others. GLOSS: In keeping with what I said before, that justice should begin with oneself, the authority forbids the prince or person dispensing justice to take anything belonging to another. O how this word can be understood in a variety of ways! It is not taking something from another when you receive what is due you through traditional well-regulated custom such as signorial rights, which were established for the well-being and protection of everyone, nor to those dispensing justice in recompense for the efforts and responsibilities of the position, but it is rather to take from another by imposing excessive charges because of greed or extortion when done under the guise of some entitlement or presumed protection of public welfare. And if some of you do such things, or place or assign new charges for personal profit without just cause or public benefit, then this is undoubtedly taking what belongs to others and you damn yourselves hopelessly.[5]

And as for judges, if they impose unreasonable and unjustified fines and other expenses, or if they take gifts that are intended to corrupt them, whereby justice becomes fraudulent, or if they charge the poor and simple by a different system from others and fail to punish their officials who do this sort of thing but rather use their influence to protect such wrongdoing because these belong to their court, and in other ways do, or allow to be done, various wrongs and extortions, such people are not ministers of justice, but of the devil himself, who is prince and author of fraud and deceit. But nevertheless, God knows how often one sees these tricks in many courts of justice, and obviously simple folk who have no favor nor indeed any particular malice are consumed by various devices. In many church courts there are the high and mighty, and it is a great wonder what tricks they have found at the devil's instigation to deceive and devour the ordinary people in particular, without conscience or regard for God, which is indeed a manifest sign of little faith or fear of the Lord. And such people, in spite of calling themselves servants of the Church, are certainly not, indeed quite the opposite, when they act against its recommendations. There is no doubt that such as these will be punished, for this is what God says, and Earth and Heaven will perish sooner than His Holy Word.

It is not enough, as the authority says, to avoid taking from another; it is necessary for the prince or dispenser of justice to make criminals give back what they have taken and to punish them. I refer to a true situation and to many who know that favor often misleads both princes and judges in such cases, for if the thief is powerful and well-connected, or perhaps even the one who has himself made the judgment concerning the restitution and the punishment, God knows how it may turn out; in the case of some unimportant and ordinary thing, and of the most wretched of mortals, punishment and restitution are indeed carried out. And if I speak too plainly, according to fact although not according to the pleasure of some, I am nevertheless telling the truth. Some know this well, as do I, who happen to have been beaten by this rod.[6]

TEXT: Do not incite controversy through any ambiguity of the voice, but rather note and consider the quality of your courage. GLOSS: What is the meaning of not showing ambiguity through a double voice, except that the prince or administrator of justice should not in any way pretend by covert language the opposite of what is truth and what he knows for certain to be the case? And why, I ask, the prince or administrator of justice more than anyone else? Because although it is unsuitable for anyone, nevertheless it is worse for such as these because more faith is placed in what they say, and since they are in a more important situation they are more able to deceive if they want to, and as they really have less reason to do so, pretense and deception are truly unworthy of them. For the one who profits from such a situation should be clear and readily understood in all deeds and words, as befits those who should have nothing to fear, for pretense seems to come from fear and servility. And speaking of such a cover and pretense, isn't it a form of treason to show oneself in word and aspect different from fact? And does one believe that it is suitable in any way except that it can perhaps be excused in this way; that is, as it seems to me, if it should happen that an individual has any reason to deal with a powerful man, hard and brusque and without pity, as is all too common, one who could cause him harm and grief, nevertheless this individual passes through his hands and he knows very well that he will gain nothing by complaining and that there is no possibility except to endure and plead, even if very little attention will be paid to him. There is no doubt that his heart aches and that he doesn't like this important person, but what of it? He knows very well that if he showed his true feelings it would be all the worse for him, and he would gain nothing. If such a person speaks well and shows a good face to the one who has wronged him, even if he doesn't like him, I insist that this is strong and useful courage and that it makes sense, because it is necessary for him. Such dissimulation or pretense is not wrong. Still, to keep God's commandment he should not pursue wrong under the guise of friendship, but should expect God's punishment and should not want to do this if he wants to be perfect. Thus one can practice licit pretense to guard one's honor, as the following text shows, or to achieve some good end, but as for deceiving, harming, or betraying another because of greed or spite, that is a wicked, ugly, and despicable vice.

TEXT: Do not make a distinction between affirming something and swearing to it, for it is a part of religion and reverence for God to speak the truth, for even if God is called to witness to the one not swearing, nevertheless do not overstep truth nor the laws of justice. GLOSS: The simple word of the prince or administrator of justice and what he affirms, if he is just, should not be different from a sworn oath, for it is essential to his position that he be believed, and also to the religion of which he is a part (which is to say God and Christianity) that he speak the truth to everyone, for when he speaks the truth, God (who is truth itself) is his witness even if he does not call on Him, nor does he need to swear to it. The reason is that when a man swears a strong oath one supposes that his simple word would not be believed and that therefore his authority is not very great. This should not be the case among those in authority, and if they overstep the law of justice by speaking falsely this is against both their duty and their honor.

Nor is there any doubt that all Christians should do the same, but many today do not observe this principle, for great deceptions and other wrongs are perpetuated while calling God's name to witness in great oaths in order to make what is said more believable, and so they deceive and cover falsehood with sovereign truth, which is God's. This is against His commandment, which forbids that His name be taken in vain, when they perjure themselves to disguise falsehood. The worst of these have such bad habits that it is a great scandal to hear coming from the mouths of Christians such expressions as "the worthy blood," "the wounds" and the "holy body" of their Savior and Redeemer by whom they have been ransomed, irreverently recalled, injuriously, or in anger, or to bear false witness. One wonders that princes or other officials allow it, or even curse and insult God themselves, as is sometimes done. Alas! Anyone who might speak of them in such a manner would certainly be punished. But in order to do away with such a custom, the prince would have to make an edict and law and he himself would have to observe it, as formerly those who established the laws did in the past, so that he could enforce it on others under pain of punishment.[7]

TEXT: If in spite of everything, you are occasionally obliged to resort to lying, do it not in misrepresentation but rather in the service of protecting something. GLOSS: Here it appears how circumstances worsen a matter, or may perhaps justify it and excuse it. For according to the meaning of the text, it seems that the author wishes to give license to lying in certain cases, but at the same time falsehood cannot be excused unless there is no harm done, in which case this wise man permits deception. Thus we should understand that he wishes to say that of two ills one should choose the lesser, for however bad lying may be, it is still possible to speak the truth in such a way to do more harm than falsehood. As the common proverb says: All truths are not pleasant to speak.[8] It is as if I knew something about myself or about another that would be very harmful if I were to say it. In that case, if someone were to ask me, or to insist that I tell what I know, I would excuse myself, saying that I didn't know anything or that there's nothing to tell. It seems to me that in this case it is a lesser evil to lie than to say something whereby I would dishonor or harm myself or another. Such a case might come about if I were to see a man with a drawn knife chase another in great anger. If the other should escape and hide in a certain place, if I were to tell the aggressor, should he ask me, that I don't know where the other is, even if I knew perfectly well, isn't this a lesser evil than if I told the truth and the other man was killed? Wouldn't I be the cause of the death of both? And so it might happen in other cases. For this reason the authority says: Use lies not for falsehood but for the protection of something, for in the case of actual falsehood or distortion, it is not to be excused in any way.

TEXT: However much loyalty sometimes seems to require that one lie, do not actually lie but excuse yourself in a better way, for the honest person does not reveal his secrets but remains silent about what should not be said and says only what should be said. GLOSS: Here the authority distinguishes between something that is of particular significance and something that is of less importance, for although he has already given license to lie, that is to say, to avoid a greater evil, he says afterwards that one does not lie even if loyalty requires it. How are we to understand this? I believe his meaning can be illustrated by such a case as this: A man serves his lord or another, and because he serves him he owes him allegiance and loyalty. The situation arises where loyalty requires that for certain reasons he lie on his master's behalf. He will not lie, because it is not a question of death or dishonor, but he will excuse him so wisely and eloquently that he will protect his master better than if he had lied for him. If he is required to reveal his master's secret or his own, he will not do so but will reply so wisely that those who ask will not know any more afterwards than before.

As we happen to be speaking of this matter, I cannot avoid smiling to myself, thinking that in this situation the rule is not very well observed today in France, for lying is not only used to protect oneself or another in some trial or need but it is also used in many other cases, and even worse, I insist, by everyone generally and in all sections of society.[9] Indeed, from the greatest to the least important, there are few who can claim that in all their actions and words they stick to the truth, and this is done more often to mislead than for other reasons. For when it is a question of excusing another, unless in exchange for some unmerited favor, there are few who will lie, but in the opposite case, it is common practice. This allows the great to make promises, and with fine words to make offers that will never be fulfilled. Churchmen make use of lying for deception and pretense, noblemen for bragging of trifles and vanities, merchants for trickery and deception, the common people to invent stories or happenings that have taken place, or might take place, involving lords and ladies, their situations and their morals, their possessions and how they conduct themselves. God knows how stupidly they talk about these things, spreading about falsehoods. So it is with all sorts of people, but I reserve especially for the last people involved with money, treasures, and other such people. This is their proper place. It is not entirely unbecoming to them, for it is their business, and truly they are good at it. Good Lord, would that it would please Him that their ways should displease the most powerful! I insist that it would be to their advantage, and that others would follow their example and thus everything would improve. It is a grievous misfortune that today one has the greatest difficulty in finding truth in anyone. Certainly nobody who is guilty of such a vice can be virtuous or worthy of praise.

TEXT: And so peace and tranquility are assured to the righteous at the same time that the others are vanquished by their own sins and evildoings. GLOSS: Those who follow the rule of virtue and good conduct truly acquire all prosperity, and those who follow the opposite destroy and ruin themselves according to their just deserts. So the virtuous overcome evils and the wicked are overcome by them.

Thus the authority speaks fully and finally concludes clearly concerning the reward of the merit of perfection, and so it is that in this way he who desires merit should direct his deeds in order to arrive at the place for which he is intended, which is to say Heaven.

CCW

(Translated from Vatican Library Ms. Reg. Lat. 1238)

NOTES

1. This text is also known as *The Book of Prudence,* the title given to it by Christine in later manuscripts, notably after the death of Louis d'Orleans in 1407.
2. Justice was an essential trait expected of a ruler in the late Middle Ages. See J. Krynens, *Idéal du Prince et Pouvoir Royal, 1380–1440* (Paris, 1981), pp. 184–99. See also Christine's *Book of the Body of Policy,* I, chap. 19 (Bornstein ed., pp. 60–63), where she refers to what she had already said in this work; she also discusses Justice in *The Book of Peace,* II, chaps. 6 and 7 (Willard ed., pp. 95–97). Several chapters on the virtue of Justice are also to be found in one of her principal sources, the French translation of Egidio Colonna's *De Regimine Principium (The Government of Kings).* See *Li Livres dou Gouvernement des Rois; a XIIIth Century French Version of Egidio Colonna's Treatise de Regimine Principium,* ed S. P. Molenaer (New York, 1899).
3. In *The City of Ladies,* Justice is presented as carrying a measuring cup intended to give everyone his due.
4. Fear as the beginning of Wisdom is not from the Psalms, but rather from the Book of Proverbs 1:7 and 9:10.
5. Among others who spoke of the troubles of the day might be mentioned in particular Philippe de Mézières in the *Songe du Vieil Pèlerin,* ed. G. W. Coopland (Cambridge, 1969), 2 vols., and Jean Gerson in his sermon *Vivat Rex,* delivered before the royal court on 7 November 1405, in which he proposed a reform for the realm (*Oeuvres Complètes,* ed. Mgr Glorieux, Vol. VII, 2, pp. 1137–85). Christine would undoubtedly have been familiar with the ideas of both.
6. It will be recalled here that Christine describes her own troubles with justice in her *Vision* (see p. 21).
7. Extravagant oaths were a trait of the day and were frequently denounced by contemporary preachers.
8. Hassell, *Middle French Proverbs* (p. 247) gives the proverb, citing both Machaut and Deschamps, but without reference to Christine.
9. Christine complains about this sort of dishonesty in describing various sections of society in Book III of *The Mutation of Fortune* (Solente ed., II, pp. 31–79). At about the same time that she was writing the present treatise, she composed a ballade complaining about the widespread habit of lying in France (*Autres Balades* XVI, Roy ed., I, pp. 254–55).

CCW

LETTER TO THE QUEEN
OF FRANCE,
ISABEL OF BAVARIA

❦

H ERE FOLLOWS a letter that Christine de Pizan ... wrote
to the Queen of France at Melun, where she had been accompanied by my Lord of Orleans, who had there assembled a great number
of men-at-arms, in opposition to the dukes of Burgundy and Limbourg
and the Count of Nevers, brothers who were at that time in Paris
likewise assembling men-at-arms from all quarters. And there were on
the one side and the other a good ten thousand soldiers, a situation
fraught with danger of destruction for the good city of Paris and the
realm at large, had not God seen fit to supply a remedy, but with the
aid of the kings of Sicily and Navarre, and with them the dukes of
Bourbon and Berry, and the good counsel of the king, a right and
peaceful solution was achieved, the men-at-arms on both sides dispersing, with no harmful incident occurring upon their departure.

Most excellent, respected, and sovereign princess, my Lady Isabel, by
the grace of God, Queen of France.

Most high, sovereign, and mighty princess, may your worthy Highness not disdain or despise the piteous voice of your humble servant,
Christine, but rather deign to receive attentively kind words from
whatever good source they may come, even though it may seem to
you unfitting that so humble, ignorant, and unworthy a person should
undertake to speak of such high matters; yet, as it is a common
occurrence for people suffering from an illness to seek diligently for
a remedy, so that we see the ill seeking cures and the hungry searching
for food and likewise each thing its proper remedy, therefore you
should not be amazed, most noble lady, if we turn to seek recourse in

you, who according to the word and opinion of everyone can be the medicine and sovereign remedy to cure this realm, at present sorely and piteously wounded and in peril of worse—not pleading with you on behalf of a foreign land but for your own, but for your own place and the natural inheritance of your most noble children.[1] Most worthy and reverend lady, even though your sound judgment may be aware and well advised of what the proper action is, it is nonetheless true that you, seated in royal majesty and surrounded by honors, can only know by the report of others, either in word or in deed, the common needs of your subjects. For this reason, worthy lady, let it not displease you to hear recalled the pitious complaints of your grieving French suppliants, at present oppressed by affliction and sorrow, who with humble voice drenched in tears cry out to you, their sovereign and esteemed lady, begging mercy for the love of God that humble pity reveal to the kindness of your heart what desolation and misery is theirs, that you may seek and obtain a ready peace between these two worthy princes, cousins by blood and natural friends, but at present moved by a strange fortune to contention with each other. And indeed it is a human and common enough thing, for discord often arises between father and son, yet it were the devil's work to persevere therein. In this you can note especially two great and horrible ills and misfortunes, the first, that the realm must rapidly be destroyed, for our Lord says in the Scriptures, "a house divided against itself shall perish";[2] the second, that perpetual hatred might be born and grow from this time forward among the heirs and children of the noble blood of France, which has been like a very body and pillar for the defense of this realm, long recognized as strong and powerful for this very reason. Most excellent and noble lady, may it please you to note and remember three great benefits that would accrue to you through the procurement of this peace. The first pertains to the soul, which would acquire most excellent merit if through you such great and shameful effusion of blood were avoided by God's Christian kingdom as well as the confusion that would result if such a wrong were to endure. *Item*, the second benefit, that you would be the instigator of peace and the restorer of the welfare of your noble offspring and of their loyal subjects. The third benefit, which is not to be despised, is that you would be perpetually remembered and praised in the chronicles and records of the noble deeds of France, doubly crowned with the love, gratitude, and humble thanks of your loyal subjects.[3] And, noble lady, considering the question of your rights, let us suppose that the dignity of your position may be considered to have been injured by one of the contenders, whereby your noble heart might be less inclined to work for this peace. O most noble lady, what great good sense it is occasionally, even among the very great, to sacrifice a part of one's rights to avoid a greater misfortune or to gain a superior advantage!

Ah, noble lady, the histories of your forebears who conducted themselves with discretion should provide you with examples of good conduct, as it happened in the case of a very great princess in Rome, whose son had been wrongfully and without cause banished and exiled from the city. Afterwards, when he had assembled such a large army to avenge his injury that it could have destroyed everything, didn't she go before her son to appease his wrath and reconcile him with the Romans? Alas, great lady, if pity, charity, clemency, and benignity are not to be found in a great princess, where then can they be expected? As these virtues are a natural part of the feminine condition they should rightfully abound in a noble lady, inasmuch as she receives a greater gift from God, so it is to be expected that a noble princess or lady should be the means of bringing about a treaty of peace, as can be seen in the cases of the valiant ladies praised by the Holy Scriptures:[4] the valiant and wise Queen Esther, who by her good judgment and kindliness appeased the wrath of King Ahasuerus so that he withdrew the sentence against the people condemned to death; likewise Bathsheba, didn't she appease on many occasions David's anger? Another valiant queen who advised her husband that since he could not conquer his enemies by force, he should attempt what good doctors do, for when they see that bitter medicine does not benefit their patients, they give them sweet medicine, and in this fashion the wise queen reconciled him with his enemies. Endless similar examples could be recounted, which I omit for the sake of brevity, of wise queens who are praised, but also, on the other hand, of others who were perverse, cruel, and enemies of human nature, such as the false queen Jezebel and others like her who, because of their shortcomings, are still and will always be blamed, cursed, and damned. But among the good ones useful to our purposes is also, in our opinion, without seeking further, the very wise and kindly Queen of France, Blanche, the mother of Saint Louis.[5] When the barons were discordant because of the queen's regency, didn't she take her son, still an infant, into her arms and, holding him in the midst of the barons, say: "Don't you see here your king? Do not do anything to make him displeased with you when he has reached the age of discretion." And so by her good judgment she appeased them.

Very good lady, may my words not displease you if I say further that just as the Queen of Heaven is called Mother of God by all Christendom, any good and wise queen should be called mother and comforter and advocate of her subjects and her people. But alas, where is the mother so hardhearted, if she didn't have a veritable heart of stone, who could bear to see her children kill each other, spilling each other's blood and destroying and scattering their poor arms and limbs? And if then it should happen that foreign enemies should come to persecute them everywhere and seize their heritage! And, mighty lady, you may be quite certain that it would come about if an end were not put to this affair. May God forbid, for there is no doubt that the kingdom's enemies, overjoyed by this turn of events, would rush in with a great army to destroy everything.[6] Lord, how sad for such a noble realm to lose and allow to perish its knighthood! Alas, it would become necessary for the poor people to pay heavily for a sin of which they were innocent and for poor little nurslings and other small children to cry after their weary mothers, widowed and grief-stricken, dying of hunger, who, deprived of their possessions, would have nothing with which to comfort them so that their voice crying out to God, as the Scriptures tell us in several places, would pierce the Heavens piteously before a just God to draw justice on the heads of those who were the cause of it all. And in addition to everything else, what a shame for this kingdom if the poor, deprived of their possessions, should have to be driven by famine to foreign countries, telling how those who should have protected them have destroyed them! Lord, how would this ugly blemish, so unaccustomed for this noble land, be repaired or atoned for? Surely, most noble lady, we already see the effect of these mortal judgments, which are already sufficiently present that right now there are those who are ruined and deprived of their property, and more and more are ruined all the time so that any Christian ought to take pity on them. Moreover, no prince or princess whose heart is so hardened in sin should hold God accountable for any such griefs; it is rather the most capricious turn of Fortune's wheel that can change everything in a single instant. Heavens, of what blows would Queen Olympias have thought, she who was the great Alexander's mother, during the days when she saw the whole world at her feet, that Fortune had the power to inflict to the point where she ended her days pitiously and in great shame.[7] And one could say the same of many others. For what happens when Fortune has received thus some powerful person? If he has not behaved wisely, in times past, with regard to love, pity, and charity so that he has made peace with God first and then the good will of the world, all his life and his actions are retold in public with great reproach, like a dog that is being chased is pursued by everyone, and he is divested of everything with shouts that his losses are well deserved.

Most excellent and mighty lady, endless reasons could be stated that should move you to pity and to sue for peace, of which your good judgment makes you well aware. So I will end my letter by begging Your Majesty to accept it willingly and to view favorably the tearful request written by me on behalf of your poor, loyal French subjects. And just as it is more charitable to give the poor a piece of bread in times of scarcity and famine than a whole loaf in times of fertility and abundance, be pleased to give your poor people in this time of tribulation a measure of the word and effort of your might and power, which will be enough to reassure them and feed their hungry desire for peace. And they will pray God on your behalf, for which good deed and many others on your part may God grant you His grace for a long and good life and at its end everlasting glory.

Written the fifth day of October in the year 1405.

Your humble and most obedient servingmaid,

Christine de Pizan

CCW

(Translated from Paris B. N. Ms. fr. 580)

NOTES

1. The loyalty of the German queen was somewhat open to question. She is known to have acted in favor of members of her own family, notably her brother, Louis of Bavaria, who was established at the French court. The citizens of Metz accused her of sending considerable sums of money to Germany. See Religieux de Saint-Denis, *Les Grandes Chroniques de France, III,* pp. 229–33; J. Verdon, *Isabeau de Bavière,* (Paris, 1957), p. 138.
2. Matthew 12:25. Christine later cites the same passage in *The Book of Peace* (Willard ed., I, 3, p. 61); its application to France at that time is obvious.
3. On a number of occasions, Christine shows a humanistic concern for renown. This is especially noteworthy in the biography of Charles V. She speaks of her own hope of being remembered in the future, especially in the last chapter of *The Treasury of the City of Ladies.*
4. Christine had already cited the example of Queen Esther in *The City of Ladies* (II, chap. 32, Richards trans., pp. 145–46). Bathsheba is the mother of Solomon by King

David, whom she had married after he had sent her first husband, Uriah, to his death in battle (2 Samuel 2). Jezebel is the wicked woman who married Ahab, king of Israel (1 Kings 16, 19; 2 Kings 9: 7–10, 30–37).

5. Blanche of Castile appears in *The City of Ladies* (Richards trans. I, chap. 13, p. 34 and II, chap. 65, pp. 207–8) and again in *The Treasury of the City of Ladies* (Willard ed., I, 13, p. 86).

6. This is a reference to the threat of an invasion by the English, which would indeed come about several years later.

7. Olympias was for some years the virtual queen of Epiraus. After Alexander's death she seized power over Macedonia and made her grandson, Alexander IV, king. Finally a victim of her unbridled ambition, she was killed by her enemies. Christine had already told this story in *The Mutation of Fortune* (Solente ed., Vol. IV, pp. 67–68, vv. 23251–23272) with a comment on the perversity of Fortune:

> O all men, much vain glory
> Behold, see in this story
> How cruel Fortune from renown
> In brief time, perversely casts down.

CCW

THE BOOK OF
THE BODY OF POLICY

❧

HERE BEGINS the Book of the Body of Policy, which speaks of virtues and good manners and is divided into three parts. The first part is addressed to princes, the second to knights and noblemen, and the third to the common people.

The First Chapter Describes the Body of Policy (I)

If it is possible for virtue to grow from vice, it pleases me well in this part to have the feelings of a woman.[1] Since many men claim that women do not know how to keep quiet or restrain the abundance of their spirits, let me now come forth boldly and show by several streams the source and inexhaustible fountain of my spirit, which cannot staunch its desire for virtue. O virtue, noble and godlike, how do I dare to speak of you when I know my mind does not know you well enough to fully understand or explain you? But this comforts me and makes me bold; I know you to be so benign that it will not displease you if I speak of you not in regard to the most subtle things, but only those which I can conceive and understand. I will call you to mind to the best of my ability in the teaching of good manners, speaking first of the occupations and rule of living of our betters, that is to say the princes, whom I humbly beseech not to be displeased or disdainful that so simple a mind and so humble a creature should dare to speak of the manners of so high an estate. May it please them to keep in mind the teaching of the philosopher, who says, do not have disdain for the insignificance of someone who speaks good words, no matter how great you are.[2] Afterwards I hope to speak, by the grace of God, of the order of living pertaining to noblemen and knights, and thirdly, of the common people.

These three estates ought to be united in one commonwealth, like a living body, according to the saying of Plutarch, who sent a letter to the Emperor Trajan comparing the commonwealth to a living body,[3] of which the prince holds the place of the head, since he is or ought to be the ruler, and from him come the laws, as from the mind of man come the plans that the limbs achieve. The knights and noblemen hold the place of the hands and arms. As the arms of a man are strong to sustain labor and pain, they must defend the right of the prince and the commonwealth; and they are also the hands because as the hands discard harmful things, they must get rid of all that is destructive or unprofitable. The common people are like the stomach, feet, and legs. As the stomach receives all that sustains the head and the limbs, the deeds of the prince and the nobles must turn to the good and the love of the commonwealth, as will be declared hereafter. As the legs and feet support the actions of the human body, similarly the laborers support all the other estates.

Here the Image of Virtuous Felicity Is Discussed (II)

Now we must discuss virtue for the profit of the three different estates, by which human life must be ruled in all its endeavors and without which no man can attain honor. To show that it is the proper kind of honor, Valerius Maximus says that the cultivation of virtue is honor.[4] To this purpose, Aristotle says that reverence is due to honor in recognition of virtue, which is to say that honor should be given only to the virtuous, for he does not say to power or riches but to virtue. For according to him, only the good should be honored; and there is no thing so much desired by noble hearts as honor. As he says in the fourth book of *Ethics,* power and riches are desired only for honor.[5] Thus it can be seen that honor and consequently virtue pertain particularly to kings and great princes.

Now we must analyze the nature of virtue. In the twentieth chapter of *The Book of the City of God,* Saint Augustine explains it in the following manner.[6] He states that the philosophers say virtue is the end of human good and evil. That is to say, human felicity consists in being virtuous. Now it must be so that there is great delight in felicity, or else it would not be felicity, and of this joy and felicity the ancient philosophers made figures and painted the image in such a manner: it was in the form of a beautiful, delicate queen who sat on a royal throne, and the virtues sat on the earth around her regarding her face to perceive her commandments and to serve and obey her. She commanded Prudence to inquire diligently how she could reign long and be healthy and in sure estate. She commanded Justice to do what she should and guard the laws so that there would be peace. She commanded Fortitude that if any affliction came to her body, she should moderate it through resistance and virtuous thought. She commanded Temperance to take wine, food, and other pleasant things so temperately that by taking no more than reason demanded, no harm would come to her. Thus by this description, one can see that to be virtuous is nothing else than to have in oneself all the things which draw toward goodness and withdraw from evil and vice.

Now it is necessary to govern effectively the body of policy so that the head will be healthy, that is to say virtuous. For if it is sick, all the rest shall feel it. We will begin to speak of the medicine for the head, that is to say the king or princes; and since our work begins with the head, we will take the first head of age, that is to say the childhood of the prince when he is nourished under the guidance of his relatives.

How One Must Bring Up Children of Princes [7] (III)

Since we are expressly commanded to love God, we must introduce the son of the prince to this love when his understanding first begins to grow and teach him to serve God with short, simple prayers according to his ability. For the things one gets accustomed to in childhood are difficult to abandon. To show that such a thing is agreeable to God, the Psalmist says that in the mouth of babes and sucklings God receives his perfect praise, that is to say it is pleasing to him. [8] Furthermore, when he is older, it is necessary to teach him letters and the divine service so that God may be praised. It is a very commendable custom that the princes of France, more than those of other countries, teach their children to hear mass and say their prayers. One must provide a master for him who is wise and prudent, more in manners than in great learning. In former times, the children of princes were taught by philosophers, as it is written of Philip, King of Macedon and father of Alexander the Great, who wrote to Aristotle that he had great joy that a son was born to him; but he had still greater joy because he was born in Aristotle's time since he would be able to inform and instruct him, which happened afterwards, for Aristotle was master to Alexander the Great. [9] Nevertheless, nowadays princes are not so eager to be taught the sciences, which I wish they were, if it pleased God.

It is best to find a master who is a discreet, wise man with good manners who loves God, even if he is not the most excellent or subtle philosopher; that is more important than if one could find a great scholar who was less prudent and well-mannered. The princes must diligently inquire about the man's character, for the good manners that the child sees in the master and the wise words and expressions are like a lesson and a mirror to him. The wise master must maintain himself in his office by great prudence. For although the nature of children can be disciplined only by fear, another manner is suitable for the son of a prince than to make him afraid by beating him severely. By too harsh a manner of correction, a child who is brought up in luxury, and already feels the grandeur of his rank through the honor that is paid to him, might become indignant instead of being chastised and feel resentment toward his master as well as his lessons, which would be to the great harm of his learning and a peril to his master and might even hurt the health of a child who is delicately brought up. What must the wise master do? He must act toward the young prince as one acts toward the lion. Other children are customarily brought up along with the sons of princes, sons of barons who are his schoolmates. The master must be harsh to them when they misbehave in the same way the son of the prince has, and beat them suitably but threaten them more with angry looks than by beatings. Similarly, he must use such threats with the son of the prince if he will not correct himself and sometimes make him feel the rod, and by such means he will make him feel ashamed of his misbehavior and fearful and obedient. The wise master must not be too familiar or intimate with his student, for he will fear him the less, and the child should not see him playing idle games, or laughing or speaking foolishly, or being too familiar, but he should act as if he were half master over everyone. His countenance should be serious and sedate, his clothes clean and honorable. In front of his student, he should speak words that are not vain but profitable and should tell of good examples, but he should not always have a harsh expression or use proud words. Thus he should amiably draw the child to him with kind words when he learns his lessons well or does something good. Moreover, the master should please him by giving him some little things that children like and sometimes telling him children's tales about some trifle to make him laugh, and all this so that he will like his studies as much as his own amusements. [10] The master must establish a suitable hour and schedule in a set period of time when the child will apply himself to his studies and afterwards give him space to play for a while before dinner, which should be well regulated, without too many delicate or rich foods and wines, which are sometimes a cause of indigestion or sickness.[11] When the child begins to study grammar, then the master must use more subtle words in his instruction according to the ability of the child to understand them, so that little by little he will give him more and more, as the nurse increases the food of a child according to his growth.

Indeed, I suppose that the prince would want his child to be sufficiently instructed in letters to know the rules of grammar and understand Latin, which I wish were a general custom for all the children of princes in the present and future, if it pleased God.[12] I believe that great good would result from it for them and their subjects, and they would increase in virtue. The prince should have his children learn logic and continue further in their studies, like the wise prince the Duke of Orleans who now lives, and the wise, good, and virtuous duchess his wife, who appreciates and honors the value of learning and is diligent, like a prudent mother, to see that her children are well instructed in letters.[13]

When the understanding of the child begins to grow and is able to conceive more, then the above mentioned master should feed him with wise doctrine, particularly in regard to good manners, by telling him of examples or having him read of them in books. He should make him understand the difference between good and evil, and teach him the way to follow good manners and virtue, like the valiant, famous princes, his predecessors, and others, and show him the great benefits that come from being good and follow those who govern themselves well, and by contrast the evils that follow the bad or vicious. If he sees him to be at all clever or inclined toward learning, he should show him the great felicity that is in learning to make it more appealing to him and open the ways of philosophy. That is to say, he should make him understand the various sciences. With such a master at the beginning, the son of the prince will attain great learning, which will lead to virtue and fame in his maturity if he continues.

What Kind of Men Should Be Entrusted with the Governance of the Children of Princes [14] (IV)

When the son of the prince is sufficiently grown up, then he must be separated from the women who have nourished him and given to the care principally of a mature knight of great authority. One must make sure that this knight is a wise, loyal, brave man of good life, and with him others who are similar. This knight must diligently watch over the manners of the child as much as or more than his body. He must make sure that he gets up at a reasonable hour, hears mass, says his prayers, has a pleasant and well assured countenance, speaks courteously to the people, salutes them benignly, and renders to each one who speaks to him the honor due to his rank. This knight must often show him the honor and valor of chivalry and tell him of the brave deeds of valiant men. He should let him know who are the good men and the best men of his father's house and who ought to be most honored, explain to him the nature of honor in arms and the proper manner of battle and knighthood, how men fight, assault, and defend themselves, for what quarrels one should take arms, what harness is best, the strongest or the most secure and most easy, how one must arm differently for different kinds of battle or feats of arms, how men fought formerly and how they fight today, and how he must praise the good and valiant men and draw them toward him, honor and love them.

These things done, the knight should take care that around the prince's son, who is already growing up, there are no reporters of evil or dishonest tales who might introduce him to folly, and if he knows of any such men, he should keep them from him. He must see that the children around him are well brought up so that they do not lead him to misbehave or commit childish pranks. If the son of the prince misbehaves, he must correct him, saying that it does not suit the rank of a prince to do that, and if he does not correct himself he will be shamed and dishonored, and a prince without honor is worth nothing, and if he does not act differently he will leave him. Thus he must speak to him and admonish him, and the sons of princes and noblemen must be governed in this way if they are to attain honor in the time to come.

Valerius Maximus affirms this in his book, which tells how the ancients trained their young people to have good manners and to undertake great enterprises and deeds of honor and bravery. They told them of the deeds of prowess of good men and showed them good examples, saying that none could achieve honor without virtue. At meal times they had sung the deeds of heroes of the past and the good works of their ancestors so that the will of young people would be encouraged. Thus, says Valerius, the ancients held schools of knighthood and good manners from which issued the Caesars and the noble lines famous for prowess and bravery.[15] It is no doubt that by good examples and wise instruction often seen and heard in childhood a man can come to great virtue, and similarly by bad instruction he can be led to perdition. For Averroes[16] says in his second book of *Physics* that a man can acquire a second nature by long exposure to good or evil. Because of this, relatives should to the best of their ability prevent children from adopting bad customs in their youth. For as Orosius says, the earthen pot will keep for a long time the scent of that which it has once held.[17] For this reason the Greeks, who formerly governed themselves with great wisdom and cunning, took pains to see that those they hated would take great delight in evil customs, and by this means they found a way to seek revenge.

The Exhortations One Must Make to the Children of Princes (V)

Even when he is still a child, the son of the prince should be brought to the council where are assembled the wise men and counselors who determine the needs of the country, and the matters that are discussed, and the order of effectively governing the commonwealth, so that from his childhood he is accustomed to hearing about the governance of the land that belongs to him and to which he is heir, and by observing he can learn to speak about what pertains to him.[18] The knights and wise men who have charge of him should tell him to pay attention to what he hears and keep it in mind. Moreover, those who have charge of him should have all things discussed before him: diverse countries, customs of men of war, battles, the government of different places, various deeds of arms, the deeds of the clergy, the pope, and the church, and theologians should explain to him the law of the commandments and what one must believe as a Christian. At times he should hear sermons and homilies by clerks, at times hear of the deeds of the common people and laborers, of merchants and how they do business, of the poor and the rich, and thus of all things so that his mind will not be ignorant of anything that may be virtuously known, for the philosopher says that he is not wise who does not understand all things.

It is good for him to exercise his body at times in some work or labor and in some games such as palm play[19] and other similar games, but he should do this in moderation. He should make sure that he does not become flabby, heavy, or gouty by too much rest, and that he does not let superfluous humors gather in him. Similarly, one must speak to him of the poor and indigent and show him that he should have pity and compassion for them and do them good for the love of God if he wishes to go to paradise, and also that he should have pity for poor noblewomen, widows, and orphans, and help them in their needs for the love of God and nobility, and also help all poor women and men to the best of his ability and hear their requests graciously.

One should instruct him to be benign, humble, and truthful, and show him that although he is raised to a high rank by the grace and will of God, he is as mortal as another, and the only thing he will take with him is the good or evil he has done, and because he is of greater rank, he will have a greater account to render. He must not become proud or haughty in spirit although people do him great honor, but render thanks to God and acknowledge all the benefits he receives from him. All such exhortations and other good and virtuous things must often be shown to the prince's son. Nevertheless, one must let him play and amuse himself sometimes, as said before. Yet one must never forget to remind him and instruct him in virtue and good manners.

What the Young Prince Must Do When He Begins to Govern (VI)

When the son of the prince is grown up and has come to the age when he receives his lordship and becomes heir of his heritage, whether it is a realm or another territory, just as the trees show their fruit after their flowers, then will appear in him the perfection of virtue, as in the case of Charles V, the wise king of France, who diligently followed the path of virtue. For from the time that he was crowned, even though it was in the flower of his youth, never could anyone accuse him of doing anything displeasing, for he always occupied his time with virtuous and proper things, as I have written of him more fully in the book that tells of his deeds and good manners.[20]

The virtue of the prince must be shown especially in three things, which are most necessary for him, for without them he cannot acquire the crown of praise and good fame, and consequently of honor. The first, and the main one, is to love God, fear him, and serve him without feigning, and to serve him more by good works than by remaining long in prayer. Second, he must singularly love the good and profit of his country and people, and this ought to occupy all of his attention rather than his private profit. The third is that he must supremely love justice and keep it without infraction, and give equity to all people, and by well observing these three points, the prince will be crowned with glory in heaven and on earth. Now henceforth we will continue our work in this first part which speaks of the head, that is to say of the prince, and we will base our discussion on these three points. We will begin by speaking of the first, which is to love God, from which we will draw many branches of virtue that depend upon it, all to our purpose, and similarly of the other two.

The Wise Advice That Is Suitable for a Young Prince to Have (VII)

The good prince who loves God will fear to do anything against his reverence and commandment and will take pains to know all the things he should do and those he should not do. By learning these things, he will perceive and know his fragility, and that he is a mortal man subject to a brief life, concerned with mortal things, and frail as another man without any difference except for the goods of fortune. But when he studies the law of God to be well informed as a good Christian ought to be, he will be advised of the peril of those goods in regard to his soul; that is to say, if he does not use them well, he is lost, and the great lordship he has is nothing but a transitory office of brief duration that he must leave shortly, that is to say through death, a dark and fearful passage that he must cross, and he must render his account before the judge from whom nothing is secret or hidden, who will pay him according to his merit. Such thoughts will give him little reason to praise those goods and honors that are so perilous and of such brief duration. Such thoughts the good prince will have in his heart, which will keep him from pride and lack of self-knowledge. Nevertheless, since God has chosen him for his office of lordship, it is fitting for him to maintain his worldly position, with moral discretion. If he thinks in this way, he will live and govern himself by the law of a virtuous, well-mannered prince, and will perform his duties for the common good of his realm or country to the best of his ability, and will use the wealth and honors the world has given him so discreetly that his heart will not be hindered or raised against God.

As the vicar of God on earth, this good prince must diligently take heed of the state of the church so that his Creator can be served properly, as is right. If any discord arises through the instigation of the enemy, he should do whatever is necessary to make peace, and he should make sure in promoting his ministers that he grant no request for any of his servants, no matter how good a friend he may be, if he does not know him to be a good clerk and a wise man suitable to serve God and perform his service in the office he requests. The prince should diligently inquire about this before he grants the request, or else he will burden his conscience heavily and be the cause of the damnation of those who by his promotion are given benefices of which they are not worthy, as it is decreed. But now such a rule is not kept, which is a pity, for God knows if knowledge, wisdom, and a just life are now the causes for the promotion of clerks. Certainly not, but often they are given by means of flattery, adulation, and other evils, and the petitions of great lords, and it thus appears in the ruin of the ship by what wind it is struck. For covetousness is the reason for their promotions, which holds them in the detestable error and blindness that now characterizes the deeds of the clergy.[21] Alas, as Jesus Christ said in the gospel speaking to the Pharisees, the Queen of Sheba who came from a distant land to see the wisdom of Solomon will condemn you, who have with you more than Solomon and do not know it.[22] Similarly, the pagans who formerly kept their law without breaking it and carefully guarded it and observed all their ceremonies with great reverence, even though this law was false and reproved by God, will be the reproach of the Christians, who have such a worthy and holy law and yet keep and observe it so badly.

Is it not written that the ancient pagans had such great devotion to their idols and gods that in all things they were diligent and careful that the ordinances of their establishments were well kept, and that the priests who made the sacrifices were people of good and honest life, or if not they punished them so severely and reproved them so strongly that they would not allow them to be negligent or vicious? This was well shown at Rome, as Valerius Maximus says in the first chapter of his book,[23] when one time the chaplet fell from the head of one of their priests while he was making the sacrifice (the chaplet was a proper ornament that they wore, as we might say a miter). They considered him negligent and unworthy to have the office, and so they deposed him. They did the same thing to a virgin dedicated to the temple of one of their goddesses named Vesta; because this virgin, who was as we might say a nun, was negligent in seeing that the lamp that should always be lit not be extinguished, and it was extinguished because of lack of oil, she was grievously punished and deposed from her office. Thus I could tell you of many other examples. But in our bishops and priests one can openly see many detestable faults. There is no prince or any other who will reproach them, but they themselves excuse them before they are accused, saying that they are men and not angels, and that it is human to sin. Alas, they are not truly men, for the body of a man is a small vessel that may easily be filled, but they are devils and ghouls of hell, for as the mouth of the inferno cannot be satiated or filled no matter how much it receives, the desires of these men cannot be satisfied, they are so covetous for money and all delights, for which reason all evils are common to them. One can well verify the words of Valerius in them, who says: What is it that avarice or the insatiable hunger for gold will not cause men to do? The good prince must take heed of all these things. For even though the correction of the clergy does not pertain to him, nevertheless, where is the prelate who is so elevated, or any other priest or clerk, who will dare resist or murmur against the prince if he reproaches him for his vice and sin?

The king or the good prince should take care that the temple and house of God are not polluted or soiled by diverse sins committed there, as Christians do nowadays, like nobles, merchants, and people of all estates who have no shame to hold their meetings in the church and arrange their parliaments and worldly matters, and God knows if many foolish and false contracts are made there. Jesus Christ spoke of these in the gospel when he said, do you wish to make the temple of my father, which is a house of prayer, into a cave of thieves and a place for worldly things? [24] Yet more against us and to our damnation is the order that the ancient pagans held, as Valerius tells regarding the devotion that the Romans had for their gods, speaking of two consuls, that is to say two princes and dukes of Rome, who were with a large army in a strange country; but only because they held their military council in the temple, the Senate of Rome, that is to say the great council of rulers, deposed them from their office, in spite of the fact that they were very brave men. They did the same thing to Fabius Maximus, who was a very valiant, brave man of arms. They deposed him from the highest office in Rome, which they called the dictator, for from all the other offices one could appeal to the dictator, according to their rules and regulations, but from the dictator one could not appeal. He was deposed because he heard questions regarding various things in the temple. For the same reason they deposed Caius Flamius from his high position,[25] who was a great captain of men of arms. Alas, nowadays one does not depose those who not only hold their parliaments and assemblies in the church but also make it a foul stable for horses.

The Observances Toward God and Toward the Law That a Good Prince Ought to Hold (VIII)

The good prince who loves God will keep in mind his commandments and how the worthy name of God should not be taken in vain. For this purpose, he will make a proclamation throughout his land in which he will forbid anyone to swear, curse, or renounce his Creator, on pain of great punishment. Alas, there is great need now for such an edict to be made in France, for it is disgraceful that among Christians there is such irreverence toward the Savior. For one scarcely hears any other language, be it in earnest or in game, but horrible cursing by the torments of the passion of our Savior at the expression of every word, and swearing and forswearing. I believe that the pagans of ancient times would have taken great displeasure in speaking so of their gods and idols. The good prince must forbid all such things, for they are against the Christian religion and can cause the anger of God and the destruction of realms and countries, as it is said in various prophecies.

Thus the good prince who loves God will diligently keep the divine law and proper observances in all holy things, which I will cease speaking of for the sake of brevity, and also because many people find it annoying to hear these things discussed. By thus properly observing and keeping the laws, the good prince can have firm faith that God will defend and protect him and increase his soul and body in virtue. And why should he not have faith in the living, almighty, and just God, when the pagans had faith that by the worship of their gods and idols they would be greatly exalted, as it appears by what Valerius says, who praises the city of Rome for having such great zeal and desire for the service of the gods.[26] He says thus: Our city has always put everything aside for the service of the gods, even those things regarding the honor and sovereign majesty of the emperor. For he says they had a firm belief that by doing this, they acquired the rule and government of the world. For this reason, the emperors of our city and all others generally have not been negligent in constantly following the practices of their religion. This suffices for the first point of Part I, which tells how the virtue of the prince must be mainly founded on the love and worship of God.

How the Good Prince Must Resemble the Good Shepherd[27] (IX)

We have touched upon the first point on which the goodness of the prince ought to be mainly founded. Now we must speak of the second point, which is that he must singularly love the common good and the increase of it more than his own, according to the doctrine of Aristotle in his book of *Politics,* who says that tyranny is when the prince seeks his own profit more than the common good, and that this is against the office of the prince, who must care more for the profit of his people than his own. We must consider in what manner he will demonstrate this love.

The good prince who loves his country will guard his people carefully, like a good shepherd who guards his sheep and takes great care to defend them from the wolves and other wild beasts, and sees that they are kept clean and in good health so that they can grow and bring profit and yield good wool, made healthy and fat by the earth by which they are nourished, and that the shepherd may be well paid by their fleeces, gathered at the proper time and season. But since the rich good shepherd who has great wealth to guard cannot watch all his flocks himself, he procures competent and suitable help. He hires diligent, wise servants whom he well knows to be loyal and desirous of his profit. He will ordain that these servants be provided with good, strong dogs with iron collars, who are trained to go out in the fields and chase the wolves. At night they will be left untied in the sheepfold so that if robbers come to steal the sheep, they will run upon them. By day the servants will keep them tied with their leashes while the sheep graze peacefully in the fields. But if it happens that the servants hear the noise of wolves or wild beasts coming out of the woods or mountains, they will untie the dogs and let them run and urge them on often, and to give them greater boldness run after them with iron staffs, chasing the wolf or the wild beast. Or if it should happen that any sheep go astray and leave the flock, the dogs, who are trained to do this, will run after him and without hurting him call him and bring him back to the flock. By these means, the wise servants defend and watch the sheep so well that they render a good account to the chief shepherd who closely watches over them.

Likewise, to our purpose, is the good prince who cares for the defense and safeguard of his country and people, for whom it is impossible to be personally in all places and positions. He provides himself with good help for the deeds of knighthood and other things, that is to say with valiant officers whom he knows to be good and loyal and who love him, such as a constable, marshal, admiral, and others, whom he charges to hire good men of arms, instructed in and accustomed to warfare, whom they tie to them by oaths, who cannot depart without their leave, who they hold ready so that if the need occurs they can go out against their enemies, so that the country is not attacked and the people not killed or pillaged.

That is not to say that the men of arms themselves should pillage and lay waste the country as they now do in France, which they do not dare do elsewhere. It is a great evil and a perverse practice that those who are established to defend the people should themselves pillage and rob them. There are some who are so cruel that except for killing the people and setting their houses on fire, their enemies could do no worse. This is not the right way to make war, which should be just and without extortion. The soldiers and the princes who send them to war are in great peril that the wrath of God will fall upon them and grievously punish them, for there is no doubt that the curse of the people because of too much oppression rightfully given before God can cause many evils to befall, as it is found by examples in Holy Scripture and elsewhere. For everyone knows that God is just. All this fault comes from bad ordinances. For if the men of arms were paid properly, one could pass a law that would forbid them from taking anything without paying on pain of serious punishment. By this means, they would find food and everything they needed cheap enough and in great plenty. It is a great marvel how the people can live under such an ordinance, and there is no compassion for them. May the Holy Spirit, father of the poor, visit them. Regarding the above, if a shepherd had a dog that ran on his sheep, he would strike him at once with his staff. It is not a thing that a good prince who loves God and his people should allow.

As one keeps the dogs untied at night in the sheepfold to guard against robbers, the officers should keep guards and spies on the frontiers and send them far about so that the country and the people are not secretly surprised by any trick, for they know the plan of their enemies. The men of arms have another office, which is as the good dog brings back the sheep that goes astray, they must do the same if they see common people or others who because of fear or ill will wish to rebel and go over to the enemy. They must bring them back to the right road, be it by threats or by taking them into custody.

Although it may displease some who may wonder that I compare the noble office of the knight to the nature of a dog, this comparison is without blame, for the dog truly has many qualities that the good man of arms ought to have. The dog greatly loves his master and is very loyal to him. It is necessary that the good man of arms be this way. He is bold and exposes himself to death to defend his master, and when he is given any place to guard, he listens very carefully and is soon awakened to run on evildoers or robbers. He does not bite the friends of his master but sniffs them amiably; nor does he bite neighbors nor those of the house in which he is nourished, but he protects them. He is very brave and fights with great virtue. He has great understanding and knowledge and is very amiable to those who show him friendship. A good man of arms should have all of these qualities.

Diane Bornstein

(Translated from Middle English translation, Cambridge U. Lib. Ms. Kk. 1.5)

NOTES

1. The pleasure in being a woman expressed by Christine here is in marked contrast to her presumably ironic despair at her female condition at the beginning of *The City of Ladies* (p. 172–74)

2. This recalls the end of *The Letter of Othea*, which speaks of the Cumaean sibyl's announcement of Christ's birth to the Emperor Augustus. She points out that he has learned this from a woman, for it is the message that counts and that the wise man listens to it regardless of the messenger's identity (British Museum, Harley Ms. 4431, fol. 141).

3. Christine is referring here to the *Policraticus* by John of Salisbury, where the organic analogy of the state to the human body purports to be based on this letter written by Plutarch to the Emperor Trajan. However, no trace of such a letter has been found. It is thus thought to have been John of Salisbury's invention. See John of Salisbury, *Policraticus*, ed. and trans. by C. J. Nederman (pp. 65–68 and Introduction, p. xxi).

4. One of Christine's principal sources for this book was the *Memorable Deeds and Sayings*, the Roman history of Valerius Maximus, which she knew through the

translations of Simon de Hesdin and Nicholas Gonesse for the Duke of Berry in 1401.

5. *Ethics*, Book IV, chap. 3.

6. Christine is here referring to Book IV, chap. 20 of Saint Augustine's *City of God*, which she knew through the translation of Raoul de Presles.

7. In discussing the upbringing of royal children, Christine undoubtedly had in mind the example of Egidio Colonna's *De Regimine Principium*, composed in the thirteenth century for Philip III when this Augustinian friar was tutor to Philip the Fair. The French translation, known as the *Gouvernement des Rois* by Gilles de Rome, was made soon afterwards by Henri de Gauchi, which is undoubtedly the version used by Christine. Here she is referring to Book II, Part II, chap. 6. See *Li Livres dou Gouvernement des Rois*, ed. S. P. Molenaer, pp. 195–97.

8. Psalms 8:2.

9. This account is to be found in the *Policraticus*, Book IV, chap. 6 (Nederman ed., p. 45).

10. This recalls the advice given by Christine in *The Treasury of the City of Ladies* for the early education of a princess (Book I, chap. 15).

11. Gilles de Rome, Book II, Part II, chaps. 12–13 (pp. 210–15).

12. Gilles de Rome, Book II, Part II, chap. 7 (pp. 197–99).

13. This evidence that the Duke of Orleans was still alive indicates that the book was finished before the end of November 1407, when he was murdered in the streets of Paris. The duchess, Valentina Visconti, was known to be an educated woman.

14. Suggested by Gilles de Rome, Book II, Part II, chap. 9 (pp. 202–6) and chap. 17 (pp. 222–23).

15. Christine refers to the custom of having deeds of heroes recounted during meals in *The Treasury of the City of Ladies* (I, 12). An account of the Roman custom of initiating the young into arms is developed in *The Deeds of Arms and of Chivalry* (I, 9). For the text and translation of this chapter see *The Study of Chivalry*, ed. A. H. Chickering and T. H. Seiler (Kalamazoo, 1988), pp. 520–29.

16. This reference to Averroes is to be found in the commentary on the translation of Valerius Maximus (B.N. Ms. fr. 282, fol. 278).

17. This saying attributed to Orosius had become a common proverb. See B. J. Whiting, *Sentences and Proverbial Phrases from English Writings Mainly before 1500* (Cambridge, MA, 1968) p. 468.

18. From the age of nine the Duke of Guyenne did indeed sit in on council meetings.

19. Palm play was a game resembling tennis where the ball was struck with the palm of the hand rather than with a racquet. According to contemporary accounts, the Duke of Guyenne was not fond of exercise and needed to be admonished on this subject. Exercise is also recommended by Gilles de Rome in Book II, Part II, chap. 13 (pp. 212–15).

20. A reference to *The Deeds and Good Character of King Charles V the Wise*, Part I, chap. 8 (Solente ed., pp. 20–22).

21. This recalls Christine's remarks about the greed of the clergy in *The Book of Man's Integrity* (see p. 263 of selection).

22. Matthew 12: 38–42; Luke 11: 29–32.

23. These two examples come from Valerius Maximus, Book I, chap. 10.

24. John 2: 16.

25. From the commentary on Valerius Maximus, f.fr. 282, fol. 7v°.

26. Valerius Maximus, Book I, chap. 1.

27. Christine was fond of this comparison and would use it again in *The Deeds of Arms and of Chivalry* I, chap. 14 (Brussels Ms. 10476, fol. 5v°) and *The Book of Peace* (see p. 315) In *The Long Road to Learning* she had already written:

In Ethics Aristotle says
That all princes authentic
Should be, and they should appear
Like a father who holds his children dear
And as a shepherd to his sheep
Who would them from all harm keep.
(C. C. Willard,
trans., Püschel ed., vv.5511–16, [p. 234])

It seems probable that Christine had read Jean de Brie's *Vray Regime et Gouvernement des Bergers et Bergeres,* composed for Charles V's library in 1379. Its forty-seven chapters give detailed directions for care to be given sheep month by month. Christine had already shown a knowledge of a shepherd's life in the "Dit de la Pastoure" (*The Tale of the Shepherdess*) composed in 1403, and had given instructions to the lady managing her manor in the *Treasury of the City of Ladies* (II.10) concerning the care of sheep. She had also compared a king to a good shepherd at the beginning of *The Book of the Deeds of Arms and of Chivalry.*

CCW

THE BOOK OF
THE DEEDS OF ARMS
AND OF CHIVALRY

Concerning the Prime Causes of Wars and Battles (I. iv)[1]

As it belongs to sovereign princes to undertake and carry on wars and battles, we must now consider the causes by which, according to lawful means, they may be undertaken and pursued. In this matter one is well advised, it seems to me, to remember that five grounds are commonly held to be the basis of wars, three of which rest on law and the remaining two on will. The first lawful ground upon which wars may be undertaken or pursued is to sustain law and justice; the second is to counteract evildoers who befoul, injure, and oppress the land and the people; and the third is to recover lands, lordships, or other things stolen or usurped for unjust cause by others who are under the jurisdiction of the prince, the country, or its subjects. As for the two of will, one is because of revenge for any loss or damage incurred; the other to conquer and take over foreign lands or lordships.

But going back to the first of these points, which is one of justice: it should be remembered that there are three chief causes under which the king or prince is empowered to undertake and carry out wars and battles. The first is to uphold and defend the Church and its patrimony against anyone who would defile it; this is expected of all Christian princes. The second is on behalf of his vassal, if he should require it in cases where the prince must settle a quarrel and in which the prince is duly forced to bring about an agreement among various parties, but then only if the adversary proves to be intractable. And the third is that the prince may, if it pleases him, justly go to the aid of any prince, baron, or any other ally or friend of his, or to help any country or land if the need arises and if the quarrel is just; and in this point are included widows, orphans, and all who are unjustly trampled under foot by another power.

For this ground and likewise for the other two aforementioned grounds — that is, one to counteract evildoers and the other to recover lost property — it is not only permissible for the prince to start a war or maintain it, indeed he is obliged to do so, through his obligation incurred by his title to lordship and jurisdiction in accordance with his rightful duty.

But as for the other two points — that is, one for revenge for some damage or loss inflicted by another prince, and the other to acquire foreign lands without title to them — even though conquerors in the past, such as Alexander, the Romans, and others who have been greatly praised and accorded titles of chivalry, as well as those who wreaked great vengeance upon their enemies, for better or for worse, and despite the fact that such actions are commonly undertaken, I do not find in divine law or in any other text that, for these causes, without any other ground, it is proper to start any kind of war or battle upon any Christian land, but rather the contrary.

For according to God's law it is not proper for man either to seize or usurp anything belonging to another, nor even to covet it. Likewise, vengeance is reserved for God, and in no way does any man have the right to carry it out.

But in order to set forth our ideas on this subject more clearly and to answer any questions that might arise, it is true that it is lawful for the prince to keep for himself the same right that is granted to others. And as for what the just prince will do if he considers himself wronged by some other power, should he simply depart, in order to obey divine law, without taking any further action? In God's name, no. For divine law does not deny justice, but rather commands that it should be carried out and requires punishment for misdeeds.[2] And in order that a prince may go about the matter justly, he will follow this course: he will gather together a great council of wise men in his parliament, or in that of his sovereign if he is a subject, and not only will he assemble those of his own country, but in order that there may be no suspicion of favor, he will also call upon those from foreign countries who are known not to take sides, elder statesmen as well as legal advisers and others;[3] and he will propose or have proposed the whole matter in full and without holding any of it back, for God cannot be deceived, everything according to what may be right or wrong, and he will conclude by saying that he wishes to recount everything and to hold to the determination of doing right. In short, by these points the affair will be put in order, clearly seen and discussed, and if through such a process it appears that his cause is just, he will summon his adversary to demand of him restitution and amendment for his injuries and the wrong done him. Now if it comes about that the aforesaid adversary puts up a defense and tries to contradict what has been said, let him be heard fully without special favor, but also without willfulness nor spite. If these things are duly done, and if the adversary should refuse to appear—as the law requires—then the just prince may surely undertake war, which should on no account be called vengeance but rather the entire carrying out of due justice.

∞

A Discussion of the Qualities a Good Constable or Leader Should Demonstrate in the Conduct of His Office (I. xii)

So it is in the event of war having been set in motion, after the prince's deliberation and with the usual hindrances encountered, that the wise leader will, to begin with, order that the frontiers should be well garrisoned, with both good men-at-arms and with artillerymen, as well as with all the other necessary things and preparations, depending on the skill of the enemy. Cities and fortresses should be prepared so that nothing further will be needed. The leader will then determine what number of men will be necessary, according to the nature of the undertaking. He will then select the best among his men-at-arms, archers and likewise gunners, and others according to the number considered necessary.

Regarding the fact that nowadays it is held that victory in battle can reasonably be expected to fall to the side that has the most men, Vegetius says on the contrary that in an ordinary battle it is sufficient to lead one legion of men-at-arms with their aides.[4] A legion numbers 6,666 of what we should call spears, or helmets. All authors who have written on this matter agree with Vegetius that too great a number of men encourages confusion, so that the most needed against even a greater number of enemies would be no more than two legions of good men-at-arms, but that they must be led by an excellent commander. This would amount to no more than thirteen thousand helmets. One finds that many armies have been thrown into disarray more by their own great number than by enemy forces. And why is this so? Certainly there are good reasons, for a great multitude is more difficult to maintain in good order, and is often in trouble because it requires more provisions, is more quarrelsome, and is subject to more delays on the road. Thus it can easily happen that the enemy, though fewer in number, is likely to surprise-attack at narrow passages or rivers, and there is the difficulty, for the large army cannot move forward, but rather get in the way of each other, and in battle formation they lunge forward so hastily that they mingle needlessly with the enemy and are exterminated. For this reason, as has been said, the Ancients who had mastered such things useful in battle and knowing the perils from experience, valued higher an army well taught and well led than a great multitude.[5]

The good commander shall place over such men as he has assembled various captains and constables, under each of whom he will commit a certain number of men-at-arms, to some more than others according to their capabilities. And he will also arrange for himself and his subordinates to observe his foot-soldiers and archers in the field on various days. Care should be taken there that none are be included who are not acceptable, so that nothing will be at fault either in the people or in the equipment or mounts, regardless of social status. There should also be wise clerks who see to it that there are no deceptions with regard to pay, so that those who are not accepted will not be rewarded.[6] From the earliest times the leaders were under strict oath to serve that prince or the country loyally, without fleeing or abandoning the battlefield because of fear of death or some other peril. These would likewise receive the oath of each man-at-arms when they accept them for pay.

When these things have been well and duly accomplished, when there is good security and the pay of the men-at-arms has been established for whatever length of time they are expected to be needed (for the leaders must have due regard for this matter, as it will mean the achievement or failure of their undertaking; for nobody can expect to have good soldiers who are badly paid because their courage will decline along with their pay), the leaders will take leave of the prince and in the field will put these people into such action as circumstances require.

Here Vegetius Speaks of Sea Battles (II. xxxix)[7]

In accordance with matters referred to at the end of his book, Vegetius touches rather briefly upon some issues pertaining to battles that are fought at sea or on rivers. First of all, concerning the construction of ships and galleys, he says that in March and April trees are full of sap and should not be cut down to build ships but that they must be cut down in July and August, when the sap has ceased to run. They may be sawn and made ready and left to dry out until they are no longer green and can shrink no more.[8] Furthermore, he says that to nail the boards, brass is better than iron, even though iron is stronger; but brass withstands moisture better without rusting. Also he states that those who wish to fight at sea, either in an army or by whatever other arrangement, must be provided with expert night sailors, masters in the office of nocturnal navigation; skilled in the knowledge of the source and dangers of winds; knowledgeable in the perils of the sea, being familiar with channels and dangerous places and harbor facilities; in map reading and in celestial signs and stars. Without all such knowledge sailors set out to their woe. They should be able to recognize those signs that indicate the fortunes of the sea, what the future holds in respect to the sun, the moon, the winds, the birds, and even the fish; they should be masters of the sails and ropes, and know when to drop anchor and weigh anchor. All of this is necessary, for many times armed men find themselves in sea battles under perilous conditions, faced with unforeseen adventures.[9]

If all provisions are duly made to arm ships or such vessels, they must be manned by skilled men-at-arms. It is said that those who depart to fight on sea should be better and more strongly armed than those who fight on land; for the former are more interested in their movement and must send little corsair vessels ahead to reconnoiter and to find out by means of spies what they can of the enemy.[10] And when they close in, they must "greet" [the enemy] with bombardment of stones hurled from various devices, such as strong crossbows, and as the ships approach the valiant men-at-arms, who are confident of their strength, the ships having been joined together, jump the decks and pass over to the adversaries' ship and there, using good swords, axes, and daggers, engage in violent hand-to-hand combat. In their greatest vessels, towers and barbicans are erected so that from on high they can hurl down objects and injure and kill as many as possible. Inasmuch as a battle is indeed a cruel thing, in which men perish not only by force of arms but also by fire and water, without any possibility of fleeing or even of turning aside, whole and living creatures are often cast overboard to feed fish. There are burning arrows and darts, wrapped in pitch and oil; the railings of vessels, made of seasoned wood, are covered in pitch, which easily catches fire. [11] Thus it is that some perish by fire or by iron, others are burned, still others are forced mercilessly to leap into the water; hence by these means many perish who fight on sea; it is a most piteous and bitter affair.

∽

The Defense Garrisons That Equip Men Who Fight at Sea (II. xl)

Sea fighters must be equipped with vessels full of pitch, resin, sulfur, brimstone, all of which must be melded together and bottled; these vessels then must be set afire and sent in the direction of enemy ships and galleys, attacking them at once before they have time to extinguish the fire. It must be remembered that there is one way of making a certain fire, which some call Greek fire, invented by the Greeks during the siege of Troy; [12] some have been heard to say, "This fire burns even in water; stones, iron, and all manner of things burn, nor can it be extinguished except by certain mixtures made for this purpose, but not by water." In addition, certain poisons can be made that are so powerful and lethal that if they contaminate iron, a mortal wound will result. But since such things should not be taught because of the evil that could result from them, they should be forbidden and cursed; it is not good to put them in books or otherwise reduce them to writing, because no Christian soldier should use such inhumane weapons that are in fact contrary to the laws of war. [13] Furthermore those who fight must always do everything in their power to drive the enemy towards land while maintaining their own position in deep water.

Additionally, to the ship's mast a trefoil must be attached, completely armored with iron, and maneuvered with a device that can raise and lower it, thereby striking great blows against enemy ships, and in this way it may be hacked to pieces, serving as the aforementioned battering ram. In addition, they must have an abundant supply of arrows with iron tips to pierce the sail so badly that it cannot retain the wind and thus can no longer advance. And a crooked piece of iron fashioned like a sickle, with a sharp edge, by which the sailors can cut the ship's ropes. And if one has the upper hand, one should use iron hooks to lash enemy ships to one's own so that they cannot escape. And it is good to have a great supply of pots full of soft soap, which can be hurled into the enemy ship, with the result that sailors cannot stand up but slip and fall into the water if they are near the ship's edge; then it is good to throw pots of quicklime, which upon breaking fills their eyes and mouths so that they can scarcely see. Additionally they must be equipped with certain men trained and outfitted to plunge into the water and remain beneath the surface;[14] these men, as long as the battle lasts, swim under water and pierce the ship with great augers so that water enters in various parts. And many large stones and sharp irons should be hurled, along with anything else that might damage the ship as much as possible.

Having stated the above things, I can use Vegetius' very words at the end of his book: "I think that henceforth I can remain silent on the discipline of arms, for in these matters common practice often reveals more of the art of warfare than ancient doctrine demonstrates."[15]

Here Inquiry Is Made into Whether It Is Right to Seize in Enemy Territory Simple Peasants Who Are Not Engaged in Warfare (III. xviii)[16]

I ask you whether, whenever a king or prince is warring against another, even though it be just, he has the right to overrun the enemy land and take prisoner all manner of people, common people, that is, peasants, shepherds, and such like; it would appear not. Why should they bear the burden of profession of arms, of which they know nothing? It is not for them to pass judgment about war; common people are not called on to bear arms; rather, it is distasteful to them for they say they want to live in peace and ask no more. They should be free, it seems to me, just as all priests and churchmen are, because their estate is outside military activity. What honor can accrue to a prince to kill, overrun, or seize people who have never borne arms nor could they make use of them, or poor innocent people who do nothing else but till the land and watch over animals?

To this I would answer with a supposition like this: let us suppose that the people of England wished to give no aid to their king in order to injure the king of France, and the French fell upon them instantly with right and reason on their side, and in accordance with lawful practice they should not in any way cause bodily harm or injure the property of the people nor of those who may come to aid the king, offering both goods and counsel. But if the subjects of that king or of another in a similar situation, be they poor or rich, farmers or anything else, give aid and comfort to keep up the war, according to military right the French may overrun their country, seize what they find, that is prisoners of whatever class and all manner of things, without being held by any law to return the same. For I tell you that this is determined as a matter of law, that is the law of war. For if a war is judged by the counsellors of both kings or princes, the men-at-arms can win one over the other. And occasionally the poor and simple folk, who do not bear arms, are injured — it cannot be otherwise, for weeds cannot take root among good plants, because the latter are so close together that the good ones do not sense their presence. But in truth it is right that the valiant and good gentlemen-at-arms must take every precaution not to destroy the poor and simple folk, nor suffer them to be tyrannized or mistreated. For they are Christians and not Saracens. And if I have said that pity is due to some, remember that not less is due the others; those who engage in warfare may be hurt but the humble and peaceful should be shielded from their force.

∞

Here It Is Asked Whether an English Student Studying in Paris or in Some Other Enemy Territory May Be Seized and Held for Ransom (IV. xix) [17]

But as we are engaged in a discussion of prisoners of war, I wish you to be the judge of a little debate, herewith proposed. It is well known, even notorious, how the kings of France and England frequently are at war with each other. Let us take as an example a student given leave by the city of London to come to Paris to study for a graduate degree in law or theology. It happens that a French man-at-arms realizes that the student is English and takes him prisoner, an act formally resisted by the victim. The matter is finally brought before justice. There the English student, basing his reasons on law, says that it is expressly stated by the law that on account of the great privileges accorded students, no harm may be done to them but rather honor and reverence. Here he states the underlying reasons: Who is he who would not recommend scholars, who for learning and the general acquisition of knowledge have abandoned riches and all bodily comforts, their close friends and their country, have taken on poverty, and given up all worldly goods, and everything else for the love of knowledge? He would resist anyone who would do such a student evil. To this line of reasoning a man-at-arms would reply in these terms: Brother, I tell you that among us French we do not enforce the laws of the emperor, to whom we are neither subject nor obedient. The student responds: Laws are nothing more than right reason ordered in accordance with wisdom, and if you do not care about this, it is not because the king and lords of France do not use reason concerning reasonable matters that they themselves have commanded. For when at the Pope's request Charlemagne transferred the General Study of Rome [Studium Generale] to Paris, the lords gave great and notable privileges to this school.[18] For this reason the king sent out into all parts in search of masters and students of all languages, and all were agreed on these privileges: why, then, cannot they come from all countries when they are given royal permission to do so, as all kings swear upon their assumption of power to maintain these privileges? In God's name, says the man-at-arms, assuming what you have said is true, you should know that since the general war has been waged between your king and ours, no Englishman may come into France for such a reason as you give, nor any other person without a safe conduct; and the reason for that is a good one, for you could, under pretext of studying, write and make known in your land the state of affairs here and commit all sorts of undercover deeds if you wished. Indeed it is not right that any kind of privilege should turn into prejudice against the king or his realm.

Hear these reasons and tell me, my dear friend, what you think.

Straightaway, master, since it pleases you that my humble opinion may serve the cause, I say to you that the person of whom you speak is a true student. That is to say, he did not pretend to come under false colors to spy or to do harm. I consider his motive to be good and that he should not be taken prisoner unless the king had issued a special order that no Englishman or any sort should come to study in his kingdom, and that such an order has been widely published and known in all places.

You have shown excellent judgment and made a wise distinction. For even if the bishopric of Paris or the archbishopric of Rouen, of Sens, or any other should become vacant and an English priest were to be elected, the king would have the right to quash the election for the reason that it is not expedient for the king or for his realm to have enemies in their midst.

But still another question.[19] Answer me this: suppose the student may not be taken prisoner. What about his servants, if he brings along several from England? After all, the privilege given to students was never extended in good faith to servants.

Master, subject to your correction, that reason notwithstanding, it seems to me that part of the privilege of the master, if he be a true student, would be that his servants should be included, as in the case where the king grants privilege to his officers, their servants and their whole families are included.

But master, I should like to ask something that may cast doubt upon this matter. Suppose the student were ill: could his father by right come to visit him without danger?[20]

To this I respond that according to written law, even if he came under false pretenses, he should be able to come safely. The reason is that the law of nature is greater than that of war. Love of father and mother for the child is privileged; no right of arms can take precedence over it. An even stronger argument may be advanced that if the father were to go and see his son, who was quite well and at work at his studies, or even if this were elsewhere than Paris, to take him books and money, he may not for that reason be arrested, seized, imprisoned in any country whatsoever, friendly or enemy. This judgment is set forth in written law, just as I have said. And for the same reason are included brother, relative, or servant, who may take money or books to him, under the provisions of the aforementioned clauses; and all this is by virtue of privileges reserved for students generally.

SUMNER WILLARD

(Translated from Brussels Royal Library Ms. 10476)

N O T E S

1. The first seven chapters of the book are a discussion of the concept of the Just War from a medieval point of view. This was a subject popular with jurists and theologians of the day. Although Christine's immediate source here was Honoré Bouvet's *Tree of Battles*, the subject owed much of its development to the rediscovery of Roman law by jurists at the University of Bologna (where Christine's father and grandfather had been educated) and the publication of Gratian's *Decretals* around 1140. Christine, in accord with many of her contemporaries, was particularly opposed to private wars and duels, which had indeed been outlawed in France in 1406 (Solente, *Histoire de la littérature française*, p. 64).

2. The basis for this idea came from Saint Augustine and Isidore of Seville as their ideas were developed by the Italian legists.

3. This practice was followed by Charles V. See the *Fais et Bonnes Meurs du Sage Roy Charles V* (Solente ed., II, pp. 118–20.).

4. Vegetius II, chap. 5. See *Vegetius: Epitome of Military Science,* trans. N. P. Milner (Liverpool, 1993). Christine frequently contrasts the theories of Vegetius with the ideas of her own day.

5. A particular irony of history is that the French defeat at Agincourt was caused in large measure by the fact that the French army was too large for the available terrain. Leadership was also notably lacking, for few of the commanders, notably the Count of Armagnac, had had experience in actual battle. Had Christine's book been taken more seriously at the time it was written, it might have provided a useful warning. See J. Keegan, *The Face of Battle* (London, 1976), pp. 79–116 for a good account of this battle.

6. Christine had insisted in *The Body of Policy* (p. 288) on the necessity of rewarding services fairly. For conditions governing the ordinary soldier see P. Contamine, *War in the Middle Ages* (Oxford, 1984), pp. 150–65.

7. Although the naval engagements during Charles VI's reign were of little consequence, Charles V had created a regular royal navy under the command of an admiral, Jean de Vienne. This was based at an arsenal, the Clos des Galées at Rouen. The royal fleet was thus able to take part in the military operations that Christine speaks of in the *Livre des Fais et Bonnes Meurs* (Solente ed., I, pp. 239–42.)

8. Vegetius V, 6; also quoted in the *Fais et Bonnes Meurs* (I, p. 240.)

9. This advice on the skills needed by sailors is condensed from Vegetius V, chaps. 8–12.

10. Vegetius V, chap. 14. These points are also mentioned in the *Fais et Bonnes Meurs* I, pp. 240–41.

11. Vegetius V, chap. 14. Solente (I, p. 240n) also calls attention to the influence here of the French translation of Egidio Colonna's *De Regimine Principium.*

12. Christine's idea that Greek Fire was first used at Troy is based on legend. It was probably developed at the end of the seventh century by a certain Callimacus, a Greek architect living in Syria. The formula was indeed kept secret but was probably a combination of naphtha, sulfur, and quicklime that exploded on contact with water. It was fired through siphons with high-velocity nozzles, or in hand grenades made of earthenware vessels. It came to be one of the most effective Byzantine weapons and was used for several centuries in defense of Constantinople. See J. R. Partington, *A History of Greek Fire and Gunpowder* (Cambridge, 1960); W. H. Spears, Jr., *Greek Fire, the Fabulous Secret Weapon that Saved Europe* (Chicago, 1969).

13. Contamine (p. 274n) is of the opinion that reservations against certain weapons arose more from chivalric ideology than pacifist sentiments, although this might not be the explanation for Christine's attitude, for she was certainly an advocate of peace. It is nevertheless interesting to find that her views are echoed by Jean de Bueil in *Le Jouvencel,* written around the middle of the fifteenth century (ed. C. Favre and L. Lecestre [Paris, 1887–1889], II, p. 58). See also Contamine, p. 274n.

14. This suggestion does not appear to come from Vegetius; it must have been a recommendation from one of Christine's contemporaries.

15. Vegetius V, 15.

16. Books III and IV are based on Honoré Bouvet's *Tree of Battles.* This chapter is a considerably revised version of Part IV, chap. 48 of Bouvet's text: "Whether on account of war between the kings of France and England the French may lawfully overrun the lands of the English and take their goods." See G. W. Coopland trans. (Liverpool, 1949), pp. 153–54. Christine is more outspoken in her defense of the poor.

17. *Tree of Battles*, IV, chap. 56. Here Christine adds her own comments to an extended summary of Bouvet's chapter.
18. This transfer of studies was an idea attractive to early French humanists, Gerson among others, whose ideas had an important influence on Christine. She had already mentioned it in the *Chemin de Long Estude* (vv. 5893–5906, p. 250) and the *Fais et Bonnes Meurs* (II, pp. 46–49). For the history of this idea see E. Gilson, *Les Idées et les Lettres* (Paris, 1932), pp. 183–85; F. Simone, *Il Renascimento Francese* (Turin, 1961), pp. 47–54.
19. *Tree of Battles*, IV, chap. 27, where Christine again expands the comments of her model.
20. *Tree of Battles*, IV, chap. 28.

CCW

LAMENTATION ON THE WOES OF FRANCE

❧

Lamentation of Christine de Pizan
May whoever has pity put it to work
This is the time that requires it!

ALONE AND APART, restraining with great difficulty the tears that obscure my vision and flow like a fountain over my face, so that I can barely manage to write this sorrowful complaint, while the pity of the misfortune that threatens effaces the writing with bitter drops. For I am completely overwhelmed and say in complaint: "Oh how can it be possible that human heart can reduce man to the level of a bloodthirsty and cruel beast, can Fortune be so strange? What sort of reason calls him a rational animal? How is it in Nature's power to change man so greatly that he is transformed into a viper, human nature's enemy? Alas, noble French princes, the possibility exists. And may it not displease you if I ask, where is now the sweet natural blood among you, which was formerly the best in the world's kindness, with which true stories have been filled from time immemorial, and about which Fame used to trumpet throughout the world? What has happened to the clear vision of noble understanding that naturally and through long custom made you work with the council of worthy men of good conscience? Are you fathers of French unity now blinded, as it would seem, whose ancestors formerly guarded, protected, and nourished the numerous children of this once blessed land, about to be transmuted into desolation, if pity doesn't alter the situation? What have those who have adored you like gods done wrong that you who were greatly renowned for your honor should now seem to treat them less like your children than like mortal enemies in your mutual talks that lead only to sorrow, battle, and war for them?

For Heaven's sake! For Heaven's sake! Mighty princes, open your eyes through knowledge such as this so that you can see what can happen by your taking up arms. Thus you will see cities in ruins, towns and castles destroyed, fortresses thrown to the ground! And where? In the very midst of France! The noble chivalry and youth of France which as one body and soul used to stand ready to defend the crown and public good, now assembled in shameful ranks against each other, father against son, brother against brother, one relative against the next, their deadly swords drenching the battlefields with blood, with dead and dismembered bodies! What a dishonorable victory, whoever may gain it! To whom will it bring glorious renown? Will the victors be crowned with laurel? Alas, their heads might rather be encircled with black thorns, not conquerers but genocides for which they should wear black as for the death of members of their own families.

And you, sir knight, who comes from such a battle, pray tell me, what honors do you bear? Will it be said of you, for your honor, that on that day you were on the side of victory? Or will that peril from which you managed to escape be placed against your other more creditable deeds, for you will not be praised for that day. Ah, may it be pleasing to men, for God would not wish that anyone should be so bold as to arm himself for either one side or the other.

And then what next, in God's name? Famine because of the pillaging and destruction of property that will follow, and failure to cultivate the fields, from which will result rebellion of the people because they are harassed by the soldiers, deprived, too hard pressed and robbed of this and that; subversion in the cities where, for the need of money, it will be necessary to impose outrageous taxes on citizens and inhabitants; and above all, the English, who for their part will checkmate if Fortune permits; and there will still be the dissensions and mortal hatreds entrenched in many hearts that will lead to treason. Is this what is intended? Indeed, yes.[1]

Weep, then weep, beating together your palms with great cries, ladies, maidens, and other women of France, as was once done in a similar case by the sorrowing Argine and the women of Argos,[2] for the blades are already sharpened that will make you widows and deprive you of both children and fathers! O Sabine women,[3] there is need for you in this case, for wasn't the peril even greater and the quarrel already existing among your relatives when with great prudence you played your part in establishing peace, when you rushed disheveled in great swarms to the battlefield, your infants in your arms, crying out: Have mercy on our dear friends and relatives, make peace!

Ah, Queen of France, are you asleep?[4] What prevents you from trying to check and make this deadly undertaking cease? Don't you see the heritage of your noble children threatened? Mighty princess, mother of the noble heirs of France, who but you can act? Who would disobey your power and authority, if you truly wished to establish peace?

Come, come, sages of the kingdom, join with your queen! What good are you doing in the king's council? Let everyone lend a hand. Now you merely occupy yourself with details. Why should France pride itself on so many wise heads if no way can be found now to protect the country, fountain of wisdom, from perdition. Where then are your enterprise and your wise opinions? Ah, French clergy, will you allow Fortune's influence to go unchecked? Why don't you organize processions and devout prayers? Don't you perceive the need for them? It now seems like Nineveh,[5] which God condemned to perdition because of his great wrath at the grave sins that abounded in the city; the outcome here will be most dreadful if the sentence isn't revoked through the intercession of devout prayers.

Surely then, people, devout women, you should cry misericord for this distressing tempest. Ah, France! France! Formerly glorious kingdom! Alas! What more can I say? Bitter tears fall unceasing like rivulets on my page so that there is no dry place left where I can continue writing this piteous lament that my overflowing heart yearns to unburden. My weary hands are kept busy, frequently laying down the pen with which I write to restore the sight of my grieving eyes, wiping away the tears that are so abundant that I am dampened to my waist, when I think what will be said of you in the future. For won't you henceforth be compared with strange countries, those where brothers, cousins, and other relatives jealously and greedily kill each other like dogs? Won't it be said reproachfully: Come, come, you French, you boast of the gentle blood of your princes who are not tyrants, and mock us because of the ways of our Guelphs and Ghibellines![6] Now they are produced by your country also. The seed has germinated, your provinces have come to the same pass as ours. Now lower your horns, for your glory is tarnished. Alas, sweet France, can it be that you are really in such straits? Indeed you are, but there is still a remedy. God is merciful. However great the peril, all is not lost.

O Duke of Berry, noble prince, excellent forebear of the royal princes, son of the king of France as well as brother and uncle, father of the tradition of the French lily, how is it possible that your kindly heart can allow you to see yourself, on a given day, in battle array bearing arms against your nephews? I do not believe that the memory of your great natural love for their parents, your beloved late brothers and sisters, could stop the tears from flowing like a fountain down the length of your face, nor could your noble heart fail to be dissolved by pity to the point where it could scarcely sustain you. Alas! How distressing to see the most noble kinsman alive today, uncle of three kings, six dukes, and innumerable counts murderously arrayed against his own flesh and blood, and the nephews who should revere him as their own fathers, facing him in battle![7] O noble French blood above reproach, how can you permit such a shameful thing to happen (and may that day never come) that those who were once the pillars of faith, supporters of the Church by whose virtue, fortitude, and knowledge it has always been sustained and pacified, and which among all nations has been called the most Christian promoter of peace, friend of concord, should now come to such a predicament?

Come then, come, noble Duke of Berry, most excellent prince, and follow the divine law that advocates peace! Seize the bridle firmly and put a stop to this disgraceful army, at least until you have spoken with the two factions.[8] Come to Paris, to your father's city where you were born, which is crying out to you in its tears, sighs and anguish, begging and beseeching you. Comfort the grief-stricken city and return to your children speaking the language of correction, if you find them at fault, like a good father. Calm them while reproving them as is your duty, pointing out to one side and then the other how, whatever their quarrel, they should be the defenders, pillars, and supporters of the noble crown and shield of the kingdom that never harmed them, nor should this be compared with what they demand of each other, nor should they wish to destroy it!

For the love of God, noble duke, warn them soon that although there is talk of victory on both sides — "We will conquer and we will carry on thus and so" — that such boasting is folly, for it should not be forgotten how uncertain and unpredictable is the outcome of any battle. Though man proposes, Fortune disposes. What did it avail the king of Thebes to leave the battle victorious with three of his knights only, leaving all the rest dead on the battlefield, lying amidst his many enemies, all decimated by the swords of their relatives and princes?[9] Lord, what a victory! It was pitiable! The king of Athens mortally wounded in battle — what good was his victory to him?[10] What has it profited many people in such circumstances? Was not Xerxes undone, he who had so many troops that the valleys and mountains were covered with them?[11] Does a good and just cause then prevail? If this were so, the king Saint Louis, who had won so many great victories, would not have been defeated by the infidels before Tunis.[12] What better example could there be of God's remarkable disposition to let a battle run its course, where the evil is certain and the good that might come of it is highly uncertain? And above all, even though war and battles are always very perilous and difficult to carry out, there can be no doubt that among such close relatives, which nature has united as if by one bond of affection, it is completely perverse, dishonorable, and outrageous, and no good can ever come of it. Alas! If this is so, and it is indeed the case that for various motives and quarrels wars often break out, there are even better and stronger reasons why they should be shunned and avoided and that peace should be sought instead.

Now may virtue overcome vice. A way should be found to pacify natural friends who accidentally become enemies. Alas! Would to God that the trouble and effort exerted at present were as devoted to seeking a peaceful solution as to promoting strife. I think it could be achieved with less cost, and with a common will and true spirit of union this army might be turned on those who are our natural enemies, where good, loyal Frenchmen might better employ themselves than in killing each other. Lord! What a joy that would be and what great and eternal honor to the kingdom!

Ah most honored prince, noble Duke of Berry, pray hear this, for there is little that the human heart undertakes, especially with just intent, that cannot be accomplished. If you were to work toward this end henceforth you would be called father of the realm, preserver of the crown and of the royal lily, custodian of its high nobility, protector of the nobles against slaughter, comforter of the people, guardian of noble ladies, widows, and orphans, to which purpose may the blessed Holy Spirit, source of all peace, give you heart and courage to bring trouble to a speedy conclusion.[13] Amen. And to me, poor voice crying in this realm, desirous of peace and of universal good, your humble servant Christine, moved by good will, may it be given to see that day. Amen.

Written the twenty-third day of August, the year of grace, 1410.

CCW

(Translated from Paris B.N. Ms. fr. 24864)

NOTES

1. Christine discusses here the same three parts of the state as in *The Body of Policy:* the princes, the knights, and the suffering common people. These last will face famine if they cannot cultivate their lands. In addition, the possibility that the English may be waiting for an opportunity to attack is a pervasive fear. Christine's view was only too accurate.

2. Argia, daughter of the king of Argos, was the widow of Polyneices, who had been killed by his brother Etiocles. In the course of the fratricidal war between these two sons of Oedipus, all the Arginians perished except Adrastus. Christine had already referred to this episode in the history of Thebes in *The Mutation of Fortune* (Solente ed., II, pp. 319–28) and in *The Book of the City of Ladies* (II, chap. 17, Richards trans., pp. 125–26).

3. The example of the Sabine women had also been cited in *The Mutation of Fortune* (III, p. 183), and *The City of Ladies* (II, chap. 33, Richards trans., pp. 147–50).

4. It is evident that Isabeau of Bavaria had not persisted in any peacekeeping efforts, despite Christine's exhortation in 1405.

5. Nineveh was saved from destruction by Jonah's warning (Jonah 3). Christine had also referred to this episode in *The Mutation of Fortune* (I, pp. 152–53).

6. Christine is referring to her Italian birth, and also to the long political struggle in Italy between the Guelphs (supporters of the popes) and the Ghibellines (supporters of the emperors). Christine had written more of this conflict in *The Mutation of Fortune* (II, pp. 14–18 and S. Solente's notes, pp. 337–38). She was perhaps also recalling Dante's *Purgatory*, Canto 26, vv. 76 and following, for she does refer to Dante in the passage in *The Mutation of Fortune.*

7. The Duke of Berry was the uncle of the king, the Duke of Burgundy, and the murdered Duke of Orleans.

8. Christine is presumably referring to the duke's initiative in the formation of the League of Gien against the Duke of Burgundy in the spring of 1410. He responded immediately by gathering together an army to oppose this alliance. In July, the king's mental condition stabilized long enough for him to be alarmed by the state of affairs, and he immediately tried to calm the situation. The Duke of Burgundy was more receptive to his pleas than was the Duke of Berry, who refused to come to Paris to discuss a truce. (F. Lehoux, *Jean de France, Duc de Berry*, [Paris, 1968] III, pp. 166ff.) Christine's letter should perhaps be considered as part of the king's effort to bring the Duke of Berry to Paris.

9. Christine apparently took Adrastus, king of Argos, to be a king of Thebes, as it would appear from her account of these events in *The Mutation of Fortune* (II, pp. 284–328).

10. She had already told the story of the death of King Codrus in the biography of Charles V (Solente ed. I, pp. 186–87).

11. Christine had recalled the defeat of Xerxes in *The Mutation of Fortune* (Solente ed. II, pp. 242–56).

12. S. Solente considered Joinville's *Vie de Saint Louis* one of Christine's sources for her biography of Charles V. Both this and the *Histoire de Saint Louis* by Guillaume de Saint-Pathus were available in the library of the Louvre, to which Christine would undoubtedly have had access through her connections with the royal librarian, Gilles Malet (*Les Fais et Bonnes Meurs de Sage Roy Charles V*, I, pp. lxix–lxx.)

13. Christine is obviously trying here not only to remind the duke of his duties but to flatter the vanity of the elderly prince.

CCW

THE BOOK OF PEACE

❦

*Here We Speak to My Lord of Guyenne, Urging Him to Continue
Keeping the Peace* (I. iii)

OMNE REGNUM IN SE DIVISUM DESOLIBITUR ET OMNIS
CIVITAS VEL DOMUS DIVISA CONTRA SE NON STABIT.
IN EUVANGELIO.[1]

No kingdom divided can stand; nor can cities or households divided
against their own good endure. The Holy Scriptures show this by
accounts of various examples. This could also be said of Troy, Rome,
and various lands that for the sake of brevity I won't mention, but that
were once of such great strength if they were in agreement that
nobody in the world would harm them; yet they perished through
discord. So let us once more, noble prince, praise your efforts on behalf
of this worthy peace; for while it is true that where there is dissension
any kingdom will undoubtedly perish, it is also certain that peace and
love will preserved it. Thus you, being wise and well-advised, could
find no better medicine or effective remedy for preserving this noble
kingdom, which is your heritage, than by re-establishing peace. Along
with safeguarding what is yours, you have gained merit both in
Heaven and on Earth, for as the Scriptures say: Blessed are the peace-
makers, for they shall be called children of God.[2] Likewise you will
benefit on Earth because it is also said that the glory of a ruler is
greatly enhanced when his subjects are at peace, without thought of
war.[3] Therefore, as joy and tranquility exist where there is no such
preoccupation, you will enjoy an increasing abundance of goods for,
as the Psalmist says: An abundance of all good things will be found in
your storage houses, which is to say in your possession.[4] And David
said: Seek peace and pursue it, and that you have certainly done, for
you have indeed sought it until you have found it. And so you must
continue forever to pursue it, as the Scriptures say: Great merit to the
prince when he is able to make use of the benefits of peace for the
profit of all and without prejudice to any. He will be loved by all.[5] So

you must strive for the continuation of peace with great prudence, which means that if you can attract and maintain all things necessary for the preservation of peace, and use such good advice as is necessary, avoiding all eventualities that might come about because of the chance of not foreseeing them. As a philosopher has said: Such great skill is not necessary to acquire what one wants as to keep it. Nothing is more true than this, for when a fire is kindled and burns brightly in a town, it is difficult to extinguish it so completely that no tinder remains that might easily re-ignite in a few days and cause further damage.[6] In the same way, the resentment and ill will demonstrated by a show of arms is difficult to turn aside and appease (it is as destructive as the fire), so that to put it out there is need for a continuation of the water of kindness and good will to pour over it, and this must come from you as from a true fountain of clemency, joy, and benignity. You must always serve as a means of conducting peace gently, not for just a month or two, but forever, so that you can gain and touch people's hearts to the point where the residue of past bitterness will be effaced as much for devotion to you and your concern for them as for their own good. Then all may be changed into good will and good fellowship. Thus, noble prince, by following such ways as these and any others that are suitable, have no doubt that God, by whose help (may it be praised) you have done the essential part, will permit you to carry out the rest in such a way that henceforth you can live gloriously in the affection of your people and their prosperity, as God may grant it to you.

CCW

In the Following Chapter Reasons Are Given to Show That No One Needs Greater Knowledge Than the Prince of the Realm, and the First Example Is That of King Charles, Fifth of the Name (I. vi)

NON QUAEQUAM MAGIS DECET, VEL MELIORA SCIRE, VEL PLURA, QUAM PRINCIPEM CUIUS DOCTRINA OMNIBUS POTEST PRODESSE SUBJECTIS.

VEGETIUS, De Re Militari, in primo
capitulo[7]

Concerning what was said in the preceding chapter, most noble prince, the authority quoted above offers sufficient justification for my having made so lengthy a description of Prudence, for it is surely certain that no man needs to know more things or be better informed than does the leader of the realm, since all his subjects can profit by his prudence and the good example of his life. And therefore, so that your fame, both for the present and times to come, be not only resplendent through all the world on account of your worthy rank, but greater still because of your virtues and wisdom, the virtue of prudence is of the greatest necessity, and all your actions should be governed by circumspection, which the sage will follow in all such matters, before taking up whatever cause, as we have previously said.

And that this be true, surely I could find examples enough among the great men of antiquity, as the worthy Caesar, or Pompey, or Cicero, or other men of great nobility — whose every effort was spent in knowing as much as possible before undertaking any action, and in becoming wise, so that much good came of their policies, being conducted by profound knowledge rather than by force of arms. But the example of your good forebear, Charles the Wise, fifth of the name, should be sufficient — and may God give you the grace to resemble him! For then none of the qualities which can be asked of the wise and perfect prince would be lacking in you. Who can mention any wiser than he, with better upbringing and grace, or any more perfect in all things? For in the very flower of his youth, understanding by the grace of God how noble and necessary a thing it is for a prince, however young in years, to be of mature character and to know those things which must be done and those one should refrain from doing, he abandoned the manner of youth, giving himself entirely to those things which wisdom teaches.[8] And having made this decision, in order to put his good intentions to work, he cast out of himself all desires contrary to his good resolve, seeking to attract from all countries wise men and worthy, of upright conduct; such men he would find and take to his service, keeping them in all manner of state with great honor and profit.[9] Thus to be well instructed in those things relating to spiritual welfare, which is the most important of all, he wished to have at his service weighty and worthy theologians, as for example a most wise master in divinity, one Jean de la Chaleur,[10] him and others he would often hear, and at regular hours and days would receive their lessons in morality. Such teaching led him to give himself entirely to God's service, fearing and loving Him above all things, so that he completed his learning by virtuous works, both in acts of charity to the poor and in the construction of churches or establishing prayers or other acts of devotion his whole life long, as can still be seen in many places.

Again, in order that his realm be well governed in political matters, he sought to engage renowned clerics, expert in legal matters, so that by their counsel he might govern all things according to the law; and thus it happened that as long as he reigned, by following the procedures appropriate to a well ordered royal government, he kept his realm in the greatest of splendor, growing ever more prosperous. And this was done by observing strict justice, by keeping his army active and engaged in such training and actions as are fitting, by respecting the privileges and the province of the clergy, showing love to the citizens of his towns, and keeping a just peace among the merchants whether foreign or his own, with the people at rest, not occupying them with other matters than their work or trade, as right government prescribes, neither exacting unjust sums nor allowing others to do so.

Again, that the realm be well defended and aggrandized in his hands, he sought to engage good men at arms in his service, wherever they might be called to his attention, the flower of chivalry, setting the best of them in command with the honors and provisions due them, as many who are still alive can testify. And as for the results, my noble lord, it is obvious enough that you yourself have profited thereby, as (may it please God) the crown will ever profit, and his merits and good fame forever endure.

ERIC HICKS

∽

Christine Speaks of the Peril in Which the Kingdom of France Has Been Because of the Recent Civil War in the Hope of Avoiding a Repetition (III. xiv)

AD PAUCA ADVERTENTES DE FACILI PARALOGIZANTUR.
ARISTOTILES IN *ELENCHIS.* [11]

Aristotle means to say here that those who pay little attention, or who fail to protect themselves, easily and often find themselves deceived. So it is with the nobility, because they cannot communicate well about the matter already mentioned. They face the danger of unreasonable popular uprisings. Through the example of the present case, or former events, may they learn to behave in such a manner that a similar incident—or one even worse—could not happen again. Good Heavens! What heart would not tremble thinking of the great danger in which the kingdom stands to lose everything because of this pitiful war? [12] There is no reason to recall it, or put it into writing, except, as has been mentioned, so that it may serve as a warning to wise people who are now living or to those in future times who may hear about it, for, as Aristotle says, examples serve as lessons to those who listen. So let us give a little thought to what it would have been like to see assembled in deadly conflict so many princes and other noblemen in a body under a noble leader, killing each other and perishing piteously because of Fortune's intervention in the dwelling of Mischance.[13] Let us consider the absolute folly of seeing a man driven so greatly by anger that he wants to destroy himself: his teeth tearing at his own feet, his hands striking great blows at each other, and his feet tripping each other up and kicking out his eyes, so that the whole body seemed to be in an insane spasm against itself.[14] Indeed, one would have reason to say that such a person was completely mad. Alas! Is that not the case of civil war in a country, and especially in this one, where noblemen were formerly a single body, as they should indeed still be? And then after the slaughter and rout come the diabolical commoners with their picks and maces, which they are so unwisely allowed to own and carry, who would have massacred the remaining noble ladies, maidens, and children, lacking sufficient good sense to be aware that some foreign lord would soon arrive to subjugate them and kill them because the death of the nobles would leave them without anyone to resist the invader. So France would be ruined and enslaved just as other kingdoms have been. So I, still trembling from fright when I think of it, pray God that this may never come about. Oh what a pitiful state of affairs! For God's sake, for God's sake, noble and worthy French princes, knights, and all noblemen living or to be born, may this crisis and mortal peril never fade from your memories for your own sakes! May strife never again be permitted or such a dreadful misfortune ever come about. Nor should the ruin, destruction, bloodshed, unspeakable cruelty, impoverishment, popular lack of respect toward sovereign lords, ladies, young girls, widows, and orphans, which can result from this mischief, be forgotten or overlooked. Poor Christine, your humble servant, has already said this in *The Vision of the Cock* and in her tearful and piteous letters,[15] and she is still fearful of worse to come, so that she cannot remain silent. But even in this danger she does not dare to rely on common sense, but hopes for divine intervention through an evident miracle, for which Heaven be praised!

How a Prince Should Deal with the Common People in Order to Keep Them from Presumption and a Reason for Rebellion (III. xv)

SI VOLUNTAS DIVERSOREM VAGA RELINQUATUR CONFUSIO CULPARUM AMICA GENERATUR. EXEMPLA 2ª. LIBRO Iᵉ SENECE.

In order to complete what I began earlier, for it is sometimes necessary to postpone conclusions in order to explain the problem more fully, in this case the sort of government that a prince should follow in order to keep his subjects in peace, we can thus interpret the authority cited above to mean that bad deeds cannot be ignored until the desires and wishes of certain other things cease, so that those who were enemies become friends. A will for certain things truly exists in the common people, and so to satisfy their vague desires, in order that troubles like those just past are not repeated, it seems to me a good policy for the prince to fulfill his duty towards God as well as to make sure that the people have no further cause to complain and be discontented. He should govern suitably with especially deep respect for justice, not allowing the commoners to be mistreated nor pilfered by the militia nor by anybody else.[16] He should protect them diligently from all enemies, just as the good shepherd looks after his sheep,[17] and he should make sure that if anything is taken from them or denied them because of their labor, they should be promptly paid and given satisfaction, for a wise man says: Do not withhold the pay of the workers from evening until the next morning so that you will not be cursed by them. Do not demand any subsidy from them nor impose taxes or any other charges upon them beyond what is necessary to pay for just wars. Maintain them in peace and do not allow anyone else to oppress or injure them, thus causing them to become aroused or distracted by anything beyond their tasks and specialties. The prince should be kindly in word if he has occasion to speak to them, and favorable to their rightful requests. He should not be guilty of cruelty, but should rather see to it that they are kindly treated. And when he goes about the city, or elsewhere, if they come to see him and greet him, he should return their greeting in a friendly fashion and with a pleasant look.

At the same time, he should order that they should not wear outrageous clothing, nor anything that is unsuitable to their station in life, such as embroideries or coats of arms such as rightfully belong to gentlemen, for pride of this sort can be harmful and indeed has perhaps already been so.[18]

Likewise, so that they may learn to be more courteous, he should forbid them, on pain of punishment, to indulge in blasphemy, profanity, or outrageous oaths on the name of Our Lord. This should apply to all, great as well as humble, even the courtiers. . . . Likewise, as idleness often encourages bad habits in the young and also foolish conspiracies, certain people should be appointed in the cause of justice to search out and make sure that no trouble is concocted in the town, and that those wastrels who wander about frequenting taverns in idleness should be arrested if they do not go to their jobs on work days. [19]

Furthermore, false rumors such as those that have circulated should be forbidden, and those who use them against others should be punished.

In short, through such means as these, and other good and suitable ordinances, the prince can maintain his people in peace and promote their welfare. They would not be wasting their time as they have been doing recently; instead, everyone would stick to his appointed task, and all would be pleased with the prince for protecting their peace with justice. In this way they could improve themselves financially, so that they would be in a better position to come to his assistance if he should have need of it. [20] In this way the people would live gloriously under a good ruler.

CCW

(Translated from Brussels Royal Library Ms. 10366)

NOTES

1. Matthew 12: 25. Christine had already cited the same passage in her *Letter to the Queen* (see p. 270)
2. Matthew 5: 9.
3. Psalm 121: 7.
4. Psalm 33: 15.
5. A note in the margin of the manuscript attributes this to Cassiodorus.
6. Christine is recalling a proverb that says that it is better to prevent a fire than to try to extinguish it once it is burning. She had already cited it in *The Treasury of the City of Ladies* (Part I, chap. 23).
7. *The Art of Warfare* by Vegetius had been a principal source for *The Deeds of Arms and of Chivalry*. This reference is interesting, however, for it shows that Christine knew the Latin original as well as a translation of the text. It is also noteworthy that Nicole Oresme made use of this same passage in the Prologue to his translation of Aristotle's *Ethics*, (ed. A. A. Menut [New York, 1940], p. 40) with reference to Charles V. It is at this point that Christine begins once more to hold up the example of the former king to his grandson.

8. Christine had already made this point in both the biography of Charles V and in *The Body of Policy*. It is not difficult to understand what she was trying to impress on the mind of a rather frivolous young man.

9. Christine had also spoken of this in the biography of Charles V. Of course Christine's father had been one of the men attracted to his court.

10. Jean de la Chaleur was appointed Chancellor of the University of Paris on October 3, 1370 (Delachenal, *Histoire de Charles V*, p. 101n).

11. A reference to Aristotle's *Sophistici Elenchi*, although Christine undoubtedly knew it through some compilation of quotations such as the *Manipulus Florum*. The error in the spelling of Aristotle's name and other errors in the Latin are in the original text.

12. Christine is here recalling the events of the Cabochien uprising, led by the violent guild of butchers, which lasted from the end of March until August 1413. The same events are discussed by Jean Gerson in a sermon preached before the court on September 4 of the same year: "*Rex in sempiternum vive*" (*Long Live the King*). See Jean Gerson, *Oeuvres complètes*, VII, pp. 1005–30.

13. The reference is to Fortune and her brother Mischance (Meseur) as described in *The Mutation of Fortune* I, pp. 71–74 (vv. 1805–1910); pp. 82–86 (vv. 2165–2282).

14. This obviously recalls once more the image of the "body politic." A similar image of the various members destroying each other was used by Gerson in his sermon "*Rex in Sempiternum vive*" (ed. cit. pp. 1029–1030).

15. Christine is here recalling not only her letters to the queen and the Duke of Berry but also a work of which no trace has been found beyond this reference. See K. Sneyders de Vogel, "Une oeuvre inconnue de Christine de Pisan," in *Mélanges . . . offerts à Ernst Hoepffner* (Paris, 1949), pp. 369–70.

16. Christine was not alone in her concern over the undisciplined state of the military. It was a preoccupation of Philippe de Mézières in the *Songe du Vieil Pèlerin*, of Nicolas de Clamanges in letters to Gerson, of Gerson himself in his sermon *Vivat Rex* preached before the court in 1405, and also several ballades of Eustache Deschamps. For a detailed description of this problem, see P. Contamine, *Etat et Société à la fin du Moyen Age: Etude sur les armées des rois de France* (Paris, 1972), pp. 205–73.

17. Once more Christine uses the figure she has developed already on several occasions. Gerson had also used it in his sermon "*Vivat Rex*" (*Oeuvres* VII, p. 1160).

18. Christine had expressed a similar sentiment with regard to clothing suitable for women in the *Treasury of the City of Ladies* (II, chap. 11). From around the middle of the fourteenth century, styles had become increasingly elaborate, especially as the middle class prospered. See. P. Contamine, *Le Vie Quotidienne pendant la Guerre de Cent Ans* (Paris, 1976), pp. 203–06; I. Brook, *Western European Costume: Thirteenth to Seventeenth Century* (London, 1939), pp. 85–90.

19. Christine had remarked on the bad habits of some workers in *The Body of Policy* (III, chap. 9), and in *The Treasury of the City of Ladies* she admonished wives to try to keep their husbands in order (III, chap. 8). Christine also believed that the middle class had a duty to help keep the workers under control.

20. Christine believed that the bourgeoisie, and especially the merchants, should support the legitimate activities of the prince. Their increasing importance and prosperity eventually led to the French Revolution. An especially interesting study of the rise of the middle class is J. Bartier, *Légistes et Gens de Finances au XVᵉ siècle* (Brussels, 1952).

CCW

VII

THE LIFE OF THE SPIRIT

❦

A CRITICAL overview of Christine de Pizan's writings does not provide an impression of any great piety, and certainly not more than might be expected in any observant medieval woman; religious faith was a fundamental aspect of any such life. Especially in her early years, she attributed her difficulties to Fortune more readily than to Divine Providence, and she favored action and resolve more than prayer as a means of response to them. This secular impression must be somewhat modified, however, by a few works that are distinctly spiritual in character, even if they are not entirely devoid of worldly overtones. The selections included here represent a considerable span of her life, for the *Prayers to Our Lady* date from 1402–1403, the *Allegorized Psalms* from the end of 1409, whereas the *Letter Concerning the Prison of Human Life* is dated January 20, 1417.

The *Prayers to Our Lady* was first published in 1838 by Raimond Thomassy,[1] who was of the opinion that it had been written in 1414, when the Council of Constance had been convened to try to bring an end to the Schism that had so seriously divided the Catholic Church. He also believed that Christine was seeking comfort in religion from the political trials that were facing France at that period. His dating of the poems is, however, unlikely, because of the prayer for the Duke of Orleans, who had been murdered in November 1407, and because these prayers were included in the earliest manuscripts of Christine's collected poetry; therefore they must have been written before 1402 or the beginning of 1403. Maurice Roy suggested more plausibly that the prayer referring to peace within the Church could have been inspired by negotiations then in progress between the French crown and the anti-pope Benedict XIII, which led to France's declaring obedience to him in May 1403.[2] Other details in this series of sixteen prayers, of which four are included here, support such a date. Christine prays, for instance, for Charles d'Albret, who was named constable of France at the end of February 1403 and to whom she dedicates

Ballade XXV of her *Cent Ballades*. At the same time it is interesting that she should have included prayers for all levels of French society: the knights, the clergy, the bourgeoisie, and those who work on the land. One already glimpses the idea of the body politic, which she would develop in *The Book of the Body of Policy*. There is also a prayer for all women, heralding *The Book of The City of Ladies*, on which, in fact, she might already have been at work.

Her references to the doctors of the Church is interesting, although they have generally been overlooked. She had already shown an interest in their writings by quoting a goodly number in her *Letter of Othea*. One need not be overly impressed by this display of erudition, however, for it has been repeatedly demonstrated that Christine made constant use of the *Manipulus Florum*, a manual of quotations much consulted by preachers.[3] These references, however, are a reminder that her piety was neither simple nor altogether conventional, for she evokes a whole army of early Christian writers. In the *Letter Concerning the Prison of Human Life*, she includes quotations from the best known philosophers of antiquity, including Plato, whose writings she could scarcely have known directly any more than did most of her contemporaries. Her desire to reconcile Christian and classical philosophic thought is a constant theme in her writing, a trait marking her as an early humanist. It is noteworthy that the very concept of the escape through death from the prison of human life is Platonic, and is more frequently associated with poets of the sixteenth century than of the fifteenth. Nevertheless, these earlier prayers reflect, in a rather curious way, Christine's intellectual and worldly concerns at the time she composed them.

By 1409 France was in even greater need of prayer; the country was in danger of civil war. After the Duke of Orleans' assassination at the end of 1407, the rival Duke of Burgundy was for a time banished from Paris, but after a resounding military victory over his brother-in-law's rebellious subjects near Liège, this triumph paved the way for a return to Paris. This return was aided by the support of the King of Navarre, Charles the Noble, the king's cousin, who was instrumental in bringing about the Treaty of Chartres on March 9, 1409. This ceremony of reconciliation between the Duke of Burgundy and the dead duke's son, more important as a gesture than as a remedy for the divided government, indeed brought the Duke of Burgundy back to the French capital.

On July 7 of the same year, a formal treaty was signed by the Duke of Burgundy and the King of Navarre, who promised to support the duke in his opposition to the House of Orleans in return for a promise of help against the King of Castile or the Count of Armagnac, who was by now the father-in-law of the young Duke Charles of Orleans. At the beginning of September, there was a further agreement to rid France of certain malefactors and traitors. This provided the Duke of Burgundy with the excuse he wanted to arrest and have summarily executed one of his most powerful opponents, John of Montagu, Grand Master of the Royal Household. This was followed by a purge of other royal officials who were Orleans' supporters.[4]

Charles the Noble, among others who witnessed Burgundy's machinations, was shocked by the brutality of his acts. It seems probable that at this time he commissioned Christine to write the *Seven Allegorized Psalms*. References in the text make it evident that they were composed in the latter half of the year, and a copy was presented to the Duke of Berry on New Year's Day.

It must be remembered that the Seven Penitential Psalms, which form the basis for this work, were traditionally recited in times of great trial and misfortune, and their use at that particular moment would be a significant reflection of the consternation in Paris after brutal events, as recorded in the *Journal* of the anonymous Bourgeois of Paris as well as by the chronicler Jouvenal des Ursins.[5]

What is known of Charles the Noble suggests that along with being a notable patron of the arts, he was a very pious man. Entries in his official accounts record the purchase of a number of religious books, of which the best known today is his handsome *Book of Hours,* now in the Cleveland Museum of Art.[6] This volume includes the Penitential Psalms introduced by a remarkable miniature representing the punishments of Hell. It is not surprising that such a man as Charles the Noble should have reflected on these psalms, especially in the late fall of 1409.

To understand what Christine meant by an allegorization of the psalms, one must return to her definition of allegory at the beginning of the *Letter of Othea* as "the use of Holy Scripture for the edification of the soul residing in this miserable world." What she was apparently undertaking to do was to interpret these Old Testament Psalms in the light of texts from the New Testament and also the Articles of Faith, which formed the basis of the religious training of the period. She had made use of the same Articles of Faith in the program of education for a young knight in the *Letter of Othea*. She seems to be reminding her readers of their duties as Christians as she offers prayers for their salvation in a time of trouble. She includes prayers for the souls of such departed leaders as Charles V and the Duke of Bourbon, along with the leaders of the present government on whom France depends for its future, and the ordinary people of France. It is notable that no mention is made of Duke Louis of Orleans.

Commentaries on the Penitential Psalms were far from unknown in Christine's day. In 1355 Boccaccio had given to his friend Petrarch a valuable manuscript of Saint Augustine's commentary, which still exists today.[7] It provided the inspiration for Petrarch's own very personal paraphrase of these psalms. Although it is not certain that Christine knew these, there was a copy in the Duke of Berry's celebrated library. Pierre d'Ailly, Christine's contemporary and one of France's early humanists, had also written a commentary on the Penitential Psalms. An interesting point of difference between Petrarch's interpretation and Christine's is that whereas his is intensely personal, her primary concern is for the fate of France and for the rulers who require the strength to govern and save the country. Her self-interest is of little weight.

This detachment from self and concern for the welfare of others is even more significant in her *Letter Concerning the Prison of Human Life*, written after the French disaster at Agincourt (November 1415) and dedicated to Marie of Berry, Duchess of Bourbon, who had not only lost a number of relatives in the slaughter of French knights ordered by Henry V, but whose husband and son-in-law were both captives in England, from whence they would never return.

Christine speaks to the duchess and to all the other women affected by this human tragedy with great understanding and compassion. It is evident that she has come a long way from the personal grief of her own widowhood as expressed in her early poetry. Indeed, in a certain sense she speaks here to the widows of all wars, telling them that they have no choice but to cultivate patience and hope for their husbands' salvation. Although her numerous quotations from the Scriptures and other theological texts may seem unduly ponderous to modern readers, her psychology is remarkably timeless and universal. Her development of the Platonic idea of the release of the soul from the constraints of the body by death is especially interesting, and she dwells on the conviction that traditional Christian values are comforting in the face of sorrow due to Fortune, rather than complaining as she did earlier of Fortune's constantly turning wheel. The evolution of Christine's thinking across the years, based on her reading and illuminating her writing, is one of her most appealing qualities. It reminds us once more of her intensely sympathetic human traits.

These same qualities are to be seen in *The Hours of Contemplation on the Passion of Our Lord,* composed at Poissy,[8] possibly after the Treaty of Troyes in 1422 when the French throne was taken over by the English, dispossessing the dauphin Charles, or after the death of Christine's son Jean in 1426. Rather than personal sorrow, however, this reflects compassion for the sufferings of all women in France in one of the country's darkest hours. This text has never been published and is little known, but it is an important revelation of Christine's state of mind in the years leading to the appearance of Joan of Arc.

NOTES

1. *Essai sur les Ecrits Politiques de Christine de Pisan* (Paris, 1838), pp. xxxvi–xxxviii; 171–82.
2. *Oeuvres poétiques de Christine de Pisan,* III (Paris, 1896), pp. ii–iii.
3. R. and M. A. Rouse, *Preachers, Floriligia and Sermons,* pp. 213–15.
4. R. Vaughan, *John the Fearless* (London, 1966), pp. 79–80.
5. *Journal d'un Bourgeois de Paris, 1405–49,* ed. A. Tuetey (Paris, 1881), p. 6; J. Juvenal des Ursins, *Histoire de Charles VI,* ed. J.A.C. Buchon (Paris, 1875), p. 201; F. Lehoux, *Jean de France, duc de Berri,* III (Paris, 1968), pp. 156–58.
6. See P. de Winter, "Art, Devotion and Satire: The Book of Hours of Charles III, the Noble, King of Navarre, at the Cleveland Museum of Art," *The Gamut* 2 (1981), 42–59.
7. E. H. Wilkins, *Life of Petrarch* (Chicago, 1961), pp. 37–38; 145.
8. The French text was transcribed by Liliane Dulac from Paris, B.N. ms. nouv. acq. 10059 (fol. 114), and will eventually be published by her.

PRAYERS TO OUR LADY

❧

V

O you, Virgin decreed
Long before you were born,
As Saint Augustine said,
You, by the Trinity ordained,
To bring us salvation,
Predestined pure and perfect,
To you I pray that our Queen
Of France will never know
Infernal punishment, give her
Joy and peace, in this world
Keep her from suffering; and
After death, protect her soul.
Ave Maria

VI

Most courteous lady of angels,
As Saint Ambrose has testified,
Mirror of all virtue,
True humility which quells
The noise of pride and calms
Immoderate anger, virtue,
Peace, a good life, and good purpose
Give to my lord the Dauphin,
Give him the wisdom to govern
The people who give their love
With loyal hearts, and to such ends
May he reign after his father!
Ave Maria

∞

VIII

Most pure, whom we cannot praise
Sufficiently, there is so much
To revere, even if one knows nothing,
Saint Jerome said, of the parlor
Of doctrine and the mirror of honor,
The pillar of faith and the universe:
For the noble duke of Orléans
I pray for protection from the enemies
Within, who watch him constantly;
I pray that your son will conduct
Himself and his people with virtue,
And his soul be welcomed into paradise.

Ave Maria

☙

XVII

Virgin Mother, servant of god,
In shed and temple of the Trinity,
As Saint Jerome has noted,
Maiden still after giving birth,
Of all women you are the one
Who was predestined for grace:
For all devout women
I pray you keep their bodies
And their souls in your holy
Protection, be they maidens or wives
Or others, keep them from slander
And let no fire of hell burn them.

Ave Maria

REGINA DeCORMIER

(Translated from *Oeuvres Poétiques de Christine de Pisan*, ed. Maurice Roy)

THE SEVEN ALLEGORIZED PSALMS
Psalm V

(BASED ON PSALM 102)

❧

I. *Lord, hear my prayer and let my cry come to Thee.*

Let the cry of my prayer come to Thee, Lord, whereby I beg thee, because of that Annunciation that the Angel Gabriel made to the Virgin Mary of thy incarnation in her for our salvation,[1] that it may please Thee to turn my heart toward Thee, whom it loves above all things,[2] so that it may not love any other thing save through thy love and because of Thee. Let not its desire be for money, precious jewels, worldly honors, nor any earthly happiness. Let all its affection reach out to Thee, Lord, and pray forgive such errors as I've made to the contrary.

II. *Do not hide Thy face from me in the day of my distress; incline Thy ear to me.*

Incline thine ear to me, my God, and turn not thy face from my prayer, for today I call on Thee and pray in the name of thy glorious Nativity,[3] for the humility where Thou, God, King of Heaven and Earth, humbled thyself when Thou deigned to be born of a woman in a poor common place among dumb beasts; and Thou, precious Godly One, sovereign Wisdom, were willing to take on our flesh, to assume a childish body and be nourished at a virgin's breast. Thou who didst lay upon hay in a manger, may it please Thee to give me grace in thy Holy Name, which the heavenly angels and saints hold in such great reverence. May I never take it in vain,[4] in accepting or swearing a falsehood, not even inadvertently; may I not bear false witness against Thee, who art perfect and complete truth. Pardon me, Lord, where I have failed Thee.

III. *In whatever day I may have called on Thee, forgive me without delay.*

I call on Thee once more today and now, my God; pray forgive me. I beg it in honor of that very great benevolence that made Thee humble thyself when Thou didst allow Thy blessed birth to be announced by the angels to the shepherds, by whom Thou chosest to be first visited and adored.[5] Keep me from breaking Thy holy commandment that teaches me not to forget Thy holy days.[6] So give me grace that on those days I may rest my body and give myself to prayer, avoiding all sin with a peaceful conscience; and pray forget, Lord, my past delinquencies.

IV. *For my days have been consumed like smoke, and my bones are burned like dry wood.*

My days are brief, Lord, and pass like smoke, and death is near, wherefore I beg of Thee to implant in me the thought of this, so that I may hold in contempt the world and its pleasures,[7] and this I beg of Thee in honor of the blessed blood Thou didst shed at the time of Thy worthy circumcision. May I fulfill my duty in honoring my family, friends, and benefactors suitably,[8] succoring them in their needs, helping them in their old age, and praying for them, so that this may be an alleviation of their pains and a help in their necessity, an honor to their bodies and also my salvation. May I be no longer lacking as I have been, for which shortcoming pray forgive me, my Lord.

V. *I am withered like grass and my heart is smitten, for I have forgotten to eat my bread.*

I am smitten because my heart is wounded unto death by sin, and dry of devotion, O Lord. And Thou sayest: Thou shalt not kill,[9] and if I kill my own soul, I should be considered a homicide. But Thou who canst revive me, I call upon Thy help in this. Making oblation to Thy infancy, I pray in contemplation of the offering and adoration of the

Three Kings, when they found Thee wrapped in swaddling clothes in the manger, with Thy Virgin Mother. [10] May it please Thee to revive me from the death of sin to life in a state of grace, and pray see to it that henceforth I kill neither myself or another.

VI. *Through the voice of my groaning my bones cling to my skin.*

My mouth cries unto Thee with groaning, begging forgiveness for all sings committed by the flesh, sweet Savior. I beg of Thee forgiveness for anything I may have done to overstep Thy commandment: Thou shalt not commit adultery [11] nor fornication (by which is forbidden all union other than in marriage, and all illicit and improper use of the body, whether in act or in thought), that I may be pardoned in remembrance of that worthy offering made by Thy mother in Thy infancy, in the temple, in the arms of Saint Simeon, [12] and may I never relapse.

VII. *I am like a pelican in the wilderness; I am like an owl in its habitation.*

The pelican, Lord, sacrifices itself for its young, and gives its blood to revive them, but Thou, Lord, art the true Pelican, [13] who willingly exposed Thy body on the cross, obedient unto death, in order for Thy young (that is Thy people) to be saved, Thou didst sprinkle them with Thy blood. O my sweet Savior, I beg in honor of Thy blessed child-hood, spotless and pure, and Thy virtuous and worthy adolescence, [14] that Thou will defend my heart, my body, and my hands from seduction by foul covetousness of the belongings of others in any sort of grasping action, be it thievery, fraud, violence, or anything taken by force from the people. [15] Guard me from this sin, my God, I beg of Thee, and if I have failed in any way, I beg Thy forgiveness.

VIII. *I have watched and am as the sparrow alone upon the housetop.*

Lord, take no notice of my flesh, which is heavy and sunken in sin, but notice my spirit, which is alert and wakened in solitude; receive, if it may please Thee, its oblation, for I pray to Thee in honor of Thy holy baptism, which Thou didst deign to receive in the river Jordan at the hand of Saint John, and of that voice from Heaven, heard coming from God the Father, which said: Here is my Son, with whom I am well pleased.[16] Pray protect me and make sure that false witness against my neighbor may never be on my lips,[17] nor any other untruthful accusation, nor complaint, criticism, evil report, or defamation of others. If I have committed this sin, pray may I be pardoned, my sweet Lord.

IX. *All day my enemies reproach me, and they that are mad against me have sworn against me.*

I know that I have no enemies so mortal as my most recent sins, even though they flatter me while giving my body various pleasures. But Thou, Lord, by Thy holy mercy, deliver me from these sins, and prevent me, among other sins, from coveting the wife, daughter, relative, or servingmaid of my neighbor,[18] or that I should stray into such sin in thought, word, or deed. Pray extinguish in me the flames of fornication, and pardon any occasion in the past when I may have faltered. Grant this to me by the holy fast Thou didst make during forty days.[19]

X. *For I have eaten ashes as well as bread and mingled my drink with weeping.*

Lord, give me such distaste for my sins and such great contrition that I may say, when I am forgiven them, that I have eaten bread tasting of ashes and drunk wine mixed with tears because of distaste for my shortcomings and because I have been forgiven. And I beg of Thee, in virtue of all the holy miracles Thou didst perform during Thy stay in this mortal world, and for Thy blessed sermons and holy words, that I may never falter in thought or deed into the sin of coveting what belongs to others,[20] be it house, heritage, or anything else, that I gain not anything fraudulently, by cleverness or any other sort of extortion. May it please Thee to pardon me if I have mistakenly done any such thing, and permit me to make restitution.

XI. *May I be far from Thy indignation and Thy wrath, for Thou hast raised me up and cast me down.*

Protect me from seeking Thy wrath, O God who created me, and bestow on me the gifts of Thy Holy Spirit, by which I may receive wisdom to fear and know Thee,[21] and have such remembrance of Thy piteous passion that the recollection will never leave me and be the purgatory of my sins.

XII. *My days are like a shadow that declineth; and I am withered like grass.*

As I am already full of days and old, my Lord, it is time for me to repose in Thee, without other cares. So I beg of Thee, for that holy supper Thou didst hold the Thursday before Thy passion with the blessed apostles, and for the blessed sacrament of Thy glorious body and blood instituted in the form of bread and wine given them,[22] that Thou may fix in me the virtue of fearing to offend Thee,[23] through which I may be prevented from falling into sin.

XIII. *And Thou, O Lord, shalt endure for ever; and Thy remembrance from generation to generation.*

To Thee, God the Father all powerful, who art in Heaven, enduring there through all generations, I beg in honor and recollection of the prayer made to Thee by Thy blessed Son, sweet Jesus Christ, in the garden on the Mount of Olives before His passion, asking Thee if He must drink this bitter cup, knowing the terrible death He was to suffer He trembled so greatly that bloody sweat flowed from His body onto the ground,[24] may it please Thee to implant in me such compassion that the suffering He endured may never leave my thoughts and be useful in wiping out my sins. And grant that for the love of Him I may have such pity and compassion for my neighbors[25] that I may help them in their needs as charitably as I am able.

XIV. *Sire, in arising Thou shalt have mercy upon Zion, for it is time to pardon her; the appointed time is come.*

Zion is Thy Christian people, Lord, who praise and bless Thee in the bosom of Thy Holy Church, which may it please Thee to preserve evermore in Thy service; grant that it may increase and multiply in faith; give it power and strength over miscreants, and may Thy people be not overcome by Thy enemies. Grant me also this request, sweet Jesus Christ, who at the hour of matins accepted to be taken and bound by his enemies.[26]

XV. *For Thy servants take pleasure in her stones, and favor the dust thereof.*

In the time when the King of Nineveh wept from contrition before Thee, and Thy prophet Jonah, and with him groaned his people who had been as obstinate as stone, Thou didst have pity on them, Lord. [27] Thou willst not be more cruel to Thy Christian people, if they repent in begging forgiveness. My God, hear the cries of Thy Holy Church which prays for its flock, and I, with the others, beg for thy holy humility shown by Thee in the hour that false Judas betrayed Thee in blessing Thee and Thou didst say: "Friend, why hast thou come?" [28] Give us strength and vigor to resist the temptations of the enemy. [29]

XVI. *O Lord, the people shall fear Thy name, and all the kings of the Earth Thy glory.*

By virtue of Thy holy name, Lord, Thou didst give power to the apostles and to their followers, to resuscitate, and to perform miracles in the presence of kings and their peoples. [30] Lord, I beg of Thee, by this same virtue that Thou mayst raise me up in contemplation and recollection of Thy holy neck and worthy hands that were so tightly bound by wicked enemies who beat Thee. [31] Give me grace to acquire knowledge, [32] by which I may be able to govern and instruct myself and others.

XVII. *For our Lord has built up Zion, where He shall appear in His glory.*

Lord, who hast built the holy Church Militant, which will be seen above in Thy holy glory as Triumphant, may Thou give it peace and maintain it without faltering in Thy bosom. May Thy people be nourished by the milk of Thy holy doctrine. [33] Lord, Thou wast led away by Thy enemies, on the night when first taken, to the house of Anne, where Thou wast bound, struck, and mistreated until daybreak, [34] may it please Thee to enlighten my understanding of Thy holy grace [35] so that I may see more clearly all things which ought to be done or not to be done.

XVIII. *He has regarded the prayer of the humble and has not despised their prayer.*

Sweet Jesus Christ, who liftest up the prayers of the humble and dost not disdain them, I beg of Thee in remembrance of when Thou wast led at daybreak to the bishop Caiphas, where they accused Thee and struck Thee,[36] that Thou hear my plea, wherein I beg once more for Thy holy Catholic Church, from which it has seemed for a long time that Thou hast withdrawn Thy hand, that Thou may give to Thy servant Alexander, newly elected Thy vicar,[37] and to those who may follow him judgment, power, strength, and good will so to govern the holy papal office that it may be to the profit of their souls and the furtherance and augmentation of Thy holy faith, for the health of Christianity, and the restitution of its past ruin. Protect them in particular from the evil spirit of pride, vainglory, and greed. I beg this likewise for all prelates, priests, and those who have charge of souls, and indeed for all clergy. And mark me with the virtue of pity,[38] so that I may be inclined to help, as I am able, all those who are in need.

XIX. *These things will be written and ordained for the generations to come: and the people yet unborn shall praise our Lord.*

By the prophets, Sire, Thy holy advent was foretold, also Thy death and passion, and as we praise Thee we believe it firmly, for which holy mystery, and in honor of the patience with which Thou didst bear the blows before Caiphas,[39] may Thou regard those in Purgatory, the souls of my parents, those near to me, friends and benefactors, especially King Charles V, Duke Philip of Burgundy,[40] and all their friends and relations, pray give them peace, lighten their pains, and grant them pardon, as with others so with me after my death. And bestow on me the gift of counsel,[41] that I may direct towards salvation myself and others.

XX. *Our Lord has looked down from the height of His sanctuary; He beholds the Earth.*

Sire, from Thy holy heights, look earthward on Thy Catholic king of France and may it please Thee to grant him health in soul and body.[42]

Give him wisdom and sense to govern himself and his subjects to the profit of his soul. Keep his subjects in peace and love, without extortion, so that he may govern them for the welfare and prosperity of the public good. Protect him from his enemies, seen and unseen. This I beg of Thee for the dignity with which Thou didst allow Thyself to be led before Pilate at the hour of prime,[43] where Thou wast falsely accused. Would that Thou might truly bestow on me the seven Works of Mercy,[44] so that I could visit Thy poor sick members.

XXI. *He hears the groaning of the prisoners and loosens the bonds of slaves and those doomed to die.*

Jesus, who of Thine own volition didst choose to suffer death and passion so that Thou might hear the groans of those in Limbo, I beg of Thee, in remembrance of the torment Thou didst suffer, bound to a pillar and flagellated so that the blood flowed from Thy worthy body,[45] that to our Queen of France,[46] and those who will come after her, Thou may grant grace so to live in this world that their morals and manner of life may serve as good example. May the voice of good report carry their good names to all lands. Give them descendants in prosperity and with such charity that the poor may be succored by them; and give them in the end Paradise. Likewise, permit me to bring solace to Thy poor who are dying of thirst.[47]

XXII. *Therefore they declare the name of our Lord in Zion, and His praise in Jerusalem.*

Thou who in reality dost rescue souls from Limbo, so that in the vision of peace that is in Heaven they may praise Thy name, I beg of Thee, for the merit of that crown of thorns so hard and piercing that was put upon Thy head,[48] that the King's children, present and to come, may be recommended to Thee. Give them fair growth in body, and even more in habits and wisdom to fear and serve Thee, sense to govern themselves and keep their subjects in peace and love, prosperity, health in body and soul, increasing worldly possessions, due authority, and, in the end, Paradise. And also grant me grace to want, and to be able, to feed the hungry for love of Thee.[49]

XXIII. *Gathering the people together, and the kings, to serve our Lord.*

Sire, I pray Thee, in memory and compassion for the mocking, the purple mantle, and the blows received,[50] that all kings, Christian princes, especially those of the French royal blood, including their children and relatives, Thou may take unto Thy holy protection: King Charles of France, King Louis of Sicily, King Charles of Navarre, by whose command this present work is written (may it be to the profit of his soul as well as mine), Duke John of Berry, Duke John of Burgundy, their children, and all their lineage.[51] Be favorable and kindly towards them, causing them to govern themselves and their subjects with good judgment and in fear of Thee, and may they direct this kingdom well. Keep them from all obstacles, giving them too Paradise in the end. Likewise I pray for all Christian emperors and other rulers. Grant me, along with them, the will to clothe Thy naked and deprived members.[52]

XXIV. *He replied, tell me the scarcity of my Days in the way of virtue.*

My God, Thou who will announce to me truly the scarcity of the days I have yet to live, so may it please Thee to give me perpetual memory of death, that it may be always before my eyes so that I may amend my life. To this end I beg Thee to give me grace, in honor of Thy most glorious bandaged eyes, of Thy holy face, struck and spat upon for our sake,[53] that Thou willst keep under Thy protection all the clerks, masters, and students of Thy noble and honored University of Paris; theologians, or those of whatever faculty, and likewise those of all other Christian universities. Give them strength to endure the demands of their studies, to gain knowledge and use it profitably, to instruct the ignorant and all people for their salvation.[54] Look Thou after their needs, and give me the possibility, for Thy sake, to lodge Thy poor wayfarers.[55]

XXV. *Do not take me away in the midst of my days: Thy years are through all generations.*

Sire, when Thou hast raised me up and withdrawn me from the path of sin, revoke not my good deeds when I am in the midst of them (which is to say, do not let me falter again). I beg this of Thee, sweet spotless Lamb, who willingly suffered the rabble to cry against Thee: Take Him away! Crucify Him![56] Pray give grace to all the counsellors of rulers, of cities, towns, or countries, indeed of private individuals, to advise them so well that salvation and prosperity will be theirs and those they advise.[57] And grant me such charity that I will expose my hands to burying the dead.[58]

XXVI. *In the beginning, Lord, Thou laid the foundation of the Earth: and the Heavens are the work of Thy hand.*

God who truly made all things, I beg of Thee in compassion and remembrance of that pitiful condemnation to death on the cross, which was given at the hour of tierce to thy blessed Son by Pilate washing his hands,[59] that Thou mayst have under Thy care all Christendom generally, increasing and protecting it against its adversaries. And grant me that (for love of Thee) I may use my own wealth to ransom captives.[60]

XXVII. *They will perish, but Thou shalt endure; Yea, all of them shall wear out like a garment.*

My God, who wast before all things and shall endure forever, and for whom nothing is impossible to change through Thy holy will, I beg of Thee for the great and heavy cross which Thy blessed Son suffered to be laid on His shoulders, leading Him to martyrdom,[61] that Thou mayst protect from evil and peril all people of good will in France; increase in fact and desire this good will, grant them grace for their salvation and joy in this life, and grant me such displeasure at hearing falsehood spoken that I will admonish those who speak such evil.[62]

XXVIII. *Like the vessel without a cover, Thou willst change them and they will be changed; but Thou art the same, and Thy years shall have no end.*

Oh Lord, whose years will have no ending, but by whom all things are changed, who alone art unchangeable and art to be adored and cherished, I pray to Thee in honor of the pity Thou didst have for that city Thou knewest would be destroyed (when Thou didst say: Daughters of Jerusalem, weep not for me, but rather for yourselves and your children,[63] that Thou mayst protect from evil and peril all those who are on official missions for this kingdom of France or elsewhere, to bring peace and tranquility to the Church and also between princes and prelates,[64] as well as others, and give them grace to accomplish all treaties of peace that Thou, the author of all peace, may be praised and all people filled with joy. And grant me the possibility of avoiding all uprisings, of encouraging peace wherever I may go, and for the love of Thee to bear all things patiently.[65]

XXIX. *The children of Thy servants shall dwell secure, and their seed shall be established before Thee.*

The children of Thy servants whose seed shall grow are the just, for whose merit, and in honor of the sacred tears Thou didst shed over the city of Jerusalem,[66] permit me to weep abundantly for my sins. And through the merit of those tears, sweet Jesus Christ, I pray Thee once more for all nobles of the kingdom of France, and likewise for those elsewhere: give them strength and force to battle against the assaults of the enemy in this world, so that they may be led into the knighthood of Heaven. Guard and defend the kingdom or land from which they come, and all Christendom, so that no enemies may harm them. Bestow on them honors and possessions, without undue pride, protecting their bodies and limbs from harm. And grant me strength, for love of Thee, to forgive all offenses willingly.[67]

CCW

(Translated from *Sept Psaumes Allegorisés*, ed. Ruth Ringland Rains)

NOTES

1. Luke 1: 26–33. This is the beginning of a meditation on the Life of Christ. Books of Hours, intended for individual worship, sometimes had illustrations of these episodes. One is reminded that Christine worked in collaboration with artists who illustrated such Books of Hours.
2. Reference to the first of the Ten Commandments: You shall have no other gods before me.
3. Luke 2: 6–8.
4. The Second Commandment: You shall not take the name of the Lord in vain.
5. Luke 2: 8–20.

6. The Third Commandment: Keep the Sabbath day holy.
7. John 12:25.
8. The Fourth Commandment: Honor your father and your mother.
9. The Fifth Commandment: You shall not kill.
10. Matthew 2:11. One suspects that Christine was thinking here of the miniatures representing the Adoration of the Magi.
11. The Sixth Commandment: You shall not commit adultery.
12. Luke 2: 22–23. The Presentation in the Temple was another popular subject for manuscript illustrators.
13. The pelican was a symbol of sacrifice, selflessness, and generosity. In Saint Thomas Aquinas's hymn *Adoro Te*, for instance, he addresses Christ: "Pelican of Mercy, cleanse me in Thy Precious Blood."
14. Luke 2: 40–52.
15. The Seventh Commandment: You shall not steal.
16. Matthew 3: 13–17; Mark 1: 9–11.
17. The Eighth Commandment: You shall not bear false witness against your neighbor.
18. The Ninth Commandment: You shall not covet your neighbor's wife.
19. Matthew 4: 2.
20. The Tenth Commandment: You shall not covet what belongs to your neighbor.
21. Wisdom is not only one of the Seven Virtues, but also one of the Seven Gifts of the Holy Spirit.
22. Matthew 26: 17–29.
23. Christine continues her meditation on the Seven Gifts of the Holy Spirit, of which Fear of the Lord is one. These are based on Isaiah 11: 2 and are presented in contrast to the Moral Virtues. Sometimes they are presented in contrast to the Seven Deadly Sins.
24. Luke 22: 39–44.
25. Misericord, or compassion, is the Fifth Gift of the Holy Spirit.
26. Matthew 26: 47–50.
27. Jonah 3.
28. Matthew 26: 48–50.
29. Fortitude is the Fourth Gift of the Holy Spirit.
30. Matthew 10: 8.
31. Luke 23: 63–64.
32. Knowledge is the Third Gift of the Holy Spirit.
33. This is a reference to Saint Paul's words in 1 Corinthians 3: 2.
34. John 18: 13–24.
35. Intelligence or Understanding is the Sixth Gift of the Holy Spirit.
36. Matthew 26: 57–75.
37. Christine is referring here to the Papal Schism, which began in 1378. Alexander V, who was elected pope on June 26, 1409 with the support of most of Western Europe (with the exception of Scotland, Spain, and a few parts of Italy), lived for only ten months afterwards, so the conflict was not resolved.
38. Here Christine, possibly following the example of Jean Gerson in his *ABC of Simple Souls,* interprets the Second Gift of the Holy Spirit *(pietas)* as Pity rather than Piety.
39. Matthew 26: 67; John 18: 22–23.
40. The former king and the Duke of Burgundy were among Christine's greatest benefactors, so it is suitable that she begins by remembering them.
41. *Consilium,* the Fifth Gift of the Holy Spirit, is considered by Gerson to be the equivalent of Prudence.
42. This would seem to be a tactful reference to Charles VI's increasing periods of insanity.

43. Matthew 27: 1 and 11–14.
44. Christine now passes to the Seven Acts of Mercy, based on Christ's predictions about the Last Judgment in Matthew 26: 35–45. The first of these is to visit the sick.
45. Matthew 27: 25; Mark 15: 15; John 19: 1.
46. The queen, Isabeau of Bavaria, was noted for her frivolity and cupidity as well as her extravagance. One suspects Christine of making a veiled reference here to these shortcomings.
47. Giving drink to the thirsty is the second Act of Mercy.
48. Matthew 27: 29; Mark 15: 17; John 19: 2.
49. Feeding the hungry is also an Act of Mercy.
50. Mark 15: 17; John 19: 2; Matthew 27: 28.
51. This assembly of noblemen to serve the Lord is particularly interesting. All had been involved in one way or another in the effort to keep peace in France. Louis of Anjou, Charles VI's cousin, was King of Sicily in name only. His father had laid claim to the throne as the adopted heir of Queen Johanna, but she had been deposed by her cousin Charles of Durazzo in 1381. Charles, king of Navarre, was also the king's cousin; he was in France trying to settle his claims there as Count of Evreux. His father had been Charles V's principal rival for the French throne, to which his claim had merit. He had been defeated by DuGuesclin at the Battle of Cocherel. His son, however, had quite a different nature, and was notable for his talents as a peacemaker, a role he had had the opportunity to exercise during a sojourn in France in 1405.
52. The third Act of Mercy is clothing the naked.
53. Luke 22: 64; Matthew 27: 30.
54. Instructing the ignorant is one of the Works of Spiritual Mercy.
55. Sheltering the homeless is an Act of Corporal Mercy.
56. Mark 15: 13–14; Luke 23: 18–21.
57. Counseling the doubtful is an Act of Spiritual Mercy.
58. Burying the dead is an Act of Corporal Mercy.
59. Matthew 27: 24.
60. This is a variant of the admonishment in the Acts of Corporal Mercy to visit those in prison. Ransoming captives of the Muslims was an important issue throughout the crusading period and was the particular work of certain religious groups.
61. John 19: 17.
62. Admonishing sinners is an Act of Spiritual Mercy.
63. Luke 23: 28.
64. This was written shortly after the Council of Pisa, which attempted to deal with the Schism and restore unity in the Church as well as the Treaty of Chartres (March 1409), which achieved a temporary reconciliation between the Armagnac and Burgundian factions in the government.
65. Bearing wrongs patiently is an Act of Spiritual Mercy.
66. Luke 20: 41–44.
67. Forgiving offenses willingly is also an Act of Spiritual Mercy.

CCW

A LETTER CONCERNING THE PRISON OF HUMAN LIFE

❧

IN THE HOPE of finding some sort of remedy and medicine for the grievous illness, bitterness of heart, and sadness of mind that manifests itself in floods of tears, in no way benefiting either body or soul, so that they may be dried even though they have continued to flow and still do not cease (which is a great pity) on the part of queens, princesses, baronesses, ladies, and maidens of the noble royal blood of France, and among all the women who are suffering from such great misfortune in the kingdom of France, because of so many deaths or the captivity of those near to them — husbands, children, brothers, uncles, cousins, other relatives and friends, some of them killed in battle and others dead from natural causes in their own beds. As so many such losses and other sorts of misfortunes and misadventures have occurred unjustly in recent times, I am wondering whether there is anything I can propose or recall that might serve any use in bringing some small comfort. And among the throng of those who grieve, my lady, Marie of Berry, Duchess of Bourbon and of Auvergne, you have been neither spared nor excluded [1] (to my great sorrow). Because of your gracious charity to me in this time of affliction when so many friends have left us, and as you have also been of particular help to my own humble state of widowhood (may God reward you for it!), therefore, in recognition of your kindness, for which I am in no way ungrateful, and because I should like to serve you in some way, you the first among the princesses of this realm (even though this was suggested by someone else), [2] my letter will be addressed to you, with the hope that it will also serve the many other women afflicted by similar troubles.

Therefore, mighty princess, I, your humble servant, moved by pity as well as by loyal and true affection, began this present work some time ago. I will explain presently the reason I have not finished it sooner, but better late than never and the time of the sickle after the harvest is not yet upon us in view of the misfortunes that continue.[3] Therefore, I have taken it up again with the intention of finishing it, by God's grace. As the death of friends, which has been all too frequent, is the principal grief to wound the hearts of so many loyal and loving ladies, and as this is a sorrow without remedy and not easily forgotten, it will form the principal theme of my letter, which discusses this problem and aims to bring comfort. Thus in your person, which has indeed borne its share of sorrow, I shall be speaking to all the others, attempting by my words and my modest learning and wisdom to remind you of certain useful facts selected from history and also from the Holy Scriptures. These may, and indeed should, help in stemming the flow of tears, which grief makes stream so freely down your face because of the great loss of French knighthood and so many noble and worthy royal princes of France, near to you and even those blood relatives who are dead or have been taken prisoner—husband, son, father, cousins, so many dukes and counts and other noblemen[4]—that you find yourself quite alone as well as bereaved, although by God's grace all are beyond reproach, having died honorably, some naturally as good Catholics in a glorious end, acknowledging their Creator in Christian humility, and the others assaulting the English enemy on the one hand and defending themselves on the other, all elected to be God's martyrs in the just defense of battle, obedient unto death in order to sustain justice, along with the rights of the French crown and their sovereign lord, like those of whom and for whom the Scriptures say: Blessed are those who suffer for Righteousness . . .[5]

O great lady! Shall we not believe truly in the Holy Scriptures and the faith in God without which, as Saint Paul said, none can be pleasing to God nor be saved?[6] Nevertheless, Saint Bernard says[7] of this that our mortal life can be represented to each of us as a prison, for just as the prison encloses the prisoner so tightly that he cannot carry out his wishes nor fulfill his desires, so the reasonable soul, which is man's most noble part, and without which the body is no more than clay and corruption, is held imprisoned and bound within the body, so that it is indeed so constricted and inhibited by the weight and roughness of its enclosure, that it is able to make use of only a small portion of its inclinations and desires, and is obliged to obey quite contrary impulses. So the wise Helbertus[8] says very appropriately that when a man dies the soul is unbound and set free, and as it is the case that all beings living in this mortal world are equal, whether they be great, of middle status, or humble, all are equal with regard to being prisoners. And now we shall see if in that prison man, of whatever status he may be, is assured of everything, at his ease and without peril . . .

Ah, World! Does it then bring such great joy and profit to reign in you? Indeed, who serves you best is often worse rewarded and not without pain. In short, one could easily think of endless examples of various perils and trials that mark this grievous prison of human life. And it must be noted, moreover, that just as there are storms in the atmosphere and tempests blown about by various winds that strike first and assault high places and the tops of high towers, blowing them down more readily than things on lower levels, likewise the winds of Fortune, when contrary, blow more dangerously on highly placed persons than on lesser ones. Because of this, Boethius says in the second book of *Consolation*[9] that ill Fortune is more profitable than its opposite, for good Fortune blinds with its prosperity and gives confidence in security, whereas adverse Fortune reveals the truth of its fickleness and shows that one should not depend on it.

∞

The Principal Causes That Should Move One to Have Patience on the Death of Friends (III)

Returning to our first matter, my Gracious Lady, those examples presented for the purpose of encouraging you to have patience and take comfort in your grief at the death of your good friends, as you see that you should not weep for them but rather praise God joyfully for several reasons.

The first is that through God's grace they were never blamed for cruelty, and thus you can think that the just Judge through His holy mercy has ended their days as good and of good repute, not like the wicked ones spoken of earlier.

The second cause has to do with the prison of human life, from which by God's gift they have escaped. Of this prison Saint Paul says[10] that there is no security in any of its estates nor in any location, as has already been mentioned, and experience bears this out, even for the most fortunate and those we think to be the happiest, for who is the person, however great, who can boast of passing through life without various illnesses or without great stress of body or mind, or without disagreeable subjections or some sort of care that includes much bitterness and unpleasant tribulation? Boethius says:[11] There was never anybody in this world so fortunate that he did not experience a share of great trials, perils, displeasure, and much bitterness, and Maximien says: O human life! How wretched—always in peril of death, without security or stability!

As for all this, my Lady, you yourself, even though you are a great princess, have known very well by experience on several occasions, I doubt not, and through many trials, as Paradise is not given to anyone in this world. For this reason the wise men of antiquity disdained this life, concerning which Lactantius said that death is the wish of wise men.[12] Maximien said: O human life! how foolish is anyone who prizes you, for you are wretched and have three particularly unpleasant qualities: first, you are very brief; second, you offer no repose; finally, many things are always lacking in you. Therefore Macrobius says that true philosophy is to have before one's eyes the brevity of this life, for thinking of death makes man wise and helps him to know himself.[13] Seneca says that the wise man should always have in mind his final hour, just as the pilgrim has in view, and cannot forget, the dangerous precipice that he must cross before returning home.[14] Thus, most noble Lady, these considerations and others I omit for the sake of brevity should comfort you and make you somewhat content that those you have loved have now departed from this wretched prison.

∞

Returning to Those Who Die Well (IX)

The doctors say of the pains of Purgatory that they can be shortened by friends who offer gifts, prayers, pilgrimages, and all good deeds, things that should not be forgotten by friends still living. Oh! how happy are those who have escaped from that peril, whatever torment they may have experienced, for at least they have to comfort them the hope of arriving presently at the joy that never ends and the consolation of being sure of their salvation; doubtless this is no small joy, giving great solace and alleviation of any torments suffered. Oh! fortunate is anyone who is already in that glorious company, for there is security and no fear of the horrible sentence to damnation that is never revoked, of which no creature living in this world can be certain for the abundance of sins into which we so often fall, and we do not know our final hour, or how we will be taken. God says: Where I find you, there will I judge you,[15] which is indeed a thought for reflection and fear. For this reason the Holy Scriptures say fittingly:[16] Blessed are the dead who die in the Lord, which matter of dying well, according to Boethius,[17] is accomplished by knowing oneself well, giving little thought to the body, as there is nothing more vile, and much care to the soul, as there is nothing more noble.

As for those dying well, and against those who weep for them, an authority says that more worthy is the day of death for a human being who dies well than the day of his birth, and it is more joyful, for as he says, man is born in sin and would be lost if he should die without the regeneration and cleansing of baptism. But afterwards, if he arrives at the age of discretion, he may die in grace and may even have acquired such merit that he may go directly to Heaven, as the blessed saints have done. The day of birth is thus an entrance into misery and tribulation; the final day, if one dies well, is a departure from all affliction and misery. Man is born ignorant and without knowledge, but at death he knows God more than ever, if he repents and begs mercy and is thus saved, and so he escapes from the peril in which he has lived. And nevertheless, he says, great ignorance makes one weep, as does lack of faith in the friends who mourn for the dead they see following the path of salvation. To say, as some express it, that when one dies one doesn't know where one is going is wrong and something to be reproved, as we are not Christians, nor worthy of being so called, if we don't have faith and a firm belief in what the Holy Scriptures tell us concerning the salvation or damnation of souls according to their deeds, and they command us to believe the faith and law of God. And as for what our eyes can't see, as fools say, or that we don't know anything about these matters except what we are told, certainly anyone who relies on such an opinion resembles those who have troubled vision, who put in their eyes harmful medicines to clear it and so become completely blind. Likewise those who doubt what they can't see can become lost in the blindness of error through questioning too much and wishing to know more, and they are like the Pharisees who demanded that Our Lord show them signs, for which he reproached them, and scolded and blamed them.[18] God's law says that the Catholic faith should be entirely, firmly, and uniquely believed, as our Holy

Mother Church commands us, if we wish to be participants in the merit of what Jesus Christ said to Saint Thomas: Blessed are those who do not see me and yet believe in me.[19]

In addition to all this, in approval of our faith, the philosopher Plato, although he was a pagan who lived long before the establishment of Christian law, in his book called the *Phaedo*[20] proves by reason, showing how the reasonable soul, through virtue, should attain Paradise after leaving this world. Prosper in his book called *Epigrammatum*[21] says that after death those who die well will find endless joy, light without shadows, a single will, health without sickness. Of that holy city of Paradise Saint Gregory says in the twenty-third chapter of his *Morals*[22] that God has shown the path of this life to be harsh so that those who are tempted to go astray do not take such delight in it that they forget, because of a passage too relaxed and joyous, to keep to the straight and narrow way that leads to the sky. He says after that: The hearts of the elect who await the great joys of Paradise take courage against the assaults of adversaries, for the greater the struggle the more eagerly they await the glorious victory, and they are strengthened by tribulations, like the fire whose flames are diminished by the wind, so that it seems to be dying down but is rather increasing, just so the tribulations increase the strength of their desire for God.

∽

Written in Paris by me, Christine de Pizan, your humble and obedient servant, who begs you that you do not take it amiss, nor think the less of her because you have not received this letter sooner. May you receive it now graciously, it being my fault that it has been so long delayed although it has long been composed with you in mind. If it may please you to know, several great trials and confusions of spirit since I started this letter some time ago have upset my poor understanding with its shortcomings and have held it so bound by sad imaginings and other thoughts that I have been unable to finish before today, January 20, 1417.

CCW

(Translated from Paris B. N. Ms. fr. 24786)

NOTES

1. Marie of Berry, Duchess of Bourbon, was bereft not only because her husband and other members of her family had been killed or taken prisoner at Agincourt, but because of the death of her father, the Duke of Berry, on June 16, 1416.

2. Suzanne Solente (BEC 84, 1924, 270−71) was of the opinion that Christine's letter had originally been commissioned by the Duke of Berry before his death, but there is no firm evidence of this.

3. Christine, too, had lost friends at Agincourt, and the state of France in the months following the defeat had only deteriorated. The Armagnacs, who were now in power in Paris, had instituted a virtual reign of terror, and Henry V continued his conquest of Normandy. The dauphin, Louis of Guyenne, in whom Christine had put such hopes in her *Book of Peace,* had died unexpectedly at the end of 1415.

4. Not only were her husband, Duke Jean de Bourbon, and a son by an earlier marriage, Charles, Count of Eu, prisoners in England, but her son-in-law Philip of Nevers, the Duke of Burgundy's younger brother, had been killed. Other relatives were Charles of Albret and Antoine of Brabant, who had been killed, and John Harcourt and Charles of Orleans, who had been captured by the English.

5. Matthew 5:10.

6. Hebrews 11:6.

7. S. Solente gives as the source here Saint Bernard's *On the Virtue of Obedience,* but it is probable that Christine was following her frequent practice of quoting from the *Manipulus Florum.*

8. A reference to Albertus Magnus, which probably also came from the *Manipulus Florum.*

9. See *The Consolation of Philosophy,* ed. H. F. Stewart (Cambridge and London, 1946, pp. 220−21) for this passage, which was also cited by Christine in her *Vision.*

10. Hebrews 13:14.

11. As it has been impossible to identify this reference exactly, perhaps Christine was quoting from memory, as she frequently did, but the line attributed to Boethius may have been inspired by a passage in *The Consolation of Philosophy,* Book II (Stewart ed., p. 192).

12. A reference to the *Divine Institutions,* the most important work of this early Christian writer, who has sometimes been called the Christian Cicero. See Book IV (Of True Wisdom and Religion) and Book VII (Of the Blessed Life).

13. Apparently a reference to *The Dream of Scipio.* See *Macrobius' Commentary on the Dream of Scipio,* trans. W. H. Stahl (New York, 1952), p. 138.

14. Refers to the dialogue on the Pilgrimage of Life in the pseudo-Senecan *Remedies of Fortune.* All these references, except to Boethius, probably come from the *Manipulus Florum.*

15. Ezekiel 21:30.

16. Revelations 14:31.

17. This seems to be a reference to the general philosophy of Boethius rather than to a specific passage.

18. Matthew 16:1−4; 13:28.

19. John 20:29.

20. The central theme of Plato's *Phaedo* is the immortality of the soul. Christine had shown a fondness for quoting Plato ever since the *Letter of Othea,* but there is no reason to believe that she could have known his writings directly. P.G.C. Campbell has shown convincingly that she must have known them by way of her contempo-

rary, Guillaume de Tignonville, who translated the *Dicta Philosophorum* of John of Procida.

21. This is apparently a reference to Prosper of Aquitaine, a fifth-century lay theologian of some distinction, noted especially for upholding Saint Augustine's teachings. Christine undoubtedly knew him by way of the *Manipulus Florum.*

22. Christine had already cited this passage from the Commentary on the Book of Job in her *Vision.* Although her quotations from Saint Gregory are numerous throughout her writings, there is no reason to suppose that she knew his works directly. Once more it must be assumed that she was making use of the *Manipulus Florum.*

CCW

THE HOURS OF CONTEMPLATION ON THE PASSION OF OUR LORD

❦

CHRISTINE, having taken pity on and felt compassion for ladies and young women especially, but on all women in general who are grieved by troubles past and present, in order to instruct and encourage them to patience, has written and compiled in the following order these present Hours and so puts at the beginning this letter addressed to them:

To you, my ladies and young women, and to all of the feminine sex whom this may touch and prove useful, I humbly recommend myself as your servant, always desiring to help you through natural inclination and pure love to bring you at least some comfort in the misery of the endless tribulations which have existed far too long and, sadly, gone from bad to worse. For you, who in various ways have been cast down, especially in this kingdom of France, both through the death of friends and through various events, and through other losses: exile, displacements, and many other hardships and dreadful perils, I continue my previous writings in which I have already spoken to you about these same matters, and having seen the need now greater than ever, I have undertaken to search out in the Holy Scriptures something capable of giving you guidance and inciting you to seek the treasure and richness of patience, which is profitable above all other things. And as a great ill requires a great remedy, and as I have not been able to find a more suitable and useful resource, I have written for you what follows as outstanding medicine, the recipe of the precious potion which may be useful for the alleviation of your ills and sorrows, if you use it well, which is to say by reflecting through pious meditation on the pains and griefs suffered for us so patiently by the King of Heaven, Creator of all things, in His very holy and worthy humanity. So I have, through pity and concern for you, translated from Latin into French,* and put into the form of the reading of the Hours, according to the texts of Sacred History and the words of several holy doctors, arranged in such a way that they can be the themes of meditation. So may it please you, my friends, to sample and make use of this glorious and useful remedy so that it may serve as a double benefit for you, that is to say, in the alleviation of your bodily pains by accepting them patiently for love of Him, and also in the benefit for your soul through compassion for the suffering Jesus. May He by His grace give you all this.

May whoever thirsts for patience come to this fountain.

CCW

(Translated from Paris B. N. Nouv. Acq. fr. 10059)

*This is the definite evidence that Christine de Pizan did indeed read Latin.

VIII

THE MIRACLE OF
JOAN OF ARC

❧

CHRISTINE'S career as a writer ended in an unexpectedly dramatic fashion. She lived to witness the appearance of Joan of Arc and the coronation of Charles VII as king of France, and to write the first poem in celebration of this great miracle. [1]

After 1418, when Burgundian forces had recaptured Paris from Armagnac domination and had introduced a new reign of terror in the city, Christine sought refuge in a convent, probably the royal Abbey of Poissy where her daughter had been a nun for many years. Although Christine had earlier enjoyed the patronage of the Duke of Burgundy, her son had subsequently become one of the dauphin's secretaries. As his name first appears on official documents in 1409, it is possible that John the Fearless at least facilitated his appointment. Because the dauphin Charles was supported by the Armagnacs, he was obliged to make his escape from Paris on the arrival of the Burgundians, at which time Jean du Castel followed him into exile. It was undoubtedly this situation that made it necessary for Christine to seek refuge beyond the walls of Paris. A note written in a book by Sir John Fastolf's secretary, William Worcester, who had been with the English army during its occupation of Paris, speaks of Christine's presence at Poissy, which was also occupied for a time by the English. [2] It thus seems likely that she was not as isolated from the world as the first lines of her poem about Joan of Arc would suggest.

This poem celebrating the appearance of Joan of Arc is dated July 31, 1429; it mentions her journey to Chinon to meet the dauphin, the raising of the siege of Orleans on May 8, and the royal coronation at Rheims on July 17. In addition to recounting these events, Christine expresses the hope that all true Frenchmen will now show loyalty to their proclaimed king so that the country may return once more to peace and prosperity; indeed, she hopes that Joan will not only restore peace to France but to all of Christendom as well by leading a crusade for the recapture of the Holy Land.

Not only does Christine rejoice at the official coronation of this king, but her pleasure is all the greater because of the remarkable fact that it has been made possible by a young woman. Joan's triumph at Rheims is Christine's vindication that women are capable of great deeds. It is especially interesting to find that she compares Joan with some of the same heroines she had recommended as models to the queen of France more than twenty-five years earlier. Christine has great reason to rejoice.

Unfortunately, there is also a darker side to this picture, for although the coronation at Rheims restored to the heir of the Valois kings the throne that had been lost by the Treaty of Troyes, there was the problem of the Parisians and the inhabitants of other towns under English domination, who had to be convinced to reject the English and accept the new king. Christine, Parisian that she was, particularly addresses herself to the lack of loyalty to their rightful monarch; in 1418 he had been obliged to escape from the city under cover of night. She admonishes them:

> O Paris, city ill-advised,
> Foolish people undone by fear,
> Would you now rather be despised
> Than your own royal prince revere?
> In truth, you so perverse appear
> You'll be destroyed, aren't you aware
> Unless with contrite hearts sincere
> You beg mercy? If not, beware.[3]

She is unfortunately all too correct in her suspicions, for although she speaks of the imminent return of the king to Paris, when the royal army undertook to recapture the city at the beginning of September, the undertaking failed. Even the fact that Charles was negotiating a period of truce with the Duke of Burgundy, now John's son, Philip the Good, the Parisians did not have enough spirit to rise up against their occupiers. Christine must have been aware of these negotiations, for she points out to the Parisians that they should not consider the Burgundian duke their enemy.

Christine's apparent inside knowledge of what was going on, taken together with the only manuscripts in which this poem is preserved, raises interesting questions about another source of inspiration for her final poem. The Berne Manuscript,[4] the best of the three still known, is contemporary with events. It is in a compilation of texts copied by a certain Nicolas du Plessy at Sens at the beginning of 1430, shortly after the city had declared its loyalty to the king. Du Plessy, a public official, was obviously a supporter of both Charles VII and Joan of Arc, and other documents in the manuscript are quite evidently propaganda in favor of them both, raising an interesting question about the ultimate purpose of Christine's poem.

Another fifteenth-century manuscript now in Carpentras once belonged to a lawyer named Pierre Parent, and a fragment in Grenoble, though copied later, belonged to a collection of documents compiled by an official of Charles VII's court in 1456, shortly after the Rehabilitation of Joan of Arc.[5] It is significant that these men were officials with duties and political affiliations similar to those of Christine's son, Jean du Castel.

Even closer to the world of Christine's son was the poet, Alain Chartier, who also belonged to the exiled court of Charles VII. There still exists a letter written by him to an unidentified prince in July 1429 that gives an enthusiastic account of Joan of Arc's miraculous appearance in terms comparable to those in Christine's poem.[6] This must lead one to the conclusion that more than Christine's feminism fuels her poem's passion; it is also informed by her ardent desire to see France restored to its proper destiny under its hereditary king. If Christine was not actually composing official propaganda, her writing would certainly find sponsors in the supporters of the newly crowned Charles VII, who had yet to be accepted by all his subjects. One can only guess at the contacts with this world that Christine maintained even in the Abbey of Poissy.

This poem, then, should be seen as her final effort on behalf of France, a last attempt to point the way towards peace and prosperity. She had firmly believed that it was the role of poets and philosophers to speak the truth to kings and other public officials in order to recall them to their duties. This she had done ever since composing *The Long Road to Learning* in 1403. So it was that she raised her voice once more to point out to the country that had caused its subjects so much suffering the path it must now follow for its own well-being. Yet the most touching aspect of her message is the sense of rejoicing and relief expressed by the poet who has found a reason to laugh again in the sun that is shining once more. The poem crowns a long career of writing in the affirmation of integrity, of women, and of France.

One can only hope that her life ended on this triumphant note, for nothing further is heard from her. The permission granted to her daughter-in-law by the English occupier to return to Paris in 1431 suggests that Christine's voice had finally been silenced by death.

NOTES

1. There were, however, a contemporary "Ballade contre les Anglais" (published by Paul Meyer in *Romania* 21, 1892), and an anonymous "Ballade faite quant le Roy Charles VII fut couronné à Rains du temps de Jehanne dicte la Pucelle" (Eduard von Jan, *Das literarische Bild des Jeanne d'Arc*, [Halle, 1928], p. 11).
2. P. Maurice-Garçon, *Poissy: Historique et Touristique*, (Paris, 1979), pp. 5–6.
3. *Le Ditié de Jeanne d'Arc*, eds. A. J. Kennedy and K. Varty (Oxford, 1977), pp. 38–39 (vv. 433–40); Willard, *Christine de Pizan*, p. 206.
4. Kennedy, Varty, eds., pp. 2–4.
5. Kennedy, Varty, eds., pp. 4–5; C. de Roche and G. Wissler, "Documents relatifs à Jeanne d'Arc et à son époque extraits d'un manuscrit du XVe siècle de la Bibliothèque de la ville de Berne," in *Festschrift Louis Gauchat* (Aarau, 1926), pp. 329–52.
6. P. Champion, *Histoire poétique de XVe siècle* (Paris, 1933), Vol. I, pp. 153–54.

THE POEM OF
JOAN OF ARC

I

Now I, Christine, who've shed my tears
In this closed abbey where I've lived
Eleven years, since Charles, the king's
4   Own son — and dare I say that now? — [1]
Took flight from Paris hastily
(And what a strange event that was!);
Enclosed in here by that foul play,
8   It's only now I start to laugh.

II

I take to laughing joyously
Because the wintry season has
Been spent; it was my custom then
12   To stay, lamenting, in my cage.
But now I'll change my tearful sounds
To song, because again I've found
The pleasing season . . .
16   I have indeed endured my share.

III

The year of fourteen twenty-nine
The sun came out to shine again.
It brings the season new and good,
20   Which we had not directly seen
Too long a time, while many passed
Their lives in sorrow; I am one.
But now, no longer do I grieve,
24   Because I see what pleases me.

IV

For since the day I came to stay
In here the temper of the time
Has turned from mournfulness to joy.
28 And so, thanks be to God that spring
(The name we give the loveliest
Of seasons, which I've so desired,
When living things are born anew)
32 Has turned the wasted land to green.

V

It's all because the cast-out child,[2]
The son of France's rightful king,
Who has for long endured so much
36 Adversity, approaches now;
He rose as one who goes to prime,
Arriving like a king who's crowned
In all his might and majesty,
40 And fitted out with golden spurs.

VI

And now let us receive our king![3]
May his return be welcomed here!
Rejoicing in his regal style
44 Let all of us, the great and small,
Advance (let none shrink back from this!)
To offer greetings happily
While praising God, who guarded him,
48 And crying out aloud, "Noël!"

VII

But now I want to tell just how
God made that happen, through His grace.
(I pray to Him for guidance so
52 That I won't miss a single point.)
Let word go out to every place,
For this deserves recall; and may
The chronicles and histories
56 Record it, never mind who's irked!

VIII

    Now hear throughout the world around
This thing most marvelous of all!
And see if God, in whom all grace

60   Abounds, does not support what's right,
When all is done. That's notable,
Considering the case at hand!
And may this hearten the dismayed,

64   The ones whom Fortune's trampled down!

IX

    Take note that none should feel cast down
By adverse Fortune, even when,
Unjustly, one is scorned and then

68   Attacked by all, from every side!
Observe how Fortune always is
Capricious, who has harmed such scores!
For God, who stands opposed to wrong,

72   Upraises those who keep their hope.

X

    Has anyone seen anything
More singular and rare occur
(That every region would do well

76   To recognize and to recall)
Than that this France (of whom they said
That she was overthrown and done)
Be brought from evil days to fair

80   By means of God's divine command,

XI

    Through such a miracle, indeed,
That if the facts were not well-known
And evident in every way,

84   There's none who would put faith in them?
Indeed this is a thing quite worth
Remembering, that God had wished
To grant such mercy unto France

88   (Yes, truly!) through a tender maid.

XII

Oh, what an honor to the crown
Of France, this proof divinely sent,
For by the blessings He bestows
92   It's clear how He approves of France:
For in the royal house of France
He finds the strongest faith — I've read
That France's Lilies never lost
96   Belief (but nothing's new in that!)

XIII

And you, the King of France, King Charles,
The seventh of that noble name,
Who fought a mighty war before
100   Good fortune came at all to you:
Do, now, observe your dignity
Exalted by the Maid, who bent
Your enemies beneath your flag
104   In record time (that's something new!)

XIV

And people thought that it would be
Impossible indeed for you
To ever have your country back,
108   For it was nearly lost; but now,
It's clearly yours; no matter who
Has done you wrong, it's yours once more,
And through the clever Maid who did
112   Her part therein — thanks be to God!

∽

XXII

You, Joan, were born propitiously;
May He be blessed who gave you life!
Young maid who was ordained of God,
172   In you the Holy Spirit poured
His ample grace (in whom there was
And is divine munificence),

Refusing none of your requests.
176   Who'll grant reward enough to you?

XXIII

Could more be said about the men
And thrilling deeds of bygone times?
In Moses God who's bountiful
180   Instilled great moral force and grace;
Then tirelessly did he escort
God's people out of Egypt's land
By miracle. Just so have you
184   Saved us from ill, elected Maid!

XXIV

When I reflect upon your state,
The youthful maiden that you are,
To whom God gives the force and strength
188   To be the champion and the one
To suckle France upon her milk
Of peace, the sweetest nourishment,
To overthrow the rebel host:
192   The wonder passes Nature's work!

XXV

That is, if God, through Joshua
Performed so many miracles[4]
In conquering those places where
196   So many met defeat—a man
Of strength was Joshua. But she's
A woman—simple shepherdess—
More brave than ever man at Rome!
200   An easy thing for God to do!

XXVI

But as for us, we've never heard
About a marvel quite so great,
For all the heroes who have lived
204   In history can't measure up
In bravery against the Maid,
Who strives to rout our enemies.

It's God does that, who's guiding her
208 Whose courage passes that of men.

XXVII

We set great store in Gideon,[5]
Who was a simple laborer.
Now God caused him, the story says,
212 To fight, so none could hold him off,
And thus he conquered everything.
Whatever word God gave to him,
The miracle was never quite
216 So clear as now He works for her.

XXVIII

And Esther, Judith, Deborah,[6]
Those ladies of enormous worth,
Through them it was that God restored
220 His people, who were solely pressed;
Of many others I have learned,
Courageous ladies, valiant all,
Through whom God worked his miracles.
224 But through the Maid He's done much more.

XXIX

By miracle has she appeared,
Divine commandment sent her here.
God's angel led her in before
228 The king, to bring her help to him.[7]
There's no illusion in her case
Because it's been indeed borne out
In council (in conclusion, then,
232 A thing is proved by its effect);

XXX

They questioned her most carefully
Before they would believe her words,
To priests and wise men she was led;
236 They searched the truth of her account
Before it might be told about
That God had sent her to the king.[8]

And in recorded history
240   They found her destined just for this.

XXXI

The Sybil, Bede, and Merlin, too,
Five hundred years ago and more
Foresaw her in their minds,[9] and as
244   The cure for France's plight they wrote
Of her, and of her prophesied,
Predicting that she'd bear the flag
In France's wars, as they foretold
248   The way of her accomplishments.

XXXII

Her life of beauty in the faith
Attests the grace of God in her,
A sign by which we place more trust
252   In her: Whatever she may do,
She's always keeping God before
Her eyes; she calls on Him, and serves
And supplicates in word, in deed;
256   And nowhere does her faith grow weak.

XXXIII

How evident it was when at
Orleans the siege was laid, for there
Her strength was first made manifest![10]
260   For never clearer miracle
Was seen: God helped his own, so that
The foe could help each other fight
No more than lifeless dogs might do;
264   Thus they were caught and put to death.

XXXIV

What honor for the female sex!
God's love for it appears quite clear,
Because the kingdom laid to waste
268   By all those wretched people now
Stands safe, a woman rescued it
(A hundred thousand men could not

Do that) and killed the hostile foe!
272 A thing beyond belief before!

XXXV

A little girl of sixteen years
(And doesn't that pass nature's ken?)
For whom no arm's too great to bear,
276 She seems to have been reared to this,
So strong and resolute is she.
In front of her the enemy
Goes fleeing, not a one remains.
280 She acts, in sight of many eyes,

XXXVI

While ridding France of enemies,
Retaking town and castle both.
No force was ever quite so great,
284 If hundreds or if thousands strong!
Among our men so brave and apt
She's captain over all; such strength
No Hector or Achilles had.[11]
288 All this God does, who's guiding her.

∞

XXXIX

Lay down, oh Englishmen, your horns,[12]
For you'll not bag the precious game!
Don't bring your business into France!
308 For your advance is stopped — a thing
You'd scarcely thought a while ago
When you were acting bellicose,
But you had not yet reached that path
312 Where God strikes down the arrogant.

XL

You thought you'd taken over France,
That she belonged to you by right.
But things are otherwise, false lot!

316 You'll beat your drums some other place,
    Unless you want to have a taste
    Of death, like your confederates,
    Who're provender out there for wolves,
320 Among the furrows, lying dead.

XLI

    The English will be crushed through her,
    And never will they rise again
    For God who wills it hears the voice
324 Of guiltless folk they tried to harm!
    The blood of those they've killed, who'll walk
    No more, cries out. God wants an end
    To this; instead He has resolved
328 To chastise them as evil men.

XLII

    In Christendom and in the Church
    She'll kindle harmony anew,[13]
    The faithless we have heard about,
332 And heretics, who lead base lives,
    She will destroy, for thus it's said
    In prophecy, which in advance
    Could see all this; and she'll forgive
336 No place that vilifies God's faith.

⚭

XLIX

    In regal triumph and in force
    Did Charles receive the crown at Rheims,
    Without a doubt, quite safe and sound,
388 With men-at-arms and many lords,
    The year was fourteen twenty-nine,
    July the seventeenth, to be
    Exact, and there he stayed awhile,
392 A sojourn of about five days,[14]

L

Along with him the Virgin Maid.
Then coming back across his land
No city, castle, nor small town
396   Resists. For whether he's despised
Or loved, and whether they are stunned
Or reassured, the citizens
Surrender. Few require attack,
400   So much his power makes them quail!

LI

Some in their foolishness believe
That they'll resist; it's pointless, though,
For in the end, whoever stands
404   Opposed pays for his faults to God.
It's futile. Thus they must give in,
No matter what they will. For no
Resistance can be strong enough
408   To last beyond the Maid's assault,

LII

Assembling in their mass they thought
They could prohibit his return
By launching a surprise attack;
412   But now they need no healer's balm
For one by one they've all been caught,
Opponents who are dead and gone—
Dispatched, as I have heard it said,
416   To either Hell or Paradise.

∞

LIX

Alas! He's so magnanimous
He wants to pardon everyone!
And it's the Maid, obeying God,
468   Who causes him to act that way.
Now give yourselves, your hearts, to him,
As loyal Frenchmen ought to do![15]

And when you listen to him speak,
472   No man will remonstrate with you.

LX

I pray to God that He'll inspire
In you the wish to act that way
So that the cruel storm of wars
476   We've known may be erased from thought;
And that you spend your life in peace,
The subjects of your king supreme,
So that you never give offense
480   To him; and may he lead you well.
    Amen.

LXI

This poem's offered by Christine,
The year of fourteen twenty-nine,
As said above, July's last day.
484   But now I understand indeed
That some will be displeased to hear
What it contains, for he whose head
Is bowed, whose eyes remain upon
488   The ground, cannot behold the light.

Here ends a very fine poem written by Christine.

THELMA S. FENSTER

(Translated from *Le Ditié de Jehanne d'Arc*,
eds. Angus J. Kennedy and Kenneth Varty)

NOTES

1. Christine is undoubtedly referring here to the fact that the Treaty of Troyes (May 21, 1420) had forced Charles VI to disinherit the dauphin and to recognize his son-in-law, the English King Henry V, as his heir.
2. The dauphin was also disinherited by the French Parliament in January 1421.
3. Charles VI had died on October 21, 1422, so the question of the proper succession was already several years old.
4. Joshua's most celebrated miracle was making the sun stand still, thus allowing him to achieve victory over the Amorites. (Joshua 10: 12–14).
5. Gideon was entrusted with a divinely ordained mission to deliver his country from the Midianites (Judges 6–7).

6. Christine not only recommends these women to Isabeau of Bavaria as models in her *Letter to the Queen of France*, but she also writes of them in *The Mutation of Fortune* and *The Book of the City of Ladies*. It is interesting to note that Jean Gerson, in his treatise on Joan of Arc, *De quadam puella*, written during the spring of 1429 in support of the supernatural nature of her mission, likewise cites these same examples.

7. Reference to Joan's arrival at the dauphin's court in Chinon, probably on March 6, 1429.

8. This reference is to the interrogation and examinations to which she was subjected at Poitiers in the spring of 1429.

9. For a discussion of these prophecies, see Andrew Lang, *The Maid of France* (London, 1909), pp. 32–33; 308–11.

10. The siege of Orleans was raised on May 8, 1429.

11. Those who question Christine's feminism are surely overlooking these verses. It is noteworthy that she cites both biblical and pagan examples here.

12. This sort of characterization of the English was common in the period of the Hundred Years' War. See C. Lenient, *La Poésie patriotique en France au moyen âge* (Paris, 1891).

13. These lines refer to the belief that Joan's mission included not only the transfer of imperial power to France, but also the restoration of the Church after the Schism. The "heretics" are apparently the Hussites, who had embarked on a campaign of revenge after the burning of John Huss in 1415.

14. Christine was obviously well informed concerning these events. Accompanied by Joan, Charles arrived in Rheims on July 16 and left on July 21, 1429.

15. These lines are a final appeal to the French to heal their divisiveness and unite before the new king, a culmination that was not achieved for some time although by the end of his reign it had generally come about. The last lines of the poem also allude to division among the French.

CCW

BIOGRAPHICAL NOTES
ON THE TRANSLATORS

❦

BARBARA K. ALTMANN is an Assistant Professor of French and Medieval Studies at the University of Oregon. She has published on Christine de Pizan and Guillaume de Machaut, and is currently preparing an edition of Christine de Pizan's three love debate poems.

Before her untimely death, DIANE BORNSTEIN was an associate professor at Queens College-The City University of New York. Having received a Ph.D. from New York University, her special interests were medieval literature and linguistics. In addition to articles on Christine de Pizan, Chaucer, Caxton, Malory, Lydgate, Hoccleve, and Shakespeare, her publications included *Mirrors of Courtesy* (1975), *The Middle English Translation of Christine de Pizan's Livre du Corps de Policie* (1977), and *The Lady in the Tower* (1983). She also edited *Ideals for Women in the Works of Christine de Pizan* (1981).

REGINA DECORMIER is the author of *Growing Toward Peace* (Random House); *Discovering Israel* (Random House), which received a National Jewish Book Award; and, most recently, *Hoofbeats on the Door* (Helicon Nine Editions). Her work has been published in numerous anthologies and periodicals, including *American Poetry Review, The Nation,* and *Salmagundi.*

THELMA FENSTER has edited and translated works by Christine de Pizan in *Poems of Cupid, God of Love: Christine de Pizan's* Letter of the God of Love *and* Tale of the Rose; *Thomas Hoccleve's* The Letter of Cupid; *with George Sewell's* The Proclamation of Cupid (with Mary Erler, ed. and trans. of Hoccleve; E. J. Brill, 1990). She translated Christine de Pizan's *Book of the Duke of True Lovers* (Persea Books, 1991). Her new edition of Christine de Pizan's *Livre du Duc des vrais amans* is forthcoming from SUNY-Binghamton Press, in the series Medieval and Renaissance Texts and Studies. She teaches French medieval literature at Fordham University.

ERIC HICKS is the editor of the original French and Latin documents in the Quarrel of the Rose; co-editor, with Charity Cannon Willard, of Christine de Pizan's *Livre des Trois Vertus;* co-translator, with Thérèse Moreau, of the modern French translation of *La Cité des Dames;* and most recently, editor of the Latin texts of the *Letters* of Heloise and Abelard, with the thirteenth-century translation attributed to Jean de Meun. He has taught at Yale University, the universities of Kentucky and Maryland, and presently holds the chair of Medieval French Language and Literature at the Université de Lausanne.

NADIA MARGOLIS received her training in various aspects of medieval culture in both the United States and France, specializing in French medieval language and literature. She has taught at several universities, currently in Comparative Literature at the University of Massachusetts, Amherst, where she is also an adjunct fellow at the Institute for Advanced Study in the Humanities. In addition to a sourcebook, *Joan of Arc in History, Literature and Film,* she has also authored articles and translations dealing with Christine de Pizan and related topics.

JUNE HALL MCCASH is a Professor of French at Middle Tennessee State University. Her publications include *Love's Fools: Aucassin, Troilus, Calisto, and the Parody of the Courtly Lover* and articles in a variety of journals, including *Speculum, Medievalia et Humanistica* and *Medieval Perspectives.* She is now editing a book on women's cultural patronage in the Middle Ages.

GLENDA MCLEOD holds a doctorate in Comparative Literature from the University of Georgia, and teaches at Gainesville College. She has published several essays on early women writers. Her books include *Virtue and Venom* and *Christine's Vision,* a translation of Christine de Pizan's *Avision-Christine.*

CHRISTINE RENO is Associate Professor of French and Director of the Medieval and Renaissance Studies Program at Vassar College. She has published numerous articles on Christine de Pizan. She and Liliane Dulac have just completed the first French critical edition of the *Avision-Christine*, and she is working with Gilbert Ouy on an album studying the manuscripts produced by Christine's workshop.

EARL JEFFREY RICHARDS received his doctorate in Comparative Literature from Princeton University in 1978 and now teaches French at Tulane University. Besides translating Christine de Pizan's *Book of the City of Ladies* (Persea, 1982), he has also published *Dante and the "Roman de la Rose": An Investigation into the Vernacular Narrative Context of the "Commedia"* (1981), and *Modernism, Medievalism and Humanism: A Research Bibliography on the Reception of the Works of Ernst Robert Curtius* (1983). In 1992 he edited a series of essays dedicated to Charity Cannon Willard and entitled *Reinterpreting Christine de Pizan*. His latest book, *European Literature and the Labyrinth of National Images: Literary Nationalism and the Limits of Enlightenment*, is forthcoming from Niemeyer.

KITTYE DELLE ROBBINS-HERRING, Associate Professor of Foreign Languages at Mississippi State University, has a special interest in medieval, renaissance, and neoclassical French literature, particularly women's writings, and in medieval themes in modern literature. Her publications include the *trobairitz*, Hélisenne de Crenne, and Anna de Noailles.

SANDRA SIDER has published translations of poetry by Diane de Poitiers (French), Sor Juana Inés de la Cruz (Spanish), and Philodemus (classical Greek). She has taught Renaissance art history at Sarah Lawrence College, published several works on Renaissance humanism and iconography, and is head of the department of manuscripts and rare books at The Hispanic Society of America, New York.

JAMES J. WILHELM is the author of numerous medieval books, including *The Cruelest Month, Seven Troubadours, Dante and Pound*, and *Il Miglior Fabbro*. His translations of Christine de Pizan's lyrics are most accessible in his *Lyrics of the Middle Ages: An Anthology* (Garland, 1990), which includes Rondeau XLVI, also published here.

CHARITY CANNON WILLARD, the editor of this volume, has devoted herself primarily to research and writing since her retirement from her position as Professor of French and Spanish Literature at Ladycliff College, adding substantially to earlier publications on Christine de Pizan, Isabel of Portugal, and the literature of the Court of Burgundy. She is the author of the biography *Christine de Pizan: Her Life and Works* (Persea, 1984) and the editor (with Eric Hicks) of the critical edition of *Livre des Trois Vertus* (1989) which she also translated into English under the title *A Medieval Woman's Mirror of Honor: The Treasury of the City of Ladies* (Persea, 1989). In recognition of her long and distinguished career in the service of French language, literature, and culture, in 1983 she was awarded the Order of Academic Palms by the French government.

SUMNER WILLARD holds three degrees from Harvard University, where he started his teaching career as Teaching Fellow and Tutor in Romance Languages. Called to national duty soon after the bombing of Pearl Harbor, he received an Army commission and was assigned to teach at the United States Military Academy at West Point, where he spent the major part of his teaching career, eventually becoming Professor and Chairman of the Foreign Languages Department. Upon his retirement, he was promoted to Brigadier General and awarded the Distinquished Service Medal. With Lady Sheila Southern, he translated J. F. Verbruggren's *Art of War in the Middle Ages*. He is now preparing an edition and a translation of Christine de Pizan's *Livre des faits d'armes et de chevalerie* with his wife, Charity Cannon Willard.

BIBLIOGRAPHY

❦

I. Biography and Bibliography

Du Castel, Françoise. *Damoiselle Christine de Pizan, veuve de M. Estienne du Castel* (Paris, 1972).

———. *Ma Grand-mère Christine de Pizan* (Paris, 1936).

Favier, Marguerite. *Christine de Pisan: Muse des Cours Souveraines* (Lausanne, 1967).

Kennedy, Angus J. *Christine de Pizan. A Bibliographical Guide* (London, 1984; 2nd ed., 1994).

McLeod, Enid. *The Order of the Rose. The Life and Ideals of Christine de Pizan* (London, 1976).

Nys, Ernest. *Christine de Pisan et ses Principales Oeuvres* (Brussels, 1914).

Pernoud, Régine. *Christine de Pisan* (Paris, 1982).

Pinet, Marie-Josèphe. *Christine de Pisan 1364–1430: étude biographique et littéraire* (Paris, 1927).

Solente, Suzanne. "Christine de Pisan," *Histoire Littéraire de la France* XL (Paris, 1969), 335–422.

Willard, Charity Cannon. *Christine de Pizan. Her Life and Works* (New York, 1984).

Yenal, Edith. *Christine de Pizan: A Bibliography of Writings by Her and about Her* (Metuchen, NJ and London, 1982). Second edition: *Christine de Pizan: A Bibliography.* Scarecrow Author Bibliographies 63 (1989).

II. Modern Editions of Writings

Ballades, Rondeaux, and Virelais: An Anthology, ed. Kenneth Varty (Leicester University, 1966).

Lavision-Christine. Introduction and Text, ed. Sister Mary Louise Towner (Washington, DC, 1932).

Cent Ballades d'Amant et de Dame, ed. Jacqueline Cerquiglini (Paris, 1982).

Christine de Pisan (Choix de Poésies), Introduction, Choix et Adaptation par Jeanine Moulin (Paris, 1962).

"Christine de Pizan's 'Epistre à la Reine,' " ed. Angus J. Kennedy in *La Revue des Langues Romanes* 92 (1988), 253–264.

Le Débat sur le Roman de la Rose, ed. Eric Hicks (Paris, 1977).

Le Ditié de Jehanne d'Arc: Christine de Pisan, eds. Angus J. Kennedy and Kenneth Varty (Oxford, 1977).

The Epistle of the Prison of Human Life with an Epistle to the Queen of France and Lament on the Evils of the Civil War, ed. Josette Wisman (New York, 1984).

Epistre de la Prison de Vie Humaine, ed. Angus Kennedy (Glasgow, 1984).
"Lettre à Isabeau de Bavière," in *Anglo-Norman Letters and Positions from All Souls Ms. 182,* ed. M. Dominica Legge (Oxford, 1971).
Le Livre du Chemin de Long Estude, ed. Robert Püschel (Berlin-Paris, 1887; rpt. Geneva, 1974).
Le Livre du Corps de Policie, ed. Robert H. Lucas (Geneva, 1967).
Le Livre des Fais et Bonnes Meurs du Sage Roy Charles V, ed. Suzanne Solente, 2 vols. (Paris, 1936–1940).
Le Livre de la Mutacion de Fortune, ed. Suzanne Solente, 4 vols. (Paris, 1959–1966).
Le Livre de la Paix, ed. Charity Cannon Willard (The Hague, 1958).
Le Livre des Trois Vertus, ed. Charity Cannon Willard and Eric Hicks (Paris, 1989).
Oeuvres Poétiques de Christine de Pisan, ed. Maurice Roy, 3 vols. (Paris, 1886–1896).
Poems of Cupid, God of Love: Christine de Pizan's "Epistre au Dieu d'Amours" and "Dit de la Rose"; *Thomas Hoccleve's "The Letter of Cupid"; with George Sewell's "The Proclamation of Cupid,"* eds. Thelma S. Fenster and Mary Carpenter Erler (Leiden, 1990).
Sept Psaumes Allegorisés, ed. Ruth Ringland Rains (Washington, DC, 1956).

III. Translations into English and Modern French

The Boke of the Cyte of Ladies, trans. Brian Anslay (London, 1521). Reprinted in *Distaves and Dames: Renaissance Treatises for and about Women,* ed. Diane Bornstein (Delmar, NY, 1978).
The Book of the City of Ladies, trans. Earl Jeffrey Richards (New York, 1982).
The Book of the Duke of True Lovers, Now First Translated from the Middle French of Christine de Pisan, trans. Alice Kemp-Welch with Lawrence Binyon and Eric R.D. Maclagan (London, 1908; rpt. New York, 1966).
The Book of the Duke of True Lovers, trans. Thelma S. Fenster, with lyric poetry translated by Nadia Margolis (New York, 1991).
The Book of the Three Virtues: See *A Medieval Woman's Mirror of Honor: The Treasury of the City of Ladies.*
Christine's Vision, trans. Glenda K. McLeod (New York, 1993).
The Fayttes of Arms and of Chyvalrye. Facsimile of Caxton's 1489 edition (Amsterdam, NY, 1968).
The Epistle of Othea to Hector, trans. Anthony Babington, ed. James D. Gordon (Philadelphia, 1942).
The "Epistle of Othea." Translated from the French Text of Christine de Pizan by Stephan Scrope, ed. Curt F. Buhler (London, 1970).
Christine de Pizan's Letter of Othea to Hector, trans. Jane Chance (Cambridge, MA, 1990).
The Epistle of the Prison of Human Life, trans. Josette Wisman (New York, 1985).
Le Livre de la Cité des Dames, trans. Thérèse Moreau and Eric Hicks (Paris, 1986).
A Medieval Woman's Mirror of Honor: The Treasury of the City of Ladies, ed. Madeleine Cosman, trans. Charity C. Willard (New York, 1989).
The Middle English Translation of Christine de Pisan's Livre du Corps de Policie, trans. Diane Bornstein (Heidelberg, 1977).
Morale Proverbs of Chrystine. Facsimile of Caxton's edition of Anthony Woodville's translation (Amsterdam, NY, 1970).
L'Oroyson Nostre Dame: Prayer to Our Lady by Christine de Pisan, trans. Jean Misrahi and Margaret Marks (New York, 1953).
Poems of Cupid, God of Love: Christine de Pizan's "Epistre au dieu d'Amours" and "Dit de la Rose"; *Thomas Hoccleve's "The Letter of Cupid"; with George Sewell's "The Proclamation of*

Cupid," eds. and trans. Thelma S. Fenster and Mary Carpenter Erler (Leiden, 1990).

The Treasure of the City of Ladies, trans. Sara Lawson (London, 1985).

La Querelle de la Rose: Letters and Documents, trans. Joseph L. Baird and John R. Kane (Chapel Hill, 1978).

IV. Selected Studies of Christine de Pizan's Writings

Altmann, Barbara K. "Reopening the Case: Machaut's *Judgment Poems* as a Source in Christine de Pizan," in *Reinterpreting Christine de Pizan*, ed. E.J. Richards (Athens, GA, 1992), 137–156.

Bornstein, Diane, ed. *Ideals for Women in the Works of Christine de Pizan* (Kalamazoo, MI, 1981).

———. *The Lady in the Tower: Medieval Courtesy Literature for Women* (Hamden, CT, 1983).

Bozzolo, Carla. " 'Il Decamerone' come fonte de Livre de la Cité des Dames," *Miscellanea di Studi e Recerche sul Quattrocento Francese*, ed. Franco Simone (Turin, 1967).

Brownlee, Kevin. "Discourses of the Self: Christine de Pizan and the Rose," *Romanic Review* 78 (1988), 199–221.

Campbell, P.G.C., *L'Epître d'Othéa: étude sur les sources de Christine de Pisan* (Paris, 1924).

Cropp, Glynnis M. "Boèce et Christine de Pizan," *Medium Aevum* 37 (1981), 387–417.

Delany, Sheila. "Rewriting Woman Good: Gender and Anxiety of Influence in Two Late-Medieval Texts," *Chaucer in the Eighties*, eds. J.N. Wasserman and R.J. Blanch (Syracuse, 1986), 83–86.

Dulac, Liliane. "Inspiration mystique et savoir politique: les conseils aux veuves chez Francesco da Barbarino et chez Christine de Pizan," *Mélanges à la mémoire de Franco Simone* (Geneva, 1980), 113–141; English trans. by Thelma Fenster in *Upon My Husband's Death: Widows in Literature and Histories of Medieval Europe*, ed. Louise Mirrer (Ann Arbor, 1992).

———. "Un Mythe didactique chez Christine de Pizan: Semiramus ou la veuve héroïque," *Mélanges de Pilologie Romane offerts à Charles Campoux* (Montpellier, 1978), 315–343.

Erhart, Margaret J. "Christine de Pizan and the Judgment of Paris," *The Mythographic Art*, ed. J. Chance (Gainesville, FL, 1990), 125–156.

Fraoli, Deborah A. "The Literary Image of Joan of Arc: Prior Influences," *Speculum* 56 (1981), 811–830.

Gauvard, Claude. "Féministe ou Bas-Bleu? Le Cas de Christine de Pizan," *L'Histoire* 62 (1983), 94–96.

Hindman, Sandra L. *Christine de Pizan's "Epistre d'Othea." Painting and Politics at the Court of Charles VI* (Toronto, 1988).

Huot, Sylvia. "Seduction and Sublimation: Christine de Pizan, Jean de Meun, and Dante," *Romance Notes* 25 (1985), 361–373.

Kellogg, Judith L. "Christine de Pizan as Chivalric Mythographer," *The Mythographic Art*, ed. J. Chance, 100–124.

Kelly, Douglas. "Reflections on the Role of Christine de Pizan as a Feminist Writer," *Sub-stance* 2 (1972), 63–71.

Kelly, Joan. "Early Feminist Theory and the Querelle des Femmes, 1400–1789," *Women, History and Theory* (Chicago, 1984), 65–109.

Laidlaw, James C. "Christine de Pizan—An Author's Progress," *Modern Language Review* 78 (1983), 532–550.

————. "Christine de Pizan, the Earl of Salisbury, and Henry IV," *French Studies* 36 (1982), 129–143.

————. "Christine de Pizan—A Publisher's Progress," *Modern Language Review* 82 (1987), 35–75.

Margolis, Nadia. "Christine de Pizan and the Jews: Political and Poetic Implications," *Politics, Gender and Genre,* ed. Margaret Brabant (Boulder, CO, San Francisco, Oxford, 1992), 53–73.

————. "The Poetess as Historian," *Journal of the History of Ideas* 47 (1986), 361–375.

Laigle, Mathilde. *Le Livre des Trois Vertus de Christine de Pisan et son Milieu Historique et Littéraire* (Paris, 1912).

McLeod, Glenda. *Virtue and Venom: Catalogues of Women from Antiquity to the Renaissance* (Ann Arbor, 1991).

Nicolini, Elena. "Cristina da Pizzano, l'origine e il nome," *Cultura Neolatina* 1 (1941), 143–150.

Poirion, Daniel. *Le Poète et le Prince: L'Evolution du lyrisme courtois de Guillaume de Machaut à Charles d'Orléans* (Paris, 1965).

Quilligan, Maureen. *The Allegory of Female Authority in Christine de Pizan's Cité des Dames* (Ithaca, NY, 1991).

Reno, Christine. "Christine de Pizan: Feminism and Irony," *Seconda Miscellanea di Studi e Ricerche sul Quattrocento Francese* (Chambéry-Turin, 1981), 127–133.

————. "Feminist Aspects of Christine de Pizan's 'Epistre d'Othéa à Hector,'" *Studi Francesi* 71 (1980), 271–276.

Thomassy, Raymond. *Essai sur les Ecrits Politiques de Christine de Pisan* (Paris, 1838).

Willard, Charity C. "Women and Marriage around 1400: Three Views," *Fifteenth Century Studies* 7 (1990), 475–484.

————. "Christine de Pizan: the Astrologer's Daughter," *Mélanges à la mémoire de Franco Simone* (Geneva, 1980), 95–111.

————. "Une Source Oubliée du Voyage Imaginaire de Christine de Pizan," *Et C'est la Fin Pour quoy Nous Sommes Ensemble: Hommage à Jean Dufournet* (Paris, 1993), 321–326.

————. "Christine de Pizan's *Cent Ballades d'Amant et de Dame:* Criticism of Courtly Love," *Court and Poet,* ed. G.S. Burgess (Liverpool, 1981), 357–364.

————. "Jean de Werchin, Seneschal de Hainaut: Reader and Writer of Courtly Literature," *Courtly Literature: Culture and Context,* eds. K. Busby and E. Cooper (Amsterdam and Philadelphia, 1992), 595–605.

Wilkins, Nigel. "The Structure of Ballades, Rondeaux and Virelais in Froissart and Christine de Pizan," *French Studies* 23 (1969), 337–348.

Winter, Patrick M. de. "Christine de Pizan: Ses Enlumineurs et ses Rapports avec le Milieu Bourguignon," *Actes du 104ᵉ Congrès des Sociétés Savantes: Archéologie* (Paris, 1982), 335–376.

V. General Background

Abensour, Léon. *La Femme et le féminisme avant la Révolution,* (Paris, 1923).

Alain de Lille. *The Plaint of Nature,* trans. J.J. Sheridan (Toronto, 1980).

Avril, François. "La Peinture française au temps de Jean de Berry," *Revue de l'Art* 28 (1975), 40–52.

Badel, Pierre-Yves. *Le Roman de la Rose au XIVᵉ siècle; Etude de la réception de l'oeuvre* (Geneva, 1980).

Boccaccio, Giovanni. *Concerning Famous Women,* trans. Guido A. Guarino (New Brunswick, NJ 1963).

Capellanus, Andreas. *The Art of Courtly Love*, trans. John Jay Parry (New York, 1959).

Constantinidis, Elizabeth. "Amazons and Other Female Warriors," *The Classical Outlook* (October–November, 1988), 3–6.

Coopland, F.W. *The Tree of Battles of Honoré Bonet* (Liverpool, 1949).

Coville, A. *Les Cabochiens et l'Ordonnance de 1413* (Paris, 1888).

Delachenal, Roland, ed. *Les Grandes Chroniques de France: Chroniques des règnes de Jean II et de Charles V*, 4 vols. (Paris, 1910–1920).

Delachenal, Roland. *Histoire de Charles V*, 5 vols. (Paris, 1909–1930).

Delisle, Léopold. *Recherches sur la librairie de Charles V*, 2 vols. (Paris, 1907).

Dupuy, R.E. and T.N. *The Encyclopedia of Military History from 3500 B.C. to the Present*, second edition (New York, 1986).

Deschamps, Eustache. *Oeuvres Complètes*, ed. G. Reynaud, 11 vols. (Paris, 1878–1903).

Dow, Blanche Hinman. *The Varying Attitude toward Women in French Literature of the Fifteenth Century* (New York, 1936).

Colonna, Egidio. *Les Livres du Gouvernement de Rois, a XIIIth Century Version of Egidio Colonna's Treatise de Regimine Principium*, ed. S.P. Molenoer (New York, 1899; reprint 1966).

Fleming, John F. *The Roman de la Rose: A Study in Allegory and Iconography* (Princeton, 1969).

Gerson, Jean. *Oeuvres complètes*, ed. P. Glorieux, 11 vols. (Paris, 1962–1973).

Gilmore, Myron P. "The Renaissance Conception of the Lessons of History," *Humanists and Jurists: Six Studies in the Renaissance* (Cambridge, MA, 1963), 1–31.

Hassell, James W., Jr. *Middle French Proverbs, Sentences and Proverbial Phrases* (Toronto, 1982).

Henneman, J.B. "The Age of Charles V," *Froissart Historian.*, ed. J.J.N. Palmer (Woodbridge, Eng. and Totowa, NJ, 1981).

Legnano, John of. *Tractatus de Bello, de Represaliis et de Duello*, ed. T.E. Holland and trans. J.L. Brierly (Oxford, 1917).

Salisbury, John of. *Policraticus; Of the Frivolities of Courtiers and the Footprints of Philosophers*, ed. and trans. C.J. Nederman (Cambridge, 1990).

La Librairie de Charles V (Paris, Bibliothèque Nationale, 1968).

Maurice-Garçon, Pierre. *Poissy: Historique et Touristique* (Paris, 1979).

Meiss, Millard. *French Painting in the Time of Jean de Berry: the Limbourgs and their Contemporaries* (New York, 1974).

Hicks, Eric and Ornato, Egidio. "Jean de Montreuil et le débat sur le *Roman de la Rose*," *Romania* 98 (1977), 216–219.

Histoire des Femmes en Occident II: Le Moyen Age, ed. Christiane Klapisch-Zuker (Paris, 1990).

Journal d'un Bourgeois de Paris, 1405–1409, ed. A. Tuetey (Paris, 1875).

Juvenal des Ursins, J. *Histoire de Charles VI*, ed. J.A.C. Buchon (Paris, 1878).

Krynen, Jacques. *Idéal du Prince et Pouvoir Royal en France à la fin du Moyen Age, 1380–1440* (Paris, 1981).

Lehoux, Françoise. *Jean de France, duc de Berri*, 3 vols. (Paris, 1968).

Lenient, C. *La Poésie patriotique en France au Moyen Age* (Paris, 1891).

Le Roux de Lincy, A.J.V. *Le Livre des Proverbes français*, 2 vols., second edition (Paris, 1859).

Margolis, Nadia. *Joan of Arc in History, Literature, and Film* (New York, 1991).

Mirot, L. "L'Enlèvement du Dauphin et le premier conflit entre Jean sans Peur et Louis d'Orléans, Juillet-Octobre, 1405," *Revue des Questions Historiques* 95 (1914), 329–355; 96 (1914), 47–68, 369–419.

Nordberg, Michael. *Les Ducs et la Royauté* (Uppsala, 1964).

Ouy, Gilbert. "Honoré Bouvet (appelé à tort Bonet), prieur de Selonnet," *Romania* 35 (1959), 255–259.

Ovide Moralisé, poème du commencement du quatorzième siècle, ed. C. de Boer, 5 vols. (Amsterdam, 1915–1936).

Partington, J. R. *A History of Greek Fire and Gunpowder* (Cambridge, 1960).

Patch, Howard R. *The Goddess Fortuna in Medieval Literature* (Cambridge, MA, 1927; reprint New York, 1967).

Philippe de Mézières. *Le Songe du Vieil Pèlerin*, ed. G.W. Coopland (Cambridge, 1969).

Préaud, Maxime. *Les Astrologues à la fin du Moyen Age* (Paris, 1984).

Richardson, Lulu McDowell. *The Forerunners of Feminism in French Literature of the Renaissance from Christine de Pisan to Marie de Gournay* (Baltimore, 1929).

Roche, C. de and Wissler, G. "Documents relatifs à Jeanne d'Arc et à son époque extraits d'un manuscrit duXV siècle de la Bibliothèque de la ville de Berne," *Festschrift Louis Gauchet* (Arrau, 1926), 329–352.

The Romance of the Rose, trans. Harry Robbins (New York, 1962).

Rouse, Richard H. and Mary A. *Preachers, Florilegia, and Sermons: Studies on the "Manipulus Florum" of Thomas of Ireland* (Toronto, 1979).

Spears, W.H., Jr. *Greek Fire, the Fabulous Secret Weapon that Saved Europe* (Chicago, 1969).

Spearing, A.C. *Medieval Dream Poetry* (Cambridge, 1976).

Thorndike, Lynn. *A History of Magic and Experimental Science*, 8 vols. (New York, 1923–1958).

Tuve, Rosemond. *Allegorical Imagery* (Princeton, 1966).

Van Hamel, A.C. *Les Lamentations de Mathéolus et le Livre de Leesce de Jean LeFèvre de Ressons*, 2 vols. (Paris, 1905).

Vaughan, Richard. *John the Fearless* (London, 1966).

Vegetius, Publius Flavius. *Epitome of Military Science*, trans. N.P. Milner (Liverpool, 1993).

Verdon, Jean. *Isabeau de Bavière* (Paris, 1957).

Wilkins, Ernest Hatch. *Life of Petrarch* (Chicago, 1961).

Wilkins, Nigel. *One Hundred Ballades, Rondeaux and Virelais* (Cambridge, 1969).

Willard, Charity C. "Raoul de Presles's Translation of Saint Augustine's *De Civitate Dei*," *Medieval Translators and their Craft*, ed. Jeanette Beer (Kalamazoo, MI, 1989), 329–346.

Wilson, Katharina M., ed. *Women Writers of the Renaissance and Reformation* (Athens, GA, 1987).

Winter, Patrick M. de. "Art, Devotion and Satire: The Book of Hours of Charles III, the Noble, King of Navarre, at the Cleveland Museum of Art," *The Gamut* 2 (1981), 42–59.

Woodward, William H. *Vittorino da Feltre and Other Humanist Educators* (New York, 1963).

Wright, A.R. "The Tree of Battles of Honoré Bouvet and the Laws of War," in *War, Literature and Politics in the Late Middle Ages*, ed. C.T. Allmand (Liverpool, 1976), 12–31.

INDEX

Othea, *see Letter of Othea to Hector, The*
Ovid, 29, 42, 45, 89, 90, 138
  Christine's view of, 31, 90, 138

Pallas, 49–50, 99
Parent, Pierre, 350
Paris (city), 137, 250
  book trade in, xi–xii
  Burgundians vs. Armagnacs in,
    251–252, 257, 258, 269, 319, 320,
    348
  English occupation of, 348, 349
  violence in, 258
Paris (prince), 99–100
Paris, University of, x, 4, 139, 333
Paul, Saint, 159, 204, 205, 339, 340
peace, 214–216, 284
  see also Book of Peace, The
peasants, *see* common people
Penitential Psalms, 320, 321
Peter, Saint, 98, 204
Petrarch (Francesco Petrarca), x, 3,
    190, 230, 321
Phaedo (Plato), 343
Philip, King of Macedon, 277
Philip I, King of France, 215
Philippe de Mézières, 251
Philip the Bold, Duke of Burgundy, 92,
    142, 331, 348
  Charles V's biography commissioned
    by, 20, 30, 94, 229–230, 233–234,
    251
  death of, 20, 30, 251
  Jean du Castel and, xii, 20, 30, 141,
    251
Philip the Good, Duke of Burgundy,
    349
philosophy, 16, 239–240
  Christian thought and, 319
Philosophy, Dame, 4, 6–24
Physics (Averroes), 281
Pierre d'Ailly, 321
Pizan, Christine de, *see* Christine de
  Pizan
Pizan, Thomas de, *see* Thomas de Pizan
Plato, 98, 174, 319, 321, 343
Plautilla, 205
Plutarch, 276
Poem of Joan of Arc, The (Christine de
  Pizan), 348–351, 352–363
poetry, 17, 29
  allegorical, 17, 89–90
  contests of, 28, 34, 139
  Court of Love and, 34

in education, 31
fixed forms of, xiv, 27, 38, 30
poetry, of Christine, xiv, 27–40, 318
  Book of the Duke of True Lovers, xiv,
    29, 33, 35–36, 70–81
  *Christine's Teachings for Her Son, Jean
    du Castel*, 59–60
  dedications of, 29–30
  early, 15, 17–18, 27–29
  emotions reflected in verse forms of,
    37–38
  experimentation in, 28, 30, 37–38
  forms used in, 27, 28, 30, 37–38
  gossips in, 32, 33, 36, 38
  love as theme in, 31–39
  May Day, 28
  monologue and dialogue used in, 32–
    33, 37–38
  moral teachings and proverbs, 30–31
  rondeaux, 27, 28, 30, 32, 33, 52–55
  Songs for Sale, 30, 57–58
  Tale of Poissy, 34–35, 61–69
  topical, 29
  virelays, 27, 30, 55–56
  widowhood and, 27–28, 31, 53, 89
  see also allegorical poetry, of
    Christine; ballades, of Christine
Poissy, Abbey of:
  Christine at, 322, 348, 350, 352
  Christine's daughter at, 23, 34,
    348
  Tale of, 34–35, 61–69
Policraticus, The (John of Salisbury), ix–
  x, 241, 253
Politics (Aristotle), 241, 287
Prayers to Our Lady (Christine de
  Pizan), 318–319, 323–324
princes, 253
  Book of the Body of Policy addressed to,
    253–254, 275–291
  causes of warfare and, 292–294
  Christine as advisor to, 92, 249
  common people and, 315–316
  God and, 277–278, 282–285, 286–
    287
  health of, 281–282
  instruction in government and
    customs for, 281
  knights as teachers for, 279–281
  Lamentation on the Woes of France
    addressed to, 304–305
  pride of, 282, 283
  role of, in body of state, ix–x, 253,
    276, 277